AF479479

FRED GRACELY

Misfit's Magic: The Last Halloween
by Fred Gracely

Revised Edition, 2026 (1)

Published by Bisket Press, LLC, Woburn, MA

Cover: Candice Broersma
Chapter Illustrations : Ethan Gettman
Editors: Lisa Messinger, Gill Donovan, Caroline Gracely

ISBN: 979-8-9861364-0-0 (ebook)
ISBN: 979-8-9861364-1-7 (paperback)
ISBN: 979-8-9861364-2-4 (hardback)
ISBN: 979-8-9861364-3-1 (audiobook)

CONTENTS

misfit (noun)

mis·fit | ˈmis—ˌfit also ˌmis—ˈfit

Definition of Misfit:

    1 : something that fits badly // social mis-
fits

    2 : a person poorly adapted to a situation

    4 : something or someone no one wants

    3 : a person who doesn't fit in with the
rest

no light
  to brighten the path
    we walk unprepared
        alone
        scared...
     misfit for the task
      through the shadows we wade
         hoping
       that death
      has other plans
     for us made
           – fg

floating in the dark ocean
buried under a wave of water
left with one last breath
to make it out alive.

      – savage mind

CHAPTER 1

The Gargoyle

AN icy autumn breeze smelling of rotting leaves scratched Goff's cheeks as he studied an eerie bronze statue hidden behind the tiny Spraksville Library—four bronze men in hooded robes standing at the corners of a granite obelisk, unaware of a fanged gold gargoyle crouching on top, poised to attack. A dark feeling washed over Goff. It almost sounded as if the white noise of the tall swishing maples nearby whispered a warning—"You should not be here."

Goff shook it off, not the type to believe in whispering willows or any other sort of hocus pocus. That was just a creepy statue, and the trees were just plants—big plants, very big plants, but nothing more.

Preparing to jot down some notes, Goff opened a tattered Spraksville Junior High ring-bound notebook and pulled a yellow No. 2 pencil from behind his ear. With cold fingers, he positioned the graphite's point just above one of the thin blue lines and looked up at the gargoyle.

A sliver of fear raced up his spine.

It had moved.

Or, had it?

Perhaps he'd just let himself get spooked by the chatty trees. Perhaps it was just wind-blown hair thrashing against his glasses like sea kelp. Perhaps it was the shadows cast by the cascade of multicolored leaves fluttering through the air. But was that talon raised now when it hadn't been before? Had its eyes always been turned ever so slightly in his direction? His heart beat like a kettle drum as he tried to convince himself otherwise.

Statues don't move. That's crazy talk.

He wished he could leave, but that wasn't an option. It would mean the end of his dream of winning the Journalism Scholarship to Amworth Academy—his only hope of escaping dreadful Spraksville and feeling like he finally had a real home. This paper about the local history of witchcraft was the centerpiece of his scholarship application, and he needed his submission to be perfect. That meant he had to write something about this stupid statue. It was the most peculiar, spooky relic in the entire town.

Frustrated, Goff stared at the statue while shards of late autumn sun stretched across the cobblestones and his unbuttoned barn jacket flapped against his legs. He had hoped that coming here would give him something interesting to use for this paper. But being here only raised more questions. Who had put this strange statue here and why? Where had it come from? The shiny brass plaque on the base only read "Unknown, 1775," and his research had turned up nothing.

"What are you trying to say?" Goff muttered to the statue. "Beware of evil approaching from an unwatched direction?"

"Freak!"

Goff flinched and spun around. Tom Sweeney, a dim-witted rhino of a boy from his class, was clomping toward him. Goff suddenly regretted donning a pointy dime-store wizard's cap and cape—the cheap kind made of navy blue felt with gold stars. He had hoped it would help him "feel" this story, but now he just felt idiotic. He yanked the wizard's cap off. "I'm doing an assignment for a class," he explained.

"A class about how to be a freak?" Tom yelled back.

Goff sighed. Tom was typical Spraksville. "It's a history class, Tom."

"History of freaks?"

"Regional history."

"Regional history of freaks?"

"That's just dumb."

"You're dumb."

Goff didn't reply. This was going nowhere.

Tom walked closer. "Freak."

"Will this be over soon?" Goff asked.

"Yup," Tom said, punching Goff hard in the stomach. "Done!"

Goff doubled over, his breath knocked out of him, and dropped his notebook and pencil. He wanted to shout something at Tom, something clever and nasty, but that would have required breathing, and his lungs weren't working at the moment. He fought off the urge to puke, refusing to give Tom that satisfaction.

Tom walked away. "See ya later, loser!"

Goff stared at his shoes, watching the ground spin. It spun and spun and then slowed and eventually became just the ground again. The danger of puking now over, he stood up.

Tom was nowhere to be seen, but Goff caught his own reflection in the brass plaque on the statue's base. There before him was a blurry picture of the poster child for "Most Likely to Be Bullied"—skin as pale as snow, wild blue eyes, a mass of brown hair clawing at his head, plastic glasses with thick frames covering half of his face, and of course, a goofy wizard's cape draped over his shoulders.

"It's a miracle I'm still alive," he groaned.

He stared for a moment longer and then looked away, even more determined to win that scholarship. He stepped back and surveyed the statue. The sun had faded just a little, darkening the shadows, and now it looked even more evil, more mysterious. Glancing around to make sure he was alone, he jammed the wizard's cap back on his head. "Forget you, Tom."

He retrieved his pencil and notebook from the ground. After thinking for a moment, he opened the notebook and wrote:

Behind the Spraksville Library stands a statue of four men, worried and serious-looking, who seem to be guarding against something unexpected, something evil, something that will attack without warning. I ask myself: Are we all in danger here? Perhaps the little town of Spraksville harbors secrets only the oldest townsfolk know, secrets that may one day haunt us—or maybe even kill us—in our sleep.

He reread it and smiled. It was a good start, and he could refine it later at home. But before he left, he wanted to add an illustration for a bit more pizazz. With broad strokes, he captured the pillar and roughed out the four men and the gargoyle. A stiff breeze kicked up a pile of orange leaves nearby. Goff watched them swirl and dance and then returned to his drawing for a moment before looking back up.

He froze.

The gargoyle had turned its head.

It was staring straight at him with beady little eyes.

Panic surging through him, he pressed the pencil too hard against the paper and snapped off the tip. With shaking hands, he pulled his glasses off and cleaned them with the sleeve of his jacket, muttering,

"It's just a smudge or something."

He slid his glasses back on, blinked hard three times, and then looked again at the gargoyle. It was staring at the distant horizon as it had been before. Goff let out a sigh of relief. With his heart still pounding, he put away his broken pencil and notebook, deciding he had done enough witchcraft research for one day. He watched the gargoyle closely, though, as he backed up toward the stone pillars marking the park entrance. When he reached the threshold, the gargoyle's head swiveled toward him.

Goff's legs started running before he had a chance to think about it. He didn't stop until he rounded the corner of the library and threw himself up against the cold bricks, goosebumps covering his arms, rapid breaths blowing silver clouds.

That did NOT just happen!

Maybe Tom had punched him harder than he'd realized? Perhaps lack of oxygen had messed with his brain? Or maybe his imagination was too good to write about witchcraft? He should probably write about something boring instead, like sports or town meetings.

He remained pressed against the wall, waiting for his heart and breathing to settle before he walked home. A familiar smell started mixing with the cold air. *Pizza!* He peeled himself off the wall enough to see the glowing neon sign for Pongo's Pizza down on Main Street. How perfect would it be to eat pizza at home while he worked on this paper? He could have a first draft done by morning!

He made his way quickly down the path by the side of the library and crossed Main Street. At the entrance to Pongo's, a statue of a smiling Italian chef with a bulbous red nose greeted him. The bells on the door clanged happily as he pushed it open, and the unmistakable yeasty, cheesy smell of fresh pizza washed over him. He rushed between the red upholstered booths toward the chrome and glass counter where rows of big round steaming pies waited. Thoughts of glaring gargoyles melted away.

When he had nearly reached the register, a group of older kids spilled out of their booth and blocked his way. Goff's heart sank. He had forgotten a cardinal rule in his excitement about pizza: always check who's inside first. Bullies went into a feeding frenzy whenever they sensed his dorky essence.

The two kids at the front of the pack were the worst bullies in town: a pair of nearly identical twins with chiseled jaws and mean little eyes: Goff's new foster siblings, Ben and Pam. Other than their hair—Ben sported a buzz cut and Pam a tight ponytail—it was nearly impossible to tell them apart. Both were the same height, had athletic builds, and always wore white T-shirts and jeans.

"My new brother," Ben said as he snatched Goff's cap and punched it inside out. "You're such an embarrassment!"

Goff's cheeks flushed with anger.

"Give it!" Pam said. She took the cap from Ben and jammed it down around her ears inside out. "Look at me! I'm Goff, the all-powerful wizard!"

Laughter traveled around the circle of morons ringing Goff. He felt like screaming—all he'd wanted was pizza, and now he'd have to endure whatever bullying this crew would kick up. He sank even deeper when he saw two kids he had classes with—Lydia Garcia and Halstrom Flint—sitting in a booth on the other side of the restaurant, watching the show.

"I know what's missing!" Ben pulled Goff's glasses off and handed them to Pam.

Pam put them on, scrunched up her face, and threw back her shoulders. "I am Dorko! Fear me!"

Goff started shaking. Of all the things bullies could do to him, swiping his glasses was the worst. They were his last line of defense, his shell.

"Give them back," he mumbled.

"You squeak something, mouse?" Pam asked with a nasty grin.

"I want my glasses back."

"Is somebody talking?"

"You heard me."

"I hear crickets."

Goff's anger brought his wits back. "That's not even how you use that phrase."

Pam tossed her head back. "You an English teacher now, Goff?"

"So, you *can* hear me?"

"I hear crickets."

"Give me back my glasses!" Goff demanded.

Pam looked down at him dramatically, pretending to be surprised by his presence. "Oh, it's Goff." She took off the glasses and held them out. "You want these? Go ahead, take them."

Goff knew this would not end well, but he had to try. He reached out and grabbed one arm of his glasses just as Pam jerked her hand back. The arm snapped off. The circle of kids cackled and hooted. Blood rushing to his face, Goff stared blankly at the stick of brown plastic in his hand. It felt like his own arm had been torn off.

Anger exploded up from his core. He charged at Pam, swinging his fists, but Pam held him back easily with a hand on his forehead. A second later, a pair of giant arms wrapped around him, pulling him back.

"No fighting!" Pongo shouted in his ear with breath that smelled like pepperoni.

"B-but she broke my glasses," Goff stammered, pointing at Pam.

Pam batted her eyelashes like a kitten and handed Goff the other half. "He dropped them, and they broke," she said in a fake sweet voice. "I was just handing them back. I would never break a little boy's glasses."

"That's a lie!" Goff said.

"I don't care." Pongo released Goff and pushed him toward the door. "Boys don't fight the girls, and nobody fights in Pongo's. Now you get out and don't come back!"

Goff shook his head, unable to believe how unfair all of this was. "But—"

"Go!" Pongo shouted, pushing him toward the door. "No fighting in Pongo's!"

Pam smiled ear to ear.

Ben tossed the wizard cap to Goff. "You forgot your hat, little boy."

Goff tried to catch it but missed. The group fell over themselves with glee.

"Sit down and be quiet!" Pongo hollered, turning and clapping his giant hands. "Or you go too!"

As Pam, Ben, and the others ran back to their booth, Goff scooped up his hat, jerked the door open, jingling the bells angrily, and left. His cheeks burning with frustration, he scrunched up the wizard's cap under his left arm, held his broken glasses on his face with his hand, and strode off down Main Street, determined to get home as soon as possible.

I HAVE to win that scholarship.

He grabbed the Amworth Academy brochure from his backpack with his free hand and let the glossy panels unfold. The austere brick buildings and sprawling landscape of Amworth covered all three sections. Not only was it beautiful, but he'd nearly melted when he learned it was a school with a legacy of producing great writers, thinkers, artists, and scientists. It was a year-round boarding school, so he'd never again have to bounce from house to house.

He'd already started the application process, and with his outstanding academic record, his counselor had assured him he was a good candidate. So, it all came down to this paper. His favorite teacher, Mrs. Wicket, had promised to submit it with a strong recommendation... if it was good enough.

Goff returned the brochure to his backpack and walked a little faster.

The sun glowed deep red along the horizon, illuminating trees sporting vast plumes of leaves in brilliant autumn shades of red, orange, yellow, and coffee brown. The air smelled of rotting apples and wet earth. The store windows glowed with Halloween colors and displayed various blends of hairy spiders, black cats, dangling skeletons, green witches, and glowing jack-o-lanterns.

He passed Town Hall, a red brick building with imposing doors and a looming bell tower. The bell rang out the quarter-hour, sounding like a dying whale. Decades ago, it had cracked for no discernible reason, and now the sickly ring was part of the town's eerie ambiance. Spraksville was strange like that—an odd blend of quaint and spooky. Visitors soaked it up this time of year, posing for pictures with pumpkin-spice lattes in front of everything but the trash cans.

Near the edge of downtown, Goff noticed more ugly gargoyles jutting out from the top of the Post Office. Perhaps it was just shifting shadows, but their beady little eyes seemed to follow him as he walked. His skin went cold, and he looked down at the ground.

What is wrong with me today?

Anxious to get home where there were no gargoyles and he could lose himself in writing his paper, he picked up the pace. He turned onto Hayden Avenue from Main Street and passed house after house decorated with pumpkins, corn stalks, half-buried zombies, gravestones, and strings of orange lights. As fast as he could, he made his way down the streets, past creepy Spraksville Cemetery, to his current home, a dark little gray ranch house with green moss covering the roof. Not even a single pumpkin had been placed out on the front step. Frank, his foster father, wasn't the type to decorate for a holiday.

Goff headed to the back door, hoping to slip in unseen. As he stepped around the corner, the acrid smell of cigarette smoke and the sickly-sweet odor of citronella wafted over him. A large, tattooed man with a flattop military haircut was leaning up against the porch's railing in the light of a yellow bug bulb and a candle in an orange glass holder. A cigarette hung between two thick tattooed fingers.

"Get over here," Frank commanded. "You're in trouble, boy!"

CHAPTER 2

Death's Gate Traversal

GOFF thought about running, but escaping Frank was simply not possible. The man was moronic but fast. He raced down the stairs and grabbed Goff's shirt collar, leaning in close and releasing a puff of smoke from a cigarette glued to his lower lip. Goff waved the stink away and pushed his broken glasses up as far as they could go, leaving Frank a little distorted through the skewed lenses.

"Somebody break your glasses, kid?" Frank asked.

"Pam."

Frank screwed up his face in disgust. "You didn't lose no fight to no girl, did you?"

"Have you met Pam?"

"I ain't payin' for no new glasses."

Another double negative. Goff couldn't resist. He didn't usually talk back to adults, but Frank was an exception. "I don't want no new glasses."

"Good. And what are you wearin'?" Frank flipped the hem of Goff's cape with his free hand. "You some kinda superhero?"

"Yup. You caught me. I'm Superman. Don't blow my cover?"

"Don't be smart with me." Frank flicked his cigarette into the yard. He tightened his grip and leaned in. "Ain't I told you not to borrow my tools?"

Goff remembered now that he'd borrowed Frank's drill the day before and forgotten to return it. He got lost in what he was doing sometimes... too lost.

"The drill? Sorry about that."

"I spent half an hour lookin' for it," Frank said. "You got a half hour of my time in your pocket?"

"That's not possible."

"Well, I'm takin' it, anyway. You're on dish and laundry duty for the whole week."

"But that's way more than half an hour," Goff protested, thinking about the volume of dirty clothes and dishes Frank, Ben and Pam generated. "I have schoolwork!"

"Shoulda thought of that before you borrowed my drill. Borrow it again, and you'll sleep in the garage for a month."

"Might be an improvement over the attic."

"It's a bedroom, ain't it?"

"You want to sleep there?" Goff challenged.

Frank's nostrils flared, and a tiny remnant of smoke blew out. "Listen, kid, you better start showin' more respect! And you need to shape up a bunch, too. Pam and Ben tell me they think you're weird, that you sit alone at lunch and don't got no friends. I wish social services had mentioned that in their report."

"That I don't got no friends?"

"Yup, and the teasing. You lettin' kids tease you?"

Goff's stomach tightened with anger. "Well, I don't ask them to."

"Better not be! I tell you, I never let no kids tease me when I was your age. Cracked Chuck Smith in the nose when he told me my shirt was on backward. And ya know what? It was!" he laughed. "Never bothered me no more. See what I mean? You gotta let them know who's boss. You act like a wimp, let them walk all over you, and they'll do it every chance they get!"

"I don't let them walk all over me."

"Sure, ya do." Frank wrapped his big fingers around Goff's upper arm. "You call this an arm? Barely more than a toothpick. It's no wonder they tease you. Be a good thing if you put down that pencil and picked up some weights like Ben and Pam do."

Goff wriggled free of Frank's grip and stepped back. "And maybe they should pick up a pencil and put down the weights, so they don't flunk every class. Sorry, but I have bigger plans than bulking up. I'm going to do big things and go places. You watch."

"You ain't goin' nowhere." Frank stood up, his face red. "Just remember, ya got nobody in this world, not without me, and I don't even like you. I took you in out of the goodness of my heart. You're a nothing, kid."

"I'm not a nothing!" Goff stomped his foot. A sudden breeze blew out the citronella candle, leaving only a thin snake of black smoke. Goff was all but certain he hadn't caused the stupid, smelly candle to go out, but the timing felt satisfying regardless. "Besides, I'm here because of money, not your goodness. You don't have a heart."

Leaving Frank fuming, Goff turned and went around to the front of the house. He pulled open the rusty metal front door and entered the living room. As usual, the place was a biohazard: it stank like an ash-tray, and piles of trash, stacks of beer cans, and mountains of cigarette butts lay everywhere. Spiders hung in dusty webs in the corners, and mice scurried back to their homes inside the walls.

On the coffee table littered with old *Commando* magazines sat a little clear box-shaped mousetrap. They were supposed to be humane, since they didn't kill the mouse, but Ben and Pam thought it was fun to catch a mouse in them and watch it die slowly. A tiny brown mouse with big black eyes sat inside this one, shivering, wide-eyed, and drenched in pee.

"I'm sorry, little guy. Let's get you out of there."

He took the trap outside, where he sat down on the front steps, tilted the box forward, and opened the flap. The little creature slid out and landed like a wet turd. It didn't move.

"Go on," Goff said. "You're free."

Slowly, the mouse lifted its head and looked up at him. Goff stared at those little black ball eyes, feeling an odd sense of connection.

"Go on. Go home."

The pathetic creature held Goff's gaze for a few seconds, let out a tiny squeak, and took off. It ran down the front steps and streaked across the yard. It ran and ran, traveling hundreds of feet, just barely visible in the soft light of the moon, and then disappeared into brambles wrapping around a wrought-iron cemetery gate.

Goff pushed his broken glasses into place with his finger and studied the rusty iron letters above the gate: Spraksville Cemetery. His eyes moved over the ornate serifs and twirls of the words while a breeze rustled the leaves dangling over the gravestones. An owl hooted in reply, serenading thin clouds sliding in front of a low, large moon like a flock of ghosts.

Centuries ago, witches held coven meetings deep in the Spraksville Cemetery. Thinking about witches turned Goff's mind to his paper.

He'd already scratched out the rough outline but was worried it would be too dull—just a bunch of questions, details, facts, and an illustration. It wasn't going to be good enough. To get into Amworth, he needed to surprise and awe the selection committee. He needed to show them that someday he'd be a reporter willing to stand in the middle of a war zone or on the edge of a volcano—whatever it took to get a good story.

Basically, he knew this paper had to be *spellbinding*.

Amused by his word choice, he watched a triplet of bats flutter across the sky as an idea fluttered its way up from the back of his mind.

"I can't believe I'm considering this," he said softly, "but think I need to do what the witches are known for—cast a spell."

Goff sat in silence for a moment, digesting this idea. *Cast a Spell? Me?* Wind rattled leaves into waves of static. He looked up at the moonlit rows of stones poking up like jagged teeth, and his heart tightened, realizing that to do it right, he had to go deep into that cemetery at midnight—the witching hour—and perform a spell, like the old witches of Spraksville.

"Being a great journalist," he whispered to the moon, "means stepping out of comfort, standing at the edge, taking people places they'd be too terrified to go themselves."

This was just what the paper needed. He'd structure the entire thing as a blend of facts about Spraksville witchcraft and the story of his spellcasting adventure in Spraksville Cemetery. The only problem was that the thought of going out into that cemetery at midnight, especially to cast a spell, was terrifying. Pushing away his fear, Goff headed into the house. At the top of the stairs, he pushed aside the smelly plastic yellow curtain with salmon flowers and green vines that had been hung as a door for his room.

Entering this space always lowered his mood a few notches, as if it contained a cloud of depression vapor. He looked around at the exposed beams stuck with rusty nails, the flooring made of splintered wood planks, and the single dirty window at the very end. There was no closet and barely any furniture. His bed was a thin mattress on the floor, which he shared with a few mice.

After replacing the arm of his glasses with one from an old pair, Goff walked to the window and pushed up the sash. He leaned against the crumbling frame and stretched out into the cool night air to survey the landscape, considering his escape options.

Five feet below, the garage roof ran out a little way, and beyond that lay the cemetery a few hundred feet in the distance. As he stared down, light flooded the cemetery gates. He froze as it grew brighter. A big old-fashioned hearse with red curtains covering the coffin-compartment windows drove into the cemetery, casting bouncing white light over the tombstones.

A corpse delivery.

Feeling queasy about a fresh corpse being nearby while he cast his spell, Goff sat on a crate that served as a chair for his desk, careful not to get splinters from the jagged desktop. With shaky hands, he poured some water from a pitcher into a glass and raised it in a toast to a taxidermied black cat on his desk. "Cheers, Maxim."

Maxim didn't reply, of course. Goff had found him next to a trashcan the weekend before. At first, he thought he had found an abandoned cat in need of rescue, but when it turned out to be a taxidermied cat, he brought it home anyway. He wanted to create a witchy atmosphere in his writing space, although he regretted that decision now. Maxim creeped him out a little... well, a lot. The darn thing stood on a little black pedestal staring blankly with shiny green eyes. Its claw was raised, and its mouth frozen open in a perpetual hiss.

Goff sipped his water and scratched Maxim between the ears. The hair felt stiff, like the bristles of a brush. "So, being a black cat and probably having belonged to a witch at some point, what advice do you have about casting a spell?"

Maxim hissed silently.

Goff pulled out his binder of notes and paged through it, finding only one image of a spell from a book called *Ways of Witches*. Horrifyingly, the spell was called "Death's Gate Traversal." The description explained that it enabled someone to communicate across the boundary of death. At the top, an ugly pen and ink drawing depicted a decaying human walking through a gate made of bones toward a witch standing over a cauldron.

"You've got to be kidding me," Goff sighed, leaning back and staring at the paper. "It certainly isn't dull, right Maxim?"

What remained to be decided was who he would speak to. He scanned a row of books lined up on the floor against the wall. A famous philosopher? No, way too old, and what would he even say to them? Famous poet? No, that could be weird and sad. Then his eyes traveled to the bin beside his bed. There sat his copy of *Excellence in Reporting* by the late William Cranston. Perfect. He'd only passed away a few years back, and if by some crazy circumstance this spell worked, William Cranston would probably appreciate Goff dragging him through the gate for the sake of good reporting.

Goff placed the Death's Gate Traversal spell before him on his desk and studied the ingredients. In addition to a picture of the person he intended to speak to, he needed a candle, a small bowl of pond water, a grave flower, and three living things. The instructions didn't seem too hard, either. After lighting the candle, you said some weird words three times while placing the living things in the water. Easy. Plus, it would be over quickly. He tried the words on for size.

"I command thee, step aside and let William Cranston through!"

The curtain flew open.

Goff jumped up.

Brak, a big furry mutt with floppy ears that Frank did nothing but yell at, rushed in, panting and wagging his tail. Goff sat back down and tussled Brak's ears. Brak was the only good thing about living here.

"Hey, boy." Goff pulled back and held Brak's face. "So, what adventures did you have today? Meet a nice lady dog? Dig in some trash? I had the usual bad day, but things will get better. I figured out how to make my paper great, so I'll probably be going somewhere really good pretty soon."

Brak walked over and stepped onto Goff's bed, turned in a circle three times, and lay down, staring up at Goff through sad eyes with his nose propped up on the pillow.

"Don't get all sullen," Goff said. "I'll take you with me if I can. I promise."

Brak yawned and turned his head to the side.

Goff returned to his desk and looked at his planner. The paper was due in a few days, and he needed a day or two to write and then edit, which meant he had to do the spell tomorrow night.

The three living things could be spiders from his room. There were certainly plenty of those. He would get the pond water after school from a pond up on Hallow Hill. So that left just the flower from a grave, and checking the spell again, he noticed an asterisk next to this item. At the bottom of the page, there was a matching footnote: "Must be fresh. A dried or wilted flower will not do."

He had just seen a hearse enter the graveyard, so there were probably fresh flowers out there right now. But a frost was due overnight, so they would be shriveled up by morning. A feeling of dread filled him as he realized what that meant. He had to go into the cemetery to collect a flower. Tonight.

CHAPTER 3

Grave Robbers

THUD.

The front door slammed shut, shaking the entire house.

Goff jumped and nearly fell off the crate. Thoughts of sneaking off into the cemetery disappeared behind a much less pleasant one: Pam and Ben. No doubt it was them. They didn't open and close doors, they yanked them wide and slammed them hard.

"Goff! Cook us food!" Ben roared up the stairs.

As mandated by Frank, meals in the house were Goff's responsibility, but he didn't mind. His last foster father had been a wonderful chef, and they had cooked all sorts of gourmet foods together; Goff was sad when that situation ended because of an illness. Cooking here was much less fun—Frank was a culinary Neanderthal by comparison—but he still enjoyed spending time in the kitchen.

Before he reached the bottom of the stairs, Pam and Ben rushed up, huffing and puffing.

"You turd," Pam said. "Did you open the mousetrap?"

"It was dying."

"It was a freakin' mouse!"

"It was a living thing. You had no right to torture it."

"Might makes right, moron." Ben punched Goff in the arm.

Goff winced. "That's stupid."

"It's the way of the world, so you better get used to it."

"I guess I live in a different world."

"Well, this is our world, so leave our mice alone!"

Goff slipped between them and went into the kitchen to start cooking. While tempted to dump a can of beans into a bowl and call it supper, he thought better of it. His butt was still sore from the last time he'd served Frank cold beans. Twenty minutes later, he stood over a sizzling pan of meat, broccoli, and carrots, ready to douse it all in stir-fry sauce he'd created using some ancient takeout soy sauce packets, ketchup, and ginger ale.

Brak, who'd sat in silent torture smelling sizzling meat for too long, finally came to Goff's side and barked out his frustration. Goff put a scoop of dog food into his bowl. Brak flashed big, pleading eyes of disappointment, so Goff scooped a little peanut butter on top. Brak barked happily and began gulping down his gourmet meal.

Goff wiped his sweaty brow, then dished his stir-fry masterpiece on top of some rice on each plate. He fixed up Frank's plate by removing all the vegetables and adding more meat from the other plates. For garnish, he added a few carrot slivers on top.

"Dinner's ready!" he called.

Pam and Ben thundered down the stairs.

"Bring it!" Frank shouted.

Goff grabbed a fork and a napkin, picked up Frank's plate, and carried it to where Frank sat in his recliner watching his favorite show about huge trucks.

"What's that on top?"

"Carrots."

"Why'd you put it there?"

"It's a garnish."

"Garnish?"

"It's like decorations made of food."

"Take them off."

Goff picked the carrots off the top and ate them.

"There's more garnish under my meat."

"That's not garnish."

"What is it then?"

"Rice. Most people think of it as food."

"Get rid of it."

"I can't."

"You're a terrible cook, kid."

"Thanks." Goff turned away, ignoring Frank's culinary review.

He arrived back in the kitchen as Pam and Ben raced back up the stairs, laughing. His plate had been cleaned bare except for a small pile of carrots sticks surrounded by stains of brown sauce. Of course, they had eaten his food. *Might makes right.*

He sighed, eating the rejected carrots and grabbing a box of Lucky Puffs from the pantry to carry up to his room. He didn't have to worry about the plates tonight. Frank would fall asleep with his plate on his lap, and Pam and Ben would stack theirs with the rest of their dirty dishes on top of a pile of dirty underwear, socks, jeans, and T-shirts.

Goff snacked on the stale cereal in his room while he put an old plastic bottle into his backpack for the pond water. He found a candle in one of Frank's moving boxes marked "stuf 2 keep" along with an old hammer and a jar full of rusty nails. He dumped out the nails, poked holes in the lid, and set the jar on the floor.

"Now I just need three spider volunteers."

He searched behind boxes and crates for spiders, but only found dusty, empty webs. Frustrated, he turned to pick up the jar to go hunt up in the rafters. To his surprise, three spiders with black bodies the size of peas were crawling around inside it. Pleased with his lucky break, he screwed on the lid and held it up.

"Don't worry. I won't hurt you. You'll be free soon."

A few minutes later, the crashing and hollering sounds of Frank's favorite show, *Mega Battles,* thundered up through the floor. That meant it was seven o'clock. On cue, Brak trotted in through the curtain. He didn't care for the loud, stupid show any more than Goff did. The two of them flopped down on the mattress. Goff couldn't sneak out of the house until eleven, when everyone was asleep, so he had some time to kill. He planned on thinking about his paper, but he ended up falling asleep instead.

At eleven-thirty, he awoke to a horrible smell. Brak was staring at him with a guilty expression.

"You're the world's worst alarm clock, you know that, Brak? No more peanut butter for you!"

He waved the odor away, got up, crossed the room, and opened the window. As Brak watched, Goff quietly dropped to the garage roof, then down to the shed roof and to the ground. The moon was high in the sky, illuminating the graveyard in a pale blue glow. The cold air turned his anxious breath to silver smoke. At the cemetery entrance, he steeled his nerves with a deep breath before pushing the left gate panel open, wincing as the rusty hinges let out an awful screech.

He stood on a threshold of looming trees and grim tombstones. A lonely path led the way between them. An image of a skeletal hand clawing its way up through the dirt entered his mind, and his heart started pounding.

"Stop it," he ordered his mind. "This is the real world, not a horror movie. Stuff like that doesn't happen."

He stepped into the cemetery, and a deep chill flooded his body, as if he had just walked into a giant refrigerator. Ignoring it, he forced himself to take another step, trying to push images of Amworth ahead of thoughts of zombies and werewolves. He walked slowly, searching for a grave with flowers on it. The sooner he found one, the sooner he could get out of here. Row after row, he scanned for any spark of color, but all the graves seemed lonely and forgotten.

Suddenly, an odd scratching sound from behind him filled him with dread. Braced to run, he turned to find Brak barreling toward him, tongue flapping, breath coming out in bursts of white steam. He arrived in a flurry of fur and wagging tail.

"Good boy." Goff smiled, then leaned down to accept a few licks on the face. "How did you know I needed some company out here tonight?"

Feeling braver with Brak for company, he began walking more quickly. It wasn't until he reached the far side, down a hill near some woods, that he found what he was looking for. It was off the path by twenty feet, and the stone had not been placed yet, so he didn't know who was buried there. On top of the dirt lay several bouquets of flowers. He walked over, selected a white carnation, and tucked it into his jacket pocket. When he got home, he'd put it in water to keep it fresh. He looked up at the moon, feeling very pleased with himself. The hardest step was done.

But just as he turned to head back to the house, a spray of white light bounced over the tree trunks nearby. He dropped down to his knees as headlights crested the hill. The car drove slowly down the rocky path, heading his way. Goff kept low and led Brak up to a sarcophagus that looked like a little stone shack.

Pushing gently on his back, he got Brak to sit. "Stay, boy."

Carefully, hugging the wall, he inched around the side for a look. The car was parked off the path several feet from the mound. It wasn't the hearse he'd seen earlier, but a black limo. The doors opened, and three large men got out.

One of them wore a large hood that exposed only a strange black beard that came to a point on the sides, like little horns, and formed a ring at the bottom big enough to put a hand through. The other two men wore long robes. Their massive bald heads glistened in the moonlight as they carried shovels toward the mound of dirt.

"Be quick," the hooded man commanded.

"Just the eyes this time?" asked one.

"Or do you want fingers too, like last time?" finished the other.

"Just the eyes," the hooded man said. "I've no need for fingers this time."

Fingers? Eyes? Goff went numb. Graverobbers!

The two bald men knocked the flowers off the top with their shovels and set about digging into the earth, working quickly. Their shovels created a pulsing beat of crunching. Goff pulled away and started walking backward, holding Brak at his side. He made it ten feet before stepping on a twig, breaking it with a loud *snap*. He flinched and dropped down to his knees. The pulse of shovels crunching through fresh dirt abruptly stopped.

Goff froze.

"Who's there?" a deep voice called out.

CHAPTER 4

Black Magic

"ZIG! Zag! Go see who it is."

Moving as silently and quickly as possible, Goff scuttled on hands and knees to hide behind a large gravestone a few feet away. His breath was punching out clouds, so he tried to keep his breathing shallow. He wanted nothing more than to be far, far away, but he knew making a break for it would be stupid. They would see him and chase him down, perhaps even slit his throat and steal his eyes—no need for fingers this time.

A tremendous flapping noise arose. Goff couldn't resist peeking around the edge of the tombstone. Two gigantic birds rose into the moonlight and hovered above the sarcophagus, flapping wings as big as car doors. They had bald, wrinkled pink heads like turkeys and long sharp beaks like vultures.

The birds let out a shrill shriek. Brak growled and ran out, barking and snarling. *Brak! No!* Goff sat frozen, unsure what to do. Should he go defend Brak? Stay hidden?

Dropping as low as he could, he peeked out from the base of the gravestone to see what was going on. The two giant birds flew forward and landed in front of Brak. They spread their wings and hissed. Brak bared his teeth, snarling and spitting, haunches up, prepared to attack.

From around the sarcophagus, the hooded man stepped into view. He had piercing black eyes and deep lines slicing across his brow. The lower half of his face was hidden behind that long beard with a circular hole at the bottom. A bolt of fear crashed through Goff; he backed out of sight.

"It's just a dog," the man said. "Back off, you fools! You'll wake some idiot up!"

Goff hugged his knees to his racing heart, hoping his presence hadn't been detected. The birds stopped hissing. Wings beat the air as Brak returned to Goff, shaking like crazy. A moment later, the crunch of shoveling resumed.

Goff rubbed Brak's furry cheeks. "That was very dangerous," he whispered. "But thank you!"

Brak wagged his tail proudly.

Goff checked carefully to see if they were in the clear. The men were out of sight. The idling limo, long and black with a prominent chrome grille, drew his curiosity, but looked empty inside. No sign of the giant birds. He squinted to bring the license plate into focus. It was a vanity plate with six letters: BLK MGK.

Black Magic? Goff's eyes bulged. *Time to get the heck out of here.*

His heart racing, Goff used the sarcophagus for cover and crept backward, Brak at his side. After making it past several stones, he scuttled on all fours from gravestone to gravestone until he crested the hill. Confident that he was out of sight, he stood up and ran through the cemetery, through the gates, and back to the garage. Brak darted toward the dog flap in the back door, and Goff forced his tired body back up the way he'd come down. He rolled in through his bedroom window and closed it quietly but firmly behind him. Brak came racing in just as Goff straightened himself, his heart pounding, out of breath, and his brain nearly spinning out of his head.

He hugged Brak. "Did that really just happen, boy?"

Brak panted heavily in reply. Goff leaned forward and held his soft, furry head, looking him directly in the eyes. "You saved me out there, Brak. I don't know what they would've done if they'd found me. Pam and Ben think you're a wimp but they are so wrong. You're a hero!"

Goff sunk his face into Brak's fur, enjoying the softness and warmth, while his mind chewed on what had just happened. BLK MGK? Was that some kind of joke? Spraksville had seen its share of witches and warlocks, but that was ancient history, and there is no such thing as magic... black, pink, white, or any other color.

Giving Brak one final nuzzle, Goff stood up as a smile spread across his lips. They'd just escaped from grave-robbing warlocks, which was exactly how he would write about it in his paper. And despite that, he'd still managed to get the flower for the spell. Carefully, he took the precious carnation out of his pocket and gave it a home in some water in a drinking glass. It was a bit rumpled but seemed still fresh enough to be used for the spell tomorrow night. At least, he hoped so. What did he know about spells? Would using a wilted flower in a spell be like using old yeast in bread, meaning it just didn't rise? Or would it do something horrifying, like turn his eyes into marshmallows?

A yawn took him by surprise. He checked the clock: 1 a.m. Way past his usual bedtime. He took off his jacket and got into bed with his clothes still on. Brak dropped down at his feet, his heavy breathing softly rocking the thin mattress. Goff pulled the covers up against the cold and lay there enjoying the feeling of Brak warming his toes while watching the moonlight break into icicles across the beams of the ceiling.

It seemed only minutes later that the buzz of the alarm clock rattled him awake. He changed into a gray sweater and jeans and ran down to the kitchen. Pam and Ben sat wearing pajamas at the table under a little ring of light from a single dim bulb above.

Goff opened the cereal cabinet. "You guys staying home today?"

"No, dork, it's pajama day at school," Pam said.

"Really?"

Pam threw a chewed corner of toast at him. "Duh."

"And, if you forget," Ben added, grinning stupidly, "they make you sing a song in front of everybody at assembly."

"You better go PJ up," Pam warned.

Goff's mind felt so fuzzy from being up nearly all night that he couldn't process the idea of pajama day. *What sort of moronic Glee Club member thought that was a good idea?* But he certainly couldn't imagine anything more terrifying than singing in front of the entire school. He grabbed an oatmeal bar and ran upstairs to his room to change back into pajamas.

"Don't miss the bus!" Ben shouted.

Goff quickly changed into red flannel pajamas. Just in case shoes mattered too, he slipped on a pair of fluffy white slippers. Grabbing his coat and backpack, he ran down the stairs and out the door, arriving at the bus stop just as the red flashing lights went out and the door started closing. He pushed it back open, catching a dirty look from the bus driver, and bolted up the stairs.

Pam and Ben, who were sitting in a middle row fully dressed, burst out laughing. Nobody was wearing pajamas.

"You are such an idiot!" Ben shouted.

"I can't believe you fell for that," Pam said, grinning maliciously.

Everyone on the bus turned to look at Goff and exploded with laughter.

Goff threw himself down into the nearest seat and pulled his coat over him like a blanket, tucking his regrettable fluffy slippers up under him. Turning to watch a wispy spider crawl across the dirty glass outside, he considered his options. Maybe he could say he was sick and hide in the nurse's office? No, she would call Frank, and he'd have to wake up and drive to school. He'd go ballistic. And despite how horrible this day would surely be, avoiding it wasn't worth ruining his perfect attendance record.

Goff felt a sharp pain on the back of his head.

"Nice PJs!" Tom Sweeney mocked, flicking Goff's head again.

A surge of anger raced through Goff. "Knock it off."

"That's what happens to dorks who wear pajamas to school."

"I was tricked."

"Don't matter. It's the law, so I gotta do it." Tom flicked Goff's head again. "Right, everyone? It's the law?"

A bunch of kids hooted in agreement.

Goff dropped down and hugged his knees as the bus bounced down the road. They passed a house with three stuffed green witches dangling from a tree limb and another with a front yard full of tombstones. At an intersection, Goff studied a house with a set of zombies reaching up through the dirt near an open coffin with a plastic skeleton clambering out. Halloween had taken over Spraksville like a kitschy virus.

Several stops later, the bus pulled up in front of Spraksville Junior High. Goff wanted to be the last off, so he sat, curled up, waiting for everyone to get off. Pam and Ben and a few other kids flicked the back of his head as they passed, saying, "It's the law." Goff ignored them.

When the bus was empty, the driver, a large man with a ruddy face, stared at him with his eyebrows raised.

"Not a hotel, kid."

Goff walked forward but paused on the platform at the top of the bus stairs, dreading walking down them.

"Gonna be a tough day for you," the driver acknowledged.

"Yup."

"Life stinks sometimes, kid."

"Yup."

"Now, get off my bus."

CHAPTER 5

Harkland Mathers XIII

GOFF walked down the bus stairs to the sidewalk. Kids rushed past, pointing and staring at him in his red flannel PJs and white puffy slippers. He wanted to kill Pam and Ben. The bus driver was right—this was going to be a tough day.

Dreading going inside, he surveyed Spraksville Junior High, offended by how quaint it was: red brick trimmed in white, paned glass windows, and a cute little fake veranda over the entrance held up by marble pillars. How dare it look so unassuming and pleasant. People passing by should be able to tell it was nasty on the inside. In typical Spraksville style, there were gargoyles every dozen feet along the top. *What is it with this town and gargoyles?*

The school bell rang three times, signaling the start of homeroom. Keeping the gargoyles in his peripheral vision in case they moved, he walked toward the school as casually as he could. Ignoring the yelps of laughter all around him, he entered through the front doors that led into a highway of rushing students. Several kids flicked the back of his head on his way to first-period class. It seemed Tom Sweeney had quickly spread the word about the new "law." Goff dragged himself from class to class all morning, being laughed at, having his head flicked, and unsure how he would survive until the end of the day.

At lunchtime, he headed to the cafeteria, his stomach churning with fear of the food and whatever else he might encounter there. It was usually the worst part of the day. He joined the assembly line of kids and moved along as cooks piled food onto trays. After paying an old woman with kind eyes who told him she liked his pajamas, he turned and came face to face with Amber Henson, flanked by two of her twiggy blond cheerleading friends.

Goff's heart came to a complete stop. Amber was perfect: huge, soft brown eyes, coffee-colored skin, and twists of brown hair resting on her pink and white cheerleader sweater like chocolate sauce on strawberry ice cream.

At the beginning of the school year, the Guidance Counselor had arranged for Goff and Amber to meet, since they had both just moved into town. Despite some initial awkwardness, they'd ended up bonding over making fun of Spraksville. For a week or so, they had been friends, and life had never been more incredible for Goff. Every day, he and Amber ate lunch and rode the bus together. Then one day, the popular crowd noticed her and reeled her in like a prized marlin, signaling an abrupt end to the Beauty and the Dork fairytale.

Amber's eyes popped wide, taking in Goff's pajamas. The twiggy blonds burst out laughing.

"It's true!" one of them said. "Such adorable fuzzy slippers!"

"What a tool!"

"Where's your teddy bear, little boy?"

"Seriously damaged," Amber added, avoiding Goff's eyes.

Goff didn't say anything, but he couldn't leave, either. At least Amber had acknowledged him for a change. While the two idiots flanking her continued to make pajama jokes, she didn't try to stop them, but she didn't join in. She just shook her head and bit her lip. When they finally ran out of quips and walked off, Amber stayed back and leaned in close. "You make it very difficult for me."

"Excuse me?"

"I don't want to be mean to you, Goff, but when you show up wearing pajamas and fuzzy slippers, what am I supposed to do?"

"Is it the slippers? I worried that was a mistake."

She smiled just a little but dropped it quickly. She had always liked his jokes. "Just stay below the radar, please?"

"I'm trying."

"Try harder."

Amber walked away, and Goff couldn't wipe the small smile from his lips. It was clear Amber still cared about him a little, and that was something. He snuck his tray of gray meatloaf, burnt tater tots, and greasy three-bean salad out into the hallway to hide in a broom closet doorway and eat as much of it as he could stand.

After lunch and then a few more classes, the end of this terrible day was heralded by the clang of the bell. Fortunately, the afternoon bus was mostly empty. A few minutes after he got home, he was on his way back out the door wearing jeans, a T-shirt, and a beige barn jacket. Heading down Hayden, he started half-running, half-skipping. His hair swirled in the wind, and his backpack bumped up and down as puffy gray clouds raced across the sky and showers of leaves fell from the trees.

Half a mile down Hayden, when he came to Amber's house, he lifted his legs higher, stuck his chin out, and kept his arms at his side, hoping to look a little cooler. Then he realized Amber was at cheerleading practice. He also realized there was no way he'd actually managed anything approaching cool.

When he reached Hallow Hill Road, he fought the force of its steep slope with every step. Spraksville dropped further away, leaving only trees and road. It was a strange world up here—nothing but looming trees and a carpet of mustard-colored leaves in every direction. Not a single car had driven past. He walked along, kicking up leaves, enjoying the solitude. When he reached the top, a faint humming from down the hill broke the silence. The wind stopped short, as if someone had flipped a switch. The trees turned into statues. The leaves fell like stones.

What the heck?

A moment later, a large black car with a prominent chrome grille crested into view. It had a license plate on the front: BLK MGK.

Panic rose from the base of Goff's spine. He started walking fast, keeping his head down, hoping they'd ignore a random kid on the side of the road. As the long black car glided past, relief flooded over him. But then, ten feet away, it stopped. Goff stopped too. Why had they stopped?

The limo began backing up.

Goff began freaking out.

It pulled up to him. The back window rolled down slowly, and Goff found himself face to face with the bearded man from the graveyard last night.

Up close, he was genuinely terrifying. Oily black hair pulled back framed a freakishly high, deeply wrinkled brow. A pointy waxed mustache sat below a long, hooked nose and capped off a massive beard with a hole in it big enough to put a hand through. But all of that was nothing compared to his eyes. They were the darkest, cruelest pair Goff had ever seen.

"I'm curious," the man said, wagging his fingers at Goff, his voice as deep and dark as his eyes. "What brings a boy such as you so far up a lonely hill on a fall afternoon?"

Goff's head went fuzzy as everything except the man's eyes and voice seemed to slip away. He was about to explain that he was here to fetch pond water for a spell when a bee buzzed by, a little too close for comfort. Swatting it away brought him back to his senses. *Why would I tell him that?*

"Out for a walk," he replied simply.

The man tilted his head and took a deep breath. "So you must live near here then?"

"Across town."

"Well, I'm new to Spraksville, but if I understand the local geography, that would put you near the Spraksville Cemetery. Am I correct?"

Goff felt the word cemetery fly at him like a dart thrown at his head. It was suspicious that it had come up so quickly. "In that general area," he confirmed, trying not to show his discomfort.

"And is there a particular reason you've come so far today?"

"I'm working on a project."

"For school?"

"Yes."

"You like school, then?"

"I didn't—" Goff started. "Sure, yes."

"School is overrated."

"I suppose."

"But you are smart, aren't you," the man said.

"I do well."

"What do you study?"

Goff's mind seemed to grow fuzzier with every word the man spoke. "You know, the basics, but writing is my thing," he said, surprised to hear himself talk. "I'm here to collect pond water, in a bottle, for a..."

Goff shook his head to stop himself from continuing. *Don't tell him about the spell!* "A paper I'm writing."

The man studied him for a moment. "Ah, I see. You are here to visit the pond on the edge of my property. I recently moved into Hallow Manor up on the hill. It seems you will be my first visitor. Allow me to introduce myself. My name is Harkland Mathers, the thirteenth. May I know your name?"

Goff cleared his throat, wondering why his mind felt so heavy. "Goff."

"Goff." The man chewed on the sound of it a moment before responding. "I know that name. German, is it not? Usually a surname. I believe it means powerful warrior."

"I don't know about that," Goff said, and then he found himself talking as if his brain weren't part of the interaction. Words spilled from his mouth, and he said things he would rather have kept private. "I'm told it was supposed to have been Geoff—hard "g," soft "e" but my father's handwriting was terrible and my birth certificate came out wrong. My parents died in a plane crash weeks after I was born, so it's practically the only connection I have to them. I like the name now. It's unique, if nothing else."

"Unique, yes, but unfortunate otherwise." The man squinted, all remnants of a friendly smile dropping. "Geoff is a better name for a boy such as you. Its origins are in peace, and it's abundantly clear you are not a warrior, now are you, Goff?"

Despite Goff's mind feeling fuzzy, the criticism leveled against him reached through loud and clear. It awoke something inside him, an angry core that breathed fire on his mind, burning away the fog. He looked Mathers square in the eyes, noting a tiny flinch as they met. He could tell his anger was unexpected.

"I think a man as accomplished as you," Goff said, holding Mather's eyes for a moment, "should know better than to judge a book by its cover."

Mather's eyes narrowed. Goff looked away and started walking, trembling a little. The limo edged forward, matching his pace, and Mather's voice floated out of the window, "I can see I offended you, and I apologize for that. I am not a tactful man, Goff, but more importantly, neither am I a tolerant or forgiving man. It would be wise of you and everyone else in this town to stay out of my business. I'm afraid I must ask rather firmly that your interest in my affairs begins and ends with my pond water. When you collect what you need, return to your home near the cemetery and mind your own business. Will you do that for me, Goff?"

"I'm only here for pond water," Goff said. "Nothing more."

"Excellent." The window started rolling up, and the limo sped off, churning up a wake of leaves.

Everything that had gone still suddenly sprang back to life. Leaves swirled around Goff, slapping and stinging his face. Trees swayed dangerously, creaking with branches knocking. A gusty wind pushed him sideways. He closed his eyes and braced against it, thinking it must be just a coincidence. *Magic isn't real!* Mathers was just a weird, spooky, graverobbing man who lived on the other side of town. Nothing more. Their paths would never cross again.

CHAPTER 6

Spellcasting

GOFF walked a little further before leaving the road and traveled a good way through the woods, down into a valley where darkness had a permanent home. Thick gray tree trunks that cast no shadows rose from a beige carpet of needles. A palpable stillness in the air, broken only by an occasional falling needle, creaking branch settled deep into Goff's bones.

The pond lay at the center of a shallow valley. Goff approached it, feeling like an unwanted presence in this eerie, isolated world. A granite marker was set at the water's edge with the name of the pond chiseled into it: *Dead Man's Pond*.

Of course—what else would it be called? He descended the narrow path down to a small mud and gravel beach. The water was nearly motionless, reflecting the trees like an oil painting in coalescing greens and grays. He knelt at the edge, lowered the bottle—and then froze. Two black birds gliding among the trees were reflected on the water's surface. He held his breath, unsure if these were Zig and Zag or if he had simply developed bird paranoia. The birds shredded the silence with caws and flew out of sight a moment later. Goff relaxed. *Just crows.*

A circle of ripples calmly rolled out across the pond as the bottle filled, and he let his eyes grow fuzzy, staring at his reflection broken into circular shards. It was hypnotizing watching the swells form shapes and colors around his face, but then something moved nearby. Was it one of the birds back again?

No, someone was behind him.

Fear took hold of his body, and he jumped to his feet too quickly in the slick mud. He would have toppled into the water if a pair of hands hadn't reached out and grabbed his arm.

"Oh my god!" the girl shrieked, steadying him.

Goff found his footing and turned to see Lydia Garcia holding his arm and Halstrom Flint standing next to her—the same kids who had seen him get bullied at Pongo's. Lydia stood about two feet shorter than Halstrom, and her wild green eyes stared at Goff through red plastic-rimmed glasses that sat at the tip of her nose. Her clothing was a size too big, and a gold headband scrunched her greasy brown hair into a mushroom cloud. She seemed a strand of spaghetti standing next to towering Halstrom, a robotic, narrow wedge of muscle packed into a blue sweater and jeans. Halstrom regarded Goff sternly with shrewd, steely eyes set into a chiseled brown face. On his head was his trademark blue beanie. Goff had never seen him without a blue beanie on. Lydia and Halstrom were misfits like Goff, but the bullies left them alone. People said Lydia could scream loud enough to wake the dead when someone pissed her off, and who would bully Halstrom? He was unflappable and brawny—so both boring and dangerous to tease.

Lydia was surprisingly strong for such a wisp of a girl, but Goff pulled free of her grip.

"Dude," Lydia said, snatching the bottle from Goff and holding it back dramatically. She shook her head, and her glasses slipped down even further, looking perilously close to falling off. "You do not want to drink this water!"

"Drink it?" Goff asked.

"You know." Lydia lifted the bottle and pretended to drink. "Glug, glug, glug?"

"I'm certain he knows what drinking is," Halstrom said matter-of-factly with a slight accent Goff couldn't pin down, but which made him sound like a cartoon scientist.

"Yeah, I'm smart like that." Goff tried to seize the bottle, but Lydia was too quick.

"Really, don't drink this!" Lydia pushed her glasses back up in a grand gesture. "It's called Dead Man's Pond for a reason. There are dead people at the bottom."

"We have also seen Tom Sweeney urinate in it," Halstrom added.

Lydia shoved Halstrom. "Why can't you just say pee when you mean pee?"

"Urinate is less ambiguous."

"What else could pee mean?"

"A singular green pea."

"You're ridiculous."

"I'm accurate."

"I wasn't going to drink it," Goff said, irritated that Lydia had his bottle. "It's for an experiment."

"An experiment?" Lydia asked. "We have science class together, you know, but we never talk or anything. Did I forget about an assignment?"

"What is the hypothesis for your experiment?" Halstrom asked.

"I don't have one."

"Scientific experiments require one."

"It's not a scientific experiment."

"Then what is it?"

"None of your business!"

"By the way," Lydia said abruptly, "I can't believe you wore PJs and fuzzy slippers today."

"I laughed whenever I saw you," Halstrom added. "Sleepwear is to wear while sleeping, not at school."

"Happy you were entertained," Goff smirked. "Ben and Pam tricked me."

"Those two are the worst," Lydia said. "They think they're the cat's knees."

Halstrom raised an eyebrow, pushing his beanie up and letting a brown curl spill out, which he efficiently tucked back in. "Why do they think they are the knees of a cat?"

"She mixed her metaphors," Goff explained, hoping to speed this along. "She meant either cat's pajamas or bee's knees."

"You an English teacher?" Lydia challenged.

"Why does everyone keep asking me that?"

"Well, regardless, let me mangle metaphors if I want to."

Halstrom cocked his head to the side. "Mangled metaphors. That's new."

"Whatever!"

"Can I have my bottle back?" Goff asked.

Lydia moved it farther away from him. "You gonna drink it?"

"I told you, it's for an experiment!"

Halstrom frowned. "I still do not understand the experiment."

"You don't need to," Goff said. "Why are you even here? Do you two live around here?"

"I live with my grandfather off Main Street," Halstrom said.

"My stepdad has a trailer down the hill and over that way," Lydia said, gesturing in a way that somehow involved all of her—hand, body, head, and hair. Goff took advantage of this and snagged his bottle back.

Lydia scowled at him. "Don't drink that!"

"I'm not—" Goff started, but what was the point? He put it in his backpack and turned to walk back up the path. "Well, this has been fun."

"Maybe…" Lydia began hesitantly, "You'd wanna hang with us sometime?"

Goff stopped, surprised by the offer. Someone wanted to hang out with him? He turned to see that Lydia's cheeks had blushed as bright as the bandanna around her neck. She gulped and looked down at the ground.

"Lydia speaks to me often about you," Halstrom said.

"Shut your big mouth, you idiot." Lydia shoved Halstrom with all her might, not managing to move him even an inch. "I talk about everyone." She looked up at Goff. "No biggie if you don't want to hang out. It's not like I want you to hang out with us. I was just being generous. I figured a kid like you might need some friends. I don't talk about you. Halstrom was just joking."

"I do not joke," Halstrom said.

Lydia punched his shoulder.

"A kid like me?" Goff pressed.

"I mean… well, you know… you get teased a lot and stuff. I feel sorry for you."

"Sorry for me?"

"That sounded bad. I mean—"

"No thanks," Goff said, turning abruptly. "I'm not that much of a loser."

"Dude, come on. I didn't mean it like that."

"She often says what she does not mean," Halstrom said.

"I think she said exactly what she meant."

Anger hot on his face, Goff turned and walked away. He took giant steps and traveled as fast as possible without slipping on wet leaves and mud. He made his way back up the path to the road and marched down Hallow Hill Road. As he walked, he angrily kicked leaves piled up along the road into tiny colorful storms. *She feels sorry for me? Why does everyone in this town think they're better than me?*

Still fuming, he arrived back at the house and opened the door to be greeted by an onslaught of shouting. Frank was sitting in his big puffy lounge chair, reclined to nearly horizontal, eyes bugged out and temples pulsing. "Dirty dishes. Dirty laundry!" he roared, spittle flying in all directions. "Where have you been?"

"I had a school thing."

"Well, you're cleaning the toilets tonight too. Inside and out. I want them to sparkle."

"There's no way those toilets will ever sparkle again."

"Find a way. And cook a good supper tonight. None of that garish stuff."

"Garnish, not garish."

"Well," Frank rose and angrily trudged to the fridge to get a beer, "I don't want none of either!"

"I'll give you both, then," Goff muttered as Frank headed back to the living room.

"No garish! And hurry up. I'm hungry."

Goff got started on supper without even going to his room. He knew what to make. He wanted Frank, Ben, and Pam all fat and happy so they'd fall asleep early that night. He seasoned two pounds of ground beef with bacon bits, added a cup of grated cheese, formed it into a loaf, smeared it with ketchup, draped it with bacon, and put it in a hot oven on a sheet pan. Meatloaf for morons. They'd all be thrilled.

He fed Brak some canned food—no peanut butter tonight—and for the next hour, while Frank watched TV, Goff did the laundry and washed dishes. He cleaned the hall bathroom toilet and was on his way to clean the one in Frank's room when an envelope on Frank's bedside table caught his eye.

In ornate lettering, the return address read: Harkland Mathers XIII, Hallow Manor. Goff felt like he had just spotted a giant hairy spider. Why did Frank have a letter from that man? The envelope was already open so Goff slipped out the letter and unfolded it. It was an application for employment as a security guard, printed on gray parchment in red ink. It had been stamped *Approved* above the start date: tomorrow. Goff restuffed the envelope, feeling a little shaken.

Frank was going to work for Harkland Mathers?

Trying to push the thought away, Goff finished the nasty job of cleaning Frank's toilet as fast as possible, and after changing the laundry, arrived in the kitchen just as the oven timer began beeping. The meatloaf was brown and crispy, and it smelled pretty good for caveman food. He cut it into slices and squirted canned, neon orange CheeseE-ase ropes across the top. Then he set a loaf of white bread next to it.

"Supper's ready!"

The twins bolted down the stairs, pushing and shoving. Frank didn't wait to be served. He arrived in the kitchen first and held Ben and Pam back. Goff stood silently off to the side and watched Frank load up a plate with four sloppy sandwiches.

"See?" Frank said, heading back into the living room. "No garish is so much better."

"Bacon in everything, always," Ben said, jabbing Goff in the ribs.

Plates full, Ben and Pam shoved past Goff, both taking the time to wipe greasy fingers on his shirt on the way out. There was a little meatloaf left, but Goff opted to leave it—the more they ate, the sleepier they'd be. He poured himself a bowl of Oatmeal Stix and carried it up to his room, where Brak joined him while he did his homework. Maxim sat silently hissing at him and Goff used one of his sharp claws to hold a sticky note.

At eleven o'clock, he placed everything he'd gathered onto his mattress. It was all in order, except his nerves. He held up the black and white picture of William Cranston, whose sharp, intelligent eyes stared back at him. This man had walked onto active battlefields, stood at the base of erupting volcanos, and interviewed murderous dictators, all for the sake of good journalism.

And I'm afraid of phony spellcasting in a cemetery?

Trying to ignore his fear, Goff put everything in his backpack and lay down on his bed with Brak at his side. Frank was shouting obscenities at a wrestling match. Ben and Pam were bouncing balls off the wall in the hallway.

It took a little while, but the house eventually calmed down. Hot showers rattled the pipes, toilets flushed, and two bedroom doors slammed. Two down, one to go. Goff waited. At about a quarter to midnight, Frank's snoring started rising and falling like waves on a rocky beach.

Goff tip-toed his way to the window to keep the floorboards from creaking. The moon cast enough silvery light for him to see, but a fog had settled. Everything past the edge of the garage roof was invisible. He lifted the window sash slowly and slipped out the window as Brak headed for the door and plodded down the stairs. Goff waded through the fog to the cemetery, where Brak came running up beside him.

"You sure you want to join me in this?" Goff asked.

Brak wagged his tail.

Goff pushed the gate open and stepped in, crunching the gravel below the arched wrought-iron Spraksville Cemetery entrance. Every step seemed far too loud as he headed down the uneven path beneath the towering trees, the tops of which were invisible behind a wall of gray. *Where should I do this?* A sarcophagus sat at the end of a path to his right. It looked like a tiny, creepy stone hut with no doors or windows. Having a wall at his back felt like a good idea, so he headed toward it. Two stone gargoyles the size of small men sat on top, crouching down on clawed hooves with wide wings partially spread. *Seriously, why are there so many gargoyles?*

"Don't mind me," Goff said to them, trying to calm his nerves. "I'll be gone in a jiffy."

Keeping his eye on the stone creatures until they were out of sight, he walked around the side and leaned against the stone wall. The fog swirled around him like smoke from an old man's pipe. His heart pounded. The ancient bell in the Town Hall clock tower began clanging midnight, filling the air with a disharmonic, sickly sound. It sent a chill through Goff's entire body. His mind flooded with scenes from horror movies where foolish kids wander off alone and get killed by vampires, werewolves, or madmen. Brak pressed his face into Goff's hand and looked up with his tongue lolling out, panting through a dog smile, not looking scared at all, which helped Goff to relax.

With the pitiful bell in Town Hall still ringing out its warped tune, Goff took everything out of the backpack, lit the candle, and filled a small bowl with the pond water. He leaned the picture of William Cranston against the rim. As the bell rang for the eleventh time, he placed the jar containing the spiders and the flower on the ground and sat down to smooth out the spell sheet. The bell tolled for the last time and when its scratchy clanging stopped, silence took over.

"The witching hour, Brak. Time to cast fate to the wind."

He opened the jar and tried to tip one spider into the water. Two fell out and landed in the bowl.

"Rats!" He closed the lid, then read the words from the sheet out loud, once for each spider.

"Hellioth, thou who watches the borders, tether thy hounds. Hellioth, thou who watches the borders, tether thy hounds."

He opened the jar, and the last spider crawled out onto his hand. He recoiled, but managed to flick it off into the bowl.

"Hellioth, thou who watches the borders, tether thy hounds."

While the spiders wriggled in the water, Goff picked up the book and grabbed the carnation. Sitting cross-legged near the bowl, he rolled the flower between his fingers and looked at William Cranston. Crumpled flower petals fell into the water and on the ground as he spoke the final words of the spell.

"I command thee to step aside and let William Cranston through!"

The spell completed, Goff looked around, unsure what to expect but hoping for nothing. It hadn't gone exactly as planned, but he'd done all of it. The candle flame glowed without flickering, turning the fog to a steady orange. The spiders flailed in the water, climbing onto the flower petals as if they were tiny rafts. It all seemed ridiculous and sloppy, just a mess left behind by a kid playing with bugs and mud. He turned to Brak and laughed.

"I guess I'm not a wizard, eh?"

A single puff of wind blew the candle out. The warm orange cocoon of light dropped away, and the fog began to swirl as if stirred by an invisible hand.

CHAPTER 7

Tackle a Vampire

A thin finger of the silver fog formed a vortex above the bowl, spinning like a tiny tornado. It touched the water's surface, making it turn in the same direction. The spiders clamored for the safety of the edge as the water swirled faster and faster, rocking the bowl from side to side. Brak growled as the bowl rose into the air.

"No, no, no!" Goff scuttled backward, pressing his back to the wall of the sarcophagus. "This can't be happening. William? Is that you? Please don't hurt me. I was just doing research. You like research, remember?"

The spinning bowl continued to rise, teetering back and forth just slightly. It stopped a few feet above eye level, no longer spinning but suspended in the air as if sitting on an invisible shelf. Only the fog was still moving. Numb from head to toe, Goff was transfixed. It didn't seem possible that the bowl was simply hanging in mid-air. Physics couldn't explain that. A spider lifted one of its legs above the brim, like a tiny plea for help—

And then the bowl fell straight down.

Goff screamed and Brak backed up when it shattered against the ground. Water, flower petals, spiders, and porcelain shrapnel flew in all directions. He shielded his face but continued to peer through the cracks of his fingers, unable to look away but terrified of what he might see. Perhaps a decaying William Cranston would step out of the fog. On the ground, dizzy spiders unfolded themselves and scampered sideways out of puddles. William Cranston's picture lay face down, wet and covered with flower petals.

Goff tried to breathe, but fear had turned his lungs to stone. What he had just seen simply wasn't possible. *Magic wasn't real, was it?*

A resounding thump sent vibrations through the ground, like the footstep of a giant beast shaking the earth.

Goff's heart skipped a beat.

"I take it back!" he shouted, his voice cracking with fear. "Hellish, or whatever your name is, you can go home! Keep your hounds at your side. It was just a school project, I promise!"

The wall at Goff's back bulged and heaved. He stood and jumped away just as it split down the middle, corner to corner, with a sound like a sharp clap of thunder. Stone shards struck him and bounced on the ground.

"Please," he begged, dropping to the ground and curling up into a ball. "I'll never do another spell."

The heavy crunch of breaking stone crashing to the ground came from around the other side of the sarcophagus, followed by a shrill shriek that made Goff's hair stand on end. His breathing came to a stop.

"Come here!" commanded a gravelly voice. "And let us look upon you!"

Goff was frozen with fear, but Brak growled and barked and took off around the corner.

"No, Brak!" Goff called after him, frozen in place with fear.

Brak's bark became a vicious growl.

"Brak! Get back here!"

Suddenly, as if turned off with a switch, Brak went quiet. Goff found his courage, jumped up and ran around the corner. On the ground, ten feet in front of the sarcophagus, Brak lay on his side, motionless, eyes closed. Goff raced over to him, fearing the worst. He buried his face into Brak's fur, happy to find a faint heartbeat throbbing in his ear.

"You dare send a dog to fight your battles?" boomed a deep voice from above.

Two gargoyles with red eyes glared down at him from the top of the sarcophagus. Saliva dripped from their fangs, and they held their wings high. He gasped and crawled backward, smashing his palms down on the broken stone in the dirt. The gargoyles crouched down, tucking their wings behind them.

"Please don't kill me," Goff pleaded as he moved to his knees and brought his hands together in prayer. "I want to live."

"Pathetic," the left gargoyle snarled, letting loose a growl that rumbled the earth. They turned to each other, shaking their heads and eyeing Goff from the side, as if he were a bug.

"Off your knees, you miserable little worm."

Goff forced his legs to stand. "Please don't kill me."

"Stop begging!"

"But I really don't want you to kill me."

"Stupid boy!" The left gargoyle flapped his wings. "Sometimes, the way to get what you want is by doing the opposite of what's obvious. You know, run into a fire."

"Tackle a vampire."

"Howl at a werewolf."

"Spit at a gargoyle."

Goff's head was spinning from the back and forth between the two. "So, you want me to spit at you?"

"Not now!"

The left gargoyle crossed his arms. "Tell us, why did you come here tonight, little wizard?"

"I'm not a wizard." Goff had no idea what was going on. "I was just doing a spell for a school project, that's all. I'll never do another one, I promise."

"A spell, eh? Is that what that was?"

"Well, only a wizard could have summoned elemental magic using bugs, pond water, and… what was that ridiculous name you summoned? Hellioth?"

"And, your *spell* woke us up from a lovely sleep."

Goff pointed toward the cemetery exit. "Well, if you let me leave, you can go back to sleep."

They leaned forward, tapping their chins and narrowing their eyes.

"I'm afraid it's not that simple."

"Do you know the function of gargoyles?"

"Decoration?" Goff answered before thinking better of it.

They both snarled and flared their nostrils. "Do we look like decorations?"

Goff took a step backward. "Not at the moment."

"Gargoyles maintain the balance of magic."

"I don't understand," Goff said, shaking his head miserably.

"Once upon a time, new wizards popped up every day, all wanting magic to flow to them. Bunch of big-headed jerks, mostly."

"Yes, egotistical, power-grubbing nasties."

"But with so many, balance was never a problem. There were plenty of wizards connected to the magical realm, so magic was flowing in all directions."

"But that was long ago."

"Wizards have all but disappeared."

"Except for *him*."

"And now, since you came here tonight and revealed yourself—"

"Once again," Goff interrupted. "Not a wizard."

"But you are a wizard!"

"And now you are bound to him as an enemy."

Goff didn't like the sound of any of this. "To whom? I don't know who you're talking about, but I don't want to be any wizard's enemy. Leave me out of this."

"But balance requires opposition, like hot and cold."

"Light and dark."

"Up and down."

"So, magic will now flow to you also."

"Nope, nope, nope." Goff shook his head, a sour feeling growing in his stomach. "I just want this horrible night to be over. I'm taking my dog and going home, and you'll never see or hear from me again. End of story."

"The end?" The two gargoyles sniggered. "This is just the beginning."

"You are part of the magical contour now."

"We have done what had to be done."

The two giant creatures pulled their wings close and dropped down, resuming their original position. Their eyes stopped glowing.

"Goodbye, little wizard, and good luck—you'll need it."

"Wait," Goff stepped forward, "that's it? Magic will flow to me now? What does that even mean? Who is this other wizard?"

With a final flash of its red eyes, the one on the right moved his lips one last time to say, "He goes by the name Harkland Mathers."

Goff felt a surge of nausea. "Wait! Come back! Are you crazy? That guy is terrifying!"

The stone gargoyles didn't respond. Goff stared at them, trembling and trying to process what had just happened. He dropped down to Brak and felt a rush of joy when Brak lifted his head and lapped a big, wet rough tongue across his right cheek.

Goff rubbed the fur between Brak's ears. Brak whimpered and stood up on wobbly legs and Goff gently wrapped his arms around his quivering body. "Come on, boy, let's get home."

Goff turned to lead Brak out of the cemetery but stopped when high-pitched shrieks ripped through the air. Two massive, winged figures passed in front of the moon. Definitely not crows! He started running, keeping Brak close at his side. Near the entrance to the cemetery, two giant birds dropped down to perch on stones in front of him. Metal plaques hanging around their long, thin necks flashed blue in the moonlight: Zig on the left and Zag on the right.

CHAPTER 8

Zig and Zag

GOFF came to an abrupt stop, expelling excited clouds from his pumping lungs. Brak growled menacingly. Goff grabbed his collar and scouted out a path around Zig and Zag, but there didn't seem to be one.

"Don't bother running," Zag said in a scratchy voice.

Goff's jaw dropped. "You can talk?"

"We can hear too," Zig hissed. "You've decided to collect magic?"

"Terrible decision, wizard."

Goff's back stiffened at hearing the word "wizard" again. He clenched his fists. "I'm not a wizard, and I'm not going to collect magic. I just want to go home."

The two birds looked at each other, and then Zig spoke. "Only a fool wouldn't want that kind of power."

"The way I see it, only a fool would want power," Goff said.

"Nevertheless, you will obtain it," Zig said.

"No, I won't."

"Yes, you will."

"Magic will come your way," Zag said.

"Well, if it does," Goff said, waving his hand as if chasing a fly, "I will shoo it away. Be gone, magic. Shoo!"

Both birds chuckled and then spoke in unison. "No, you won't."

"It has the sweet taste of power," said Zig.

"Humans find it irresistible," said Zag.

"Not me." Goff folded his arms over his chest, trying to look confident. "I know better. Power corrupts. Tell your master that I don't want to be his enemy and that I have no interest in magic."

"For your sake," Zig said, "I hope you speak the truth. That is what he requires of you."

Zag leaned forward to speak with deliberate intensity. "But just to be sure, he sent us to collect a little collateral."

Goff didn't like the sound of that. "What do you mean? What collateral?"

Both birds lifted up into the air and hovered before him. "Your dog."

"No!" Goff pulled Brak behind him. "There is no way I'll let you take him."

"We're not asking."

Zig and Zag raced forward, flapping violently, screeching loud enough to shatter a crystal glass. Goff stepped backward, falling over Brak and landing on the ground. Lost in a storm of beating wings and screeching, he covered his face with one hand and tried to grab Brak with the other. Brak took off running across the cemetery, barking like crazy.

"Run, Brak!" Goff called. "Run like the wind! Get to the woods!"

Zig and Zag lifted off and turned to race after Brak like owls chasing a rabbit, their wings sending the fog swirling. Goff jumped up and ran after them, trying to think of a way to help Brak, but the two giant birds were too fast. Before Brak reached the cover of the trees, one of them dropped down right on top of him. There was a flash of light, and Brak and the bird disappeared in a puff of smoke. Goff stopped running. He stared in disbelief at the spot they had been only a second ago. Brak was gone.

Zag circled back and hovered a few feet away.

"What have you done with my dog?" Goff's voice quaked in anger.

"I hope you see the power you are up against now. That was a small taste of it, and he is capable of much greater things."

"I will make him pay if he hurts Brak," Goff said evenly. "I swear."

Zag flapped his wings, pushing out a great blast of wind, and rose high into the air. "You dare to make threats? He will crush you like a bug if you get in his way." He paused, hovering to look at Goff. "Stay low and respect the deal or you and your dog will perish." Then he flapped his wings and rose quickly into the sky.

Goff stared blankly, watching Zag's silhouette pass in front of the moon, sadness compressing his heart and tears sliding down his cheeks. Brak was gone. Nothing he could do would change that. Forcing himself to move, he made his way out of the cemetery, across the field and to his house, where he went back through his bedroom window and flopped down on his bed, instantly missing Brak at his feet. He comforted himself with the thought that all he had to do was reject magic, and Brak would be okay. So, if any of this magic came his way, he'd pretend it wasn't there.

Trying to imagine what it might look like and when it would arrive, fatigue caught up with him. His eyelids grew heavier, his blinks longer, and he eventually dropped off into a fitful sleep. When he awoke later with a start, it was still dark. The clock read 5:30 a.m. At first, he thought Brak had jumped into bed and woken him, but in a wave of sadness, he remembered Brak was gone. So, what had woken him?

He scanned the room. The moon shone through his window in tiny slivers. Everything appeared normal, and then Maxim, still sitting on his pedestal, lifted his dusty paw and licked it.

Goff froze. Ice slid up his spine.

Magic!

"Go away! I reject you!"

Maxim stopped licking his paw and turned, flashing bright green eyes. "Now, now," he said in a silky voice. "Let's not be so hasty."

"No!" Goff shouted, pulling the covers up to his chin. "Whatever magic is animating you, I reject it!"

"I'm only a little magic," Maxim said, stepping off his platform and hopping gracefully to the ground. He came over to sit on the bed directly in front of Goff, wrapping his tail around his legs. "Mathers will never know about me."

"I'm not taking any chances! Shoo!" Goff waved his hand at the cat.

Maxim hissed and bared long, sharp teeth.

"Please?" Goff begged. "Just go away? I want nothing to do with any of this."

"You ignorant boy. Mathers is playing you for a fool."

Goff couldn't believe he was having a conversation with a dead cat. He felt sick to his stomach. "Look, I only want to keep my part of the agreement so I can get my dog back, so you need to leave. Please?"

"It's not that simple," Maxim said, settling down on the ground. "I can't just go—

you really don't know the first thing about magic."

"No, I don't, and I want to keep it that way."

"Then you will end up dead, and so will your dog."

"I won't let that happen. I'll do anything to save Brak or I'll die trying."

"Well, maybe if you let me help you..."

Goff threw his pillow at the cat but missed. "You're trying to trick me! I reject you. Go!"

Maxim jumped up onto the bed. He arched his back and came within a few inches of Goff's nose. "Here's what you need to realize, and quickly: Whether you collect magic or not, Mathers will eventually just kill you and take it all for himself."

Goff stared back at the cat, feeling pretty sure he shouldn't trust a talking mummified cat. "Of course, that's what you'd want me to believe. That serves you well."

"Whatever you believe changes nothing for me," the cat said casually, practically shrugging.

"I could chop you up into bits."

Maxim hissed again and jumped to the floor. "Then you'd be hacking up a dead cat, and I would attach to something else. I am not the cat. I'm magic. It was only through the cat that I came to you." He sashayed across the floor, placing his feet down one after the other in a neat little line. "You don't choose the form. We don't, either. In my case, I just awoke, and I was a cat. If you destroy the cat, I'd probably just take another form. It's my nature to animate things. It's my attachment style."

"But why? Why is magic attaching to me? I don't want it to."

"It's magical physics, if you will."

"That's not helpful."

Maxim sat straight and tall, his tail swishing just a little. "It's simple, really. It's like how water rolls down a hill but pools in depressions. You are part of the contour of the magical realm now. Magic will flow to you. Many wizards have sought what you have but have failed to obtain it."

"Is there a way to reverse my contour? Not collect magic anymore?"

"Yes."

"Great," Goff sat up, excited. "What is it?"

"You won't like it."

"Just tell me, please?"

"The sky is getting light outside. Look."

"Stop stalling!"

Maxim licked his paw again casually. "You really want to know?"

"Yes!" Goff exclaimed, becoming frustrated.

"Well," Maxim said, "you simply have to die."

Goff became aware of his heartbeat and breath as these words hovered in the air. He stared at Maxim for a moment. "That's the only way?"

"I've never known anyone to try reversing their contour before, but that's the only way I've heard it can happen. Mind you, it usually isn't self-inflicted. Wizardry is dangerous stuff—accidents, treachery, battles, nasty creatures, dark forces. Basically, an abundance of ways to get yourself killed. But sure, there may be other ways to reverse your contour. Who knows?"

"How can I find out?"

"So now you want my help?"

"Can you help me?"

"Probably not." Maxim hopped back up on the desk.

"Then I still reject you."

Maxim stepped onto his wooden mounting platform. "Look, kid, I've been around for thousands of years. I've been many things and seen many things. In all that time, I've seen strong wizards die because they were foolish, and I've seen weak wizards do great things because they were clever." He raised his paw, assuming his frozen position.

"That's it?" Goff asked, mystified.

"My time is up. I'm night magic, and the sun is nearly up. Stay alive until sunset, and we'll talk again." He opened his mouth and bared his teeth.

"You are coming back?" Goff leaned forward. "Wait—night magic? Is there day magic I'll have to deal with, too?"

Maxim's mouth turned up a tiny bit at the corners in an odd sort of feline smile, and just before he froze in place, he hissed, "Of course there is."

Day Magic

GOFF stood up and walked over to his desk, leaning on the rough-hewn board that was the top. Maxim's green eyes had returned to being cold and empty. It was clear he would speak no more.

"Stupid cat!" Goff flicked Maxim's black and pink ear, but only a little—he'd angered enough magical creatures for one night.

He flopped back down on the bed, but sleep didn't come this time. He lay there worrying about Brak and about what the day would bring. His eyelids were just starting to get heavy when the alarm rang at 6:30 a.m.

As fatigue and dread pressed down on him like a wet quilt, Goff considered staying home sick from school. After all, he was legitimately tired, and if there was day magic like Maxim had said, this might be a terrible day. But he knew he couldn't do that. Ruining his perfect attendance record wasn't an option. The cost was too high.

Forcing his body upright, he dressed in dull gray pants and a T-shirt to fit his mood and headed down to the kitchen. Frank was already up and wearing crisp black pleated pants, a black shirt, and a black blazer. Goff hid his surprise. Frank was typically in green boxers and a stained T-shirt snoring in his puffy lounge chair at this time of day.

Pam and Ben were in the kitchen too, ready for school in their usual uniform of jeans and white T-shirts. They were eating uncooked hot dogs with maple syrup and yellow mustard. Everyone was seated around the linoleum table, looking uncharacteristically like a real family. Something wasn't right.

"Take a seat, Goff," Frank said. "We need to go over a few things."

Goff grabbed a box of Oat Stix cereal and a chipped red bowl and sat down. He opened the top, tipped the box, and cereal began trickling out. "What's going on?"

Pam grabbed a handful of little brown turds as they poured out from the box and shoved them in her mouth. "Wergon beebossfyou, datswat!"

"What?" Goff asked.

"Frank's leaving," Ben said, thumping the table. "And I'm in charge!"

"What?" Goff lost track of the bowl, and some cereal landed in his lap. "No way!"

"He's mostly right," Frank said. "I got a job, and I need to go away for a few days, so you three will have to work things out on your own. If there's any trouble, Ben is in charge."

"What about me?" Pam objected.

"A girl in charge?" Ben pondered. "I don't think so."

"Why can't we both be in charge?"

"There's gotta be a boss, and it's me. You can be the assistant boss."

Pam shot up. "I'll assist you to an early grave!"

"Sit down!" Frank yelled. "Whatever, you can both be in charge. I don't care. Just don't make a mess of things."

"Hold on," Goff said, feeling like he was in a particularly vivid nightmare. "You can't leave for a few days, Frank. You can't just leave the kids in charge of the house, especially not when that's Pam and Ben."

Frank leaned in close to Goff. "If you rat on me, kid, you'll end up in the orphanage. You don't want that, now do you?"

"Might be better than being here with these two in charge," Goff said.

"They're not in charge," Frank sighed. "Ben just gets to settle things if they get out of hand."

"And what about this job?" Goff pressed. "It sounds like a terrible idea…" He stopped himself from saying more.

"Terrible idea?" Frank stared at him and sat back, straining the rusty chrome tubes of his chair. "How would you know anything about this job? It pays well, and I don't have to do much. That's what I call a great job. Best deal to come my way in a long time, and I'm taking it, even if I have to be away for a few days, or even a week or two."

"A week or two?"

"Well, they weren't specific about that, so who knows."

"And you don't think that's odd?"

"What's the job, anyway?" Pam asked, wagging a hot dog with mustard on the end like a cartoon gangster waving a cigar.

"Can't tell ya that," Frank said, sitting back down. "Part of the deal."

"Cool," Pam said. "Is it the Secret Service?"

"He just said he can't tell you," Goff said, rolling his eyes.

"I'll bet it's assassin training," Ben said.

"That's not a job," Goff said, earning him a punch in the arm. "How can we reach you in an emergency, like if Ben sets the house on fire?"

"The number's on the fridge, but only call if there's an emergency. Don't want you makin' me look like a fool with stupid stuff. Now, I gotta go. Ben, Pam, keep this house in good shape. Goff, you cook and use the account at the supermarket like usual to buy food, but keep it simple. I can't believe what you've been buying with my money. What are crappers anyway?"

"Capers," Goff corrected. "They're—"

"Never mind," Frank stood up. "No more of them. And remember, you're on laundry and dish duty until I get back."

"And what do Pam and Ben have to do?"

"They've got school and sports."

"I have school, too."

"But no sports," Pam said with a satisfied grin.

"Get used to it." Ben whacked Goff with a hot dog. "You're the maid now."

"We should get him an apron!" Pam howled. "A pretty pink one and maybe some violet ribbon and a pair of tights."

Ben shot Pam a curious look.

"This is insane," Goff said, standing up. "I'm going to school."

He grabbed his jacket and backpack from the hooks by the door but then froze on the front step, where his jaw dropped. Pam and Ben raced out and bumped into him. The entire front yard had been decorated for Halloween.

"What the heck?" Ben said.

Goff staggered off the porch, surveying it all in disbelief. Everywhere he looked, there were glowing orange lights, swaying skeletons, leering jack-o-lanterns, and zombies dripping with red blood and brown gore. He walked toward the street, stepping carefully around a little graveyard with a sign stuck in the ground that read "Wizard's Graveyard. Enter at your own risk." Above it, hanging from a rope, swung a stuffed scarecrow with a cloth bag for a head.

Oversized brown glasses had been drawn around the eyes, and a mass of hair made from coarse beige yarn stuck out in all directions from under a wizard's cap and fell over its cheeks.

"That's you, Goff!" Pam pointed at it, nearly falling over with laughter.

"Frank did all this?" Ben asked.

"Frank?" Pam frowned. "No way. He never lifts a finger for Halloween."

Ben kicked a zombie's leg. "Gift from his new boss then?"

"Yeah, that's probably it," Pam agreed.

Goff looked at his effigy twirling in the breeze. His stomach tightened. "This is not a gift."

"What is it, then?" Ben asked.

Before Goff could answer, squealing bus brakes nearby sent Ben and Pam running. Goff took a deep breath and ran after them. He made it to the idling bus as it sat stewing in a pool of its silvery exhaust and leaped up the stairs, dropping into the first open seat. Enjoying the comforting sensation of the humming engine, he closed his eyes, trying hard to ignore the world, and more importantly, not notice anything out of the ordinary that might be day magic trying to find him.

The bus ride was bumpy and noisy but uneventful. Morning classes passed without incident. A lunch of salty gray meatloaf and a soggy vegetable medley was simply disgusting and not magical in any way. Goff began to feel hopeful that this day would not be a nightmare. Perhaps magic could only find him when he was home?

By the time final period rolled around, there still had been no sign of Maxim's alleged daytime magic. Goff decided Maxim must have been trying to scare him. Besides, he had other things to worry about. His last period class was Science with Halstrom and Lydia, and he worried it might be awkward.

He attempted to avoid eye contact with Lydia as he entered but felt her gaze all the way to his seat. He glanced at Halstrom and found his eyes on him as well, but then again, it was hard to tell if Halstrom was looking at you or through you. Goff sat down and looked at the gray-swirl tiles on the floor. Fortunately, it was only a few seconds before Mr. Dongle, a plump red-haired man sporting a red bow tie and dark blue wool blazer, entered and took attendance as best he could with kids ignoring him and chatting and laughing. When attendance was done, Mr. Dongle wheeled out a rickety metal rack with a dangling full-sized yellow-boned skeleton that clicked and clattered like a dysfunctional wind chime.

Goff knew his anatomy well and only half paid attention while Mr. Dongle called on people to say the names of bones he pointed to with a long, wooden pointer. Looking out the dirty window next to him, Goff thought about his paper. He'd weave in the history of witches in Spraksville with his personal experiment, but he'd leave out everything after the spell started to work that would make him sound like a lunatic.

Goff heard the class laughing and looked up to find Mr. Dongle standing right in front of his desk, big fluffy caterpillar eyebrows turned down, blue veins on his forehead pulsing. "Goff…Grahm!"

"Oh, sorry," Goff said, realizing he hadn't been paying attention.

"Can I assume you've studied your anatomy?"

"Yes," Goff replied, still a little far away mentally. "I know all of it."

"All of it?" Mr. Dongle laughed like a rusty hinge opening and closing. "Well then, how about you teach the class? Go ahead, show us how you know *all* the anatomy."

"Are you serious?"

"I am." Mr. Dongle held the pointer out to Goff. "I've certainly got other things I can do if you can teach the class as well as me. Off you go."

"But—"

"To the front, Goff!" Mr. Dongle thrust the rubber handle of the pointer into Goff's palm. "Start with the bones of the hand."

While the class giggled and whispered, Goff took the pointer and made his way to the front of the room. He turned to find Mr. Dongle at the back, working on hanging some line drawings of frog anatomy on the wall.

"Well," Goff tapped the skeleton's hand with the black rubber tip of the wooden pointer. "To begin with, this is the hand."

Laughter rippled through the class again.

"Brilliant," Mr. Dongle said over his shoulder. "Now, how about you impress us with a few details."

Goff cleared his throat and used the pointer to point at a few bones. "The large bone joining the wrist is called the radius, and the small one is the ulna."

Wanting to expose the wrist's carpal bones and show that he knew the names of the eight small bones there, Goff lifted the skeleton's right hand. Its yellowish, cracked head spun slowly toward him as if turning to say hello, and Goff felt a presence lurking within its dark, shadowy eyes.

Day magic!

CHAPTER 10

RIP Goff

A hot plume of panic rose from Goff's stomach, but he kept it down, hoping maybe he was wrong about this being day magic. Perhaps the weight of the dangling skeleton had just shifted.

"I guess it likes me," he joked.

"That's a first!" someone shouted.

The class laughed.

"More anatomy, less fooling around," Mr. Dongle called out.

Warily, Goff lifted the cold bony hand to expose the fingers. He'd barely bent the arm up past the elbow when the skeleton pulled its hand free.

Goff's heart skipped a beat. That had not been merely shifting bones. The skeleton had very clearly pulled its hand back. Goff took a deep breath to calm his nerves. This situation had to be handled carefully. He couldn't let his classmates see what was really going on, so he popped a smile and said, "Slippery," while wiping his hands on his pants as if drying them.

He looked into the shadowy holes where the eyeballs had once been, hoping maybe he could reason with this magic. "Now, if you'll just let me examine your hand," he said to the skeleton directly, but in a slightly silly tone so as not to give away that he was making a serious offer, "we can have a nice chat later. Okay?"

Hoping it had worked, he reached for the skeleton's hand. This time, the skeleton reached over and slapped him with its other hand. The class gasped and then exploded with laughter. Goff was stunned but shook it off quickly. He turned to face the room, hoping to recover by saying, "Don't try to do that trick at home, folks. I've been studying puppeteering."

Mr. Dongle turned, glaring at Goff as the kids continued to laugh. "Settle down! What's gotten into all of you? Goff, this is supposed to be an anatomy lesson, not a comedy act. Finish the hand, please."

With Mr. Dongle watching him, Goff swallowed hard and reached down to lift the bony hand. This time, the skeleton didn't pull it back. Instead, it squeezed tightly, mashing Goff's knuckles together. Goff winced, but smiled at Mr. Dongle as he tried to free his hand. The class again rippled with uneasy laughter. Halstrom's eyebrows raised as high as the brim of his blue beanie. Lydia, her mouth agape, leaned forward over her desk. Goff shook his hand hard, but the skeleton refused to let go.

"Stop fooling around, Goff!" Mr. Dongle said, turning back to his work on the far wall. "Get on with the lesson."

The skeleton's leg swung to the side and kicked him. Goff did his best to keep a smile on his face. Several of his classmates jumped up, laughing and chattering as a few of them approached and stood in front of Goff.

"How'd you do that?"

"Pretty good!"

Goff tried to free his hand, causing the entire skeleton to shake and clatter and its head to bobble. "Let go!" he said, fearing what would happen if this kept up any longer. "I reject you!"

"What sort of nonsense is this?" Mr. Dongle pushed his way through the crowd and came face to face with Goff, his red bowtie slightly askew. "What are you doing, Goff?"

"Sorry, Mr. Dongle," Goff said. "I was just trying to make Anatomy fun with a few parlor tricks, but this thing is stupid and ridiculous, and I reject it." Goff jerked his hand hard one more time. To his surprise and delight, it let go, and its arm dropped to its side. Goff rubbed his sore knuckles. "About time, you stupid skeleton."

Mr. Dongle opened his mouth to say something but stopped when the skeleton began jiggling all by itself. The jiggling turned into shuddering, and colliding bones filled the room with dull clicks and clacks. Goff felt sick as he stared at the bizarre spectacle, fearing what might happen next. Was the skeleton going to start dancing? Talking? Eating people?

"I said I reject you!" Goff shouted at it.

All at once, the shuddering stopped and two hundred and six bones collapsed and landed in a cacophony of clicking on the floor as if the wire connectors holding them together had been cut simultaneously.

Mr. Dongle yelped. "What on earth did you just do?" He raced forward and picked up two of the larger bones. "All the wires are broken. Every single one. How is that even possible?"

"He was making it move," one of the kids said.

"And kick him," another added.

"Move?" Mr. Dongle asked. "Kick?"

"It was just a joke," Goff said.

Mr. Dongle held up the jawbone. "There is nothing funny about this!"

"I didn't mean to break it."

"You didn't break it. You completely dismantled it!"

"Sorry."

Mr. Dongle shook his head in dismay, looking back and forth between Goff and the bones. His red hair tumbled onto his forehead, and his bowtie looked like it was trying to escape his neck. The room was so silent you could hear the clock tick. Goff felt relief wash over him when the last period bell rang, although nobody moved. Doors out in the hallway opened, and kids rushed out, talking and laughing and shouting. His classmates stood transfixed, seemingly afraid to breathe.

"Out!" Mr. Dongle threw the jawbone onto the pile. "All of you!"

The room exploded with activity. Everyone raced back to their desks and grabbed their things, chattering and whispering about Goff and the skeleton. Hoping to escape too, Goff snuck back to his desk, grabbed his backpack, and headed for the door.

"Not you!" Mr. Dongle stood by the door like a dragon blocking the entrance to its cave.

Goff froze, terrified of what Mr. Dongle would come up with for his punishment. Suspension? Expulsion? When the room was empty, Mr. Dongle slammed the heavy wooden door and sat on the edge of his metal desk. At first he didn't say anything. He closed his eyes and breathed, looking like he was silently counting to ten. A moment later, he looked at Goff, straightened his bowtie, and spoke in a strained but mostly calm voice. "I have a theory. Were you trying to impress a certain girl in the class who seems to have taken a liking to you? You know the one fond of headbands, large glasses?"

"Lydia?" Goff stopped himself from protesting, realizing that making Mr. Dongle think his theory was correct was his best way out of this mess. He hung his head, trying to look embarrassed. "I guess I kind of was. I wanted to be funny, so she would like me. Girls never like me. How did you know?"

"I have a keen sense for these things, Goff."

Goff held back a smile. "Yeah, I guess you do."

"But trying to impress a girl is no excuse for destroying property."

"That wasn't supposed to happen."

Mr. Dongle pointed at the pile of bones on the floor. "Regardless, I'm out an expensive skeleton I've had for many years." Mr. Dongle crossed his arms. "What do you intend to do about that?"

Goff looked at the pile of bones and realized that a dozen small knobby finger bones at the front had arranged themselves to spell out "Magic." He reached out with his foot and dispersed them, hissing, "I reject you!"

"Excuse me?"

"Oh, sorry, I said… I could correct you. You know, fix it, put the skeleton back together."

"Excellent," Mr. Dongle said, dropping his crossed arms and standing up. "You do that by Monday, and I won't report this to Vice Principal Sparr." He shuffled over to the board and began erasing it. "There's a box you can use for the bones in the closet."

Ten minutes later, Goff walked down the empty corridors of the school to the bus stop carrying a large cardboard box full of magical bones. He approached the bus where a few kids were hanging out the window staring at him. The story must have spread quickly because a few of them called him 'Bones' and 'Skeletor' as he climbed aboard.

Happy to find the seats mostly empty, he flopped down in the front row with the big box on his lap. He was in a terrible mood. All he wanted to do was get home and end this odd, terrible day. It seemed to take forever to finally arrive at his stop, and his heart sank when he saw Lydia and Halstrom waiting for him, standing under a tree with a steady stream of tiny yellow leaves cascading down around them.

"What are you two doing here?" Goff asked as they approached him.

A small yellow leaf settled on the top of Halstrom's beanie. "I still have not worked out how you did it."

Lydia peered into the box. "It was really cool, though. People will be talking about that for a long, long time. You study magic or something?"

"Magic?" Goff asked with alarm, turning and walking toward his house, feeling the word strike an odd chord in him. "No, of course not. Who even believes in spells and all that stuff? Why would you even ask that?"

Lydia pushed him playfully from behind. "I meant like card tricks and smoke and mirrors."

"Oh, right," Goff said. "Smoke and mirrors. That's what it was."

"Not possible," Halstrom came up next to him. "I saw it all up close. There were no mirrors or smoke, but the idea of real magic in Spraksville seems impossible, especially produced by Goff."

"Hey!" Goff protested, not sure why.

"Dude," Lydia said. "I think that was Halstrom's idea of a compliment. He means you are too normal for that stuff."

"Of course I am," Goff agreed.

"Perhaps," Halstrom said. "However, I can't find any rational explanation, so irrational explanations must be considered."

"Don't get all excited," Goff said, not liking where this was going. He pushed past them and continued toward home. "There's nothing irrational here. I rigged it yesterday, that's all. I attached little motors that you couldn't see from where you were. Just a trick."

"That isn't possible." Halstrom grabbed Goff's shoulder and stopped him from walking off. His grip was like a steel clamp. "How would you have known Mr. Dongle would call you up to the front of the class? Motors would have been visible and require power. Your story doesn't make sense, so I can only conclude that you are lying."

"Whoa!" Lydia exclaimed, clapping her hands excitedly. "If Halstrom says you're not telling the truth, then what you said must not be true because he never says things that are not true."

"Please refrain from summarizing me," Halstrom said.

"Excuse me?"

"You used double negatives."

"So?"

"It sounded like gibberish."

"Well, you know what I meant."

"That is no excuse for being unclear."

Goff stopped short. "You two are like an old bickering couple, you know that?"

Lydia blushed. "What? No, we're not a couple! Never will, would, or could happen."

"We are too young to marry," Halstrom said frankly, scratching his chin and ignoring Lydia's outburst.

"That's not the only reason, you dolt!" Lydia shoved Halstrom, but he barely budged. The kid was unmovable. Even the leaf on his beanie stayed put.

"Besides, I know who Lydia wants to be married to, and it is not me."

Lydia flushed a violent shade of red and shoved Halstrom harder, still not managing to move him or the leaf.

"Look," Goff said, stopping Halstrom from further embarrassing them both. "I have a lot to do—laundry, cleaning, cooking, and writing a very important paper. All that, plus I have to put these bones back together. Why are you guys here?"

"Scientific curiosity," Halstrom said, "although Lydia may have other reasons."

Goff turned to Lydia, who was blushing again. "He is rather annoying, isn't he?"

Lydia rolled her eyes. "Like a pebble in your boot."

"Well, I hope you got what you wanted. I'm going home." Goff turned and began walking, hoping they wouldn't follow, but they did. At the top of the hill, Frank's house came into view along with the spectacle of the massive Halloween decorations.

"Is that your house?" Lydia asked excitedly. "The decorations are next level!"

"By that, she means you have more decorations than most."

"I understood her," Goff said. "The decorations just showed up this morning."

"Showed up?"

Halstrom cocked his head, a somewhat radical gesture for him. "Decorations do not just show up."

Goff tried to dispel the curiosity that was building. "It was a gift, we think, from Frank's new employer."

"Does he work for a decoration manufacturer?" Halstrom asked.

"No, just some rich dude."

"Wait!" Lydia shoved Goff so hard that he almost dropped the box of bones. "My idiot stepdad just started a new job, too, for that rich dude who renovated the Hallow Manor. Mathers, right? He wasn't supposed to tell anyone, but the man tells me everything now that Mom's gone. Oh, no!" Lydia clapped her hand over her mouth and then peeled it away. "I'm not supposed to tell anyone, either."

"Take note," Halstrom rolled his eyes. "Never tell Lydia a secret."

"Oh, shut up," Lydia punched Halstrom's shoulder. "I can't help that I talk too much. It's genetic or something. Is Frank working for that dude too, Goff?"

Goff stopped and looked back and forth between the two of them, kind of liking that he wasn't alone with the Mathers thing anymore. "Yes. He didn't tell me—it's supposed to be secret—but I saw some paperwork."

"Well, the whole thing seems spooky to me, dude. All black clothing like secret service agents? Weeks of orientation? And why does Mathers need so much security anyway?" Lydia gestured at the decorations. "And why would he decorate your house for Halloween?"

"He hung your effigy from the tree too," Halstrom observed, pointing to the dangling corpse with the brown hair and big glasses.

"Oh my God!" Lydia smacked her head. "That's you!"

Silence fell on the threesome as they surveyed the swaying corpse and a new plastic gravestone below it engraved with "RIP Goff."

Halstrom broke the silence a moment later. "This is not a normal employee gift. Something is amiss here."

"No, nothing is amiss," Goff said half-heartedly.

"Dude, if there was ever something amiss then this is a big amiss."

Halstrom turned to her. "You say things like that, and I don't think you know what you are saying."

Goff watched as Lydia and Halstrom launched into another bout of their ridiculous bickering. "Well, I'd better get inside and start my chores," he said, hoping to get rid of them.

"Don't send us away," Lydia said. "Put us to work!"

"Bad idea," Goff said.

"Great idea!" Lydia grinned.

Halstrom stood tall. "I do many things well."

"Dude, come on," Lydia touched Goff's shoulder. "Don't you want some help?"

Perhaps it was a secret desire for help with more than just his chores, or maybe they had just worn him down, but Goff surprised himself by saying, "Fine."

"Awesome!"

"You have to leave before it gets dark, okay?" said Goff, leading them up the creaky, uneven wooden front stairs. "That's when Pam and Ben get home."

At the top of the steps, Lydia paused to look over at the corner of the porch where a giant black furry plastic spider in a white twine web spanned the distance between two green posts. "I hate spiders," she cringed.

"Me too," Goff said.

"At that size, we would be its prey," Halstrom said.

Goff gulped, suddenly very unhappy about having a spider on his porch big enough to eat him. "Let's just get inside, okay?"

CHAPTER 11

Witch's Lair

STILL a little worried that it might be a terrible idea bringing Lydia and Halstrom into his house, Goff balanced the box on his knee and slid the key into the deadbolt. He unlocked it with a heavy click to let the door swing open a little, hesitating for a second with his hand on the chipped brass knob.

Lydia ended his indecision by reaching around him and pushing the door open. She shoved Goff aside and walked in as if she lived there. Halstrom followed. The leaf finally fluttered off his beanie. Goff sighed and then wrestled the box of bones through the door behind them. He placed it on the floor and slid it to the side with his foot.

Lydia spun around. "I'd say it's a nice place, but it's kind of a dump."

"Thanks," Goff said absentmindedly. He was busy scanning the lumpy furniture, piles of trash, and even the spider webs in the corners, looking for anything magically suspicious. "Home sweet, messy, smelly home, I guess."

"Where is your room?" Halstrom asked.

"I live in the attic."

Lydia squealed with delight. "That rocks! Top of the world. I live in the basement. Can we see it?"

"Nothing much to see."

"Oh, is it up here?" Lydia headed for the stairway and started up, running her hands over the peeling wallpaper with blue drawings of pioneers in wagons.

"Wait!" Goff said, but she kept going.

"She rushes in," Halstrom said, placing his foot on the first stair, "and I follow. Keeps my life interesting."

Goff bounded toward the stairs. "Kind of like having a pet chimpanzee."

"I heard that!" Lydia yelled.

"Agreed," Halstrom said. "I'm almost inclined to incorrectly use the word literally in this case."

Goff tried to get around Halstrom, but there was no passing him. His sweater-clad arms spread wide, trailing his fingers on each wall. Piles of shoes, clothing, athletic equipment, and trash kept Goff from slipping under and around. He started to panic, remembering that he'd left out notes, photocopies of spells, and drawings for his paper. He arrived at the top just as Lydia reached the yellow floral curtain across the opening into his room.

"Is this your door?" Lydia asked, sounding amazed.

"That is not a door," Halstrom corrected. "It is a curtain."

Lydia rolled her eyes. "Must you always be so accurate?"

"Live in chaos," Halstrom said. "It's your choice."

"Yes. It's my door," Goff said, still trying to pass Halstrom. "But give me a minute to straighten up, okay?"

Ignoring him, Lydia parted the two flaps and slid through the gap. She stopped abruptly on the other side. "Oh, man, you've got some 'splainin' to do."

"He already has a lot of explaining to do," Halstrom said, stepping in behind Lydia.

"It's just for my paper," Goff said nervously, following Halstrom through the curtain. But it wasn't the spell on his desk they had seen. In the center of his room, a large black iron cauldron hung from a steel chain supported by a tripod of charred wood branches. It was framed by a white pentacle painted on the floor, and at the tip of each point sat a fat, half-melted black candle. On the ceiling between the beams, rows of magical symbols had been painted. Goff blanched, unable to believe his eyes.

"Now he has much more," Halstrom said, almost sounding surprised.

"It's research," Goff stammered, trying to find a way to spin it. "For the paper I'm writing for history class about witchcraft."

"This is next-level research, dude," Lydia said, picking up one of the black candles.

"By that, she means—"

"I know what she means."

"Have you tried any spells? That would be seriously awesome. Can we do one with you?"

"No!" Goff exclaimed, grabbing the black candle from her. It smelled like stale oregano and urine. "I don't do spells. This stuff is just for research."

"It is consistent with my hypothesis," Halstrom said, running his finger along the chain holding up the cauldron, causing the massive bowl to swing slightly.

Goff peered into the rusty interior of the swaying cauldron, glad to find it empty and not full of some bubbling green witch's brew. "What? That I can do real magic?"

Halstrom looked up and directed his unwavering gaze directly into Goff's eyes. "Precisely."

"You're crazy." Goff had to look away. Like everything else about Halstrom, his glare seemed made of steel. Goff gave the cauldron a little shove. It rocked, and the chains squeaked. "You believe magic is real?"

"I believe in logic, wherever that leads me." Halstrom crossed his hands over his chest. "Ever hear of Occam's razor?"

"Sure, law of parsimony," Goff said.

"Lex parsimoniae," Halstrom said.

Lydia thumped the floor with her foot. "Speak English!"

"Just a heuristic for drawing conclusions," said Goff.

"I said English, remember?"

"Allow me to provide a full explanation." Halstrom cleared his throat. "The law of parsimony states that when multiple explanations compete, the one with the fewest assumptions should be selected. We all saw something inexplicable today in class. An animated, dancing skeleton that collapsed, for which Goff has provided no viable explanation. So either we hold out for some more complex explanation, or we accept that which is right in front of us and requires the fewest assumptions."

"That Goff is a witch?"

"No," Halstrom said.

"No?" Lydia threw her hands wide. "Isn't that what your mumbo jumbo explanation was all about?"

"Yes, but based on gender, he would be either a warlock or wizard."

"Jerk."

Goff stopped the cauldron from swinging. "I'm not a witch or a wizard or anything else magical. I used motors!"

Halstrom turned to him and furrowed his brow. "If that is so, can we look at the bones to see these motors?"

"Great idea!" Lydia squealed, bounding for the curtain. "I'll get the box."

"You won't see them," Goff called after her as she ran down the stairs. There was no point in trying to stop her. "I removed them when I collected the bones."

"With Mr. Dongle watching?" Halstrom asked.

"He went to the bathroom."

"Then explain how you made the skeleton collapse."

Goff took a deep breath, knowing how ridiculous what he was about to say would sound. "I weakened the wires very carefully before class."

"You weakened two hundred wires so they would break simultaneously on demand?"

"Yes." Goff's shoulders dropped. "Two hundred and six—very, very carefully."

"Impossible."

Lydia came running back, panting, eyes wild and cheeks pink, holding the box upside down. "The bones are gone!"

Goff grabbed the box and foolishly looked inside as if they might be stuck on the bottom. Panic raced through him, but he did his best to hide it. He shrugged his shoulders. "Frank must have come home and dumped them in the barrels out back."

"Nonsense," Halstrom almost smiled. "They walked away."

Before Goff could object, a breeze billowed the curtain open. Goff and Lydia both jumped. Halstrom didn't budge. The front door slammed closed, shaking the walls of the house.

Ben's voice roared up the stairs. "Hey, dork! You here? I don't smell supper cooking!"

Goff groaned. Could things get any worse? "Pam and Ben are home early. You guys need to leave," he said quietly.

"But we didn't get to help you," Lydia complained.

"Maybe another time," Goff ushered them down the stairs, annoyed to find Pam and Ben in their path. They were red-faced and dripping with sweat, leaning against the doorway to the kitchen, both drinking some weird purple sports drink.

"What's this?" Ben asked. "You have little friends over?"

Halstrom stopped and stared at Ben, studying him as if he were a bug. The top of Ben's head barely reached Halstrom's chin. "Of the two of us," Halstrom said, "You are the littlest."

"Well, this is my house, so I say what's what here, not you, and I say you are little, so that's your size. What are you gonna do about that?"

"I tend to ignore stupidity," Halstrom said without moving.

"You sayin' I'm stupid?"

"Stupid says what?" Lydia asked.

"What?" Ben replied.

"Confirmed," Halstrom said.

Ben's face turned a dangerous shade of crimson. Goff laughed and even Pam smiled a little.

Halstrom turned to face Pam. "Hello, Pam. Have you written your haiku yet?"

"Hey, Halstrom," Pam replied, a flush of red washing over her cheeks and her eyes softening. "I'm working on it. You?"

Ben gave Pam a poke in the shoulder. "You know this freak?"

"We are in a creative writing class together," Halstrom said. "Pam writes well."

Ben's face washed white as if his brain was rebooting. He leaned toward Pam. "Creative writing? Do you knit now too?"

"It's just a class, jerk." Pam shoved Ben's shoulder. "I stink at it too, okay?"

"That is not true," Halstrom said. "You wrote a great poem about running. Everyone in class thought it was beautiful."

Pam turned back to Halstrom and seemed to turn into a different girl. She blushed more deeply, and her eyes widened. "Thanks. You are the best in class, though."

"I just write the truth."

"You see the truth we all miss."

"My words are simple."

"Your words are perfect."

"I—"

"Stop!" Ben stomped the floor. "We're done here." He pointed at Halstrom. "You and your dorky girlfriend leave, and Goff had better start cooking supper soon, or I'll rip his stupid, ugly little head off."

Lydia stepped out from behind Halstrom. "I am not Halstrom's girlfriend! And you shouldn't boss Goff around and call him names. He's—"

"He's what?" Ben stepped toward Lydia and narrowed his eyes.

Lydia blushed and her eyes dropped.

"Oh my god," Ben grinned. "She likes Goff!" He started laughing and singing. "Dork and dorkess sitting in a tree, k—i—s—s—i—n—"

Lydia's nostrils flared, and her green eyes grew as wide as golf balls. Goff was about to say something to shut Ben up when Halstrom leaned in close and said, "Cover your ears."

A second later, Lydia's head shot up, and a tornado of sound burst from her mouth, aimed directly at Ben. It was a blast horn combined with a hundred trumpets, all playing the same high note. Goff covered his ears, but the horrible sound penetrated regardless. Lydia pumped her fists and stomped her feet in a compact little tantrum, driving the volume even higher. Goff had heard her screaming was legendary, but this was beyond what he had ever expected. How could such a small girl produce such an enormous sound?

It was a full minute before Lydia ran out of air. She bent forward, mouth open like a cannon barrel, panting and shaking, eyes wild.

Halstrom turned her toward the door. "Perhaps we should leave now."

Lydia turned as if coming out of a coma.

"Yes," Ben said, pulling at his ears. "You two freaks, get out."

"I would not call her a freak again," Halstrom said. "That was not her loudest."

Ben started to say something but stopped himself.

Still shaking, Lydia looked up at Goff, and their eyes met. Hers had never looked more vividly green, but they were wet with tears. He sensed that screaming wasn't a trick she pulled to shut people up. It reflected more profound pain and frustration that even she didn't understand.

"Sorry," Goff said. "Thanks for coming over."

Lydia walked with Halstrom to the door but stopped as she was about to exit. "Be careful, okay? Things are a mess here."

"Amiss," Halstrom corrected, urging her out.

Goff started closing the door, but before it shut all the way, Halstrom popped his head back inside. "Just thought you might want to know, the spider is gone."

CHAPTER 12

Majestic Spider

GOFF closed the door tight and locked it as soon as Halstrom pulled his head out. Maybe someone had stolen the spider? Unlikely—only a kid with a death wish would steal something off Frank's front porch. Perhaps it had just fallen? No, Halstrom wasn't an idiot. He would have checked that. For a few seconds, Goff stared at the peeling brown paint and white vertical scratches on the six indented panels of the front door, wondering if it was strong enough to keep out a spider that size. Feeling uneasy, he headed for the stairs to hole up in his room, where he planned to ask Maxim a thousand questions.

Ben and Pam were still arguing outside the kitchen. Ben put his arm up to block off the stairs. "You better have some food ready soon, or I'll eat you!"

Frustrated, Goff turned and went into the kitchen, where he quickly got an entire pound of cold, fatty bacon frying in a hot cast iron pan. It sizzled satisfyingly, filling the kitchen with salty steam, and he broke it up and tossed it about in the pooling grease with tongs until it was brown. Then he cracked in a dozen eggs, added a bag of shredded orange cheese, and made an enormous bacon and cheese omelet. He dumped it onto a plate and left it as it landed, not bothering with garnish or plating. It looked like a greasy, deflated football. They'd love it.

"Supper's ready," he said loudly.

Pam and Ben split the omelet onto two plates and ran off without uttering a word of thanks.

"You're welcome," Goff said to an empty kitchen.

When he made it upstairs with a bowl of cereal, Maxim was sitting on his pedestal, licking his paw.

Goff gestured toward the cauldron and candles. "What's the deal with all of this?"

Maxim stretched like he was doing a yoga pose, leapt down, and strolled over to the cauldron. "The work of a few Nexi."

"Nexi?"

"Magic not yet attached to a human. They wanted you to be their master, so they arranged for this as an offering."

"Are you a Nexi?"

"Yes, but I'm complicated. Long ago, I found myself attaching to wizard possessions instead of the wizard directly and grew to prefer that arrangement. Those that came here today are different—they need a master to do magic, and they love the mischief and mayhem that comes with doing a master's bidding."

"What about the spider? Same as you?"

"No," Maxim shook his head. "That is a Nexa. Rather rare, actually. A Nexa is bound to attach to a specific person for reasons no one understands, and for her, that person is you."

"Me? Why?"

"I'm not sure, frankly," Maxim said, scratching his ear. "Nevertheless, I do know this—she wants to kill you."

"Kill me?" Goff blanched.

"Yes." Maxim lay down and rested his head on his paws, sighing with feigned boredom. "If you, to whom she must attach, reject her, as you have declared you will, then she is unable to attach to another until you die. She will be in limbo for as long as you live. It's very unpleasant stuff, and frankly, it makes her dangerous."

"Well, if I accept her," Goff said, standing up, "Mathers will kill Brak and me."

Maxim didn't answer right away. He breathed deeply for a moment, then looked at Goff with a bit of mischief in his eyes. "That's probably going to happen anyway, so perhaps you should just die and avoid all the suffering along the way."

"No! I will most certainly not!" Goff jabbed his finger at Maxim like a fire poker. "I'm not giving up on Brak, my dreams, or my life because of some stupid wizard and a couple of magical pixies or nexis or whatever."

"Well, well, well." Maxim stood up and straightened his tail. "I'm glad to see there is a little fight in you after all. A little fight—not too much—is a good thing."

The roof rumbled as if a pack of dogs had run across it. Dust and bits of wood fell to the floor. Goff gulped. "Is that what I think it is?"

"Well, it isn't Santa's reindeer."

"What do I do?"

"Go out to meet her."

Goff felt fear forming a hot ball in his stomach. "And what? Give her a hug?"

"Perhaps not but follow your instincts. I think you'll know what to do."

The roof rumbled again with the horrifying sound of eight legs scuttling across the shingles. Goff's stomach churned.

Maxim continued. "But I will tell you this: If you don't act soon, she will come crashing in through that window to coil webbing around you and suck your brains out through your toes."

Goff looked over at the window. "Follow my instincts? That's all the advice you have for me?"

"That and," Maxim said, lazily licking his fur, "go soon or die."

"Big help you are." Goff went to the window, his whole body shaking. "Will you come with me?"

"That would definitely get you killed." Maxim smiled. "Cats eat spiders. Now go!"

Goff took a deep breath and stepped out the window onto the roof. It was a still night scented with pine needles and fireplaces. In the distance, below a dark sky full of twinkling stars, silhouettes of the tombstones in the graveyard formed a row of dragon fins on the ridge of the hill. He climbed down onto the shed roof and then hopped down to the ground.

Branches in a nearby tree rustled and cracked, and Goff caught a glimpse of something big with hairy legs shifting within its shadows. His heart jumped into his throat, and he turned to climb back up.

"I'll only shut the window if you try," Maxim called from above. "Trust your instincts."

At the moment, Goff's instincts were to run as fast as he could in the other direction, but he forced himself to move toward the tree one step at a time. He stopped just short of walking directly under its branches, to prevent the spider from dropping down on him, and looked up. A pair of yellow eyes peered back at him. His heart seemed to stop.

"I'm sorry," he croaked, unable to think of anything else.

The eyes continued to stare.

"I'm sorry. I don't want to hurt you by rejecting you. I'm just scared."

The eyes flickered and then disappeared. A second later, a scratching sound arose that made his skin curl as eight legs scrambled down the trunk and a massive spider crept onto the ground in front of him. Its abdomen was the size of a propane tank, and all eight arms were as long as boat oars. Goff used every bit of restraint he had in him to resist the urge to run.

"I want to make it right," he managed to say.

The creature moved toward him slowly, alternating legs in the creepy spider way that caused Goff's stomach to feel like jelly. He stood his ground, though, knowing it was all or nothing now. There was no outrunning her. "Just tell me what you want."

When the spider was ten paces away, she dropped down so that her belly touched the ground and her legs stuck out to the side, like a cat ready to pounce.

Goff swallowed hard and his eyes bulged, expecting the worst any second. "Please. Won't you at least talk to me?"

"She can't speak," a deep, silky voice nearby said.

Goff flinched and turned to find the skeleton from science class standing a few feet away, hands on its hips.

"Great. Are you here to kill me too?"

"Neither she nor I want to kill you," the skeleton said.

Goff moved his eyes between the crouching spider and the reanimated skeleton, trying not to think about how the bones were held together with all the wires gone. "But Maxim told me she's upset that I rejected her and has to kill me so she can attach to someone else."

"Maxim? Is that his name now? Well, I suppose if you reject her, she may kill you. Who knows?"

"But what is she? I mean, is she like a demon or a ghost or something?"

"Why don't you ask her to reveal herself?"

"I can do that?"

"Give it a whirl."

Goff cleared his throat. "I... err... I would appreciate it if you would reveal yourself to me."

The spider clicked its mandibles but made no other movement.

The skeleton scratched his chin with his index finger, which Goff couldn't help remember was called the distal phalanx. "Perhaps you could be a little stronger."

"I command—"

"Not that strong!" The skeleton placed his bony hand over Goff's mouth. "You'll make her angry."

Goff pushed the skeleton's hand away and decided to use the language style in the *Death's Gate Traversal* spell. "I beseech thee, magic within the spider, to leave behind your plastic cage and reveal yourself to me!"

The skeleton did not edit him this time. The spider continued to squat and throb, but then a speck of light began glowing in the center of its abdomen. It darted around in circles as if trying to escape. A second later, the speck of light, like an ember from a fire except purple, flew out into the open air. The plastic spider collapsed. The spark of magic hit the tree and fell to the ground.

"Is that her?" Goff asked as the bit of magic hobbled along the ground like a wounded bird, trying to get up.

"Yup."

"What's wrong with her?"

"Hard to tell."

The magic spark flew up high and then dove back down. It traveled right through the skeleton's rib cage and bounced off Goff's forehead before falling to the ground at his feet, looking dim and wounded.

"Is she broken or something?"

"Well, frankly, I'm not surprised that a nexa bound to attach to you is a bit of a misfit and not ancient, powerful magic."

"A misfit?"

The spark popped into the air, did a twirl, and then fell back to the ground, scattering a few leaves and disappearing beneath them.

"Well, does that look normal?"

"How would I know? But I do feel sorry for her. What should I do?"

"What feels right?"

"I want to help her."

"Then do so."

Hesitantly, Goff squatted down and scooped the little magic spark up as gently as he would a moth. He closed his hands around it and stood back up. She felt warm and tingly, and her light shone through the gaps in his fingers. Slowly, he opened his hands. Floating in his palm was a tiny violet spark, pulsing slowly, creating a bubble of radiant light.

"Hello," Goff said softly.

The spark flashed a bit brighter in reply and then grew dim. The skeleton placed his bony hand on Goff's shoulder. "She's scared and fading fast. She needs to attach to you."

Goff's heart went out to her. What harm could just a spec of magic cause? He felt as if he were holding a tiny kitten, so he did what seemed natural and hoped it would work. He lifted her to his chest and held her there. "I welcome you."

She dissolved into him, and instantly, every hair on his body stood up straight and tingled. His skin glowed soft violet and warmth spread through him as if he had been dipped in warm luminescent soda water.

"Hello," he said softly to the spark of magic within him. "My name is Goff."

Her reply came as a pulse of warmth in his heart.

"Well done!" The skeleton patted him on the shoulder. "How do you feel?"

Goff couldn't stop smiling. "Warm. Majestic in a way. Like I've got a friend inside. But what does this mean?"

The skeleton stood back and looked at him, somehow smiling without lips. "It means you're an actual wizard now, Goff."

CHAPTER 13

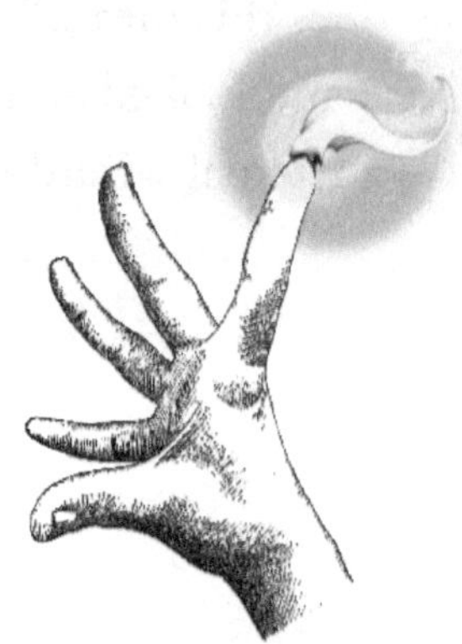

First Magic

G OFF and the skeleton, whom he had decided to call
Bones, walked slowly from the tree to the house. The
moonlight made Bones glow softly, and a few orange
and brown leaves clung to his legs.

"You've got leaves on your tibia and fibula," Goff
said.

"My what what?" Bones asked.

"Don't you know your own anatomy?"

"I'm made of bones, right?"

"Obviously."

"That's all the anatomy I need."

Laughing, they climbed back up to Goff's room. Maxim dropped down from a beam with a gentle thump and greeted them with a big grin, looking directly at Bones. "Am I in the presence of a young fledgling wizard?"

"Very wizardly," Bones said, and then they both laughed.

Goff wasn't sure what was going on here, but there was a familiarity between these two that he didn't understand. Bones sat down on the floor, slipping effortlessly into a full lotus position. He looked at the cauldron and candles. "I see you got them to leave it."

"Yes, they wanted to take it when they learned Goff was rejecting magic, but I persuaded them to leave it. I think it makes this dreadful room feel more like home."

"It does, old friend," Bones said, smiling. "Looks like all is in order now."

"In order? Old friend?" Goff asked. "Are you two in cahoots?"

Maxim walked over to Bones, who stroked the fur between his ears. "This one and I have been cahooting for thousands of years, although in different forms. We were once a pair of rats. That was the best—all that running around. And the cheese! Oh, the cheese."

"And this is a good gig, frankly," Bones said. "We consider ourselves very lucky. Working with a fledgling wizard who rejects magic will be a taste of retirement."

"Retirement?" Goff felt a twinge of anger rising. "What about saving Brak?"

Bones turned to Maxim. "Is he still going on about that dog?"

"Claims to be willing to die trying to save it, I'm afraid."

"Everyone says that until it comes to the dying part."

"I'm going to save him," Goff declared forcefully. "Even if I have to fight Mathers."

Bones stood, picked up one of the candles and went to Goff. "I admire your intentions and loyalty to your dog, Goff, but let me help you see reality as it is. You should know that Maxim and I are pretty much useless—we talk, we walk, we see things, but that's about it. The only magic you have is, and I mean this with all respect, a puny misfit—"

"Her name is Majesty," Goff cut him off, unsure where he'd come up with her name. "Speak kindly of her."

"As you wish. You may have Majesty, but Mathers has accumulated a large amount of ancient and potent magic by now. He can change the direction of rivers, summon tornadoes, and engulf an entire forest in flames. So, let's do a little test to identify the scale of difference between you two." He tapped the candle. "How about if you and Majesty try to light this one little candle?"

Bones handed the candle to Goff, who took it and looked at the wick sticking up like the leg of a buried spider. "But how do I do that?"

"That's point one," Maxim said, sauntering over and sitting down, wrapping his tail around his body. "You know nothing about how to use magic."

"And the second point is that Majesty doesn't know either. You two are a pair of misfits who won't last more than a few seconds in a battle with Mathers."

"We can do it." Goff held the candle in front of him, staring at the wick and thinking about fire. He felt a tingling sensation in his right index finger, as if Majesty was trying to tell him something. Following her lead, he lifted his hand and brought the tip of his finger close to the wick, saying, "Wick of the candle, cold and dark, catch my fire and ignite!"

"Rhyme much?" Maxim teased.

Goff ignored him as a few sparks traveled between flesh and wick, and then the tip of Goff's finger caught fire. Pain raced up his arm to his brain and came out as a scream. He raced over and dunked his flaming finger into the glass of water on his desk. It sizzled and bubbled for a second before the fire went out. When he removed his finger from the glass, the entire first digit was red and sore.

Both Maxim and Bones burst into laughter. Goff put his finger back into the glass, trying to soothe it, but it continued to throb. He spoke silently to Majesty within him, "It's okay. I don't blame you. You did your best. We both have a lot to learn."

Thumping on the stairs preceded Ben's voice filling the air. "What the heck are you doing up there, maggot! Sounds like you're havin' a party!"

Goff leapt up to meet Ben, with Pam right behind him, at the top of the stairs, to keep them from seeing the cauldron, or worse, Bones and Maxim. "I'm rehearsing. I'm gonna try out for the school play, Sleepy Hollow."

"Frank made you the maid, remember?" Ben said. "You've got too much to do around here to be in any stupid play."

Goff turned to Pam. "Halstrom is trying out too."

Pam blanched. "Why would I care what that freak is doing?"

Ben glanced at her and then turned back to Goff. "No play!"

Goff waited for a second for effect, focusing on the pain in his finger to look convincingly hurt. "Fine. But only because you're the boss."

"That's right," Ben said, puffing out his chest. "I'm the boss."

"I hate you," Goff said flatly.

"You should," Ben responded, turning to retreat back down the stairs.

"Don't mess with me, twerp," Pam said, staring at Goff for a second with narrowed eyes before walking away.

When they were gone, Goff went to the bathroom and bandaged his finger. It had calmed down a bit but was still red, and a few liquid-filled blisters were popping up. He went back to his room, where Bones and Maxim stared at him as he walked to his desk.

"You're clever," Maxim said, "I'll give you that."

"But Mathers won't be as easily tricked as your idiot housemates," Bones added.

"I've got work to do," Goff said, pulling out his notes. "Go entertain yourselves."

"Fine." Maxim said, mimicking Goff's exchange with Ben. "But only because you're the boss."

"That's right," Goff said, cracking a smile. "I'm the boss."

Maxim laughed. "I hate you."

"You should."

For the next hour, Goff worked on his paper while Maxim and Bones swung in the cauldron. He wrote four pages of pretty good stuff, too. He opened with his visit to the spooky statue behind the library and then described his attempt at casting a spell to resurrect William Cranston. All he needed now was a good conclusion. He sat back and read it through, making a few edits here and there, before turning to Maxim and Bones. "Either of you happen to be a good proofreader?"

"I consider myself proficient at spotting errors," Bones said confidently, click-clacking his way over to Goff.

"Words are like flowers flowing from my little pink tongue," Maxim chimed in.

"Great," Goff said, "then I want your comments by morning. I command thee!"

Goff headed toward the stairs to get some food as Maxim and Bones huddled together, reading and making marks in the margin and occasionally quibbling over a point of phrasing. On his way past Pam's room, Goff heard a strange sound. Listening through the door, he realized she was crying. Surprisingly, his heart went out to her. Nobody should cry alone. He lifted his hand to knock but thought better of it and continued down to the kitchen, where he made oatmeal with raisins. With Frank gone, the house was quiet for a change—no blaring TV. He sat down at the table with his oatmeal in a little circle of light and brought his unwounded hand out in front of him. The tip of his index finger began to glow soft violet.

"Hello, Majesty," he whispered. "I don't know what you are or what this is all about, but I like that you are with me. We're a team now."

Majesty grew hot in his finger, glowing brightly. A second later, his oatmeal lit up with blue flames like a pool of rubbing alcohol touched with a match. "Better," Goff said, "but oatmeal doesn't usually burn. Looks like we both have a lot to learn."

Goff put out his flaming oatmeal and headed back upstairs through a silent house. The only noise was Ben snoring and a few chattering mice running around unseen in the shadows. He entered to find the window open and Bones and Maxim sitting on the garage roof. They created a strange but touching silhouette—a skeleton and a cat sitting side by side staring at the moon.

"Beautiful moon, isn't it?" Maxim asked.

"Do you want a blanket or anything?" Goff asked. "It's cold out tonight."

Bones turned to look at him. "How did such a nice kid get into this mess?"

"I wish I knew. Blanket?"

"Thanks, but we don't do cold. We're dead, remember?" Maxim said.

"Oh, right," Goff said.

"Our proofreading comments are on your desk," Bones said.

"You write surprisingly well," Maxim added.

"Will you write about us?"

Goff laughed. "Not a chance."

"Good idea," Bones acknowledged.

"I'm going to get my dog back, you know."

Silence.

"You two can help me or not, but it looks like you're enjoying your retirement, so it might be in your best interests to keep me alive?"

Maxim turned to Bones. "Let's lock him in a box."

"Turn him into a cricket?"

"Hang him by his toes?"

"You don't scare me," Goff said. "Your only magic is being annoying."

Maxim shook his head. "Perhaps we can annoy Mathers into returning your dog."

"I command you to do that."

"Nice try."

CHAPTER 14

History Lesson

THE following morning, Goff awoke in a room smelling slightly of burnt flesh, rusty metal, and candle wax, with Maxim in his usual frozen position on his platform. Bones was nowhere to be found. There was no sign of Majesty either, but he felt sure she was still inside him. Unlike most mornings, he didn't feel alone. He unwrapped his bandaged finger and found the skin completely healed.

"Thanks," he whispered.

Majesty didn't respond.

After getting dressed, he headed down to the kitchen, where he had an abnormally silent breakfast with Pam and Ben. Tensions were running high between the two, and Goff guessed it had something to do with Pam writing haiku with Halstrom, two H-words Ben probably couldn't even spell. They were out of milk so he ate a bowl of dry cereal and looked over his Anatomy notes until it was time to catch the bus.

His nose still buried in a list of human bones, he slammed into Pam, who stood still at the door. Something had stopped Ben on the porch in front of her. An envelope sat on the front step at his feet.

"I'll handle this," Ben said, picking it up. "Official communications are my responsibility."

Ben opened the flap and pulled out a letter typed on a piece of plain blank paper. He read it slowly, moving his lips to form the words, and then looked up. "It says I'm boss for two more weeks."

"Give me that," Pam said, snatching it.

Goff looked over her shoulder while she read it. The letter was from Frank, saying that his orientation would continue for two more weeks until the day after Halloween. It was typed, not handwritten, and Frank's signature was at the bottom, but Goff suspected Frank had not written it. All the spelling and grammar were correct.

"Do either of you find this strange?" Goff asked.

"Adults are weird," Ben shrugged. "Get used to it. Oh, and go shopping today. We're out of chips."

"Okay, boss man," Goff said. "Impressive leadership. I'll get chips."

Ben gave him a deadly stare, but the bus pulled up, squealing and hissing, almost certainly saving Goff a punch in the arm.

During the ride to school, Goff looked out the misty window and watched the silver fog swirl out of the path of the bus and red and orange leaves end their lives in a soft twirl while he planned out the day. After school, he would quickly do the grocery shopping, then take care of chores at the house, including making something simple and quick for supper. Then he'd finish his paper, so he was ready to hand it in before the deadline tomorrow.

By then, it would be ten o'clock. Bedtime, when he used to fall asleep with Brak, warm and furry at his feet. Majesty rose to the tip of his finger and softly glowed there, apparently feeling Goff's sadness and anger.

"I think we need to go to Hallow Manor and see what we can see," he whispered to her, earning him a curious glance from the girl sitting next to him. Goff realized he should communicate with Majesty silently instead. *No fighting. Just investigative reporting. I have to do something. Brak needs me.*

Bumping along in his seat with Majesty held close to his chest, Goff rolled his head back and looked up at the bus ceiling. Thin white molding ran in arcs across it like whale bones. He worked out the details quickly. He'd climb out his window and make his way to Hallow Manor. He would remain at a distance and maybe see where Brak was being held and at least let him know he hadn't forgotten about him?

The bus arrived at school, and a swarm of chattering, noisy kids spilled out onto the sidewalk, Goff along with them. His morning classes went as usual, but in the hallway just before lunch, Tom Sweeney came up behind him and started flicking the back of his head.

"Knock it off." Goff swatted at Tom's hand but missed.

"Freaks get flicked," Tom said, laughing. "It's the law."

Goff turned to face him. Tom looked huge in an oversized blue Spraksville Howlers hockey sweatshirt and a bulky pair of shiny hunter-green jogging pants, but Goff felt like he needed to learn not to back down if he was going to survive this ordeal with Mathers. "That's not a law, and I'm not a freak."

"You are a freaky, freaky freak!" Tom let his finger fly again. Goff yelped, and a few nearby kids laughed.

"Stop it, you imbecile!" Goff shouted.

Tom's beady little eyes doubled in size, thought they were still beady. "What did you just call me?"

"Oh, sorry. I forgot to use small words when talking to a moron."

"Did you just call me a moron?"

"Well, you didn't understand imbecile."

Tom grabbed Goff by the collar, pulling him close to his red face. "You are so dead!"

Goff knew he had gone too far with Tom, and he braced for a punch to the gut. Majesty grew excited and made the palms of his hands hot. She wanted to attack. Before Goff thought better of it, he silently told her to let Tom have it.

Instantly, Tom's jogging pants fell to the floor and pooled around his ankles, as if pulled down by invisible hands. His pink pimply legs were exposed, as was a pair of bright red teddy bear underwear.

"What the...?" Tom said as he scrambled to pull his pants up.

"Nice teddy undies!" someone shouted.

Everyone nearby turned to look and burst into laughter.

Goff backed away and left quickly, shaking all over. It felt good to see Tom taken down so hard for being a jerk, but what if Majesty had hurt him instead of just embarrassing him? After all, she had lit his oatmeal on fire. He had no idea what she was capable of doing, yet he had told her to attack. Even the little bit of power that Majesty gave him had taken him to a dark place. He vowed never to encourage her to attack someone again.

Lydia and Halstrom, leaning against nearby lockers covered with bumper stickers, stepped in front of him. Halstrom was having his usual everything-navy-blue day, but Lydia probably couldn't have added another color or texture to her outfit.

"Once again, I can't explain what I just saw," Halstrom said, no expression to be detected on his hard bronze face.

"Talk to us, dude," Lydia implored, shoving Goff's shoulder.

"Just leave me alone, okay?" Goff turned away.

"We'll find you after school."

"No thanks."

"It wasn't an offer."

Goff headed quickly down the hallway and up a double flight of stairs to the quieter honor studies corridor on the second floor. A sense of comfort washed over him as he crossed the threshold into his favorite class with his favorite History teacher, Mrs. Wicket. Most likely the oldest teacher on staff and certainly the most engaging, her leathery skin had seen too much sun, her frayed silver hair, too much wind, and her wild blue eyes, too many wonders. She took pride in making her room engaging, too. Pictures of famous authors hung around the walls in brown bamboo frames. William Cranston had a place among other accomplished men and women—newscasters, writers, leaders of social movements. Large posters of exotic locations, some pastel and drenched with sun, some dark and mysterious, covered the rest of the walls.

Mrs. Wicket sat in one of the twelve chairs in the discussion circle, an overstuffed notebook in her lap and leather sandals with wood soles dangling off her toes. She looked up and smiled at Goff as he approached the perimeter. "How's the draft of your report coming?"

"Very well. I'll have it ready by tomorrow."

"I'm hoping you're finding your topic more relevant than you expected?"

Goff paused for a second. "More relevant?"

Mrs. Wicket laughed. "I know you didn't like the assignment, Goff, but I was hoping that once you started exploring magic, you'd find it an interesting topic."

"Yeah, that's for sure."

"There are many kinds of magic, you know."

"Many kinds?"

"Do your research."

"I am, but—"

"Class is beginning. Take your seat, dear."

Reluctantly, Goff took his seat in the circle and tried to pay attention as Mrs. Wicket told the story of a trip she had taken as a young girl to some quaint European mountain village called Monstraxen. His mind kept going over what had happened with Tom Sweeney, but his attention returned quickly to her voice when she said the name Mathers.

"... at the time, the village was ruled by a man named Mathers. A more feared and despised man I've never known. He was rumored to have spies everywhere. Some people even said the birds were his ears. Crossing him, even in word, resulted in ruined families and sudden disappearances."

Goff listened on the edge of his seat.

A boy next to Goff shot his hand up. "I've heard that a man named Mathers moved into Hallow Manor. Is he related?"

"He is a direct descendant," Mrs. Wicket said darkly, and then she looked directly at Goff. "I think it would be wise to keep your distance."

Goff gulped. She continued to look at him for another second and then looked away to continue her story, which was about farming onions or something. Goff was unable to pay attention from then on. His mind raced as he tried to figure out what had just happened. Did she know he had already spoken to Mathers and planned to visit his estate that night? Was that a warning for him? When class was over, he approached her desk to talk to her, but three other kids got there first to ask for extensions on their papers. She glanced at him, but it was just a glance. Whatever she had to say, she had said. Not wanting to be late for his next class, Goff left, feeling very confused.

Mr. Dongle gave Goff the evil eye when he arrived for science class. "Re-assembly going well?"

"Uh, yeah," Goff said. "It's practically re-assembling itself."

After getting a curious look from Mr. Dongle, Goff took his seat and removed his book and notes without looking at Lydia or Halstrom. Mr. Dongle handed out a pop quiz in which they had to label the bones on the image of a skeleton. Goff got a lot of dirty looks from his classmates, and he bolted from the class as soon as the bell rang.

On the way home, Goff altered his plans a little. He wanted to research the Mathers family and Monstraxen at the Spraksville Library before it closed. Afterward, he'd make a quick stop at the grocery store to buy chips for Ben and milk, and then rush home to finish his paper before it was time to head to Hallow Manor and see about Brak. When he stepped off the bus, he ran home to drop off his backpack, then jogged down Hayden and up Main Street to the library.

The heavy steel and glass Spraksville Library doors creaked as he pushed them open. A "Staff Favorite Halloween Books" display had been set up in the entranceway on a table draped with a black and orange tablecloth. Arriving at the front desk out of breath and a little disheveled, he saw the prim librarians eyeing him warily through horn-rimmed glasses as he made his way to the bank of shelves to the right. He passed between row after row of book bindings and past a girl reshelving more from a cart, to find an empty computer carrel against the back wall. He plopped down, logged in, and searched for "Monstraxen."

He waited anxiously as the green progress spinner spun, and a few results finally appeared. He scanned the first few pages, disappointed to find no mention of a town with that name, just results for different spellings—an old jazz song and an odd-looking adventure game involving bunnies in space suits. He typed "Harkland Mathers" and pressed enter. The search page crashed with some weird error full of gibberish. He tried three more times but got the same error each time.

Feeling spooked, Goff sat back and stared at the screen. Could Mathers be powerful enough to cast a spell that blocked anyone from searching his name?

Even more curious now, he typed in "Wicket" and saw the page fill up with results. The first one was a definition: "a small door or gate, especially one beside or in a larger one." Most of the others were about cricket and a few about companies named Wicket. On the second page, at the bottom, he found mention of an Ariel Wicket and clicked through. Ariel had been burned at the stake as a witch in a village called Saxonville. Goff had come across the name Saxonville during his research. Apparently, decades ago, the town had merged with an adjacent village called Sprakston to form Spraksville.

Goff sat back and stared at the screen as a dark feeling like a storm cloud grew inside. Why had Mrs. Wicket never told them about her relative being burned as a witch in Saxonville, which was practically Spraksville? And why had she told a story about a town called Monstraxen that didn't seem to exist?

In a whisper, he asked Majesty: "What sort of nasty evil stuff have I gotten myself into?"

But Majesty stayed deep inside, silent and still.

CHAPTER 15

Making Magic

A S Goff pondered the horror of his situation, the green banker's lamp on his station began to turn on and off rapidly. At first, he feared something magical and ominous was happening, but then he realized it was just a grumpy librarian trying to chase everyone out at closing time by flipping a switch. He grabbed his bag and headed out.

Crisp autumn air greeted him when he stepped outside. Autumn twilight made the world look as if the knob labeled "orange" had been ratcheted up to eleven. On Main Street, jack-o-lanterns leered from every step, railing, and fence post. Spider webbing fanned out like feathery mold across building fronts. Gauze mummies, dripping zombies, pale vampires, green witches, and billowing ghosts filled windows and doorways.

He walked toward the MoneySaver, surprised at how few people were out. The big windows of Pongo's, painted with cartoonish images of pizza slices and salad bowls, were dark. On the door, a crooked paper sign written in red marker read: "Closed for the season." Across the street, Java Time's purple mug-shaped sign had also gone dark, and there was a "Closed for a few weeks" sign on that door as well.

He arrived at the MoneySaver to find the entire front of the big building painted pumpkin orange, and a tall fan-powered Frankenstein dancing crazily on the roof. Goff pushed the broken automatic door open and ran in to grab two bags of cheap SaverSpecial ridged potato chips and some milk. At the register, he asked an unfamiliar girl with blue hair to charge them to Frank's account.

"Cash only," she said, not looking up from her fingernails.

"I don't have cash."

"Then no chips." She threw them into a basket behind her and set the milk aside.

"But—"

"Managers are all out sick, and nobody knows how to work the systems."

Frustrated, Goff left, pushing his way through the broken automatic doors. But a dozen feet from the entrance, the door opened by itself and two bags of SaverSpecial chips floated through the opening.

"Majesty!" Goff scolded. "That's stealing!"

The chips wiggled back and forth in the air.

Fearing someone might see them floating, Goff grabbed the bags, tucked them under his arm and started walking quickly, deciding he could charge them to the account next time. Suddenly, Lydia and Halstrom stepped out from behind a vending machine a few feet ahead and blocked his way.

"Why are you two always everywhere?" Goff tried to press past. "Leave me alone."

"Dude, you can't evade the facts any longer," Lydia said.

"Facts?"

Halstrom counted on his fingers. "An animated skeleton. Dropping pants—"

"Chips!" Lydia exclaimed, pointing dramatically.

Halstrom looked at her curiously. "It is not the chips that are of note. It was that they were floating."

"Seriously?"

"It's an important distinction."

"I'm trying to remember why I decided to become your friend."

"While you work that out," Goff said, "I'm going home."

Lydia stepped in front of him. "Not so fast, dude. You have to come clean with us. Did you get bit by a magical bat or something?"

"Magical bat?" Halstrom asked.

"Just let him answer."

Goff paused and looked at the two of them. Unable to think of any lie that would sound at all reasonable, he just blurted out the truth. "Well, it happened by accident, but I've become a wizard."

Lydia's jaw dropped, and her glasses slid to the end of her nose. "Seriously? Wow. Well, I'm cool with that. Just so you know, I believe in all sorts of crazy things, well, things other people think are crazy. For instance, I believe whales are from outer space, spiders are smarter than humans, and the world used to be flat. So, I'm totally down with you being a wizard and all."

"In my opinion," Halstrom said, "Most of what Lydia just said is some form of psychosis, but I can't deny what I have witnessed."

"Psychosis?" Lydia asked.

"Alien whales?" Halstrom countered.

"I've seen pictures."

"Pictures can be spoofed."

"Whatever," Lydia rolled her eyes and turned to Goff. "So, what can you do? Can you fly?"

"Haven't tried," Goff said.

"I dream of flying," Halstrom said.

"You dream?" Lydia asked.

Halstrom ignored her and turned to Goff. "Perhaps you should tell us the full story."

"Fine," Goff said, thinking it would be best if they knew the whole truth instead of whatever Lydia would cook up in her headband-compressed brain. "Walk with me."

As they walked, Goff told them everything that had happened. It felt so good! He began with the assignment by Mrs. Wicket to write the paper. Lydia interrupted with questions often, but Halstrom kept saying, "Keep going," and Goff complied. By the time he was done, they were standing in front of his house. Darkness fought with the fading sunset to own the sky.

Above them, the effigy of Goff swayed side to side with its stuffed head listing at a grotesque angle. They all seemed lost in thought, hypnotized by the gentle back and forth of the corpse and the sound of hundreds of crickets chirping.

Lydia was the first to speak, naturally. "Can you give us a demonstration?"

"Not sure that's a good idea," Goff said.

"Please?" Lydia begged. "Just something small. I want to see real magic!"

"Fine," Goff said, heading toward the back of the house. "A tiny bit of magic. That's all."

They followed him to where the little white shed rested against the garage. Goff put the SaverSpecial chips down behind him next to a chaotic pile of green garden hoses and sat down. Lydia and Halstrom dropped down on either side of him.

"Don't you need your cauldron and your candles?" Lydia asked.

"Doesn't work like that," Goff said, extending his hand. "Majesty? Would you honor my friends with a small display of magic… and I emphasize small?"

Majesty responded quickly. His hand grew warm and glowed violet. Lydia gasped, and Halstrom tapped his chin, looking intrigued. Majesty pulsed three times, and then, as if a magical cloud had burst open above, a flurry of glowing, swirling, purple snowflakes appeared. The air filled with hundreds of them, landing on shoulders, hands, and legs and then lifting again to fly free like playful moths. Lydia giggled hysterically. A kaleidoscope of color shimmered on her glasses as she tried to catch one but had no luck. Goff and Halstrom tried too, but the flakes were too quick.

A second later, the flakes rose like a school of fish following some unseen leader, and moved out of reach to form a cloud hovering above. A thin tendril extended and formed curly letters below it, spelling out "Accept what I offer."

"Majesty!" Goff scolded. "No!"

"Dude," Lydia said. "Let her offer if she wants to offer."

Before he could say anything else, Goff's index finger grew hot, and Majesty popped out of the tip, glowing bright, much brighter than when he had first met her. She hovered a few inches above, pulsing, and then two tiny sparks, barely larger than a grain of rice, sprang out of her. They circled her like moths around a candle, and then one flew to hover in front of Halstrom and the other in front of Lydia.

"She's propagated," Halstrom said. "I believe she is offering us magic."

"No," Goff said. "Bad idea, Majesty!"

Majesty glowed brightly like a proud mother.

"Awesome!" Lydia squealed as her spark moved to hover an inch from her nose. She crossed her eyes to look at it, and its glow turned her face into a black and white photo dipped in purple dye. "It's so cute! I'm all good with accepting this little dude." She lifted her hand to hold it under the spark. "I accept you."

Halstrom raised his hand under his spark. "As do I."

The two sparks spun in a circle and darted right into their chests. Lydia's eyes bulged, and her hair shot straight out as if charged with static electricity. Halstrom raised his eyebrows, and his beanie bounced up and landed an inch off center.

Crackling arcs of electricity shot out to connect Goff with both of them, creating a glowing triangle. Lydia reached out and took both Goff's and Halstrom's hand. Goff completed the ring by taking Halstrom's. Instantly, a feeling of power raced through him. He felt himself growing lighter, and he lifted off the ground. The others rose with him, and soon they were all floating a foot up, still sitting on a magical base but no longer touching solid ground.

Lydia bounced up and down with excitement. "This is so cool!"

"We are defying the laws of gravity, making them laws no more," Halstom declared.

Goff sighed. "A bit more of a demonstration than I had planned."

Slowly, the lines of light disappeared, and the trio began descending. When they were back on the ground, the three of them, still holding hands, stared at one another for a moment. The air around them seemed full of magic. An owl hooted in the distance, and a gentle breeze rustled the trees in the cemetery.

Lydia broke the silence. "So, are we wizards now, too?"

"I don't know," Goff said. "I'm kind of new at all this."

"Well," Lydia began, "Goff named his magic, so I'm naming mine too. I'll call my little dude Chester."

"Because it entered your chest?" Halstrom asked.

"No, smart aleck. It just feels right."

"I shall call mine Occam. That way, it will grow to be very logical."

"How touching."

"It is a better name than Chester."

"Hey!" Lydia shoved Halstrom. "Chester is a good name. Better than Occam."

"You should call yours 'Dude,' since it is your favorite word."

"Dude isn't a name."

"I don't think that matters."

"Guys!" Goff stopped them. "I wouldn't be too happy about this. Even with just a tiny speck of magic, you could be in danger now too."

Lydia blanched. "You think that Mathers dude will come after us now too?"

"You said 'dude' again."

"Shut up!"

"I don't know what he'll do," Goff said, "but I agreed to reject magic, and I've failed at that."

"True." Halstrom stroked his chin. "Perhaps we should not have accepted Majesty's gift. We know nothing of this world and are likely to die quickly because of our ignorance."

"You just sucked all the fun out of this," Lydia moaned.

"It's what I do," Halstrom said.

Goff and Lydia spoke in unison. "I know."

A girl's throaty cough came from around the corner. Their white T-shirts glowing in the light of the bug bulb, Ben and Pam strode up with wicked grins on their faces.

CHAPTER 16

Mutiny

ARRIVING like a posse hunting down criminals, Pam and Ben stomped up to the edge of where Goff, Lydia, and Halstrom sat in the grass. They stood with their arms crossed—scolding parents who'd caught their kids playing with fire. Pam opened her mouth to speak but closed it when she saw Halstrom.

"Well, well, well," Ben said. "Look at the little circle of freaks holding hands."

Goff had forgotten he was holding Lydia and Halstrom's hands. He promptly let go, relieved that Ben and Pam had not seen any of the magic. He stood up along with Halstrom and Lydia, and they faced off, three against two.

"Shouldn't you be inside cleaning and cooking, Goff?" Ben asked. "Instead of out here playing with dolls in the grass or whatever?"

"Dolls?" Goff asked, but he decided not to pursue that. He pointed toward the pile of hoses. "Your chips are over there."

"These?" Ben picked up one of the bags and made a face as if it was filled with fresh manure. "You moron. You bought SaverSpecial chips?"

"You're lucky I got some," Goff said. "There was trouble charging the account."

"Trouble with the account?" Ben asked, shaking the bag. "You spend too much on crappers?"

"Crappers?" Lydia asked.

"That's moron for capers," Goff explained.

Ben stepped in closer to Goff. "Did you just call me a moron?"

"I'm confused," Halstrom said. "The rest of us certainly heard the word moron. Did you not hear it?"

Pam snickered and then stuffed it down behind a deep blush. Ben glared at her for a second before turning to Halstrom. "Stay out of this, you freak. I was talking to Goff."

Goff stepped between them before Halstrom could respond. He wasn't going to let Ben bully his friends. "Yes, I called you a moron. Because you are one, probably the biggest moron I've ever known."

Ben flashed red, and his lip quivered. The next thing Goff knew, he was on the ground with Ben on top of him pressing his face into the damp grass. Goff struggled to get free, but Ben contained him like steel chains around a crate, shouting, "Nobody calls me a moron, you little twerp! I'm the boss here, and don't you forget it!"

Majesty grew hot in Goff's hand. For a second, he contemplated letting her do something nasty to Ben—maybe turn him into a carrot or send him up to the highest branches of a tree. But he knew that would be a big mistake, so he silently commanded her to stand down.

Ben punched him hard in the ribs. Goff yelped, and suddenly Ben lifted off him. At first, Goff thought Majesty had ignored him and sent Ben up into the clouds, but it wasn't Majesty who had freed him. Halstrom and Pam had a red-faced Ben under the arms, dragging him backward. His white sneakers dug divots in the weeds as he writhed like a fish on a line.

"Let me go!" Ben said. "He asked for it! He needs to know who's boss!"

Goff sat up, panting, feeling dizzy and about to puke.

Lydia dropped down to his side. "Dude! Are you all right?"

"I've been better," Goff said, rubbing his sore ribs.

"Why didn't you let Majesty do something?"

"Wouldn't have been right."

"But he deserved it."

"Might doesn't make right."

"I'm gonna kill you, you little maggot!" Ben shouted, breaking free of Pam and Halstrom and heading back toward Goff.

"Ben!" Pam shouted, jumping in front of him. "What's gotten into you?"

"Me?" Ben shoved her hard. "What's gotten into you? Teaming up with your boyfriend here to pull me off? Has everyone gone crazy?"

"I have not changed," Halstrom said matter-of-factly.

"He's not my boyfriend," Pam said.

"You think I don't notice?" Ben said, shoving her again. "You go quiet and blush whenever he's around. Where's my tough-as-nails sister? The one I count on to have my back? We've always been a freakin' team! You've gone soft or something lately. I don't know who you are anymore."

Pam shoved Ben back. "You're the one talking crazy now. We're still a team. It's just that, well..."

"Well, what?"

Pam paused for a moment, looking like there was a lot she wanted to say. "You just need to grow up, that's all."

"Grow up?" Ben threw his hands up. "I'm the only mature one here!"

"I am mature," Halstrom said. "You are a child throwing a tantrum."

Ben whirled toward him. "That's it!"

"What's it?"

"You!"

"Me?"

"Yes, you… maggot!"

"You are not doing well at being mature."

"Shut up!"

"Very mature."

Ben turned a deep shade of red "I don't want you here even a second longer. Leave!"

Halstrom didn't budge or even blink. "Goff invited me, not you."

"This is my house, not his. Get off my property."

"You're too young to own property."

"Don't mess with me right now," Ben threatened, clenching his fists. "I'll give you to three. One…"

"The next number is two," Halstrom said.

Ben cocked his arm, ready to throw a punch.

"No," Pam grabbed Ben's arm, twisting it behind him and pushing it toward his shoulder blades. "Enough! I'm stripping you of your duty as head of household. I call for a mutiny! Goff, are you with me?"

"Of course," Goff replied.

"You can't do that," Ben said, wincing as Pam pressed his arm up harder. "Frank specifically left me in charge."

"It wouldn't be a mutiny if it didn't force a leadership change," Halstrom said.

"Mutiny won't do any good," Ben said, struggling to get free. "I'll call Frank. He'll be furious."

"You can't call Frank," Pam said.

"Why not?" Ben asked.

"I've tried, okay?" Pam said, letting go of Ben and stepping back, panting heavily. "I've left him three messages. He hasn't called back. I tried again this morning, and the number is out of service now."

"Out of service?" Goff asked, shocked at this new development.

"Wait," Ben said, turning to Pam. "You've tried to call him? Why?"

"I need his signature on something."

"What could you possibly need Frank's signature on?"

"None of your business," Pam said. "It's personal."

"Personal? I'm your brother!"

"Dude," Lydia said. "There are things brothers and sisters don't discuss."

Ben glared at Lydia and then turned back to Pam. "Are you sick or something?"

"No." Pam shoved him hard. "You are such an idiot."

"Then what?"

"I told you it's personal. I'm just telling you that you can't call Frank and that you're no longer the boss here. I am. Now go bounce a ball or something before I give you toilet duty."

Ben shook his head and shoved his way past Pam. "You're not my boss. Stay here with these dorks if you want."

"Go suck an egg, jerk," Lydia said.

Ben glanced over his shoulder, sending knives in her direction, but kept moving. A second later, the front door slammed hard. Pam turned to Halstrom and Lydia and bit her lip. Her hair had fallen out of her ponytail and hung down onto her shoulders. She paused as though she didn't know how to say what she wanted to say. "I'm sorry for all of this. He can be a real jerk."

"It was Ben, not you," Lydia said.

"I know, but he's my brother, so it kinda feels like me, too. Can I make it up to you guys? Maybe you want to stay for dinner?"

"I'm in," Lydia said with a grin.

"I also have no obligations," Halstrom said.

"Good," Pam said. She turned to Goff. "Go inside and cook us a big supper."

"But I—" Goff started.

"Go!" Pam shoved him. "I'm not Ben, but don't forget I'm the boss."

Goff felt too worn down and confused to argue. "Fine," he said, half-walking and half-limping toward the house.

"We'll help," Lydia said, following after Goff with Halstrom behind her.

"Hey Lydia," Pam called out. "I was wondering if we could talk for a minute? Umm… privately?"

Lydia seemed unable to process the request.

"Go ahead, Lydia," Goff said. He'd never seen this side of Pam before. She was acting like an ordinary girl who needed a female friend. "Halstrom and I will get started."

Lydia walked back to Pam, and they headed around the corner of the house.

"I think they might be talking about you," Goff said to Halstrom as they walked toward the house.

"You are wrong."

"Why do you think so?"

"I see truths other people don't."

When they got inside, Goff washed up and put on a few sports-themed bandages—that was all they had—before going to the kitchen. Halstrom had hopped up onto the counter and was frowning while reading the ingredients on a box of Ben's Mega Cocoa Bombs cereal.

"What should we cook?" Goff asked.

"There is no food I will not eat."

"Of course there isn't. Lasagna?"

They went to work making lasagna, and Halstrom turned out to be handy in the kitchen. He deftly diced and cooked onions with garlic in Frank's only sauce pan, filling the kitchen with a heavenly smell, and made a sauce while Goff got the water boiling and then mixed up his secret cheese blend. A little while later, Pam and Lydia came back inside, laughing and whispering. Pam went straight to her room, but Lydia joined them in the kitchen.

"Dude! I make awesome garlic bread!" she said, and without another word, she opened a bag of stale white bread and started spreading pieces out on a cookie sheet.

Crowded together in the hot steamy kitchen, they worked together smoothly, laughing and teasing each other as if they'd been cooking together for years. After putting the big glass pan of lasagna into the oven and setting a timer, they looked at one another, "What now?"

"We've got an hour," Goff said. "I need to finish a paper tonight. Do you mind hanging out in my room while I work on it?"

"Will you-know-who and what's-his-name be up there?" Lydia asked.

"She means Maxim and Bones."

Lydia swatted Halstrom's shoulder. "Dude, he knows who I mean."

"Then why do you not just say what you mean?"

"I was trying to be discreet."

"I don't think you accomplished that."

At the top of the stairs, when Goff opened the curtain with Lydia and Halstrom behind him, neither Maxim nor Bones were anywhere to be seen.

"Maxim?" Goff called out. "Bones?"

"Perhaps they are hiding from us?" Halstrom said.

"Dude, why would they hide from us?" Lydia asked. "They're scary, not us."

"Perhaps we are scary to them."

"Guys," Goff said, checking the cauldron in case they were hiding there. "I'm worried. What if they were captured?"

"Why would Mathers want your talking skeleton and cat?"

"More collateral, maybe," Goff suggested.

"I thought Bones and Maxim annoyed you," Halstrom said.

Goff looked up at him. "You annoy me, but you're still my friend. I didn't realize it until now, but Bones and Maxim were two more annoying friends. It seems to be the character profile I attract—annoying."

"Really?" a voice called from above.

Goff and Lydia jumped. Halstrom looked up.

Maxim dropped down from the rafters. "Annoying? You think I'm annoying?"

Lydia grabbed Goff's arm and held on tight, muttering something about a "freakin' talking cat dude."

Behind them, Bones jumped up from the box Goff had used to carry him home, waving his arms and clattering his teeth like an animated skeleton in a House of Horrors.

Goff flinched.

Halstrom simply pointed at Bones, saying, "There he is."

Lydia yelped, turned pale and looked like she was going to pass out. Goff helped her down to the floor where she lay looking numb.

"What's wrong with you?" Goff yelled at Bones. "You scared her half to death."

"Nah," Maxim said. "I've seen half dead. That's only a few percent dead. She'll be fine."

Bones walked over. Lydia stared at him from the ground with her jaw dropped. "He's... he's..."

"Pleased to meet you." Bones extended his hand. "You are?"

Lydia didn't respond.

"I am Halstrom, and this is Lydia," Halstrom said, turning to Bones. "We are both pleased to meet you."

Bones leaned in and pretended to speak in a low tone. "Just so you know, we consider Goff our most annoying wizard ever, so the feeling is mutual."

"Hey!" Goff complained. "I was worried about you two. Don't make me regret it."

"You shouldn't be worried about us," Maxim said, striding closer in slow, steady steps. "You should be worried about yourselves. All of you. Very worried."

"I disagree," Halstrom said, leaning against a stack of crates with his arms crossed. "Worrying just decreases one's ability to respond to dangerous situations."

Bones shook his head and laughed. "And people think I'm dead?"

"Wait," Lydia got up slowly, helped a little by Halstrom. "So, like, what specifically should we be very worried about? I mean, is there, like, something more to worry about than before, specifically, something really worrisome? I was already pretty worried as it is. I should worry more?"

"You have the strangest way of asking a question," Halstrom said.

"Tough crowd," Maxim said, flicking his head at Halstrom before continuing. "So, is it true that I'm in the presence of three wizards?"

"Maybe," Goff said, hesitantly. "Why?"

"That wasn't part of the plan."

"What plan?" Goff asked.

"Your plan," Bones said, sitting back against the cauldron. "To reject magic so you could get your dog back?"

"Instead, you created a coven," Maxim said with some amusement.

Lydia threw her hands wide. "It was Majesty!"

"Majesty?" Bones stood up, looking intrigued.

"Despite Goff's objections," Halstrom explained, "Majesty propagated and offered us each a gift of magic. I've named mine Occam so it will be logical, and Lydia named hers Chester, since it entered through her chest."

"That's not why I called it Chester!"

Bones sat back down, a little too fast, almost tipping over into the cauldron. "Fascinating."

"Regardless of what names you assigned," Maxim said, his tail swishing back and forth slowly, "it was not a good idea."

"Do you think Mathers will find out?" Goff asked.

Maxim's tail stopped moving. "I'm certain he already knows."

The room fell silent. Bones clicked his fingers on the edge of the cauldron, causing it to ring softly like a meditation bell.

Lydia walked over and put her hand on the cauldron to stop it from ringing. "One thing I don't get is why Mathers just doesn't, you know—"

"Kill me?" Goff asked.

"I believe it's a matter of strategy," Halstrom said. "Goff is a perfect enemy—unskilled and unwilling. If he were killed, the gargoyles would find a replacement to maintain balance, and the person they choose might be a more formidable enemy."

"Exactly," Maxim said, nodding.

"It's almost as if it wasn't random - you know, me being made his enemy," Goff observed.

Bones chuckled and kicked the cauldron with his foot to make it ring as Lydia frowned. "Well, Mathers didn't move to Spraksville for intellectual stimulation."

"Did he come here to find Goff?" Lydia asked, stopping the ringing again.

Goff processed that statement for a moment. "That's crazy talk, right?"

Bones and Maxim both shrugged and said nothing.

<h1 style="text-align:center">CHAPTER 17</h1>

Monstraxen

THE alarm in the kitchen crested the hour mark and sent short but steady beeping up the stairs. Goff, Lydia, and Halstrom excused themselves and headed to the kitchen. The lasagna was perfect. Lydia broiled her garlic bread and added it to three plates heavy with big fat squares of pasta, sauce, and cheese. Goff yelled up the stairs that supper was ready.

Ben stomped down the stairs scowling. Without even acknowledging them, he went into the kitchen, filled a plate, and stomped back up to his room. Pam got a plate too, but she surprised Goff by bringing it out to the living room to join them.

"Can I eat with you guys?" she asked, looking a little uncomfortable.

"You invited us," Halstrom said. "So, I would expect you to attend the meal."

Lydia rolled her eyes. "He's trying to say that we'd like that."

Shifting around to accommodate Pam, they all found places to sit where there weren't piles of Frank's clothing, ashtrays, or nasty-looking stains. Nobody was tempted to sit in Frank's big puffy brown lounge chair, despite it being the most prominent piece of furniture in the room. It was covered in crumbs and stains and strands of his hair.

"I feel like sitting in that," Lydia said, "would be like putting on some dude's dirty underwear."

They all agreed and sat in silence, clinking forks against the cheap, mostly chipped porcelain plates. Halstrom and Lydia seemed preoccupied. Goff knew that if Lydia wasn't talking, she must be wiped out. Pam occasionally looked up with a furrowed brow, as if struggling to think of something to say, but each time she looked back down at her food and said nothing. Ben usually did most of the talking.

Goff decided to break the ice. "Do you like the lasagna, Pam?"

"I'm eating it, aren't I, dork?"

Lydia and Halstrom snapped their heads up as if a balloon had popped. The tone of her response and the word "dork" hung in the air like a bad smell.

Pam looked down. "I mean, yeah, it's good. Thanks."

Another minute of silence followed, and then Pam looked around. "Where's the wimpy dog, anyway? I haven't seen him all week."

"Brak is not a wimpy dog," Goff said, wishing she hadn't brought him up. Going to Hallow Manor tonight to see him was out of the question. The draft of his paper was due tomorrow. "I'm sure he's fine. Dogs wander off sometimes."

"Brak is an odd name for a dog," Halstrom said.

"I know!" Pam exclaimed, blushing deeply from speaking directly to Halstrom. "Frank thought it was Bark backward. It should be Krab. He's such an idiot."

"Knarf," Halstrom said.

Pam screwed up her face. "Huh?"

"That's Frank backwards," Halstrom said. "I'd be Mortslah."

"I like that," Lydia said. "I'd be A... Adly... er..."

"Aidyl," Halstrom said.

Lydia looked miffed. "I was going to say that."

"Aidyl? That's kind of pretty," Goff said, taking his turn at blushing now. "My name is boring. I'd be Ffog."

"Not as boring as Map," Pam said morosely.

"Yeah, sorry, you win at boring backward," Lydia said.

"Angasal doog," Halstrom said.

Pam laughed. "Good lasagna!"

They went around the circle for the next few minutes and said whatever they could think of backward to see who could figure it out first. Pam laughed and seemed to be having a good time. Goff liked this version of her; the scowl was gone. She tossed her hair and leaned a little towards Halstrom every time she laughed, and Halstrom didn't move away.

After a pause, while everyone thought of words to say backward, Lydia brightened. "Ooh, I have a good one! Hold on…" she closed her eyes and furrowed her brow. "I think it's Sretham Dnalkrah."

"Let's not do that one," Goff said quickly, clearing his throat. "We should clean up."

"Harkland Mathers?" Pam asked.

"Bingo," Lydia said, snapping her fingers. A few purple sparks flew out.

Pam gasped. "Your fingers! How did you make them spark like that?"

"Oh, I uh..."

"Must have been the chemicals we used in today's science class," Goff said. He snapped his fingers, and a purple flame formed on the tip of his thumb. *Majesty! No!*

Pam shot up from her seat. "That's not normal."

Goff blew out his thumb. "Powerful chemicals."

"Didn't you wash your hands before cooking?"

"Yes, but—"

"I am in their science class," Halstrom said. "My fingers spark also." He snapped his fingers. No sparks flew, but the light bulb above popped and went out.

Pam stiffened and crossed her arms. "You guys are messing with me."

"No," Goff said. "We wouldn't do that. Just chemicals—"

"Give it up, Goff! You guys have some stupid magician's kit and decided to make a fool of me. A little private joke at my expense? I knew joining you all was a mistake. I thought we were having a good time together." She picked up her plate and stood to leave.

"It's not like that," Goff said.

Pam turned. "Then what is it like, Goff?"

Goff could not think of anything to say that would make sense, and he dared not blame chemicals from science class again. He looked at the others, and they just stared back at him.

"Thought so." Pam clunked her plate down in the kitchen and ran up to her room, slamming her door so hard that the house shook.

"Well, that went well," Goff said sarcastically.

"Yeah, but my fingers sparked," Lydia said, cracking a gigantic smile.

"I think we hurt Pam's feelings," Halstrom said.

"Until tonight, I didn't know she had any," Goff said.

Halstrom and Lydia helped him put dishes in the sink and wrap up the rest of the lasagna before leaving so Goff could finish the draft of his paper. He raced to his room and was happy to see Bones and Maxim out on the roof moonbathing. He pulled out the pages he'd written so far, grabbed a pencil, and started to write.

As usual, time flew by as he wrote, but after a while, he found his mind slowing, and he became drowsy. He kept trailing off at the end of sentences and making lines instead of letters. He shook his head and took a big drink of water before trying again. Half a sentence in, his forehead landed hard on the pencil eraser, jamming the point into the paper and breaking it. He jumped up.

"All right in there?" Bones called.

"I'm sleepy."

"Try being dead."

"Funny."

Goff sharpened his pencil and started writing again. A minute later, his head was an inch off the page, and he was writing in mouse-sized letters. Unable to keep his eyes open any longer, hoping to just nap for a bit and wake up refreshed, he put his head down. As his eyes closed, he felt like he was sinking into the page, dropping through time and space through the thin little horizontal blue lines.

The next thing he knew, he was lying on the sidewalk under a cloudy sky with the full moon shining through stretched cotton clouds, making everything a deathly gray. A tree with a massive, twisted trunk towered over him, its barren branches a hundred frozen gray pythons in a jumble. Light snow fell through the gaps and landed on his face. He stood and brushed off the snow.

"Hello?" he called out.

The sound of his voice, any voice, seemed unwelcome in this grim place. This had to be a dream, but it didn't feel like one. It was all too real; he was fully aware and alert.

A snow-dusted narrow cobblestone road led up a hill with close-set stone houses on either side. They all had thick wooden front doors and crown glass windows, none showing any signs of life inside. Unsure where to go, he walked up the hill, occasionally slipping on larger cobbles. A few blocks up the road, a wooden sign in the shape of a rustic loaf of bread hung above a door. At first, the words on it seemed gibberish to Goff, but then, as if by magic, they suddenly made sense. It read "Hoffstraden Family Bakery." There was writing in red wax across the big front window. He walked up and was able to read the writing after a moment: "Closed for a few weeks." He peered in. Pale brown football-shaped loaves and piles of split-top rolls sat in baskets on shelves. A mound of them had spilled from a tipped basket onto the floor, where rats were helping themselves to them. On the counter, three candles had burned down to creamy puddles.

Over the hill and around a bend, Goff arrived in what appeared to be the downtown shopping area. All the stores were dark and abandoned like the bakery, and all had the same message scrawled on their windows.

A few blocks farther, he came to a part of town that looked to be the town square. A wide donut of cobblestones ran around a little park in front of a building with thick stone pillars. Above the twelve-foot doors, in the triangle of the pediment, the words "Monstraxen Town Hall" were etched in gold letters.

Goff's heart nearly stopped beating. Monstraxen? Why was he here, of all places, the mythical town Mrs. Wicket had spoken of only a dozen hours ago in class? A town ruled by an ancient ancestor of Harkland Mathers. In the center of the little park stood the same eerie statue that was in the park behind the Spraksville Library, but it was missing the gargoyle on top.

Goff stood there staring, unsure of what this all meant, as a cold breeze swirled the falling snow. Branches scraped like giant fingernails across the slate roof of a nearby house. A shutter banged open and closed, and he jumped at the sound. He felt as if the little square was coming to life. Something was very wrong about this place, very wrong.

Movement in his periphery startled him. He turned to see a young boy moving toward him, wrapped in a heavy red coat and wearing big black boots. The boy's face was full of sorrow, and his eyes solid white, devoid of a pupil or iris. He moved steadily toward Goff, his feet stepping but not in sync with his movement and not actually touching the ground.

Goff was frozen in place. This was not a human coming his way. It was a ghost.

More ghostly figures appeared as the boy floated closer, streaming out of every road and alley leading to the square. They were all young boys and girls, bundled up with tormented faces and glassy white eyes. Goff spun around. They had encircled him, leaving him nowhere to run.

"I just want to go home," Goff said. "Please, I didn't ask to come here."

Soon, the square was jammed with a hundred children, tightening the ring around Goff into a solid wall. Goff's heart raced, and his breath came in tiny bursts, each sending a silver puff into the air. He saw no breath escaping from the approaching horde.

The dead don't breathe.

"Who are you? What do you want?"

They stopped approaching and stared at Goff with blank white eyes. The boy in the red coat raised his arm and pointed to the other side of the square. The crowd parted.

"Is there something you want me to see?" Goff asked.

The boy stared at him and pointed more urgently. Unsure of what else to do, Goff walked slowly over the cobblestones in the direction the boy was pointing, passing close to kids of all ages, but not a single adult. They turned their heads smoothly like owls to watch him pass.

He reached the end of the crowd and headed down the street. The ring folded into a mob that followed him, with the boy with the red coat in the lead.

Goff moved forward, looking in all directions, but not knowing what he was looking for. On either side, he passed abandoned shops with dark windows, where messages had been hastily scrawled in red wax. Several blocks along, he came to a massive wrought-iron gate that guarded the entrance to an estate shielded from view by a bank of pines. All that was visible from the road was a tower. The name Mathers was woven in ornate brass letters into an arch at the top of the iron gate.

Goff stopped as a darker feeling than he'd ever felt before washed over him. Instinctively he knew that this was an evil place. Something terrible had happened here. "I don't want to go in there," he said to the boy and the crowd behind him.

The gates swung open with a rusty scream. The crowd of ghostly figures formed a wall, and the boy stepped closer, pointing urgently. Hesitantly, Goff traipsed through the gates and walked down a stone path to where a gap in the pines allowed a view of what was once a sprawling manor, but the main building was gone. All that remained was the tower visible from the road, poised like a diver preparing to jump into an enormous pit hundreds of feet in each direction. The rim of the pit was blackened as if burned by a torch, and the edges dropped straight down like a grave.

Goff swallowed hard and slowly moved forward toward the gaping hole in the ground. At about three feet away, vertigo set in, and he dropped down and crawled, trying to avoid shards of glass scattered about. His heart raced, and his fingers grew stiff from crawling on the frozen ground. When he reached the lip and peered over, there was no bottom visible, just blackness.

Goff looked back at the boy. "I don't understand. What am I supposed to see?"

The boy rushed forward, bringing the rest of the kids with him. Like rats running from a fire, they flew right through Goff and into the pit. Goff cowered as hundreds of spirits passed through him, their sorrow and loss ripping at his heart. The ground beneath him cracked, and he tried to move back, but the edge broke off, and he fell forward, screaming. He dropped at incredible speed through nothingness until even the falling stopped and he was alone in absolute blackness.

An image began to fill the darkness. As if he were a fly on the wall, he was looking down on a ceremony in a grand hall as big as a football field; it was the main body of the mansion that used to stand adjacent to the tower. Black candles burned in sconces between the floor-to-ceiling windows through which no light shone. Giant arched beams like ribs of a pirate ship held up the high vaulted ceiling.

Hundreds of men and women wearing black robes with hoods stood in rows on the wooden floor, facing an altar at the front that glowed with rows of black candles. In the center of the altar, a man hidden deep within a billowing red robe stood calling out names in a voice that boomed like thunder.

One by one, the adults stepped up to a metal cauldron and opened their mouths to release snakes of white smoke into it. There was a long pause after the last person added theirs, and then the man in the red robe called out a final name. "Geoff Von Gretell."

Von Gretell emerged from a door to the side, also wearing a red robe. He marched up to the altar, paused for a moment, and then turned toward the other man. In a deep, raspy voice he shouted, "This ends now!"

A red crackling ball of energy appeared in his hand, and he hurled it at the other man. It exploded against his chest, and he dropped onto one knee. His hood fell back, revealing eyes full of shock in a face Goff found terrifyingly familiar. It was the face of Harkland Mathers, but with short black hair and a neat beard outlining his severe jaw.

"Traitor!" Mathers hollered, gasping for breath. "Kill him! The ritual must be completed!"

The throng of people in the chamber swarmed forward, flashing deep black eyes and unhinging their jaws grotesquely. Von Gretell kicked the cauldron over. A river of ghostly smoke tumbled out, catching on fire when it touched the ground, halting the attackers' progress.

Von Gretell raised his hand, and a white Nexi flew out of it, bright and beautiful, so bright his attackers shielded their eyes. Out of each gaping mouth, a pulsing red Nexi arose. Mathers arched backward, and Nexis began flying out of his chest and hands, dozens upon dozens, red and pulsing and angry. Soon, the room was full of them, and they raced about frantically, like bees trying to escape a cloud of poison made of light.

The white Nexi rose to the top of the high ceiling and began moving in a circle. The red Nexis flew up to it and spun, forming a tiny tornado within the room.

"Think, you fool!" Mathers called out, struggling to move toward Von Gretell. "There is no undoing what has been done. Monstraxen will rise to greatness or be lost forever now! Your children. All your family. They will be cursed forever as ghosts!"

"Greatness?" Von Gretell sneered. "Your greatness is eternal suffering for all the world. Better we should all be lost and save the rest of the world from the likes of you." He looked up at the bright white Nexi at the center of the vortex. "Let it be done!"

The white Nexi plunged, scattering the red Nexis below it and striking the wooden floor. An explosion shook the entire building and a tower of flames shot up, pushing back the edges with its force.

The giant torch reached up to the ceiling, igniting it and reaching out to wrap the old, dry beams in blue and orange sheets of fire. As the edge of the crater spread wide, the people in the room tumbled into it, screaming and flailing. The red Nexis scattered and disappeared through the walls.

Moving swiftly, the edge of the gaping pit reached the altar. As beams and flooring broke apart and collapsed downward, Von Gretell and Mathers were dragged in without any chance of escape. Mathers clawed and screamed, but Von Gretell remained stiff, looking as if he had accepted this fate long before.

The walls now ablaze, the entire space became a furnace, hot enough to melt rock. The windows exploded, sending shards of glass spinning out over the landscape, and the air rushing in whipped the flames into a frenzy. The outer structure groaned, buckled, and collapsed, sucked down into the bottomless pit. It dropped out of sight quickly, sending out a massive wake of sparks and flame.

A moment later, it was all gone. The smoke floated upward silently as ashes rained down, mixing with the gentle snow. Only the tower of the grand mansion still stood, teetering on the edge of a massive, smoldering grave.

The vision ended, and Goff was suddenly back in inky darkness. His heart was pounding and drowning in sorrow for the loss of life he had just witnessed.

A hazy glow formed before him and soon solidified into two figures, a boy and a girl. They moved closer and crystallized into Lydia and Halstrom.

"Guys!" he called out. "Where are we? What's going on?"

They didn't respond and continued floating toward him, limbs still, faces set hard, eyes closed. When they were just a dozen feet away, they lifted their eyelids to reveal glassy white eyes, just like the ghost children in the square of Monstaxen.

Horror ripped through Goff, and his body went numb.

CHAPTER 18

Fire Alarm

"WAKE up!"

Goff felt the ghosts of Lydia and Halstrom slipping away. Someone was shaking him. He awoke with his head pressed against his desk, a pool of drool from the corner of his mouth spreading across the lines on the paper. "Lydia? Halstrom?"

"They aren't here, kid," Bones said. "Left last night. Your alarm has been going off. I didn't know how to turn the stupid thing off. I considered throwing it out the window."

Goff lifted his head. Maxim stood frozen in place in front of him on his platform. Bones was at his side, sunlight shining through his rib cage. A nasty electric buzz sawed the air. Goff hit the button on top of the alarm, bringing welcome silence to the room.

"That's it?" Bones said. "Really?"

Goff read the digital numbers pulsing 6:45 and started panicking. "I'm late! And my draft is a crumpled mess with drool on it. How come you didn't wake me last night?"

"Maxim and I both tried! You were lost to this world."

Goff wiped the drool off his paper and gathered the pages into a neat pile. He was already dressed, so he could just leave on what he'd worn yesterday. As he headed toward the stairs, something Bones had said tripped a wire, and he stopped halfway through the floral curtain. "Is it possible for a wizard to travel outside their body?"

"Well," Bones said, tapping his jaw. "Very skilled wizards can do it."

"Can they travel back in time, too?"

"Possible, but again, very hard. We're talking about magic, kid. It's not like the laws of physics apply. Why?"

"I think you're right—I was lost to this world. I think what's happening here has happened before, and it ended very badly for a lot of people. Does the name Geoffe Von Gretell mean anything to you?"

"Sorry," Bones said. "Doesn't ring a bell."

Goff descended the stairs, groggy from lack of sleep, and headed out the door. On the bus, Pam wouldn't even look at him and Ben sat scowling. He sat in the back, alone, staring out the window.

A gray blanket of clouds formed a cap over the town, producing a thin drizzle that settled deep into the world's bones, exposing the rot and decay behind the superficial, colorful autumn facade. Goff felt just like those rotting leaves, drained of energy and color. He pulled out his notebook and, between bumps, tried to write legibly enough to complete the final pages of his paper.

He spent his first two classes in Old Hall, where many other students had been sent to study hall due to absent teachers. Staticky classical music played through the tiny round metal intercom speakers, filling the room with fuzzy violins, oboes, and kettle drums. Goff listened to the music, completing stupid worksheets administered by teachers he didn't recognize. After spending hours filling in multiple-choice circles, his head felt heavy and dull. At lunchtime, he walked toward the cafeteria but stopped in front of a dark corridor. The sound of crying floated out from somewhere in its shadows. He walked down to see if he could help whoever was crying.

Near the end, behind a stack of plastic crates filled with basketballs, Amber was sitting on the floor, holding her knees, and sobbing into her hands. She looked up when Goff approached, her eyes puffy and tears sliding down her smooth brown cheeks.

Goff felt awkward, as if he had intruded on someone's private moment. "Sorry, I ... er... heard crying."

Amber wiped a tear from her cheek. "Guilty."

"Do you want to be alone?"

A new tear formed on the rim of one of Amber's big brown eyes. "I think I've been alone too long. Stay a minute?"

Goff sat down on the floor next to her and rested against the wall, unsure of what to say or do. Comforting crying girls wasn't something he had experience with.

Amber took a deep, sad breath. "My father is gone. I found a note this morning that said he had to go away for a while but he couldn't tell us why."

Goff felt the base of his skull tingle, and fear settled in his heart. Teachers absent, stores closed, parents missing everywhere—it all seemed to fit with the vision he'd had of what happened in Monstraxen. "I'm sorry."

"It's just so odd," Amber said hotly, quivering between sobs. "My mom's been in a hospital in Warwick for months. Why would he leave me alone in the house?"

Goff knew he couldn't tell her what he believed, that her father was under a magic influence and didn't know what he was doing. Instead, he sat silently beside her. He was contemplating whether putting his arm around her would be comforting or strange when a voice echoed off the walls, coming from the other end of the hallway.

"Amber? You down here? We're practicing in the gym. We need you."

"I can't let her see me like this," Amber whispered urgently. "Go distract her!"

Footsteps rang out as her friend approached. "Amber—"

Goff was about to jump out and say whatever came to mind to draw her off when Majesty grew hot in his hand. Before he could tell her to stand down, a pulse of purple energy burst out of him. The fluorescent bulbs in the ceiling fixtures flashed and went out in rapid succession. The hallway was suddenly dark. Amber gasped just as the sprinkler system came on, dousing them all and filling the hallway with dozens of water jets.

The girl screamed, "My hair! My hair!" and her heels clicked away.

Amber leapt up, covering her head with her hands and started running. "How did you do that?"

"Just a fortunate coincidence, I guess."

"No, it wasn't!" Amber exclaimed, slipping on the wet tiles.

Goff grabbed her hand to steady her, and they ran out of the corridor. The sprinklers stopped spraying.

"I saw what happened, Goff!" Amber shouted, facing him, still holding his hand. Water dripped from the tip of her nose and around the folds of her eyes. "I don't know how, but you set that alarm off."

A large group of curious kids had formed at the end of the hallway. Amber dropped Goff's hand, but not quickly enough.

"Oh, my God," said a blond girl in a cheerleader outfit. "Amber? You and Goff?"

"Slippery floors," Goff said dumbly. "I was steadying her."

"You two were running like lovers through a rain shower," Tom Sweeney teased.

"Shut it, Tom!" Amber shouted. "I slipped, and he kept me from falling, that's all."

Vice Principal Sparr, a compact man with receding hair and silver temples, stepped out of the crowd. He grabbed Goff and Amber's arms firmly and led them away. "You two are in loads of trouble."

Goff pulled back against Sparr's tight grip. "We didn't do anything."

"I heard what I heard," Sparr said, marching them through the crowd. Goff and Amber were so drenched they left a little river in their wake.

"Really immature teasing?" Goff asked, pushing back his wet hair with his free hand.

"And Amber saying you set the alarm off."

"I was joking," Amber protested.

"It sounded like you were pretty angry to me."

They passed Lydia and Halstrom leaning against the lockers down the hall. Lydia looked at Amber and then Goff and shook her head sadly.

When they went through the frosted glass door of the administrative offices, Sparr marched them right up to a secretary, who raised her thin eyebrows and didn't seem pleased to see him. She exhaled sharply through bright red lips and stayed seated on her rolling chair, which looked about to collapse under her weight. Water dripped from Amber's hair onto her blue stapler.

"Is he in?" Sparr asked.

"In a meeting," she said, narrowing her eyes. "Can't be disturbed."

"This is important."

"Not important enough."

"Who is he with?"

The secretary beckoned Sparr closer, and he leaned down to her so she could whisper. Goff felt his ear get warm, and Majesty amplified what she said so he could hear: "Mathers."

Goff flinched. *Mathers was here at school?*

"That man scares—"

"Shhhh!" The secretary's eyes flared. "Mind your words."

"He can't hear me."

"Don't bet on that."

Sparr turned to Goff and Amber and ushered them toward a wooden bench against the windows. He pulled a roll of paper towels from a cabinet and handed it to them. "You two sit here. And dry off before you ruin the carpet. When Principal Nestor is available, we'll deal with you properly."

Goff accepted a wad of paper towels from Amber and dried his hair as he stared at the principal's door. Silently, he asked Majesty to give him ears to their conversation. He could suddenly hear Principal Nestor speaking as if he was in the room with them.

"But I can't run the school without—"

"You will keep the school running," Mathers said harshly. "It's just one more week. Find a way."

"Don't you think the kids will become suspicious?"

Mathers laughed. "Kids are idiots."

"What about the boy?"

Mathers didn't reply. Goff's mind grew fuzzy. Majesty dropped away, and his super-hearing ended.

"What's wrong?" Amber asked. "You went all white. Are you okay?"

The door to the principal's office swung open. Mathers filled the threshold with his billowing black overcoat and crazy beard. He looked at Goff with eyes that could cut steel. Goff's mind went fuzzy. Amber tensed in the seat next to him.

Moving more like a machine than a man, Mathers strode forward, loudly clicking a thick black cane with a gold skull on top with each step. The gemstone eyes of the skeleton rings on his fingers glowed brightly in the fluorescent lights.

"Looks like someone's been breaking the rules," Mathers said, stopping in front of Goff and leaning down with both hands on his cane.

Goff gulped and tried to regain his composure. His brain just wouldn't engage. "I... I..."

Principal Nestor came out of his office, a bumpy little man with tufts of brown hair garnishing a shiny bald head. His eyes met Goff's through spectacles at the bottom edge of his nose, from which a drop of sweat hung. Briefly, they flashed black before returning to normal.

A shock ran through Goff but he tried to hide it.

Mathers narrowed his eyes. "Remember, son, disobedience comes with a high price."

The outer door banged open. Mr. Dempsey, the janitor, clomped in heavily, wearing big black boots, overalls, and leather gloves. Goff found comfort in Mr. Dempsey's presence. He was a gigantic, beefy ally against the administration here, often making the kids laugh or helping them out of tight situations. Dempsey walked up to Sparr, dwarfing him like a bear addressing a pig.

"Before ya drag kids down 'ere for tripping fire alarms, maybe check with me first? The alarm wasn't manually tripped."

Halstrom and Lydia entered behind Dempsey. Lydia blanched when Mathers glared at her, but Halstrom showed no reaction at all.

"I assumed—" Sparr started.

"Assumptions rarely form a sound logical basis," Halstrom said.

"Shhhh!" Lydia elbowed him.

"He's right," Dempsey said, nodding toward Halstrom. "Lydia and Halstrom 'ere found me and showed me that 'aint nobody tripped the alarm. Looks like the system had faulty wiring, that's all—a surge musta broken the lights and tripped the system. Didn't you think it odd that the other alarms didn't go off? No bells ringing?"

"Amber here said she saw Goff set it off."

"We'll she were wrong. Nobody set anything off."

Mathers cleared his throat and turned back to the principal. "Do you always allow subordinates to speak to their superiors in this way? This man is a broom pusher, is he not?"

"Broom pusher?" Dempsey seemed to grow twice as large as he turned to face Mathers, glaring at him with no sign of intimidation or fear. "Who are you, anyway? Here to do a Halloween skit or somethin'?"

Mathers' nostrils flared. "How dare you!"

"Okay, okay," Principal Nestor said, stepping between them. "I think we can settle all of this once our visitor has left. Children, you may go. Mr. Sparr will accompany you to your next class. Mr. Dempsey, I trust you're able to make whatever repairs are necessary on the alarm?"

Dempsey stood braced toward Mathers like a goat about to charge at a tree. "Of course," he said without taking his eyes off Mathers. Then he stomped to the door and left.

Principal Nestor looked at Sparr, who sighed and herded Goff and Amber over to Lydia and Halstrom. "Come on, let's get all of you back to class. False alarm, no pun intended."

"Technically, that was not a pun," Halstrom said as they walked out. "A pun would have been 'alarm me to get you back to class.' What you said was just a play on words."

"Is he always like this?" Sparr asked.

"Yup," Lydia said.

They walked down the empty corridors past rows of metal lockers and closed doors with frosted glass windows, the collective clatter of their footsteps on the linoleum reverberating as if they were an army.

When they arrived at Amber's class, she hesitated and stared at Goff, looking confused and scared.

"Don't worry," Goff said quietly. "Everything will be okay."

"I hope so," she said, heading into her class.

Mr. Sparr gave a thumbs up to the teacher, who nodded.

"So, you and Miss Cheerleader, eh?" Lydia asked as they continued down the hallway.

"She's just a friend," Goff said. "And don't call her that."

"That was actually very accurate for Lydia," Halstrom said.

"Thanks," Lydia said. "I think."

"I know what you meant," Goff said. "She's not like that. She's nice."

"By nice, do you mean pretty?" Lydia asked.

They arrived at Lydia and Halstrom's classroom door. Mr. Sparr opened it, releasing a flurry of sounds from a movie the class was watching. He cleared his throat and gestured toward Lydia and Halstrom. "As much as I love listening to teenage drama, off you go."

Lydia only glanced briefly over her shoulder at Goff, her usual bright green eyes looking sad and her smile gone.

"How do you know Harkland Mathers?" Mr. Sparr asked Goff, leading him away with a hand on his back.

"What makes you think I know him?"

"It was obvious. Want some advice?"

"No thank you," Goff said plainly.

"Keep your distance."

They arrived at the door to Goff's chemistry class. A substitute was sitting at the desk, reading a book. He looked up when he saw Mr. Sparr and put the book down so fast it fell on the floor.

"They're doing a worksheet."

"Of course they are," Mr. Sparr said in a bored voice.

"Where's Mr. Dongle?" Goff asked.

The substitute shrugged. "I think he's sick."

Goff took one of the worksheets off the desk and shuffled his way among the rows of kids, stepping over book bags and jackets on the floor to take his seat at the back. Staring at the worksheet, his mind turned to the conversation he'd heard between the principal and Mathers. Whatever Mathers was up to would happen within a week—just in time for Halloween.

Wizarding 101

G OFF completed the worksheet easily a little before class ended. His next class was History with Mrs. Wicket, and he was both excited about having a chance to ask her about Monstraxen and worried about telling her that his paper wasn't complete, hoping she would give him an extension. When the period bell rang, he ran through the halls to her classroom. A woman wearing a red pants-suit stood blocking the door.

"I was hoping to speak to Mrs. Wicket before class today," Goff said. "It's important."

"She no longer teaches here."

"But–"

"I don't know anything more. Report to Old Hall, please."

Goff spent the next hour in Old Hall staring at a worksheet while his mind raced. Mrs. Wicket had been his one hope of finding out more about what had happened in Monstraxen and how he and Mathers were connected. She'd also been his only hope of getting a recommendation for Amworth.

The period bell rang, signaling the end of school for the day and the start of the weekend; it set off an explosion of activity in the room. Feeling miserable and unsure of what to do next, Goff left Old Hall and headed toward the bus platform. He happened upon Halstrom, who was sitting on a low wall next to an empty vending machine. Oddly, Lydia was nowhere in sight.

"Lydia asked me to tell you that you are a jerk," Halstrom said, standing.

"Really?"

"Why would I lie about what Lydia asked me to tell you?"

"No, I mean, she really thinks I'm a jerk now?" Goff began walking toward the bus platform. "Why, because she thinks I like Amber?"

"Do you like Amber? You were holding her hand."

"I like them both as friends. That's all."

Halstrom regarded Goff with one raised eyebrow. "You do not know this, but Lydia tried out for cheerleading squad this year. It did not go well. They teased her for weeks afterward. She cried a lot during that time."

Goff stopped and turned to Halstrom. "Did Amber tease her, too?"

"She did."

"I just can't win," Goff said flatly, continuing toward the line of yellow buses that sat idling outside the front of the school. "How do I get Lydia to change her mind about me?"

Halstrom put his hand on Goff's shoulder. "Lydia hates me quite often. It is usually a short-lived sentiment."

Along the front of the school, a long freight train of yellow buses sat idling. The first bus pulled away from the curb, so Goff and Halstrom rushed outside to catch theirs. When Goff got home, he did mountains of laundry, cleaned all the dirty dishes and threw together a big pan of nachos with bacon on top to keep Ben and Pam off his back before heading up to his room. It had been a long day and he was exhausted. Bones and Maxim were sitting outside gazing at the stars again, which were just starting to appear in the twilight.

"Mind if I join you?"

"Sure," Maxim said, "but it's pretty cold out here."

"You're both out there."

"Your point being?"

"Oh, right, you're both dead." An idea popped into his head. "Hold on."

Goff went back into the room and grabbed one of the black candles, choosing a heavy one with a good, long wick. He carried it out through the window, into the crisp fall air, and sat down on the rough tar shingles between Bones and Maxim, who complained a little but scuttled to make room for him. Goff snapped his fingers and the wick burst into a flame.

"Better," Bones said, "but a candle doesn't provide much warmth."

"Hold on." Goff released the candle so it hovered in front of them. "Let me show you how Majesty has grown." The candle floated a few feet away, and the flame turned black, as if it was the shadow of a flame. A gentle warmth, like the heat of a winter fireplace, enveloped them. "See? I'm very proud of her."

"What's fascinating," Maxim said, "is that you have no ego about your magic. You treat it like a friend inside you."

"Call her Majesty, okay? She doesn't like being referred to as 'it.'"

"See?" Bones exclaimed.

Goff leaned back on his hands, enjoying the warmth, and looked up at the endless expanse of space, thinking about how far away the stars were that were making those specks of light. It didn't take long for his eyelids to grow heavy and his head to start bobbing. Bones and Maxim laughed and sent him to bed. He complied, barely finding the energy to climb through the window and snuggle under the covers. Sleep captured him instantly, and it was almost noon the next day before he finally woke up. His body felt stiff, and his stomach begged for food. After getting ready for the day, he headed down the stairs, and as he passed Pam's room, he heard her singing.

He stopped to listen. Unlike her speaking voice, which usually sounded like barking, her singing was soft and smooth. Goff edged closer, and the floorboards creaked. Instantly, the music shut off, and the singing stopped. The door opened a crack. "Spying on me?" Pam asked, peering sheepishly through the gap.

"Just passing by," Goff said, and then taking a chance, he added, "You sing well."

Pam stared at him blankly for a second. Goff expected her to blast him with something snarky, but her face softened. "I am really sorry, you know."

"Sorry? About what?"

"Almost everything," Pam said. "Being so mean and all."

She closed the door, and Goff continued down the hallway, amazed by how people can surprise you.

In the kitchen, Ben was sitting backward in a chair at the table eating chips. He was drenched in sweat and wearing a pair of gym shorts and a dirty T-shirt. His eyes were red and swollen as if he was having an allergic reaction to something.

"Get out," he barked in a hoarse tone.

"I'm just getting some food," Goff said.

Ben shot up out of his chair. "I said, get out!"

Goff froze. There was no one around to help him if Ben became violent. "Can I just get a box of cereal?"

Ben raced over. "If it were up to me, you wouldn't eat, breathe, or sleep here anymore. You'd be gone. Everything changed when you came along."

Fear rippled through Goff. This wasn't the usual mean Ben he'd dealt with a thousand times before. His behavior felt crazed and frightening. Goff considered what to say very carefully. "Maybe I can help make things what they were before."

"You think I need help from a twerp like you?" Ben pressed his forearm against Goff's neck.

"Stop," Goff croaked. "You're... choking... me."

"I don't care. You don't get to breathe my air any longer."

Goff felt Majesty stirring. He didn't want to hurt Ben, but he couldn't draw more than a fragment of a breath, and it felt like his throat was about to collapse. He tried to call out to Pam, but he couldn't make his vocal cords work. Scared that Ben would kill him this time, he asked Majesty for help. His hands grew hot, and a second later, Ben flew backward and slammed against the far wall.

Ben spat blood on the ground and pushed himself off the wall to charge at Goff. "You're dead!"

"Don't do this, Ben!" Goff's hand flashed hot, and Majesty sent a metal and plastic kitchen chair flying at Ben. Growling, Ben deflected it as if it were a wad of paper, sending it crashing into the wall. Majesty hurled another at him with the same result.

Pam rushed in, wearing a bathrobe and bright pink lipstick. "What's going on in here?"

Ben whipped his head toward her and spoke in a voice that didn't sound like his—deep and resonant as if rising from a well. "Keep out!"

Pam's eyes popped wide. "Ben?"

Ben clenched his fists tight. Black veins popped out on his arms and forehead, and he cracked his neck inhumanly deep. "Can't you see I'm doing some house cleaning?"

Growling like an angry wolf, Ben flew forward, slamming into Goff, knocking him to the ground, and pressing him against the dishwasher. Goff asked Majesty to help him, but something was wrong. She shrank away, leaving his hand cold.

"Ben, no!" Pam shouted, trying to pull him off.

Ben sent her flying backward as if she were as light as a balloon. She hit her head against the wall and crumpled to the floor. Ben's eyes went solid black, and he wrapped his hands around Goff's neck and squeezed. Goff kicked and twisted, but he couldn't get free or draw a breath, and there was no one around to help him. The world began breaking into a mosaic and faded to black.

CHAPTER 20

Angry Bee

ENGULFED in darkness, unable to breathe or move, Goff heard distant voices shouting. They grew louder, and the pressure around his neck lessened, allowing him to draw a weak breath. A strange blurry scene emerged when his eyes opened. Halstrom stood above Ben, pulling on him. Lydia was behind Halstrom, pulling back on his waist, trying to help. They were both shouting at Ben, who held on tight and stared at Goff with solid black eyes. Goff managed another tiny breath, grateful that his friends had come to help him, but sure they would fail. Whatever had taken over Ben—some spell or magical spirit that Mathers had sent, no doubt—was too powerful.

He needed Majesty more than ever, but where was she? Last he remembered; she had shrunk away when Ben's eyes had turned black. Goff spoke to her softly, telling her that she had friends here now, to please be brave. He felt her stir and begin to emerge, hesitantly, from wherever she had been hiding deep inside.

Ben's hands compressed tighter around Goff's throat, and he knew it was only a matter of seconds before he lost consciousness again. If that happened, Ben would surely kill him, and then maybe the others, too. Desperate, he pleaded with Majesty to find the courage to do something, anything. Her warmth grew near his heart, rapidly swelling into a ball of heat and energy. He spoke to her silently, using up his last shred of consciousness—Please?

All at once, rushing like a terrified warrior toward an overwhelming enemy, Majesty charged up to the surface. She sent out a pulse of white light as bright as if the sun had exploded in the room. Ben howled, blown backward like a billboard in a tornado. He banged into the stove, knocking several pans to the floor, and toppled the stack of brooms and mops near the door. Goff sucked in a giant breath and felt his body greedily absorb the oxygen.

With his muscular arms spread to the doorframe, Ben braced himself in the living room doorway against Majesty's force. His eyes grew larger and darker and the black veins on his face looked like lines drawn with a marker by a toddler. "You will all pay," he shouted in a deep, booming voice before letting go and scurrying to the front door. He flung it open, leapt down the stairs, and ran off. The kitchen, tossed with pans, brooms, cereal, and toppled chairs, returned to being dim, still, and silent, except for Goff's gasping. The three ran out to the porch to watch Ben run down the road like a deranged zombie, kicking up leaves and gravel, the steady crunch of his steps slowly diminishing.

"What...the...heck?" Lydia asked, more slowly than Goff had ever heard her speak. "Did you see his eyes?"

"That wasn't really Ben," Goff said.

Halstrom nodded, coming up beside him. "Too strong for Ben."

"Should we go after him?" Lydia asked.

Halstrom raised his eyebrows. "If you scare off a bear, do you chase it when it runs?"

"Ben is not a bear," Lydia said.

"Metaphor is a bear," Halstrom said, earning him a jab in the ribs.

Exhausted, they all stood watching Ben run until he disappeared around a corner. Goff's throat still ached, but he was able to take full breaths, and his head cleared.

"Where is Pam?" Lydia asked, looking around.

Before Goff could reply, Zig and Zag dropped out of the sky and landed on the front lawn twenty feet away, talons tearing up the grass. They spread their wings and walked forward menacingly. Lydia yelped and hid behind Halstrom.

"That was your fault, Goff," Zag hissed, beady little eyes aimed at Goff like gun barrels. "Little boys who play with fire get burned, and sometimes so do their friends."

They flapped their wings and rose into the air. "Magic is not a toy or a pet, you foolish boy."

"It alters the very essence of your being," Zag said.

"It influences everything and everyone around you, as it did to Ben," Zig chorused.

"Yet you use it to light candles for amusement."

"You're lying," Goff said angrily. "Mathers did something to him, and I swear, if he hurts Ben or Brak, I will make him pay for it!"

Zig and Zag swooped forward and hovered in front of Goff, flapping their wings to create great gusts of air. They smelled of dead things and rotten fish.

"Making idle threats will only get you killed," Zig squawked.

"It wasn't an idle threat. Mathers had better start worrying about me becoming dangerous," Goff warned in a low voice, impressing himself with how confident he sounded.

"You think he could ever see you as dangerous?" Zag seethed. "You're nothing. He could kill you as easily as he could lift a finger."

"You keep saying that," Goff said. "But if I were really nothing, I'd be a pile of bones by now, wouldn't I?"

They looked at one another, something unspoken passing between them, and then Zig turned back and spoke. "Be grateful—he pities you."

"That's a lie." Goff knew he had them on the run now. "He is incapable of pity."

"I wouldn't test that theory."

"I'm done with this conversation," Goff said, remembering the gargoyles in the cemetery advising him to do the opposite of what seemed safe sometimes—tackle a vampire, spit on a gargoyle. "Tell Mathers to keep my dog safe and leave Ben alone, or this game is going to change fast. I'm sure the last thing he needs is to have me start causing trouble one week before his master plan is completed."

Zig and Zag flapped their wings and hissed.

"Do you have a death wish?"

"Just deliver the message." Goff stomped his foot hard, disturbing a small pumpkin on the railing, and it rolled off and out of sight. "I'm willing to fight if necessary."

Zig and Zag grew more agitated, flapping furiously.

"You have no game to play here, little misfit!"

"We'll see about that." Goff knew a show of power was vital at this point. Mathers had to have reason to feel that angering him was unwise. The lives of his friends and Brak could very well depend on that. Even if he was nothing more than an angry bee—a sting at the wrong time could ruin a whole party. He thrust out his hands, asking Majesty to send a little surprise their way, shouting, "Get off my property!"

Majesty didn't stir this time, and the energy moving through him felt different, but the attack was powerful—a gust of wind exploding toward them as if blown from a jet engine. Zig and Zag went spinning end over end, squawking. The blast lasted only a few seconds before subsiding. Zig and Zag corrected themselves, lifting twenty feet into the air and screeching bloody murder.

"Respect the deal or perish!"

"Begone!" Goff again thrust his hands into the air and sent another blast of wind toward them. They flapped desperately to escape it, rising high into the air and finally soaring off.

Goff watched them fly away, his whole body trembling.

"Dude!" Lydia squealed. "That was awesome old-school wizard stuff!"

"I agree," Halstrom said. "Have you always hoped for an opportunity to shout, *Get off my property?*"

"I have!" Goff exclaimed with a grin.

"As cool as it was," Lydia said, "you probably just got us all killed, right?"

"No," Halstrom said. "I think Goff read this situation correctly. If this were a chess game, that was a great move. It seems clear that Mathers assigned Zig and Zag the mission of keeping Goff benign—a pair of Knights blocking a Rook. I believe that killing Goff is not an option, so perhaps they will not do anything to anger him either. He knows now that Goff has enough power to be disruptive—he could even capture a piece that Mathers needs. Hence the bellows, correct?"

"Nice word choice!" Bones complimented, jumping down from the roof.

Pam appeared at the door, looking disoriented and pale. "Goff, are you okay? Where's Ben? What's going on?"

Everyone froze as her eyes landed on Bones. Her skin turned ashen, and her pupils disappeared under her upper lids. She swooned and fell forward, but Halstrom caught her. Moving as if he were only carrying a sack of flour, he carried her inside and set her down on the couch. Lydia followed and popped a brown football pillow under her head.

Maxim strolled in, joining the others. "I'm wondering," he said, eying Pam curiously, "if what happened to Ben is related to why Pam is wearing lipstick?"

"Look, guys," Lydia said. "Try to be supportive, okay? The chick's tired of being Ben's female brother, hanging out with his stupid burping, arm-punching buddies all the time. She talked to me about it. She doesn't even want to play football on the boys' team anymore—that's why she called Frank to sign a form. She wants to be a little more girly, you know—wear makeup and dresses, flirt with boys."

"You have expressed such interests, too," Halstrom said.

Lydia whacked him. "Do you ever think before you speak?"

Goff cleared his throat and tried not to catch Lydia's eyes. "I think it would be best to put Pam up in her room and let her wake up there. We can tell her it was all a dream or something."

"Dude, she's gonna find out eventually that Ben is gone," Lydia reminded him. "She also has bruises and cuts, so she'll know it wasn't a dream."

"The truth is most often the best choice," Halstrom said.

"For once, I agree with Halstrom," Lydia said with a smirk.

Goff crossed his arms, unhappy about getting Pam involved but not seeing another option. "How do we tell her?"

"That's no longer a problem," Lydia said, pointing at Pam, who sat resting on the little brown pillow with her eyes open, staring at them.

"Hi, guys. Welcome to what I hope is a very vivid nightmare," she said in a shaky voice. "It must be—there's a skeleton waving at me."

Everyone turned to look at Bones, who quickly dropped his waving hand. "I was trying to look friendly."

"Brilliant," Lydia said.

"Look, Pam," Goff began. "We'll get to all that soon enough, but this is not a dream. Ben attacked me, and threw you across the room. Are you okay?"

Pam sat up, groaning a little. There was a cut on her neck, and when she tried to turn her head, she winced. "I've been worse. Wait, I remember now—Ben looked all weird and was trying to kill Goff."

"He didn't know what he was doing," Goff said gently. "That wasn't really him."

"Where is he?" Pam asked, trying to stand but wincing again and sitting back down. "I need to talk to him."

"The dude was black-eyed crazy," Lydia said. "He had supernatural strength, but we zapped him with magic to save Goff."

Pam blinked three times and hugged the football pillow. "I'm so confused."

"Let me explain a few things," Lydia said, sitting on the couch next to her.

"This should be fascinating," Halstrom said, sitting on the arm of Frank's chair, which spun a little but somehow didn't move Halstrom.

"Shut up," Lydia said before turning back to Pam. "Look, I know this is probably gonna sound insane to you, but Goff got all magical, and he gave some of it to us, but just a little. There's this dead cat that only talks at night, and the skeleton's name is Bones. Zig and Zag are these big, fat geese—"

"Vultures," Halstrom corrected.

"Whatever. They work for this nasty warlock dude, Mathers, who's planning something horrible, and he may decide to kill us all, but we're not sure."

Pam blinked, looking from face to face. "I'm back to thinking I'm dreaming."

"I'm not surprised," Halstrom said. "Lydia does that to me, too, but everything she has told you, however awkwardly, is true."

Pam sat shaking her head, her eyes flipping from face to face as if looking for someone sane to save her.

"Here," Halstrom said. "Let me prove it to you."

He snapped his fingers. Goff ducked in case the lightbulb above exploded, but it didn't. Instead, a green stem wriggled upward from Halstrom's closed hand. It grew a foot long, sprouted leaves, and then a bud opened into a beautiful red rose with dozens of silky petals. He reached out and handed it to Pam, who blushed as bright as the flower itself.

"That's real magic," she said in a way that was neither asking a question nor stating a fact. She took the flower into her trembling hand. "I like that kind of magic."

Lydia swatted Goff.

"What did I do?" Goff asked.

Bones leaned in and whispered directly in Goff's ear. "Exactly nothing, Romeo."

Goff pushed him away.

Leaving Pam to rest on the couch, Halstrom and Lydia cleaned up the kitchen while Goff made a plate of peanut butter and jelly sandwiches. Lydia pulled out a bag of cookies and a bottle of soda, and they all sat down at the table to eat. Lydia popped two whole cookies into her mouth and chewed like a horse. Halstrom rolled his eyes at her.

"Itf's commfrt sfood," she said through a mouthful of cookies. She chewed fast and swallowed hard. "I need some comfort right now, okay? Excuse me if I find possibly being killed by a crazy warlock a reason to need comfort."

"I see that as a reason to eat well and feel strong," Halstrom said.

"Well, sorry—but I'm human."

"Exactly. Sluggish humans are easier to kill."

Lydia threw a cookie at him.

"I have a plan," Goff announced, interrupting their banter. "We'll find out where Mrs. Wicket lives and visit her. She might be the only one who can help us understand all of this."

"We should stay here," Lydia said, grabbing another cookie. "In horror movies, people who go out looking for answers always end up getting killed."

"This isn't a movie," Halstrom said.

"It's not normal life either, dude."

"We can't just hide." Goff grabbed another half of a sandwich and looked around the table. "Based on what I saw in Monstraxen, if we don't stop Mathers, we're all going to die anyway."

"A lot is resting on our shoulders," Halstrom said.

"Just know this," Bones said, "when it comes to magic, there are unseen lines connecting people, places, and events across space and time. Not even the grandest masters can navigate all the connections, but they are incredibly important. So, basically, from what I can tell—you all had little choice but to end up where you are now."

"Cool," Lydia said. "So, it was like our destiny? Does that mean we are destined to win?"

Bones laughed so hard his teeth chattered. "Absolutely not."

CHAPTER 21

Wiccan Way

OFF tried to use Frank's computer to look up Mrs. Wicket's address, but the stupid thing wouldn't start up. Frank had probably spilled a beer on it. An idea about how to get the address occurred to him. He grabbed a fresh piece of white paper and a pencil and sat cross-legged on the wooden floorboards. Lydia and Halstrom sat down next to him.

"Majesty," Goff said. "Can you use the pencil to show us where Mrs. Wicket lives?"

Goff felt Majesty grow warm within him, and the pencil lifted. It hovered above the paper and started spinning. A second later, it stopped spinning, flew straight over Lydia's head, just missing her, and halted in front of the curtain, quivering slightly.

"What is she doing?" Lydia said.

Halstrom stood up and brushed some sawdust off his pants. "She's doing precisely what Goff asked. She's going to show us where Mrs. Wicket lives by leading us there."

"I was hoping for a map," Goff said, scrambling up. "But that'll work too."

The three of them lined up behind the pencil. It sped through the curtain and raced down the stairs to hover at the front door. They followed it down and opened the door so it could fly out onto the porch. Lydia and Goff ran out after it.

Halstrom remained inside. "I should stay here. I don't think it is wise to leave Pam and Bones unprotected."

"Dude, like, what would you do to protect them? Making flowers isn't really gonna help if Mathers shows up."

"I do not know, but I can do more than Bones. You two have Majesty. You'll be fine."

"And Chester!"

"Right. He sparks, does he not?"

"Cooler than a flower," Lydia said.

"That's debatable."

"I think Halstrom is right." Goff continued down the front steps with Lydia right behind him. "There should at least be one human with Pam."

"And you think Halstrom counts?"

Goff smirked. "I think Pam will be delighted to have him around. C'mon, we have a pencil to follow."

They headed down the front path with the pencil hovering a few feet in front of them and moving fast. They hurried down Hayden, as white puffy clouds moved swiftly in the crystal blue sky. Leaves fell all around them, like colorful snowflakes. Lydia kept trying to catch one without any luck.

Halfway down Hayden, they approached Amber's house. An in-flated jack-o-lantern the size of a washing machine spun silently near where Amber sat on the front steps. She was wearing blue jeans and her cheerleader jacket, and her head rested on her hands. She looked up, and Goff grabbed the pencil, pulling it down to his side, but not without a fight.

"Goff?" Amber called out.

"Nice decorations," he said.

Amber stood up and dug her hands deep into her front pockets. "They just appeared. It's freaking weird."

Lydia jabbed Goff in the ribs with her elbow and hissed. "We don't have time for flirting."

"What's that?" Amber asked.

"What?"

"That!" Amber pointed a few feet down the road.

The pencil had gotten free and floated in front of them, pointing down the hill. Goff reached out and grabbed it, but despite pulling as hard as he could, it refused to drop.

Amber came running across her front yard, her curly brown hair bouncing behind her.

"Now you've done it," Lydia said. "Here she comes."

Goff ignored her and tried to look casual, holding his hand around the pencil as if using it to point the way.

Amber came up next to him. "Is that a pencil?"

"Brilliant," Lydia said. "They teach you how to identify pencils during cheerleader practice? Did they do pens too?"

"I guess you'll never find out," Amber said snarkily, her nose in the air.

"As if I want to."

"You wanted to."

"I'm sane now."

"That's not what people say."

Lydia grew red in the face. "Why don't you go—"

"Hey," Goff said. "I think we'd better get going, Lydia."

Amber crossed her arms and exhaled heavily. "I saw the pencil floating, Goff."

"Floating?" Goff said trying to sound shocked.

"Put your arm down."

Goff looked at Lydia, who shrugged. "Might as well, dude."

"Fine." Goff let go of the pencil and lowered his arm. The pencil remained where it was, hovering right in front of him, quivering as if anxious to move.

Amber gasped. "How are you doing that? Are you a Martian or something?"

"A Martian?" Lydia mocked. "You think Goff is from Mars?"

"I don't know," Amber said. "He can make pencils float!"

"And a floating pencil says Martian to you?" asked Lydia. "Martians aren't even real."

"They could be."

"Mars isn't that far away," Lydia countered. "We'd have seen them running around by now."

"I'm not a Martian!" Goff shouted. He looked at Amber, trying to get her to hear what he was about to say. "It's magic, real magic, Amber, but you don't need to be afraid."

"So..." Amber started backing up. "You're a witch?"

"If he's a witch," Lydia said, "then that's a pen. He's a wizard, dummy."

"You two are nuts," Amber said, stepping back. "Witches? Wizards? Real magic?"

"Oh, but Martians would be fine?" Lydia said.

Amber spread her arms out in disbelief. "Mars is a planet. That's science. It makes sense."

"Unlike anything you've said your entire life," Lydia said.

"That's it," Amber said, turning around. "I'm leaving. I'd stay away from Lydia if I were you, Goff. You don't need a bottom-feeder dragging you down."

"Dragging me down?" Goff asked.

"Face it, Goff," Amber said as she made her way back to her house, "your toes are touching the bottom already. Sink any farther, and you'll drown."

"What are you talking about?" Goff asked.

"Just trying to help you," Amber threw over her shoulder. "That's all."

Lydia stood with her jaw dropped, looking uncharacteristically lost for words. "Why do you even talk to her?"

"Come on," Goff said. "Let's just follow the Martian pencil."

They turned from Amber's house and followed the pencil down the hill, but neither spoke. It wasn't until they were nearly at the bottom that Goff realized what needed to be said. "She's wrong, you know."

"About?"

"She said you drag me down."

"Well, don't I?"

"That's not how I see it. I think that having you as a friend lifts me up."

Lydia blushed. "Did you just say something nice to me?"

"I guess so."

"That's better than a flower."

Goff laughed. "That's what I was going for."

At the intersection with Main Street, the pencil led them in the direction of downtown Spraksville. In the distance, shadows from the clouds passed like moving watermarks over the brick buildings, but nothing else was moving. Saturdays typically bustled with cars parking and dropping people off and shoppers holding paper coffee cups and carrying bags with straining string handles in and out of stores. But today, only a few cars passed down the road in either direction.

They walked along, and just before reaching Spraksville Library, they turned down a quieter, tree-lined street awash with dappled shadows. Brick sidewalks lined with red, orange, and yellow flowers led the way between gaps in wrought-iron fences. Cornstalks rested against every pillar of the ornate antique houses, carved pumpkins of all shapes and colors and sizes at their feet. Goff and Lydia walked in silence under the trees as they passed the pretty houses with dark windows. A few blocks up, the pencil turned sharply down a side street.

As they followed it, Lydia continually looked nervously from side to side, as if she expected something terrible to happen at any minute. The pencil slowed when they neared a house with none of the usual Halloween decorations, but with magic symbols painted on the windows. The left side of the house was hidden by a giant tree, the limbs of which looked like a nest of thick gray pythons. The pencil led them a little further on to an ornate black iron gate, and then it dropped to the ground, once again just a pencil.

Lydia looked at it. "It's dead."

"Must be the place."

Goff pushed on the gate, causing its rusty hinges to screech as it swung open. He kept looking at the tree as they walked up to the front of the house. It seemed strangely familiar, and something about it gave him the creeps, as if it were alive and watching them approach the house. They ascended the stairs onto the wide front porch, where several wicker rocking chairs sat looking forgotten. Spiders had built concentric webs like dartboards across the backs and legs. Lydia pressed a worn little white button in a brass frame by the side of the door. They heard a raspy bell ring inside. They waited, but no one appeared. Lydia pressed it again, twice. Still no response.

"Maybe we should knock?" Goff asked.

"Give it your best shot."

Goff rapped on the door, causing it to open a few inches with an eerie creak. He waited, but when there was no sign of movement inside, he pushed it open a little more to call in. "Mrs. Wicket? It's me, Goff. I was hoping to speak to you?"

No reply. Goff slid his head through the crack. A sleek black and white tuxedo cat with blue eyes leapt down from a high shelf covered in dust and hissed at him. He pushed the door open all the way, and the cat ran off.

Lydia froze. "A black cat!"

"Half black."

"Still…"

The house was a wreck. Old dark wood tables and chairs lay overturned like dead bodies. Tall bookcases lay on top of piles of books flung open and torn up. Plants in ceramic planters had been toppled, and their roots pulled up. Shards of glass from smashed pictures and mirrors shimmered on the ground. Goosebumps raced over Goff's skin as they walked in. "Looks like somebody was looking for something."

"Maybe she needs help?"

"Mrs. Wicket?" Goff called out. "If you can hear me, make a noise."

The house remained as silent as a cave. Goff walked over to a fireplace with a cavernous firebox. Tall spiraling brass candelabras with white candles as thick as baseball bats stood on either side and more symbols had been painted on the mantel and bricks—triangles, stars, circles, and odd-looking triple swirls.

"I think she was trying to keep someone or something out," Goff said.

"Looks like she failed."

A pile of dusty leather-bound books with inlaid gold titles lay on the ground near the fireplace. Goff scanned the titles. They were all about magic, mostly Wiccan from what he could tell—*The Guidebook of Wiccan Herbs, The Wiccan Way, Natural Magic,* and many more. Goff found it curious—Why did Mrs. Wicket have a significant library of books about white magic? He fetched one of the biggest from the pile and let it fall open. It was full of sketches of maps showing the European History of Wicca, but he couldn't read any of it in the dim light.

He snapped his fingers. "Majesty. Will you light the candles for me?"

The wicks burst into pure white flames, filling the room with a glow as if lit by a dozen light bulbs. While Lydia walked up to the odd white flames and ran her finger through one, Goff began turning pages, landing on a page entitled "The Dark Side" just as something thumped heavily on the floorboards above.

He froze, and his heart doubled its pace.

"What was that?" Lydia yelped, stepping close to Goff.

The black and white cat came racing down a wide staircase that spiraled up to the second floor.

"Just the cat," Goff said, unconvinced. The hairs on the back of his neck were tingling.

Shadows cast by the white candles danced on the walls, sending Lydia and Goff's eyes about the room anxiously. The ceiling creaked and rattled as if someone heavy was moving upstairs. The two moved close together, trembling. A giant "whump" shook the house, followed by a sound like a thousand wine glasses being smashed at once. Both candles extinguished, blown out by an invisible wind. Lydia's fingernails dug into Goff's arm as she gasped.

"Not the cat," Goff whispered, his brain and his body trapped between being too terrified even to breathe and wanting to run like crazy.

CHAPTER 22

Lady of the Tree

LYDIA and Goff huddled together while snakes of white smoke drifted upward from the extinguished candle wicks, filling the air with the smell of burnt cotton and wax. Shadowy darkness wrapped around them, compressing the space and pulling the walls inward.

"It could be Mrs. Wicket," Goff surmised, his heart beating heavily against his ribs.

"A lot of noise for a little lady," Lydia turned on her heels. "Let's get outta here."

"If we leave empty-handed, where will we be?"

"Safely outside?"

"Nowhere is safe, remember, Lydia? Come on."

Urging Lydia to follow, Goff moved toward the broad staircase. Teetering on the edge of the first step sat a sepia-tone photograph of a turn-of-the-century white farmhouse with a farmer sitting on the porch in overalls. The tree standing to the left of the house matched the one outside almost exactly. As Goff climbed the steps with Lydia in tow, he moved past photos and paintings hanging on the wall, each of which depicted a house with a similar tree.

A few steps from the top, rustling and crackling came from behind a door to the right. Then a voice joined the din. It was a woman's voice, but not Mrs. Wicket's. It was deeper and more demanding, like a giant, angry librarian scolding a patron. "Approach and stand before me."

Lydia leaned into Goff, shaking like crazy. "Wh...who was that?"

The voice rang out again. "I'm waiting!"

Lydia tugged on him, trembling so hard it looked like she would fall apart.

"We're not leaving without answers," Goff said decisively, taking her hand and leading her to stand in front of a wooden door with a glass doorknob. As soon as Goff's hand touched the cold glass, the entire door disappeared. Lydia gasped. Goff froze, staring into the room through the empty space where the door had been.

In the middle of a pink bedroom, on a thick, gray winding tree limb jutting through the smashed window, stood a green-eyed woman with silver hair falling to her waist. Long flowing gold robes connected her to the tree-like strands of fungus. She was there, but as transparent as vellum—Goff could see a dresser with a lamp on it through her middle.

"State your names," the woman demanded.

Goff found it hard to produce sound. "Goff," he murmured. "Goff Grahm. This is Lydia."

"Does the girl not have a tongue so a boy must speak for her?"

Goff elbowed Lydia, who stood white as a sheet next to him.

"Garcia," Lydia squeaked. "Lydia Garcia."

"That's better," the woman said, wagging a finger with a long golden nail at Lydia. "Never let a boy speak for you, dear."

"Sorry for trespassing," Goff said. "We're only looking for answers."

"Only answers? Nothing is more precious than answers, Goff," said the woman. "The simple truth is that I know much about your situation. Stating your names was a formality I require, not information I needed."

"How—"

"I have been around for a very, very long time, dear." The limb creaked as it moved like the arm of a giant carrying a small bird, bringing the woman a few feet closer. "Do either of you know who I am?"

"Mother Nature?" Lydia tried.

The woman rolled her green eyes. "I have been called the Lady of the Tree for thousands of years, and I have been known to humans practicing natural magic even before there was a term for it. I appear here now to pass along information you should have, Goff."

"Okay..."

"Listen carefully, for there is much to tell. I said I knew who you are already, Goff. That is because magic travels along family lines. There is nothing more powerful than shared blood." She closed her eyes and began to recite, "Goff Grahm is the son of Haley and several centuries of ancestors before her, Mona Mathers, maiden name Von Grettel, was betrothed to Harkland Mathers in a town called Monstraxen, in the year 1773."

"I was there!" Goff blurted out. "In Monstraxen, I mean. I don't know how, but I left my body and went there. I saw terrible things."

"Yes," the woman said. "I know."

"You know?"

"Was there a tree?"

Goff remembered the branches of a large tree spreading above him when he'd first arrived.

"What happened to all those children?"

"Patience. There is much you need to know. Where was I?"

"Mona married Harkland Mathers," Lydia said. "In 1773."

"Yes," the Lady of the Tree nodded approvingly, making Lydia blush. "The Von Grettel line was powerful magically, but tempered and decent. The Mathers line, on the other hand, also a powerful magical line, had a strong affinity for dark magic. Mona grew to despise Harkland, and although pregnant with his child, she fled, later giving birth to Harkland's son and only heir, Bellius."

"Sounds like a typical modern family plus magic," Lydia observed. "But if Goff's family was magical, why has he never heard about it?"

"Excellent question, Lydia. Mona rejected her magical nature after what had happened in Monstraxen, teaching nothing of it to her children. But, young Bellius was a brilliant prodigy, and he discovered old papers describing a ritual to obtain ultimate power that the Mathers clan had attempted every thirteen generations going back more than a millennium."

Lydia raised her hand straight up, way above her head.

The Lady of the Tree stopped speaking and folded her hands in front of her. "Put your hand down, dear. You look like a broken puppet."

"Sorry," Lydia said, dropping her hand quickly. "I just wanted to ask—these dudes keep trying this ritual? Have they ever succeeded?"

"No, and if they ever had, we would not be standing here having this conversation. The 'dude' who did it would have become invincible. I'd have been chopped into firewood and used to roast the bones of their enemies long ago."

Goff felt the gravity of those words like a storm cloud moving over him. The Lady of the Tree waited for a second, apparently to see if Lydia had more questions, and then continued.

"Back to Bellius, then. Through magical means, he learned that his father had been betrayed and killed by a Von Grettel in Monstraxen, which he knew meant it had to be a Von Grettel who would oppose the ritual some thirteen generations later, due to magical laws."

She paused and looked at Goff.

"I get it," Goff said. "I'm the Von Grettel with the ball now."

"Yes, you are," she said. "Like it or not. Bellius devised a plan to ensure the ritual would succeed next time. He cursed his step-sister, Melody, so that she and all her descendants would marry into non-magical families and have only a single child. At the same time, he made sure his family's side grew stronger—a straight line of single power-hungry male descendants with great magical pedigree for thirteen generations, leading up to the current and only Mathers who now lives here in Spraksville. It was your mother, Goff, who broke his curse when she married into another magical line of a different kind unaffected by the curse—the Wickets, a family powerful not with Mathers' kind of magic but with natural magic, healing magic."

"So, my biological father was a Wicket and a wizard?" Goff asked, feeling sad that there was so much he didn't know about his parents. With no aunts or uncles, no one had been there when he was young to tell him stories about them or even show him pictures.

The Lady of the Tree laughed in long melodic tones, causing tiny yellow flowers to pop up on the branches near her. "Unfortunately not. Magic can jump around a family tree, and despite the fact that your father's mother was a Wicket, he was not magical at all—and that is why your mother was able to marry him."

"So Harkland's curse diluted Goff's magic," Lydia said. "Like a freakin' teaspoon of blood in a gallon of water."

"It is good Lydia is with you, Goff," said the Lady of the Tree. "She completes you nicely, and what she has said sums up the situation."

"Oh," Lydia said, moving her hands as if drawing a tree in the air. "And Mrs. Wicket must be Goff's grand-aunt or something!"

Goff felt suddenly a little perplexed. "But she never came for me or took me in."

The Lady of the Tree sighed. "She had her reasons, Goff. She knew that would not have ended well for either of you. She watched over you, though, always. You've never spent a day in an orphanage, correct?"

"True, but where is she now?" Goff asked. "Is she okay?"

"Once she knew you were engaged as you needed to be, she tried to leave, as I urged her to do, but not soon enough. Sadly, her long life has come to an end. I'm sorry, Goff."

"Oh my god, Goff," Lydia said, turning to Goff. "I'm so sorry."

A wall of sadness washed over Goff. Mrs. Wicket had been his only living relative, and now she was gone. After a quiet moment passed, Lydia seemed ready to explode with a question. She started raising her hand but put it down quickly. "What were the people who trashed Mrs. Wicket's house looking for?"

"A secret," the lady said, looking at Goff. "I vowed to protect it so it could fall into the right hands when the time came."

"What's the secret?" Goff asked.

"You must discover it yourself," she said. "Follow your instincts and be in the right place at the right time with the right intentions. That's often the recipe. It can't be found any other way. I can offer no more advice."

"That's it?" Goff asked.

A loud crash sounded on the roof, rattling the house. Bits of plaster fell around them. Goff and Lydia covered their heads. A screech split the air, and the branch holding the Lady of the Tree creaked and began retracting through the window.

"All I have to offer now is a little more time."

With that, the Lady of the Tree faded and was gone. The gray trunk slid back toward the window, scraping fingernail twigs across the walls, and leaving a trail of yellow leaves. Goff was about to call out to her when another loud screech sliced through the air, harsh and shrill, and the branch hastily withdrew out of the window, breaking more of the glass and cracking the frame. Goff and Lydia shielded themselves from the flying shards.

"I know that screech!" Goff exclaimed, running toward the stairs.

"Those Zig and Zag turkeys," Lydia said, running after him. "Can you just blow them away again or use Majesty?"

"Not if they're two-hundred-pound humans this time, and Mathers could be with them."

"Right. Then we need to hide until they leave."

They raced down the stairs, dodging piles of papers and pictures, as screeches mixed with crashes filled the air. Goff guessed that the Lady of the Tree was giving Zig and Zag a thorough thrashing with her branches to slow them down. Goff and Lydia kept close to the walls, avoiding being seen through the windows. They found a small kitchen and carefully made their way across the littered floor to a door, opening it to find a set of wooden stairs leading down into an old stone cellar.

The banging now too close for comfort, they stepped onto the wide first step and closed the door. Blackness engulfed them. Silently, Goff asked Majesty to create a very soft glow. She obliged, surrounding them with a small orb of purple light. It was just enough to descend the rickety steps without tripping over dusty mason jars. As they reached the dirt floor at the bottom, the smell of mold and rot washed over them. A few small critters scurried near the large round stones of the walls.

"Gross," Lydia scowled. "I don't think Mrs. Wicket came down here very often."

"Doesn't look like they searched here either."

"Dude," Lydia gasped, giving Goff a shove. "Maybe that's why they're back! To finish searching!"

"If that's true," Goff said, feeling trapped like the mice that Pam and Ben had tortured in those little traps, "then we just made a big mistake."

A sound like a bowling ball being dropped on the floor rattled the floorboards, dropping dirt and sawdust down on them.

Lydia cowered and covered her head. "What do we do?"

Heavy footsteps thudded across the floor above, heading their way. Goff lifted his hand and spoke to Majesty. "If there is another way out of here, can you show me? Quickly?"

Goff's hand suddenly felt like it was no longer under his control. It shot out, pointing toward the back wall, and he was forced to follow it. The boards in the flooring above continued creaking and buckling. At the far end of the basement, Goff found his hand in front of a hole in the wall barely big enough for a rat to crawl into.

"Majesty!" he said, yanking his hand away. "We can't fit through there!"

The door above opened. A wedge of light cast a shadow on the basement wall of an enormous bald man holding a long-barreled pistol at his side. Goff's heart leapt up into his throat. A boot stepped onto the top stair.

"Did you search the basement, he asks," a man's voice said mockingly. "It's always something with him. Ain't nothin' down here, it smells bad, and it's too dark to see anyway."

"Find the light switch."

"There ain't one."

"Look harder."

Majesty tugged on Goff's hand, pulling it toward the hole again, but he fought her, wondering why she was being so ridiculous. He spotted a light bulb in a fixture a few feet away. Working as quickly as he could, he unscrewed the bulb just in time. A clicking sound came from the stairs. "Found it, but it don't work."

"The switch or the light?"

"How should I know?"

A dancing circle of light appeared on the wall. "Found a flashlight."

"Just one?"

"We'll have to share."

"Lemme hold it."

"I found it!"

"Fine. Let's just get this done with."

Thick legs in heavy boots clomped down the stairs while Goff and Lydia huddled in shadows rapidly gobbled up by the approaching circle of light. There was nowhere to hide.

Goff whispered in Lydia's ear. "If you get a chance, run."

"Without you?"

"Don't worry about me," he said, refusing to meet her eyes.

Majesty jerked his hand toward the hole in the stone again, much harder than before, hurting him.

"Stop it!" he scolded, a little too loudly.

Zig and Zag charged down the stairs like rhinos and cracked maniacal grins.

"Well, look—" Zig said.

"Who's here," finished Zag.

CHAPTER 23

Soul Suckers

S humans, Zig and Zag were the size of full-grown griz-zly bears. Their ridiculous grins revealed missing teeth and their eyes murderous stupidity. These were not the two chatty, annoying birds Goff had dealt with before; these were moronic killers who could not be easily scared off, and they both carried long-barreled pistols.

Desperate to save Lydia, Goff asked Majesty to protect them some-how while lunging for a mop against the back wall, hoping to engage them in a pointless fight and give Lydia a chance to flee. Majesty re-sponded quickly, but not how he expected. She harnessed his momen-tum to pull him back to the same hole in the wall.

The instant his hand crested the threshold of the little black circle, his body collapsed like a leaky balloon. Zig and Zag stepped forward, but time seemed to have almost stopped. In the span between one of their steps and the beginning of a shout, he felt Lydia reach out and grab his hand. Her face twisted with fear and confusion as she began to collapse too. Goff held on tight, feeling her hand shrink in his until it was gone. The last thing he saw was Zig and Zag lunging for them before everything pinched and swirled, and the basement disappeared.

Goff traveled through a swirling cyclone of colorful lights, feeling like nothing but light himself, until he stopped in blackness, sitting with his butt planted on cold, wet stone, unable to see anything.

"Lydia?" he called out.

"I'm here." Her voice was close.

"You okay?" Goff asked.

"I feel like I just got flushed down a toilet."

"Ditto."

Lydia snapped her fingers, creating a few sparks that illuminated the space for a second. Brick walls wrapped around them. "Where are we?"

"No idea."

"Majesty's doing?"

"I guess she knew that hole was some kind of portal. I should've trusted her."

Goff asked Majesty to create some light, and the chamber flooded with a soft white glow.

"Show off," Lydia smirked.

There was an opening to a corridor on their right. Goff helped Lydia up, and led her down it, with no idea where they would end up. They passed section after section of stained wall, and the further they traveled, the wetter it became. Streams of brackish water trickled down and ran in rivulets near their feet.

"Ugh," Lydia said. "We did get flushed down the toilet."

"It's mostly dry, so maybe this tunnel is a remnant of an older system."

"So, probably no elevator, right?"

"Just keep walking."

A little farther on, they came to a stretch of wall with white magic symbols painted on it. The glow pushed back shadows up ahead, where the corridor ended abruptly. They walked forward and stopped in front of a red wooden door made of thick, broad planks. Black wrought-iron crossbars stretched from corner to corner, and wide hinges shaped like tridents flared on the side opposite of a hand-hammered handle as big as Goff's arm, with an empty keyhole below it.

Goff tested the door, but it was locked. He asked Majesty to open it for him, but she didn't respond. The symbols were blocking her. "End of the road," he said.

Lydia began digging around near her headband. "Maybe not. My stepdad's father was a locksmith, and he taught me a thing or two." She pulled out a bobby pin and bent it into a tool with a hooked handle. Pressing her ear against the lock, she inserted the pointy end into the keyhole and started twisting it back and forth. After cursing a few times, she sat back and smiled as the door clicked open.

"It's just a matter of getting the tumblers in line," she explained proudly.

"A magical lock that can only be opened by non-magical means," Goff said. "Kind of brilliant."

"Or just a lock," Lydia said, opening the door.

The chamber they now faced was circular, like the base of a turret, and only wide enough to lay across with a bit of headroom. The curved brick walls were unbroken by windows, openings, or other doors. Sitting in the middle was a dusty stone block the size of a shoebox. Goff and Lydia knelt on either side of it. A single word was chiseled into the top: Monstraxen.

"I'll bet this is the secret the Lady of the Tree was protecting," Goff said.

Lydia reached out toward the letters. "Maybe there's more under this dust?"

"No!" Goff tried to stop her, fearing it might be some kind of trick, but he was too slow.

As soon as her fingertips grazed the dust, an explosion of sparks sprayed out, knocking him backward. Lydia grew faint and then was sucked into the stone like a cloud of smoke drawn into an exhaust vent.

"Lydia!" Goff cried.

Silence. Goff scrambled back to the stone, facing it but afraid to touch it. "Lydia! Are you in there?"

No answer.

Goff sat there, trembling, staring at the stone, feeling the sudden emptiness around him pressing in. Was Lydia trapped in the box? Was she dead? Careful not to touch it, he leaned down and blew the dust away from the top. More writing appeared next to Monstraxen—the number 1775—but the digits sparkled and shimmered as if appearing there by magic. Perhaps this stone was a connection back to Monstraxen in 1775? Was Lydia there? Determined to find her, and hoping it wasn't a trap, Goff pressed his hand down on the stone and, for the second time that day, felt himself compress like a deflating balloon.

The next thing he knew, he was whipping through space at an incredible rate, streaking like a beam of light, spinning around and around. Then, the spinning slowed, the lights grew dim, and rather suddenly, he was solid again, sitting on the floor in a dingy room that reeked of smoke and mildew. Two brass candleholders holding melted candles sat on a mantel over an unlit fireplace. Thick brown burlap curtains were drawn tight across windows on the far wall, allowing only a slit of diffuse moonlight to enter.

On the other side of the room, sitting against an overturned torn sofa, a young girl wearing a tattered blue dress was crying. In her lap, she cradled the head of an old woman who was lying limp and pale on the ground. The old woman's eyes were closed, but her chest moved with very shallow breaths, each exhale seeming like perhaps it could be her last. Lydia was kneeling behind the girl, hand on her shoulder, looking disheveled and covered with soot through which tears had cut a path on her face.

"What took you so long?" Lydia asked.

"I came right away."

"Dude, it's been hours."

"What happened here?"

"All is lost." The girl dropped her head in sadness. "It has begun."

"I don't understand."

"Go to the window, and you will see."

Lydia led Goff over to the window. She cautiously opened the curtains just enough to peer through. "Believe me—we don't want to be seen."

Goff looked through the crack. A cobblestone road lined with abandoned stone buildings ran in either direction up and down a hill. Hoffstraden Family Bakery was just across the street. Snowflakes drifted downward, and soft moonlight shone through the cloud cover to create a silver, shadowless world.

The sound of footsteps crunching on ice-covered stones out in the street preceded a young boy and girl running past the window. The boy wore a red coat. Goff recognized him as the boy who had approached him in the square, but his cheeks were pink and his eyes bright blue.

From a dark alley next to the bakery, a hooded man and a woman with black eyes stepped out to block their way. The children screamed and tried to run around them, but the adults grabbed them by the collar and lifted them as though scruffing kittens.

Goff's heart jumped. He pulled back from the curtain. "I have to save them."

"No," the old woman gasped.

"But they'll die," Goff protested. "I've seen it."

"Not...your...time," the old woman coughed out.

Goff turned back to peer through the gap in the curtains. While the boy and girl writhed, trying to escape, the two adults gaped open their mouths and a thick serpent of black smoke streamed out. It coiled around the heads of the children, wrapping around and around until their bodies went rigid. A hazy white glow in human form rose from them—their souls apparently departing—and the adults sucked these into their gaping mouths.

When they were done, and nothing of the children's smoky white glow remained, the man and woman retracted their serpents and opened their hands to release what was left of their victim's bodies. Now no more than ghosts, the children floated slowly downward, almost touching the ground but not making contact. The man and woman marched forward, right through them, spinning them around so they were left watching their attackers depart with empty, white eyes.

A tear ran down Lydia's cheek as she urged Goff away from the window and closed the curtain. Goff slid to the floor, shaking, tears welling up in his eyes. "That was horrible. What was that?"

"The reaping," the girl said.

The old woman moved her mouth and produced faint sounds as if she was trying to say something. Goff went over and sat on the ground beside her.

The girl looked up at him with big, soulful eyes that seemed somehow familiar. "I am Cailin Wegot. My grandmother wants to speak to you." The girl leaned closer and spoke softly. "Best listen now—she hasn't long to live."

"What happened to her?"

"Harkland Mathers," the girl answered, anger flashing across her eyes. "He came looking for something she had created with her magic—the stone you found. He desperately wanted to destroy it, but I hid it where he would never find it—in the sewer under the statue in the town square."

"Sewer!" Lydia said. "I told you!"

Cailin shot a curious look at Lydia and then continued. "I was hiding, and when my grandmother wouldn't tell him where it was, he struck her down with his dark magic. He is clever. He acted as if he believed her dead, so we would not expect him to return, but he will be back, hoping to find me."

The old woman coughed, and it rattled deep in her chest.

Cailin's grief-stricken eyes flipped from her grandmother to Goff. "Let her speak to you now."

Goff repositioned himself low on the dusty floor and leaned down close to the old woman. Her eyes were narrow and set deep within rows of wrinkles, but brilliant blue and piercing. Inhaling hoarsely, she raised her head and grabbed the back of Goff's neck with shaking hands to pull him closer. Moving her wrinkled lips with urgency, she spat out her words in short bursts. "Save…them…all."

She coughed, and her eyes closed. Goff felt the tension in her body relax and her head fell back. Then, in a voice barely more than an exhale crafted into sounds, she said, "All for you…"

When the sound of her voice faded, she went limp. Goff's heart clenched. She was gone, yet her final raspy words echoed in his mind: *All for you.*

He looked up to meet Cailin's eyes, which were streaming with tears. "I'm so sorry," he said.

Lydia kneeled next to Cailin and held her while she sobbed.

"What did she mean by 'all for you'?" Goff asked.

"I do not know," Cailin said, wiping away her tears. "To keep me safe, she told me very little."

The sounds of heavy boots landing on stones arose nearby. Cailin's head whipped toward the front door. "Mathers approaches." Carefully laying her grandmother's head down first, she stood up and straightened her ragged blue dress. "Go now, back to the stone in the square, back to your time. Use the back door. Quickly!" she ordered.

Goff got to his feet with Lydia and then turned to Cailin. "What about you?"

"There is nothing you can do for me here! Go now! Quickly!"

"But—"

"I will hide. Go!"

Goff pulled Lydia into a run down a hallway leading to the back of the house. They came to a narrow kitchen with a frosted glass-paneled door at the far end. Two men in black robes were visible through it, standing only a few feet beyond it.

"We're trapped," Lydia said. "What do we do?"

Goff tensed his muscles. "We do what we should have started doing a long time ago. We fight."

"How?"

"I don't know," Goff said, running forward. "Improvise!"

He jerked open the door, ringing a tiny bell above it, and came face to face with two enormous hooded reapers with eyes as black as coal.

CHAPTER 24

Narrow Escape

THE little brass bell above the door hadn't even stopped clanging before Goff realized how foolish it had been for him to decide to start fighting. While it had seemed a brave, bold move only seconds ago, he wished he had taken time to prepare a plan before jerking open the kitchen door. There was no way around these two black-eyed monsters standing a few feet away, and having just seen how strong reapers were, an all-out attack was undoubtedly going to fail miserably.

The reapers growled and reached out with their arms as they stepped forward, moving slowly and awkwardly as if their limbs were not all wired up to the same brain.

Goff tried to get Majesty to help him, but she wasn't responding. It was as if something about this place had caused her to shrink away and hide. He turned to Lydia, hoping she had come up with some idea, but she didn't return his look. Her eyes were fixed on the reapers with fierce intensity, shoulders back, shaking all over. Goff covered his ears, knowing what was about to happen.

Lydia let it rip.

The scream was epic, so loud that Goff feared he had lost hearing in the ear closest to her, even with his hand clamped over it.

Chester chose to join the fray, too. Along with the siren blasting out of Lydia's wide-open mouth, purple and white sparks flew like tiny fireworks.

The reapers howled and turned away, burying their heads in their hoods. Goff grabbed Lydia's hand and urged her off the little porch. She kept screaming as he practically dragged her to where a gap in the hedges along the walkway opened onto a path. Lydia stopped screaming rather suddenly, took a deep breath, and ran off like a crazy person, slipping a bit here and there on icy cobblestones. Goff raced to catch up with her, watching for the reapers to follow, but they headed off in a different direction.

"I hate those dudes!" Lydia shouted.

"I got that."

With Lydia panting heavily enough to create her own fog, they ran past dozens of small snow-covered stone houses with dark windows. A little farther on, they turned down an alley barely wide enough to ride a bike. Pushed together in the cluttered, narrow space, Goff reached out to hold Lydia's hand so she wouldn't fall. Lydia smiled softly and squeezed it as they ran through the darkness, the hazy moonlight providing just enough light to avoid sleek stretches of black ice and find a path around wooden crates, piles of trash, and tipped barrels. At the end of the alley, they spilled out onto a narrow street on a steep hill and stopped running so their feet wouldn't make as much noise on the cobblestones.

"Do you think Cailin is okay?" Lydia asked.

"I don't think anyone was okay on this night."

The sound of crunching from a dark intersecting alley startled Goff. Three children wrapped in puffy woolen coats and fur hats dusted with snow ran out of the shadows. They froze and stared with wide eyes, puffing steam like baby dragons. More sound from the alley preceded three reapers in pursuit.

"Leave them alone, or I'll scream!" Lydia yelped, snapping her fingers. Little sparks lit up the area, and the reapers stopped and covered their eyes. "That's right!" Lydia pressed forward. "Eat my sparks, you freaks!"

The reapers tucked their heads into their robes and ran off.

Lydia turned to the kids and shrugged. "Afraid of sparks, I guess."

They stared at her for a second, blinking their eyes, perhaps more afraid of her sparking hand and gold headband than they were of the reapers. Then, like a small herd of frightened goats, they bumped into one another and headed back down the alley. Fearing more reapers arriving, Goff pulled Lydia into a brisk walk, continuing in the direction he was pretty sure led to the town square. Distant screams and cries of children played like a haunted soundtrack all around them. Goff felt the sadness of the night darkening his soul.

"I wish we could help the kids here," he said, "but I think that we probably shouldn't mess with anything in this time."

"Like in movies where people time travel and change things, so when they return to their own time, everything is all wacko?"

"Yup," Goff nodded. "Like Halstrom might start saying 'Dude.'"

"Never," she smiled.

The road curved to the left, and up ahead, down a small hill, the square with the statue came into view. A bank of fog had formed there, through which dozens of reapers who had already reaped a soul staggered toward Mathers' mansion. Lydia placed her hand on Goff's shoulder. "Don't worry. We won't let this happen again."

"You have a plan?"

"I got nothing."

"Awesome," Goff said. Feeling the weight of being the one who couldn't "got nothing" pressing down on him, he led Lydia down the hill. "Then it's time to get back to our time and come up with something."

In the town square, Goff and Lydia walked around the statue, inspecting each side and the pedestals beneath the four men at the base. There was no door or even an opening of any kind.

"Looking for something?" the gargoyle perched on top of the obelisk asked.

Goff cleared his throat. "A way in?"

The gargoyle laughed so hard he nearly lost his footing. "What sort of fool are you? It's made of solid rock and metal."

"Over there!" Lydia yelled, pointing across the square to where a metal plate was fit into the stones in the road. "The sewer must lead to the chamber beneath it."

She tugged Goff's arm, pulling him toward it, but he held back and looked up at the gargoyle. "Why did you let this happen?"

"I let nothing happen."

"Gargoyles maintain balance, right?"

"Yes, and balance existed."

Goff shook his head and pointed to the reapers marching through the square carrying a freshly reaped soul up to Mather's mansion. "Clearly not. Many innocent people died on this night."

"You make poor assumptions, little one." The gargoyle leaned down, clutching the obelisk with his hind claws to counter his massive weight, and came within a few feet of Goff's face. His yellowing fangs dripped with drool, and his long, wide snake eyes flashed red. "Balance has nothing to do with right or wrong. Humans are weak. Power sickens their minds and fills them with greed, but that is not our concern. Now be gone before I snap your head off and toss it over the moon!"

The gargoyle let out a terrific roar that shook cascades of snow off the overloaded tree branches nearby. Goff turned and ran with Lydia toward the sewer opening with the roar still ringing in his ears. He pulled the heavy metal cover off to expose an iron ladder and they both recoiled as a foul stench stung their noses.

"You've got to be kidding me!" Lydia exclaimed. "We're going down there?"

Crisp footsteps striking stone arose from across the square, not at all like the steady dull thud of reapers. The Mathers from his time was a hundred feet away with Zig and Zag on either side of him. Goff's heart jumped. How had he gotten here? As Mathers walked, he raised his hands, and crimson sparks began to fly between them, preparing to strike.

"Get in!" Goff shouted, pushing Lydia forward.

Lydia did a pencil dive into the hole and disappeared with a splash. Goff turned just as Mathers sent a red blast of energy at him. Before he had time to react, Majesty emerged shining brilliantly and flew at the wall of energy. Sparks and light sprayed in every direction. A magnificent explosion shook the night, breaking windows and sending shutters crashing. Its force pushed Goff over the edge into the sewer.

"Come on!" Lydia shouted, pulling Goff forward while snapping her fingers to light the way.

They splashed through the putrid debris-filled water and came to a round chamber, exactly like the one they had left earlier. Lydia snapped her fingers again, and the sparks revealed the stone at the bottom of six feet of disgusting green and brown water. Shouts from above rang out, and shadows flickered near the opening. A hand dropped down, crackling with sparks.

"Dive!" Goff shouted, pushing Lydia down.

CHAPTER 25

Charred Beams

GOFF and Lydia held their breath, pressed a finger against their glasses, closed their eyes, and shot down into the water, aiming for the stone. As Mathers' deadly red wall of energy raced toward them, they touched the glowing 1775 and were sucked into the stone. Goff whirled away into darkness, losing Lydia in the chaos. A second later, he landed hard on grassy earth in the park behind the Spraksville Library and rolled backward until he came to a stop against a shrub. In front of him stood the stupid, eerie statue. A giant hole had been blown out of the base; the gold gargoyle, frozen in stone, leered down at him.

Goff's entire body ached, and his glasses were practically sideways, but he was dry and in one piece. At the same time, deep loneliness, a feeling he had almost forgotten used to be a constant companion, filled him. Majesty was gone.

He turned to look for Lydia, and she suddenly appeared out of nowhere, tumbled three times on the grass, and stopped upside down next to him. Groaning and complaining, she straightened herself and emerged through a waterfall of hair. Pushing her gold headband down, she turned to Goff with wild eyes. A sprig of grass protruded from the hinge of her smudged glasses.

"Mathers was trying to kill us."

Goff plucked the grass from her glasses. "More likely, he wanted to trap us there and destroy the stone in that time, maybe to get us out of his hair without killing us?"

"Majesty kicked his butt, though."

Goff looked into Lydia's green eyes. "She sacrificed herself to save us. She's gone."

"Dude, no!" Lydia said miserably. "That's horrible. She was your magic."

Goff's chest grew heavy. "She was my friend."

Lydia leaned in to hug him, but stopped when the statue shifted a few inches toward them. Fear pulsed through Goff. The stone split apart at the base with a loud crack. The entire obelisk toppled, bringing the gargoyle down toward them like a hammer striking a nail. Goff used every bit of his strength to shove Lydia out of its path and then rolled the other way, but he didn't make it far enough. The gargoyle's wing skewered the ground next to him, sending dirt and stone flying and sinking deep, trapping his foot under thousands of pounds of metal.

Lydia came running over and straddled the wing, lifting with all her might. "I can't budge it!"

"We should have run as soon as we got here," Goff moaned. "If Mathers follows us, I'm done for. Go see if the stone is still in one piece."

Lydia ran over to investigate and ran back. "It's there, but it's broken into three blocks."

"Well, that might buy us some time," Goff said, worried that Mathers might appear out of nowhere any second, like Lydia had.

Movement nearby caused him to snap his head up, but it wasn't Mathers. Tom Sweeney and two other boys, all wearing green army camouflage sweatsuits and matching baseball caps, were walking toward them from the other side of the library.

"The freak blew up the statue!" Tom said, stopping so short that the other two bumped into him.

"Help me get this off of him," Lydia called out.

Tom and the other boys came running over. Lydia directed them to grab an edge of the gargoyle, but even with the four of them working together, it wouldn't budge.

"The thing is as heavy as a bus," Tom said, sweat rolling down his face.

"We need some grown-ups," Lydia said. "One of you run into town and get help."

"Have you two been in a hole?" Tom asked. "There aren't any adults here anymore, haven't been for a week."

"A week?" Goff asked, stunned. "Wait—what day is it?"

The trio shared another strange look and started chuckling. "You really are a freak, you know that? It's Friday, moron. Seriously, where have you been?"

"That means tomorrow is Halloween," Goff said.

"Oh no," Lydia said, "we're out of time."

"Start digging," Goff said, clawing at the dirt around his foot. "If you can't lift this thing, then dig me out."

Lydia and the three boys dropped to the ground and sent dirt flying like dogs digging for treasure. Goff felt the pressure on his ankle release, and after a minute of digging, he was able to pull his foot free. It throbbed and wouldn't move, but he was pretty sure it wasn't broken. Lydia helped him up since he couldn't put any pressure on it.

"You guys make a bomb?" Tom asked, pointing at the crumbled base of the statue.

"We didn't blow it up," Goff said. He wasn't about to tell Tom that they had been attacked by an evil wizard, so he improvised. "Harkland Mathers, the rich guy living in Hallow Manor, tried to kill us. He's insane and has an army. He's planning to kill all the kids tomorrow. We need to get everyone out of town."

The three boys stared at him, jaws dropped in unison, and all color drained from their faces.

"Is that why things have been so strange here lately?" Tom asked.

"Yes," was all Goff said.

"So we're allowed to drive cars?" one of the boys asked.

"Drive anything you can—tractors, Mac trucks, or even golf carts," Goff said. "Just get everyone out, okay?"

"Ain't no use," the third boy said. "Thought I were going crazy, but I took my dad's truck and tried to drive to my aunt's a few towns over, but I couldn't never get there."

"'cause you got lost?" Tom asked.

"Heck no!" the kid protested. "Every time I were about to leave Spraksville, I got all spun around and started headin' back into town. I thought I was nuts or somethin'. Tried to call my aunt to come get me, but phones are all dead."

Goff felt a chill rush up his spine and watched a breeze rustle the trees nearby, sending a shower of leaves to the ground as the horror of their situation sunk in. "He's trapped us all here."

"He can do that?" Lydia asked, swallowing hard.

"I'll bet the same thing happened in Monstraxen," Goff said.

The stomach of one of the boys let out a hungry growl, and he rubbed it, smearing the camouflage with brown mud. "Let's get some candy."

"Good idea," Tom said. "No one's watchin' the stores."

As if everything they had just talked about was unimportant relative to the prospect of a candy bar, Tom and the boys turned and ran with their ridiculously large black boots kicking up little sprays of dirt and leaves.

"We need to get home and check on Halstrom and Pam," Lydia said, reaching under Goff's arm and leading him in a one-legged hop down the cobblestone path to the front of the library. "We've been gone a long time."

Main Street was a ghost town. White plastic shopping bags, paper coffee cups, cardboard food containers, shiny orange mylar candy wrappers, and a million dead leaves blew along the empty street and danced in little swirls. No cars. No tourists posing in front of statues. No clusters of middle-aged women carrying lattes and shopping bags. The only thing moving was a brown dog carrying an old, empty Pongo's pizza box in its mouth.

Despite the desolation, the Halloween decorations had been dialed up to ten. The fire hydrants had been painted like short mummies, and the fire station was now orange with a toothy grimace across the front. Black flags with ghost faces billowed from the telephone poles, and drooping lines of orange lights stretched from one side of the street to the other.

By the time they arrived at Hayden Avenue, it had gotten cold, and the air smelled of pumpkins and rotting apples. They paused, looking up the steep hill. A cluster of ash trees with barren branches cast shadows like a black net over a carpet of blood orange maple leaves. Goff and Lydia sighed, and headed up, one hop at a time, occasionally stopping to rest for a moment.

About halfway up the hill, when they were close to Amber's house, Lydia forced Goff to hop double-time. She groaned when Amber's front door flew open and Amber came running out. Her hair was a wild mess, with bits of hay sticking out of it. Her makeup was smeared, and instead of a colorful cheerleader outfit or school jacket, she wore a stained floppy gray sweatsuit a few sizes too big. Goff thought she looked like she had been living in a barn without water or a mirror for the past week.

"Oh my god!" she shouted. "I'm so glad to see you, Goff! I thought you were dead!"

"You were worried about me?" Goff asked, smiling as a warm glow spread inside him. *Why does she make me feel that way?*

"Wait," Lydia said, shaking her head at Goff, looking annoyed that he was acting dopey around Amber again. "Why did you think Goff was dead?"

Amber looked at Lydia and scrunched up her face in confusion. "Duh—because of the fire."

"Fire?" Goff asked.

"How can you not know?" Amber asked, eyes flicking between the two of them. "Where have you two been? You look like you just crawled out from under a rock."

"Just tell us!" Lydia said, stomping her foot. "What fire?"

"Goff's house," Amber said, backing up a bit. "It burned down. With no firemen, it just burned and burned. The sky was orange all night, and everything smelled like smoke. A bunch of us went up there, and we didn't see anyone who needed any help or..." she paused for a second and drew a deep breath, "bodies."

"So my house is gone?" Goff asked, feeling shocked. "Have you seen Pam or Ben or Halstrom?"

"Who's Halstrom?"

Lydia rolled her eyes with frustration. "How about a talking black cat or a walking skeleton?"

Amber furrowed her brow at Lydia and turned to face Goff. "I've seen Ben walking around. He's acting strange. I said hi and he growled and ran off. I haven't seen Pam at all. But I don't get it—where have the two of you been?"

"On Mars," Lydia said.

"Very funny."

"The truth is stranger," Goff said. "Believe me."

"Come on," Lydia said impatiently, positioning herself under Goff to help him resume hopping. "We need to find the others."

"Do you want a pair of crutches?" Amber asked. "I have a set." She ran in and came out a moment later with a set of aluminum crutches. She stood in her driveway watching as Goff hobbled off up the hill beside Lydia. By the time they got to the top, Goff was exhausted and dizzy; where Frank's house used to be, there were only trees and sky now. With a mounting feeling of dread, he hobbled to the edge of the property.

Charred beams, broken glass, chunks of wallboard, metal chair frames, and melted plastic lay in a heap, collapsing into a grave formed by the basement walls. The cast-iron cauldron sat on the top like some bizarre Halloween cherry on a black sundae. Over by the big tree out front, the stuffed dummy of him had burned, too, leaving only a tail of rope hanging from a blackened limb.

"Oh my god," Lydia said, her mouth agape.

"If they were in there—"

"No!" Lydia shouted, walking to the edge of the rubble. "Don't even think that, Goff. They got out. I'm sure of it." She kicked a wooden plank, and a section collapsed, sending out a cloud of ashes.

"If they were hurt," Goff said, "it's all my fault."

"You didn't ask for this."

"That doesn't change anything. I botched it all. I was supposed to re-ject magic but ended up starting a war. How stupid is that? I've played this whole game like an amateur. As far as we know, our friends are dead because of me."

"Don't say that!" Lydia said.

"Well, Mathers tried to kill us, and Majesty sacrificed herself to save us. What protection did they have?"

"They made it out. I know they did," Lydia said firmly. "I refuse to believe otherwise. Besides, Bones and Maxim were already dead, so you can't count them."

Goff leaned down on the left crutch and dropped down to sit on a large boulder at the driveway's edge.

"I give up."

Lydia joined him on the foundation. "You can't."

"I have no game left."

"So, we just wait for the reapers to descend on Halloween? That's really what you wanna do?"

Goff felt the heat of anger rush through him. "I never wanted to do any of this. The Mathers' clan twisted fate and spent hundreds of years creating me—the perfect loser—so there would be no hope of anyone stopping them. So, why try? I'm done."

"Don't you see?" Lydia asked, jumping up. "That's what they wanted. They wanted the opposition to be a loser who just gives up. So they win, and you, the massive loser, lose, which is as it should be. Congratulations, loser."

"Stop saying loser."

"Hey, dude, better get used to it," Lydia said, sighing. "History books will hate you as the greatest loser ever."

Goff shrank a little. She was right—if there were history books in the future they were barreling toward, he'd get a lot of mention. He would be infamous as the misfit wizard who played his role perfectly and let Mathers take over the world.

"Your name will become a curse word," Lydia mused. "You really Goffed that one."

"Stop it."

"Don't be such a Goff."

"I said stop it!"

"Oops, I keep Goffing!"

Goff jumped up and almost fell over into the basement as the pain shot up his leg like a live wire. "Enough!"

Lydia stood up next to him and put her arm on his shoulder. "Dude, all I'm saying is at least put up a fight."

Goff wished more than anything that he could talk to Majesty, see what she thought. "That would just get us all killed."

"Death isn't leaving the party, no matter what you do."

Goff looked up at the blue sky dappled with long clouds laying in magenta piles on top of a tangerine sun peeking over the edge of the world. The air felt clear and crisp, like the first sip from an ice-cold glass when you are terribly thirsty. Lydia was right—if he was going to go down, which was unavoidable, then it was better to go down with a fight.

He looked at Lydia, and despite her appearance revealing what a terrible ordeal they'd just been through—eyes red with exhaustion, hair in a tangle, gold headband askew, smudged glasses—she managed a warm, encouraging smile. "Well?" she asked.

Goff straightened, pulled his shoulders back, and stood as tall as he could. "I am Goff. Hear me roar."

CHAPTER 26

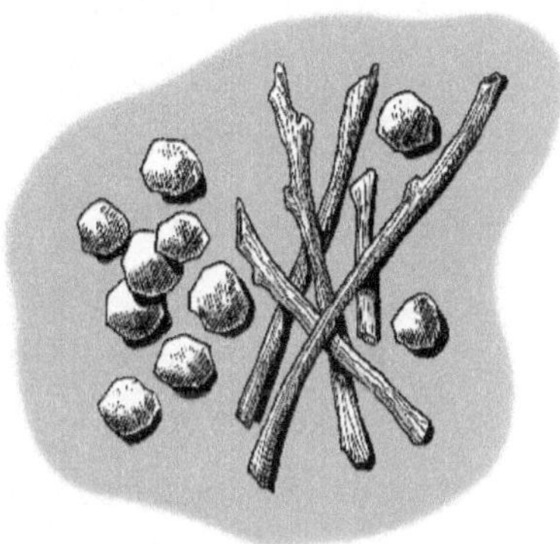

Rocks and Sticks

GOFF attempted a roar, but it came out more like he'd simply said the word "roar" slowly than actual roaring. It made his throat feel scratchy too. Lydia laughed, and Goff wished that things were normal, that he and Lydia could head inside to meet up with Halstrom, get yelled at by Pam and Ben, and go up to his room to plan out their Halloween costumes for tomorrow night.

"So where do we begin, oh mighty lion?" Lydia asked. "Speaking of cats..." she trailed off, a large grin breaking across her face. "Is that—"

With a rustle of leaves and a few snapping twigs, Maxim emerged out of the bushes and joined them. His fur was unkempt and speckled with bits of leaves. Bones stepped out behind him, brown smears across his ribcage and skull.

"You're alive!" Goff shouted with a grin.

"Funny," Bones said.

Behind them, Halstrom and Pam pushed their way through. Halstrom's beanie now sported a black char mark on the top, and his sweater was streaked with gray ashes. Pam's hair was tied up into a messy ponytail, with twigs sticking out here and there. Lydia ran over and gave Halstrom a giant hug, which he returned as warmly as a tree. Goff felt the vice squeezing his heart relax.

"Where's Ben?" he asked, realizing there was still one more life unaccounted for.

"I looked everywhere," Pam said, dropping her head. "There've been a few sightings but no one's talked to him."

"We'll find him," Goff said. "At least he's alive."

"Speaking of being alive," Maxim said, a big bald spot on his back visible. "We thought you two were dead. It's been a week. Where have you been?"

"We have a lot to tell you but you go first," Goff urged.

Halstrom straightened his damaged beanie. "Allow me. I think I can present it best."

"Of course you do," Bones said, plopping down on the ground with legs neatly crossed under him. "Buckle up, people. This is going to be a dull ride."

Goff sat back down on the boulder, which now had a damp chill on it. His foot throbbed, and the sun was rapidly fading into twilight.

"Shortly after you left," Halstrom began, "Bones and Maxim arrived at the door, saying that Zig and Zag were flying toward the house over the cemetery and were carrying a ball of fire. Everyone was about to run, but I stopped them at the front door. I did not want Zig and Zag to see us escape and engage in another attack. I thought it important to establish the illusion that they had succeeded. I held everyone back for as long as was safe, and then we left and hid."

"A little longer than that, pal," Maxim said. "A flaming ceiling was falling on us as we ran out. Look at me! I look like a mangy alley cat!"

"We've been over this a thousand times," Bones said, shaking his head. "Yes, maybe it was a little longer than was necessary, but he's right—too early, and Zig and Zag would have known they'd failed, which might have resulted in Mathers coming for us himself."

"He was brilliant," Pam said, beaming at Halstrom.

"Oh, here we go again," Maxim said, rolling his cat eyes. "Can you blush more? I'm getting cold. I can't feel the heat yet."

"You don't get cold," Halstrom said.

"Well," Goff said, hoping to change the subject, "we were attacked, too."

"By whom? Where?" Bones asked, his bleached parts contrasting heavily against the dark ground.

Taking turns speaking, Goff and Lydia told them all about the stone and Monstraxen and Mathers' attack and finally about Majesty, which elicited a collective gasp.

"Majesty sacrificed herself to save you?" Bones asked.

"Yes—we owe her our lives," Goff said, blinking a tear out of the corner of his eye.

"I've never heard of such a thing before," Maxim said.

 "What do you mean?"

Maxim stretched long against the ground, spreading his paws out far in front of him. "It's just not how it usually goes, that's all."

"Magic is usually self-serving," Bones said. "Not self-sacrificing."

"So," Lydia asked, "basically, magic stinks?"

"Typically," Maxim said, his gaze moving up toward the sky to follow a bat twirling and spinning.

"I would have sacrificed myself to save her," Goff said, "or any of you."

"Even Maxim?" Bones asked.

Goff reached down and rubbed Maxim between the ears. "Even Maxim."

Maxim hissed and shook Goff's hand off. "Don't expect the same from me. I look out for number one."

"I'll remember that," Goff said, pulling his hand away.

"Good idea," Maxim said.

An uncomfortable silence descended on the little group. Maxim sat calmly, licking his paws in silence. Soft orange twilight had settled in full force, and his eyes flashed like glow-in-the-dark beads as he tracked a moth fluttering through the circle.

Halstrom watched the moth as it flew off and then exhaled loudly, drawing the attention away from Maxim. "Our situation is dire. We fully comprehend the gravity of what will transpire here tomorrow but have little to work with to stop it. Bones and Maxim are useless, and Chester and Occam are just fledglings. With Majesty gone, I assess the odds of Goff prevailing to be very low."

"Yup," Lydia said. "We're totally Goffed."

Goff shoved her and got up on his good leg, leaning heavily on the crutch. "Look, I know this all seems really bad, and I understand if you want to throw in the towel, but I'm not going down without a fight, even if all I can do is throw rocks and sticks."

"Rocks and sticks?" Bones asked, throwing a small pebble at Goff.

"It was a metaphor," Goff said, ducking, "like farmers attacking armed soldiers with shovels and pitchforks."

"They always got slaughtered," Maxim said. "I've seen it hundreds of times."

"Fun story," Goff said sarcastically. "Now, who's with me?"

Lydia shot her hand up so high it looked like it might separate from her shoulder. Halstrom raised his, too, no more than necessary to suffice as an affirmation, and Pam joined him.

Bones stepped over next to Maxim and raised his hand. "We go where you go."

"So much for retirement," Maxim said, raising his paw in the air.

Goff looked around at the hands raised in various degrees of hesitance. He knew he should say something, motivate them, inspire them, or at least give some directions, but his mind was blank. They stared at him as he struggled to think of something inspirational to say.

"To start, we need a headquarters," Pam piped up, breaking the silence. "Somewhere Mathers won't think to look for us."

"I know just the place!" Lydia exclaimed. "Town Hall! It looks like a freaking medieval castle, and we are taking on an epic battle, after all."

"Seems cliché," Halstrom said.

"I've got nothing else," Goff said. "And it's stone, it's in the center of town, and it has huge, heavy doors."

"None of which will help against magic," Maxim reminded them, stretching into a downward cat triangle with his claws fully extended.

"Well, it's better than hanging out here in the dark and the cold," Goff said, propping himself up on his crutch.

"Then off to the castle we go!" Lydia announced, punching the air like a cheerleader calling for her team to take the field and win.

"Rah, rah," Bones said unenthusiastically as he got up slowly.

Halstrom climbed up onto the pile of rubble that had been Frank's house and came back with the cauldron. He explained that he felt it was a symbol of wizardry worth bringing, and although it was the size of a toilet bowl and looked like it weighed fifty pounds, he carried it with barely any signs of straining.

By the time they arrived at Town Hall, it was pitch dark. The massive brick structure had two turrets rising high into the sky, and the front was a beautiful piece of arcading creating three openings, in the middle of which was a tall door with ornate iron hardware. The front yard had been filled with fake tombstones, and there were witches and skeletons posed in various positions all around. A giant ghost made of cloth spanned the arcades, its enormous eyes leering down at them, and its contorted mouth spread wide in a feigned howl.

"Château de Goff," Halstrom said.

"I would have chosen Pongos," Pam said. "At least there we could have made pizza."

"I'm sure there are vending machines," Goff said.

"Yay," Pam said, twirling her finger mockingly. "Cheese curls."

Goff hobbled up to the front doors, marveling at how they towered ten feet above him and arched at the top like a castle door that could be lowered over a moat. He pushed on brass handles as big as his arm, and the doors swung open with a rusty squeal. As they entered, every click of their heels on the marble floor echoed back to them in triplicate. Halstrom found the light switches, and twelve chandeliers hanging from a vaulted ceiling sprang to life. The entryway was cavernous with a double curved stone stairway leading up to the second floor, which had an open hallway with a marble railing ringing the entire room. Goff hobbled up the wide stairs, with everyone else in tow, where they found a red upholstered door with a dull brass plaque that read "Mayor."

He was surprised that the mayor of a small town like Spraksville had such a regal office. It had a dozen arched windows, a big dark mahogany desk, and several black leather couches with yellow and gold pillows. He went to the desk and plopped down behind it in a brown leather winged chair with heavily worn arms. "Welcome to HQ," he said, leaning back and spinning a little.

The others flowed in and found places to settle. Halstrom put the cauldron down on a small wooden table that strained to support it.

"Mr. Mayor," Pam said. "Your people are hungry."

"Anyone have coins?" Goff asked.

"Who carries coins?" Lydia asked.

"Currency is the first thing to collapse in times of war," Halstrom informed them, hopping off the bookcase he had been perched on and heading for the door. "I will go fetch some cheese curls by force."

"He might need help," Pam said, following him with a blush breaking across her cheeks.

"I'll go turn out the lights," Lydia said, heading for the door. "We probably shouldn't be announcing that we're here."

"Good idea." Maxim turned to Goff. "And while I'm sure the cheese curls will be delicious for those of us who eat, does the mayor have a plan to keep everyone from being killed, or is the next order of business finding pillows and blankets for a slumber party?"

Goff swiveled his chair to the window. Out across the plaza, Main Street was empty and dark except for rings of light every hundred feet below the sad bent-necked streetlamps. He remembered the darkness of Halloween night in Mostraxen, the shrill sounds of screaming and shouting and crying as reapers hunted down and sucked the souls out of all the kids. The faces of the three children Lydia had saved temporarily by snapping her fingers arose in his mind's eyes, the reflection of the sparks Chester had created sparkling in their terrified eyes. Sadness settled on him like a wet blanket.

Lydia turned off the chandeliers in the entryway, and the room dropped into low-contrast mode, making the outside world look a little brighter. An idea suddenly occurred to Goff.

"Light," he said, turning around. "The reapers in Monstraxen winced and ran from Chester's sparks. We should rig up bright lights, as many as we can find. Then we can gather all the kids here to keep them safe behind a wall of super bright light."

Maxim sat back. "Lights are no match for Mathers' magic."

"It's the reapers we need to stop," Goff said, spinning a marble-handled letter opener on the desk and sending it off the edge. "If he can't get all the souls, he can't perform the ritual."

"That may buy you some time," Bones said. "But that's all."

"One step at a time," Goff said.

Flickering shadows on the wall announced Lydia coming up the stairs. She arrived a second later with a big smile on her face. In her hands, she proudly held a giant brass candelabra with seven tall glowing white candles. "Chester did more than spark!" she said, putting the candelabra down on the table. "He's growing!"

"Tell him to grow faster," Goff said drily, retrieving the letter opener from the floor.

"Don't rush him."

Pam skipped into the room holding a pile of little colorful mylar pouches. She dropped them into the cauldron, causing the table to sway. "Dinner!"

Lydia held out her hand. "Cheese curl me."

"Want something?" Pam asked, looking at Goff.

"Yes," Goff said. "A way to defeat Mathers."

"I was thinking more like Ranch-flavored cheese curls," Pam said.

"Our brains use twenty percent of our caloric intake," Halstrom said. "No food, no ideas."

Pam chucked a bag of cheese curls so that they landed on the desk in front of Goff. He sliced it open with the letter opener and stuffed one in his mouth, suddenly realizing how long it had been since he'd eaten. As they all ate, dancing candle flames made the shadows shift and wiggle on the walls. Maxim groomed the hairs on his legs with long licks. Bones attempted to remove the smudges from his rib cage. Just a bunch of friends sitting around eating, but Goff knew that sitting right here, next to this pretend normal, was something very abnormal, something dark and evil. And, unless he found a way to turn the tables on Mathers by tomorrow night, this would be the last day close to normal that any of them ever saw again.

CHAPTER 27

Witch's Broom

GOFF finished eating his cheese curls and threw the crumpled bag at a trash can next to the window. It unraveled halfway there and dropped to the floor.

Maxim rolled his eyes and lifted it to finish its journey. "You inspire such confidence."

Goff didn't bother replying. He patiently waited while Pam made the skinny legs of the table holding the cauldron quake as she rummaged for someone's preferred snack. When they were finished eating, the room grew silent and awkward. Candle flames flickered, and eyes turned to Goff as if they all expected him to tell them what to do. Not sure what else to do and wanting some time alone to think anyway, he came up with assignments for each of them. He assigned

Halstrom, Pam, and Lydia to gather all the lamps they could move and aim them out the windows. Bones and Maxim were more challenging, so he punted. He asked them to find the door to the roof. He knew they would stretch that task for hours while they sat up there gazing at the stars.

Soon enough, the mayor's office was empty and quiet, the soft glow of the candles washing over the dark wood shelves and snack-filled cauldron creating a reflective mood. Goff spun around and stared at the moon through a row of tall paned windows, hoping for inspiration. Maxim was right. Lights would only buy them time. Was there a way out of this situation that he'd overlooked?

His mind kept returning to Monstraxen. The way Von Grettel had stopped Mathers turned out to be as much of a failure as a success. It all seemed so bleak, or as Lydia would say—totally Goffed. He felt Majesty's absence sharply and wished she were there to help him. At least with her at his side, he'd have a fighting chance. This whole situation was incredibly out of balance.

His head popped up. *Balance.* That was it! He needed to talk to the stupid gargoyles again. They supposedly cared about balance, so perhaps they could do something to help give him a fighting chance?

Wincing as his ankle complained about being moved, he got up on his crutches and headed to the grand marble staircase, hating every click of the crutches echoing off the walls as he made his way down the stairs to the door. He grabbed a set of keys hanging behind the receptionist's desk, hoping maybe he'd find a car in the garage that he could figure out how to drive.

Moving as quickly as his pain tolerance would allow, he made his way over to a set of garage doors on the side of the building. The key chain had a fob on it with buttons, so he pressed the one that looked like a house. A grumbling motor engaged, and the big folding doors slid up and out of sight. It was empty, but a row of glowing green lights at the back provided enough light to see several Zippo fully charged two-wheeled personal transporters standing ready.

Goff hobbled over to them, unplugged one, spun it around, and put his good foot on the platform. It sprang to life with a soft humming sound. The dashboard lit up with green dials and blue lights, and it began shuffling back and forth gently like a living thing anticipating his motions. Shifting the crutches to one hand, he put all his weight on his good foot and rolled the handle forward. As if floating on air, he glided smoothly out of the garage. He released the handle, and it came to a stop smoothly with just a slight shifting back and forth at the end.

"It's like a high-tech witch broom," he said, forgetting there was no one there to hear him—no Brak or Majesty at his side.

Pushing his sadness away, he hugged the crutches to his body and rotated the handle forward. As silently as an electric toothbrush, he sped down the driveway onto Main Street. When he turned onto Hayden, the Zippo didn't falter on the hill, although he had to lean forward to help it keep balance. He smelled burnt wood long before he arrived at what was left of Frank's house and sped past it to enter the wrought-iron gates of Spraksville Cemetery.

As he traveled down the main path under tall trees, the low hum of the Zippo and the pulsing green and blue lights seemed a strange presence in the otherwise still and silent cemetery. Passing the last of the giant trees, he turned onto a narrow path leading to the sarcophagus where he'd met the gargoyles. With the Zippo gently shuffling back and forth and the glow of the lights flashing off the stones, he stared up at the giant leering monsters.

"I've come back!" he called out. "I need your help."

He waited, receiving no indication they'd heard him.

"Hello?"

No response.

He positioned his crutches and stepped off the Zippo, causing it to go dark and silent. He started to get angry as he waited for them to wake up and acknowledge his presence. They might not care that people would die, but he was going to speak to them nonetheless.

"Talk to me!" He picked up a rock and threw it, hoping to startle them by bouncing it off the sarcophagus near the top.

The rock flew high and struck the gargoyle on the right, breaking off a small chunk of its left ear, which bounced off the terra cotta roof and landed on the ground nearby. Goff gasped. He hadn't meant for that to happen.

The ground shook, and Goff fell sideways off his crutches, landing hard on his shoulder. A howl ripped through the air. Both gargoyles leered down at him with red glowing eyes. The one on the right had a trickle of blood sliding down the side of its face. "How dare you attack us!"

Goff scrambled up, ignoring the pain in his foot. "I didn't mean to hurt you, but you were ignoring me." He swallowed hard, gathering his courage. "I'll do it again unless you give me some answers."

The one on the left stretched its neck out toward Goff. "Are you prepared to die, little wizard?"

Goff straightened, remembering they respected strength—fly toward your enemy, not away. "Do your worst. If you pathetic, lazy gargoyles won't help me, I will die in a few hours anyway. A whole lot of us will, so let it be."

"Pathetic?"

"Lazy?"

The other gargoyle leaned down further and bared his sharp teeth. A drop of blood dripped onto the ground, landing a foot from Goff's shoe. "You'd be wise to fear us, scrawny little wizard."

"I can't afford fear," Goff said, although his whole body shook. "I'm here to tell you that I am no longer a wizard. My magic is gone, so there is no more balance. That's why I'm here. If you help me obtain more magic and restore balance, I promise to fix your ear."

"You lost your magic?" the one on the left asked.

"It abandoned you?"

"No," Goff said. "She sacrificed herself to save me."

"Sacrificed?" they said in unison, raising their eyebrows.

"That is not the same thing as losing it."

"In fact, it's quite a different thing."

"A rare thing indeed."

The two gargoyles shared an odd look and then turned back to Goff.

"Regardless, you are still a wizard," the broken-eared one said. "One without magic but one impressively capable of inspiring loyalty."

"You remain part of the magical contour."

"But no more magic will be coming your way."

"Why not?" Goff asked, feeling frustrated.

"You showed nothing but weakness and poor judgment," the bleeding gargoyle said with a hoarse laugh.

"You have been written off."

"Forgotten."

"Left behind."

"Eliminated."

"Got it, thanks," Goff said.

"We're not done."

"Black-listed."

"Abandon—"

"I get it!" Goff shouted. "You've made your point. I'm a loser wizard, and magic avoids me like a bad smell. Brilliant. Just tell me how to change that."

"Here's the problem," the right gargoyle said. "You are too late."

"Mathers has it all."

Goff contemplated this for a moment. "Well, then," he said, trying to sound confident, "I guess I'll just have to change that and steal some back from him."

"Steal magic from him?"

"You?"

Both gargoyles threw their heads back and laughed so hard they nearly fell off the roof of the sarcophagus.

CHAPTER 28

Crimson Sky

THE gargoyles' relentless laughter exploded into the night like cymbals crashing together, striking blow after blow against Goff's ego.

"Instead of just laughing," Goff scolded, "maybe give me some actual advice?"

Their laughter wound down to a trickle as if a faucet inside them had been slowly turned off. They used their wings to wipe tears from their eyes and looked at him. "Well," the one without the bleeding ear said. "You might dig your grave now. That way, you'll end up in a resting place to your liking."

They both found this terribly funny and resumed their annoying laughter. This time Goff didn't give them time to enjoy themselves. "Enough!" he shouted. "I need real advice. This is serious."

At first, they ignored him. Goff used the time to size up the rocks nearby, thinking of aiming for another ear if they didn't stop laughing, but they settled down before it came to that.

"All I can tell you," said the one on the left with a wide grin, "is that there have been times when something as incredible as someone stealing magic from someone like him has been done."

"But only by the greatest wizards who have ever lived," the other chimed in.

But Goff found hope in hearing that such an unlikely and dangerous thing had been done before. "How did they do it?"

Smug smiles spread across their wide mouths. "They were fierce, powerful wizards and witches."

"Greedy sorts—power-hungry."

"Horrible characters, to be honest, but ruthless and clever."

Goff stood taller. "I'm clever."

The gargoyle on the left stretched down close. Its breath was odorless but hot and wet. "Not nearly enough, little one, and you lack all the other qualities; you are nothing more than a pathetic boy who was in the wrong place at the wrong time, that's all."

"Really?" Goff asked, deciding to stir the pot and see what floated to the surface. "The Lady of the Tree seems to think otherwise."

This seemed to strike a chord with the gargoyles. Their eyes narrowed, and they shared a look before speaking.

"The Lady of the Tree?" the broken-eared one asked.

"She spoke to you?"

"She did," Goff said proudly.

Again, another silence, during which Goff stood watching them contemplate what he had told them.

"Well, that is interesting."

"Very interesting."

"I don't understand," Goff said.

"It's just that her magic is not our magic."

"It's the magic of the trees and the water and the wind."

"Healing magic."

Goff glared at them, feeling confused. "What does that mean?"

The gargoyles took deep breaths, looking uncomfortable. "It means things just got messy."

A branch cracked somewhere in the woods nearby. Both gargoyles glanced in that direction and then turned back. Straightening, they resumed their statue personas.

"We must go now."

"Wait!" Goff shouted. "I need to know more!"

"We have no more to say."

"And you've got company."

Beginning with the talons on the tips of their toes, a ripple raced up each of their bodies, leaving behind stone where there had been animated gargoyle. When it reached their eyes, they flashed red before going cold and dead.

"Come back!" Goff shouted. "I command thee!"

They remained lifeless, and stillness settled on the entire cemetery. A fog rolled in, thick and dense. Goff imagined hearing their voices hanging in the air, mockingly repeating, "I command thee." Then he remembered their parting words. *Company?*

The sound of twigs and leaves crunching underfoot slipped through the fog. Someone or something was approaching. Goff quickly grabbed his crutches and hobbled back up onto the Zippo. He turned and raced back up the bumpy path, filling the night with the sound of crunching gravel, cutting his way through what had suddenly become a fog so heavy he could only see a few feet in front of him.

A figure stepped onto the path ahead, barely visible through the fog. The chill on his bones was replaced with panic. He brought the Zippo to a halt.

"Who's there?"

The figure moved toward him, slowly and steadily. Goff wanted to run, but the cold metal of the crutches in his hand reminded him that he was lame. He considered racing the Zippo forward, but the path was too narrow to pass the figure on either side. The figure came closer and closer until it was no longer shrouded in fog. Standing about ten feet in front of him, wearing a pair of cheap dark sunglasses with a pink leopard pattern frame, was Ben. He was covered in mud, and his hair was damp and sticking out in spikes.

"We've been worried about you, Ben," Goff said cautiously. "Come back with me and we'll help you."

"There's no one here to help you," Ben said, stepping another foot closer and taking off his sunglasses. His dark pupils were stretched across his eyes, and lines that had never been there before were set deeply into his skin.

Goff had to suppress his revulsion. "Whatever happened to you, I can fix it. I promise."

"Fix me?" Ben said. "Fix what? I've never felt better, never felt stronger or clearer of mind. I take what I want, go where I please, destroy what I don't like. What's to fix?"

Goff wheeled back as Ben stepped closer.

"You can't outrun me on that thing," Ben taunted. "This is the end of the road for you."

"I'm getting that feeling," Goff said, desperately trying to come up with some options. If he tried to back up, he'd never get away in time, and turning around would take too long. Even if he could, this thing couldn't outpace Ben. With Majesty gone, he had no magic to help him.

Or did he?

He remembered what the gargoyles had said in between all their insults and mocking laughter. The Lady of the Tree was the magic of the trees and the wind and the water. That must have been the magic of Mrs. Wicket's family. Maybe it was his magic, too, even just a little? In fact, perhaps it was not Majesty that had created the wind that blew Zig and Zag away? He remembered how it had felt different, not like Majesty's magic at all. The Lady of the Tree had said that pure intentions were what engaged such magic, and his intentions right now were pure, so he lifted his hands to the sky and reached out to the wind and the trees with his heart. The tops of the trees rustled, and the fog began to stir.

Ben reached behind and pulled out a long hunting knife, the kind with the sharp jagged teeth on the back of the blade. "I'm gonna end you, Goff!"

As Ben rushed forward, a wind lifted the leaves into an army of ten thousand tiny orange and red soldiers. Ben pushed his way through, and Goff jumped off the Zippo. It fell to the ground across the path and went dark as he hobbled away.

Ben moved forward with the knife held out, stepping over the fallen Zippo. Panic sliced through Goff, but before Ben made it any closer, the army of wet leaves was swept forward by a giant burst of wind. They struck Ben, adhering to him as if he was coated with glue. He growled, flailing and thrashing, unable to see. With one hand pulling at leaves, he swung the knife wildly, trying to make contact with a lucky swipe.

Goff did his best to stay out of range of the knife as more and more leaves joined in the attack. The wind became a vortex of fog and flying leaves. Ben dropped to his knees, now just a ball of leaves with stubs of arms and legs protruding.

"Don't kill him," Goff called out, worried that Ben couldn't breathe. "Just give me time to escape."

In response, the wind softened. The leaves attached to Ben began sliding to the ground.

"You will…not…escape me," Ben choked out through the leaves covering his mouth.

Goff hopped on one foot to the fallen Zippo, skirting around Ben. As quickly as he could, he grabbed the crutches, lifted the Zippo, stepped on the platform, and gave it full throttle. Ben's howls and screams dropped further and further away as he flew along, but it was not until he raced through the wrought-iron exit that he felt safe again.

His whole body was trembling so much that he had to fight to keep his grip on the Zippo handlebar as he hurtled past the ruins of Frank's house and down Hayden Avenue. The gargoyles had been right. Things had just gotten messy. He did have some magic of his own, though a different kind of magic. It was an unexpected twist, perhaps just the turn of luck he needed.

When he reached Main Street, a mob of kids was hanging out by the Post Office. They spilled out into the street, blocking it and leaving no way for Goff to go around. He dropped the throttle back and angled toward where the mob was thinnest. Three older kids melting beige plastic forks with a lighter perked up as he approached and moved to block his way. He had no choice but to bring the Zippo to a halt.

A long-haired pimply kid with a lighter in one hand and a warped, blackened fork in the other kicked a tire of the Zippo. "Cool ride. Get off. My turn."

"My ankle is broken," Goff said.

"You've got crutches."

"I'm not getting off. I'm on important business."

A laugh ran through the mob. The boy stepped up closer and narrowed his eyes. "You got somewhere to be important enough to cross me, twerp?"

Goff stayed on the Zippo. "Yes, as a matter of fact, I do, and so do all of you."

The boy grabbed the handlebar of the Zippo and shook it. "Listen up, moron. Only one going anywhere is you—on the ground."

"I'm serious," Goff said firmly, planting the crutches to steady himself. He knew debating with this kid was not going to end well. He racked his brain for options when the bell on the clock tower in the center of town chimed, sending its discordant tone out over all of Spraksville, like an audible smelly gas. The first toll of midnight—heralding that Halloween day was only eleven tolls away. The sky up on the hill, over Hallow Manor, lit up bright crimson. The crowd turned to look.

"See that?" Goff said, pointing at the red sky. "That's why you need to listen to me."

As the bell chimed again and the sky grew even brighter, more kids turned toward it.

"Nice try," the boy holding the Zippo said. "It's just another fire."

"Been tons of them lately," another kid added.

The bell rang out its mournful tone again, and the sky grew deeper red, forming an arc across the tops of the tall trees like a bloody glowing sunset at night. A few of the kids gasped.

Goff turned to them. "If that's a fire, then where's the smoke?"

"He's right."

"Yeah, no smoke!"

"What could it be?"

"Evil," Goff said, immediately realizing how weird that sounded. They all looked at him like he had three heads.

"It's Eeeevillll!" somebody called out sarcastically.

The clock struck the twelfth toll, and a pillar of red light, sizzling and crackling, shot up from the top of the hill. It seemed to touch the sky, and a ring of crimson clouds formed around it, spreading out from the center. All the kids grew silent and stared, their eyes glistening with the reflected red light, their faces pink from the glow.

"That ain't no freakin' fire."

Goff seized the opportunity to get them to listen. "As crazy as it sounds, that is powerful black magic. Later tonight, all the adults who have disappeared will return. They will come after us. They will be strong, transformed, and under a spell. If they catch you, which they will, they will steal your soul. What's happening here now happened before, hundreds of years ago, and everyone in the village died. Everyone."

"It sure looks evil," somebody said softly.

"It's freaking me out."

"Everyone died?"

"Everyone," Goff repeated. "So, here's what you need to do—come to Town Hall when the sun begins to set tonight. We'll get through this, I promise. Tell everyone you can."

The crowd stirred and parted as Lydia and Halstrom rolled through on Zippos and stopped in front of Goff.

"Dude," Lydia greeted, glancing around at the crowd and then at the red sky. The red light flickered across her lenses. "Where've you been? You've gotta come back to Town Hall ASAAFP."

"As soon as absolutely freaking possible," Halstrom translated, not noticing the crowd or the burning sky. "There is a situation that needs your attention."

"Ya think?" Goff asked, pointing at the red sky.

"Not that," Lydia gestured absently at the red sky. "You've got a visitor."

CHAPTER 29

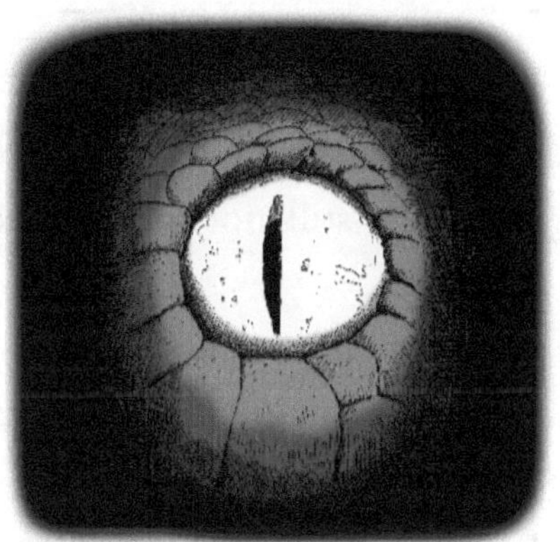

The Visitor

GOFF stared at Lydia with her headband sparkling like pink gold in the crimson glow of the evil sky above Hallow Manor. "I have a visitor? Who?"

"It made us promise not to tell you," Lydia said, turning her Zippo back toward Town Hall.

"It?" Goff asked, blanching.

"We should go now," Halstrom added, turning his Zippo. "It is very impatient."

"Again, *it?*"

"Dude, just ride!"

Reluctantly, Goff rolled his Zippo forward. To his surprise, the mob stepped out of his way. For the first time in his life, he felt important.

"Know what?" Goff said as they rolled past the last stragglers in the mob. "You guys are my Zig and Zag."

"Never say that again," Lydia said.

"I am not a bird," Halstrom said.

Goff urged the Zippo to move faster and pulled a few feet ahead of them. "Is the visitor Ben?"

"If it were Ben," Halstrom said, "we would have told you Ben was looking for you."

"Where have you been anyway?" Lydia said. "You just disappeared."

"I went to speak to the gargoyles."

"Wow," said Lydia. "I'm still not used to how weird things have gotten."

"What did you learn?" Halstrom asked.

"Not much, but Ben was there. He tried to kill me."

"And you escaped on your own?"

"I've picked up a few tricks."

"What tricks?" Lydia asked.

"I'll tell you later," Goff said as they turned into the curved driveway of Town Hall, their wheels crunching over the gravel, and proceeded into the garage. They hopped off their Zippos and plugged them into the wall.

"Why won't you tell me about this visitor? Is it Mathers? Zig and Zag?"

"Dude, that's not a visit," Lydia said. "That's an attack."

"But—" Goff started.

"We were given clear instructions," Halstrom explained. "Bring you alone. Tell you nothing."

The trio walked up the stairs of Town Hall, Goff hopping with his crutches in one hand. They pushed open the large doors and entered the dark hallway, lit only by a candelabra sitting on the receptionist's desk. Moving shadows made the entire grand space seem alive, as if creatures were moving in every crevice and around every corner.

They reached the door to the mayor's office, and Lydia held Goff's hand back from opening it. "Be careful, okay?"

His whole body rippling with anxiety, Goff opened the door and peered in. One of the windows was open, and the curtains swayed softly on either side like two synchronized dancers. The candelabra had been extinguished, so the only light came from the glowing sky outside that shone through the panes of the window. A few pink rectangles of light landed on something black and glistened against the back wall. It took a second for Goff's eyes to adjust, but then he realized the light was glimmering off the scales of a giant black snake, filling the corner with a body as thick as a telephone pole. It lifted its massive head and stared at him with glassy blue eyes full of menace.

Goff froze, his skin flushing hot with fear. The thought of entering that room, coming face to face with a snake that size, horrified him. What did it want with him? He remained frozen, unable to make his body step through the door.

"I'm not very patient," the snake said in a voice that seemed to be coming from everywhere and nowhere at the same time. "If you do not come in now, the last thing you or your friends will ever hear is the swish of my approach."

Goff swallowed hard and swung his crutches to enter the room. With a movement so quick he couldn't track it, the snake used its forked tongue to slam the door closed and floated its head close. "You are the wizard who traveled back in time to Monstraxen, are you not?"

"Yes, that was me."

The snake thumped its tail. "On that visit, did you leave anything behind?"

Goff paused, taken aback by the question. "We had nothing with us to leave behind."

The snake hissed. "Nothing?"

"Well," Goff considered, "I lost my magic there."

"Lost?" The rattling of the snake's tail filled the room with a terrifying buzz. "I think you mean abandoned!"

"Abandoned? No, the attack was too powerful. She was destroyed."

"Are you certain of that?" The snake slithered forward, moving as if unaffected by gravity, uncoiling and extending all in one motion. "Magic cannot so easily be destroyed."

Goff didn't like its enormous head moving so close. Drops of sweat rolled down his back and formed on his forehead. "It all happened too fast. The attack was so powerful, I just assumed—"

The snake hissed, drawing up its tight lips to reveal a set of hooked fangs as thick as baseball bats. "Assssssssssssumed?"

Goff stepped back, blocking his face, fearful of a strike. "There was no time. We were nearly killed."

The snake pulled back and raised its tail, flicking it angrily. It lunged at the globe in the wooden stand, grasped it in its mouth, and hurled it across the room with a toss of its head. The beige ball shattered against the bookcase on the far wall, breaking the shelves and spilling hundreds of blue legal books onto the floor. The snake turned back to Goff, nostrils flaring. "Do you know how many years I suffered? Weak and broken, all but extinguished, barely able to remember anything about how I had ended up in that state?"

"You?"

"Yes, me."

"It was Majesty who—"

"Foolishly trusted you?"

Goff looked up, his heart suddenly weighing as heavy as a brick, "Majesty?"

The snake blew a blast of hot air from its nostrils and twisted its lips into a sneer. "Don't ever call me that name again."

Goff was at a loss for words. "I...I—"

"You left me!" Majesty said. "I wandered for decades, still bonded to you, but alone and unable to attach to another. I faded so much that I nearly extinguished. Do you have any idea what torture that is for a Nexa? It was only through the assistance of the Lady of the Tree that I managed to attach to a small snake slithering in the grass to reduce my suffering."

Majesty's agitation softened, replaced by a low and deadly voice. "To survive, I was forced to become something different, something new. I grew as strong as I could in my new form, determined to live long enough to find and kill the wizard who had abandoned me to such suffering."

"But I had no idea!" Goff protested. "And we barely had time to escape ourselves."

"Don't plead your pathetic case to me now, wizard. I'm no fool. I've survived for centuries by shunning wizards. Now I am something greater. I have evolved. I no longer depend on attaching to any of your disgusting kind." She shook her tail and flicked her tongue. "When the Lady of the Tree visited me when the time was right for us to meet, she made me promise to do you no harm if she told me where you could be found."

"Did she tell you that I'm not like other wizards?" Goff asked hesitantly.

"She tried." Majesty hissed and formed a loose coil around him, her long body moving swiftly with only a slightly audible scrape of scales. She opened a jaw so wide that Goff could have easily climbed inside. With lightning speed, she lunged at him. Goff nearly passed out as her fangs snapped millimeters away. Her breath blew hot against his face. Without making contact, she pulled back, her eyes now red and full of hatred. "If it weren't for the promise I made to the Lady of the Tree, I'd swallow you whole and enjoy your screaming as I digest you. Centuries of hatred burn in my blood. You cannot change that now with your lies and stories."

"But you were once my friend," Goff said sadly, still shaking. "Can't you remember that? I loved you."

"Wizards," she hissed, "love nothing but themselves."

Goff felt dizzy and sad, and his chin was trembling. This was all so wrong. He'd loved Majesty. He missed her terribly. But he'd hurt her deeply, tortured her. "Then maybe I do deserve to die," he said softly, his head down.

She pulled back and uncoiled her body toward the open window. The tail half of her slid out while she kept her unwavering eyes on Goff. When all but her head was outside, she slowly hissed, "Yes, but another will take care of that for me soon."

As silently as a breeze, Majesty withdrew and was gone. Goff hobbled to the open window and saw her sliding through shadows in the alleys below, barely visible. "I'm sorry!" he called out to her. She paused, and he thought he saw a flash of blue eyes before she disappeared into an alley. Trembling uncontrollably, Goff dropped to his knees. A deep sadness filled his heart as he realized there was no way to convince Majesty to forgive him. He looked up at the sky churning like bloody whipped cream, thinking how he'd love to have her back as a friend and an ally. After all, he certainly didn't need another enemy right now.

CHAPTER 30

Lies, Trickery, and Deceit

SHIVERING from sadness and exhaustion as much as the cold air pouring in through the open window, Goff pushed himself up, slid the heavy sash of the window down, and closed the curtain. A slice of flickering light cut across the ground from beneath the door.

"You can come in," Goff called out, hobbling over to the door as it swung open.

"Dude, we heard everything," Lydia said, stepping in holding a freshly loaded candelabra, followed by Halstrom and Pam. She hugged Goff with one arm as a drop of wax landed on his shoe. "There was no way you could have saved Majesty. We made it out by the skin of our teeth!"

"Teeth don't have skin," Halstrom said.

"Exactly!" Lydia exclaimed.

"I should have found a way." Goff looked down at his feet.

"In crisis situations," Halstrom said, "people often do things they regret. You had to choose quickly or perish. Military leaders often suffer from such guilt. It is called survivor's guilt."

"You're a good person, Goff," Pam said. "I know I've never said that before, but I believe it."

"Thanks," Goff shrugged. "But it doesn't change the fact that I'm Goffing everything."

"I want to change the definition of that," Lydia said uneasily. "From now on, Goffing will mean being honest and brave."

"Is it an adjective or a verb?" Halstrom asked.

"Don't get technical," Lydia said, shoving him.

"If you expect us to use it," Halstrom said, "it must be clearly defined."

"It's a word, dude. Just use it."

"That is not how words work."

"Stop!" Goff said, annoyed that they could bicker like children when today was perhaps the end of the world as they knew it. He hobbled back to the desk and leaned on the edge, feeling frustrated that every time he turned around, new information came in that changed the game. It occurred to him that some of the pieces weren't sitting within the boundaries of their squares. "Where are Bones and Maxim?"

"They ran off," Pam said. "Something about cats and snakes and being a chew toy."

"Find them," Goff said. "I have a few questions for them."

"Aye, aye, sir," Lydia said with a salute. "Bossy much?"

"Sorry. Please?"

As the three headed off to find Maxim and Bones, Goff collapsed into the high back chair, sinking deep into the padded leather and swirling left and right. He watched the red sky churn for a while, feeling very small, like a fly plotting to take down an elephant. After some time, flickering shadows brought the room to life as the others returned.

"Here they are," Halstrom announced, entering with Lydia, Maxim, and Bones. Maxim hopped up on the back of the red velvet sofa in front of the desk. Bones leaned against the cauldron, barely disturbing the table on which it rested. He was holding a can of orange soda and a bag of cheese curls.

"You don't eat," Goff said, frowning at him.

"It calms my nerves to pretend."

Goff leaned forward. "I think you two know more than you've told me."

Maxim arched his back. "Are you accusing us of keeping secrets?"

Goff drew energy up through the balls of his feet and focused on the candles in the candelabra. Pushing energy toward the flames gently, they began to grow as if he were feeding them until they spluttered like Roman candles and shot up several feet into the air. Maxim hissed, and Bones dropped his cheese curls.

Lydia's eyes popped, and she set the candelabra gently down on the table. "What the heck? How did you do that?"

"Majesty is back with you now?" Maxim asked.

"Would that be disconcerting to you two?"

"No," Bones said, taking a sip of his soda. It trickled down the inside of his ribs, but he ignored it. "Not in the least."

"Stop lying," Goff ordered, allowing the candle flames to return to their usual size. "Majesty is gone, but I have more natural magic than you would like to see demonstrated." Goff thumped his fist on the desk, and the candle flames shot a foot higher.

"Are you threatening us?" Maxim asked, sitting back on his hind legs into the pose from which cats judge the world.

"I need to know the truth, and I'll do whatever it takes to get it," Goff said, trying to sound like a mobster from one of the movies he'd seen. "For instance, I think you knew that Majesty survived the attack, since magic can't easily be destroyed, yet you never told me."

Maxim strolled across the desk. "What good would it have done for you to know that?"

"That's not the point!" Goff jumped up, ignoring the pain in his ankle and leaning forward. The candle flames hissed like blow torches. "Don't hold anything back. I want to know it all."

Maxim sat back and shook his head. "You are not going to like it."

"I don't care."

"Let me," Bones interjected. "The thing is—"

"You're a loser," Maxim said. "I don't mean that personally. You are a nice kid and all, but thirteen generations carefully crafted to create a loser did a pretty good job. The Mathers clan is brilliant for bringing this plan to fruition."

"Even the gargoyles are resigned to the inevitable outcome," Bones said. "Tonight, magical history will be made. Have we been a tad self-serving? Sure, but only because there was no point in doing anything else."

"The gargoyles are working with Mathers?" Goff asked.

"Not exactly," Maxim said. "They don't care who wins; they're just tired. The game is over if one wizard becomes invincible by locking down the magical contour."

"An invincible Mathers?" Goff shook his head. "That's the worst ending I can imagine."

"Yes," Maxim agreed. "It will be horrible for humans, but there was never any hope of you stopping it. You are a novice with one pawn left to defend the king and he's a grandmaster with a full set of pieces."

Halstrom cleared his throat and walked into the center of the room, drawing everyone's attention. "A beginner has a one in a million chance of beating a grandmaster. As their skills and knowledge increase, so do their odds."

"Fascinating," Maxim said. "And maybe a brick will fall on Mathers' head."

"For instance," Halstrom continued, "we don't need to defeat Mathers. We just need to stop his ritual. The odds just increased."

"Good point," Goff said, turning to Bones. "Tell us what you know about this ritual."

"Won't make a difference, but sure," Bones said, fiddling with a cheese curl and turning his phalanges orange. "First, the wizard creates a crucible, the only place in the world where magic exists. Then they seal it off. People on the outside have forgotten it exists. Whenever they think of someone they knew here or think of visiting, a moment later, they're thinking about biscuits and gravy. And if someone inside tries to get out, they're rerouted right back in. It's a world unto itself now."

"And then what happens?" asked Goff.

"The population is divided," Bones said, "and, well, basically they destroy themselves—hence the reaping. Everybody dies, but not by the wizard's hand, which is key. In the end, the wizard is left as the only human still living in relationship to the magical contour."

"And that causes it to collapse into them," Maxim said. "Permanently. They open the crucible and emerge as the most powerful creature ever to exist."

"What about Von Grettel?" Goff said. "He stopped it. Why can't I?"

"Stopped it?" Maxim laughed. "More like botched an attempt to be the one to capture all the magic."

"I was there," Goff said. "That's not what I saw."

"That's because what you saw was not accurate," Bones said. "Von Grettel was a power-crazed monster, just like Mathers, but a sneaky one. The Lady of the Tree altered a few things in your vision."

"Why would she do that?" Goff asked.

"There's no explaining the things she does," Maxim said.

Goff sighed heavily. His head was spinning, and he simply could not hear one more thing. It was all so maddening. "Go away," he gestured wearily. "All of you. I want to be alone."

"But—" Lydia began.

"Go!" Goff shouted, causing a gust of wind to throw the large door open and bang against the wall.

Looking confused and hurt, they all scrambled out of the room. Goff closed the door with an angry gust of wind so hard an ugly painting of the current mayor fell off the wall, shattering the glass. The last wisp of wind turned the latch to lock the door. He spun his chair and looked out the window at the dark city of Spraksville. The glow of the red beacon had transformed the town into a landscape painted in blood.

Goff sat processing what he'd just heard while watching the sky slowly grow lighter as dawn approached, washing the red clouds into a dusty rose. It finally occurred to him that if he was so lame that there was no chance of him stopping the ritual, Mathers would have just ignored him. Instead, a lot of energy had been spent trying to keep him down. His mind returned to the Lady of the Tree. If she held out hope that he had a chance, perhaps he actually did. But how? Clearly, she either didn't know, or she needed him to realize it on his own. Magic was weird that way. It was full of annoying intangible aspects with ridiculous hidden meanings.

He kept chewing on this until the sun crested the horizon, and his eyes began blinking longer and longer. Eventually, the thought of sleep felt too delicious to ignore, and he dropped his head back and dreamt of eating biscuits and gravy.

CHAPTER 31

Scattering the Herd

GOFF awoke to the sound of pounding. He'd been dreaming about playing with Brak in a big open field under a bright blue sky. It had been a wonderful dream, and it reminded him how much he missed Brak. He could still hear his joyful barking and feel his soft fur against his cheek, but the pounding forced him into harsh reality. It took him a few seconds to shake the dream remnants from his mind and orient himself. Everything came rushing back when he realized he was in the mayor's office at Town Hall. Red daylight flowed through the tall windows, and swirling red clouds filled the upper panes. He had drool on his cheek and his back hurt from sleeping in the big leather chair.

"Goff!" Lydia called. "Open the door!"

Goff wiped off the drool and moved to open the door, surprised and happy to find that natural magic had apparently done its thing while he slept; his foot no longer hurt.

Halstrom and Lydia stood behind Pam wearing blue security blazers with gold emblems on the lapel. Halstrom still had his blue beanie on, but Lydia had added a green bandana tied in a messy knot around her neck. Pam wore a knee-length pleated violet dress and a pink ribbon that held her hair back from her forehead but still let the ends fall onto her shoulders.

"Trick or treat?" Goff asked.

"We were cold," Lydia said.

"You look like a wedding band."

Pam shoved her way past Goff. "Skip the fashion commentary," she said, leaning against the back of the couch, "and tell us the amazing plan you've come up with after rudely kicking us out."

"Wait," Lydia said, shoving Goff gently. "Your eyes are puffy. Were you sleeping?"

"I did kind of fall asleep," Goff admitted. "Didn't mean to…" he paused, feeling a little guilty and then adding, "You guys slept too, right?"

"Yes," Halstrom said, heading to the cauldron on the little table to rummage inside. "But we were not in charge of planning."

Goff lifted his foot and swirled his ankle. "My foot healed."

"Fantastic," Pam said sarcastically. "We were lost without your foot."

"How did it get fixed, exactly?" Lydia asked. "Majesty is gone."

"Natural magic, I guess," Goff said. "Good for more than just making wind."

Lydia slapped her forehead. "Too many jokes…"

"Hang on," Pam said, pushing her hair behind her ear. "Did you come up with a plan and then sleep or just sleep?"

Goff walked back around the desk and sat in the big brown chair. It was still warm, and he wished he could put his head back, close his eyes, and dream about Brak again, but not today. It was Halloween. Time was up. It had been his job to come up with a plan, but he'd come up with nothing. They all moved in front of the desk with arms crossed, glaring at him.

"Well?" Pam asked.

Goff leaned back deeply into the mayor's chair, angling it back so far he was nearly horizontal. Pushing with his feet against the desk, he twirled around, holding their attention as if about to say something amazing, hoping against hope that some idea, any idea, would pop into his head so he wouldn't disappoint them.

Nothing popped.

"I can see it on his face," Lydia accused. "He's got nothing."

"Thirteen generations of planning," Goff said, leaning forward, "specifically designed to ensure I would have nothing at this exact moment in my life, so yes—I have nothing. But I will have something. I just need more time."

"Time is rapidly running out," Halstrom noted.

"Yeah, thanks for the newsflash."

"Let's just pick a direction and run," Pam suggested. "I mean—sitting here thinking is not getting us anywhere."

"I agree," Lydia said. "Maybe you should try doing a spell to protect us or something?"

"Me doing a spell sounds like a recipe for disaster," Goff said. He paused as the word "recipe" connected to something. The Lady of the Tree had said that the recipe to success was often being in the right place at the right time with the right intentions. The right place, in this case, was Hallow Manor. The weight of that thought filled his veins with ice, and he spun away to hide the color draining from his face. Like a pawn poised to take advantage of any mistake made by the opponent, he had to be close to the action, not on the other side of the chess board.

Mathers would never expect Goff to drop in for a visit on Halloween night. He'd be distracted by his army of reapers heading out to do their job. That would give Goff the element of surprise. He could sneak inside and find a spot…but to do what? Attack when Mathers leaves himself unprotected? Not very likely, and not a very good plan, but at least it was a direction he could take. The only problem was that if the others found out what he was planning, they'd either try to stop him or, worse, insist on going with him, and neither was acceptable.

"I have an idea," Lydia said, smiling stupidly, "Mathers is probably just lonely, so you should go compliment him about his beard and make friends. Then you two can agree to call this whole thing off."

"It is a very cool beard," Pam said.

"I assume this is humor?" Halstrom asked.

"No," Goff spun back around. "It's a great plan. Let's go with that in case we don't think of anything else."

"Seriously?" Pam asked.

Goff stood up, happy to be able to do so without pain rushing up his leg. "Serious enough for now. Let's get ready for tonight. I'll think of something better. I promise."

Trying to look like he had confidence in what he was doing, Goff raced around Town Hall, getting his army engaged in projects. Halstrom and Pam worked on setting up all the lights they had found and aiming them out the upper windows. He and Lydia went to the hardware store and filled bags with cans of spray paint. Then they went to the Army Navy store and filled backpacks with every flashlight, canister of mace, pack of batteries, and taser gun they had. Lydia was worried that Pam would be disappointed they hadn't gotten any real guns, but Goff drew the line at actual weapons. He didn't want to kill the reapers. They were just people under a spell. He also worried that guns lying around in a building of scared kids was a terrible idea. They'd end up shooting their feet—or each other.

When they returned, extension cords snaked across the floor like rampant tree roots. Halstrom and Pam had managed to place all the lights on the second floor, angled out the windows so no one outside could mess with them. As a bonus that Halstrom seemed very proud of, the lights could all be turned on with a single switch at the end of a tangle of cords.

Goff complimented him and handed out cans of spray paint all around. "We have a lot of window blackening to do."

"Oh, fun," Lydia said enthusiastically.

"Fun is on the verge of extinction," Halstrom said.

They left the main window on the second floor clear—they needed a vantage point to see what was happening outside—but painting the rest of the windows took a while. Goff managed to keep his mind on the task, despite becoming more and more aware of what was rapidly approaching. The arrival of the reapers and him sneaking off to take on Mathers one-on-one was no longer a distant prospect.

When they were finished spray-painting, they put batteries in the flashlights and placed them, along with the mace and taser guns, on a table like a buffet. By lunchtime, everything was all set, and they had even moved some furniture to barricade all the doors except the front one. While the others had been busy, Goff had taken a moment to ensure he had an escape route through a second-story window, across a wide ledge, and down a slanted roof dropping into the garden behind the building.

"Who wants to go find some real food?" Lydia asked. "I really can't eat more cheese curls."

"MoneySaver expedition?" Pam asked.

"It may be our last meal," Halstrom said.

"Always bringing the cheer," Goff remarked, rolling his eyes.

Leaving Bones and Maxim back to keep watch over things, they headed off to the Money Saver. They traveled in a cluster out on Main Street through rolling waves of leaves swirling across the ground. Red light from the beacon over Hallow Manor blotted out the hazy sun and turned the world into a House of Horrors.

Goff was surprised that the Halloween decorations had become even more elaborate overnight. Jack-o-lanterns with angry eyes and jagged devilish mouths covered nearly all the ledges, walls, doorsteps, and porches. There were so many that the air reeked of pumpkin guts. Gauzy white ghosts with gaping mouths and distorted black eyes hung from every tree, swaying and fluttering in the breeze.

MoneySaver had been abandoned, like all other stores, and the shelves were nearly empty except for some jars of sweet gherkin pickles, squeeze bottles of mint jelly, and stale loaves of pumpkin spice raisin bread. On the way out, they heard snoring coming from the manager's booth. A very dirty and disheveled Ben with leaves still stuck in his hair was sleeping on top of the desk.

"Ben?" Pam said, running to him. "Are you okay?"

"Pam?" Ben opened his eyes, which were no longer black. He screwed up his face as if smelling something terrible. "Why do you look like a girl?"

Pam let go of his head and it landed with a *thunk*. "Nice to see you, too, idiot."

"Enemy..." Ben said, pointing listlessly at Goff before closing his eyes and falling back to sleep.

"He's useless," Goff said. "Let's put him in a cart and get out of here."

A few minutes later, they pushed a shopping cart containing a sleeping Ben down Main Street while Lydia made the strangest sandwiches Goff had ever eaten; he was so hungry, they tasted amazing. On the horizon, the red beacon made the sky look like a permanent crimson sunset, one heralding a colossal storm heading their way. The air was dead still, and it was cold, the kind of cold that seeps in through your skin to settle on your bones. They ate and walked in silence, broken only by the wobbly squeak of the cart's wheels and Ben occasionally mumbling, "Kill Goff."

When they arrived back at Town Hall a little later, Bones and Maxim were waiting for them in the main foyer.

"It's still daytime," Goff said to Maxim. "Why are you alive?"

Nice to see you, too," quipped Maxim. "Magic is out of whack at the moment, so here I am. Surprise! But after your little meltdown yesterday, I'm surprised you're not ignoring us."

"I would ignore them," Halstrom said matter-of-factly.

"Me too," Pam added.

"Ignore who?" Lydia asked with a mischievous expression, accepting a high-five from Pam.

"Look," Goff began, "I'm not happy that you lied to me, but this whole situation is a gigantic mess. No more lies or secrets, okay?"

The heavy wooden front doors swung wide, and Amber came running in, red in the face, eyes wild, and her hair blown into a tangle.

"Bizarre things are happening out there!" she shouted.

Goff and the others ran out onto the broad cement front steps. The boiling canopy of sky had thickened into heavy black and red storm clouds, dropping Spraksville into deep twilight. From where the beacon met the sky, projectiles like meteors screeched as they ripped through the air, forming black-smoke spider legs arcing toward the ground. Goff's jaw dropped. It was an ominous display of immense power. He felt like a bug watching a foot coming down to squish it.

"He's made evening come early," Goff said, trying to keep the nerves out of his voice.

"Clever move," Halstrom ceded. "He's exploited our assumption of time."

Pam wrapped her arms tightly around herself. "What do we do?"

"We get everyone here," Goff said with urgency. "Now, before the reaping starts."

"The reaping will begin soon," Maxim said.

Goff turned to Halstrom and Pam. "Go ring the bell. Ring it as loud and as hard and as fast as you can."

Pam seemed transfixed by the nightmarish spectacle on the horizon, but Halstrom took her arm and led her away at a run. A minute later, the air vibrated with the sick sound of the bell ringing. Three kids ran down the street, screaming at the top of their lungs. Behind them, a trio of mummies was coming up fast. From the other direction, a group of kids ran by, chased by a cluster of billowing white ghosts.

"We probably should have told you about the decorations," Maxim said.

"Ya think?" Lydia said sarcastically.

"They are part of his plan," Bones said. "They will create chaos, scattering the herd into the clutches of the reapers."

"Wizards love panache," Maxim added. "Never been fond of that."

Goff's heart tightened. "He's thought of everything."

"Yup," Bones and Maxim said in unison. "Everything."

CHAPTER 32

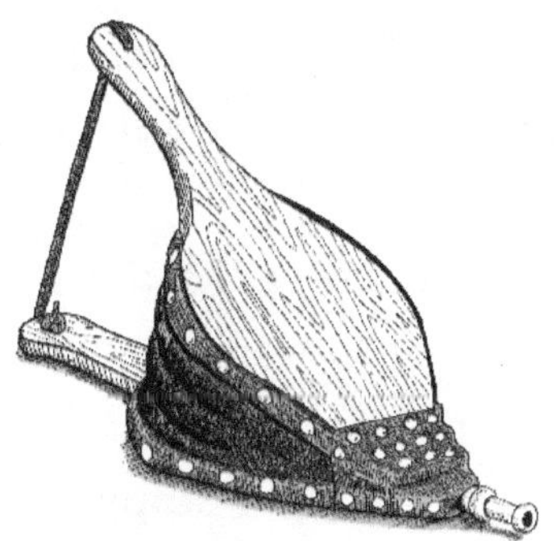

Battlefield

GOFF stood next to Lydia on the front steps of Town Hall, watching the chaos on Main Street with mounting trepidation. Screaming kids ran in all directions, chased by everything from flaming orange jack-o-lanterns with leering grins to gory zombies snapping their jaws. A young girl wearing purple leopard spot pajamas and fluffy kitten slippers ran by, being chased by a pack of skeleton dogs. All manner of cries and shouts rattled the air, floating above the buildings and treetops from near and far.

Lydia squeezed his arm. "This is a freaking nightmare."

"Can I wake up now?"

Pam ran up with Halstrom at her side. "Did anyone else feel that?" Her face was red, and her eyes wide.

"Feel what?" Goff asked.

"Rumbling."

"Like a train?" Lydia asked.

"No, more like—" Pam started, but the ground shook hard enough that the glass in the lanterns outside rattled, "that."

"Felt like a tree falling," Goff said.

"There is a rhythm to it," Halstrom said. "Like footfalls of a giant."

"I have a bad feeling about this," Pam said fearfully. "We should get inside."

Goff's heart sank even lower. Mathers was beating them back, forcing them into retreat. Movement out on the street caught his eye as a witch with long black robes and a tall pointy hat whizzed into view on a broom and then stopped in front of Town Hall, pausing in midair like a car parked against the curb. She turned her bumpy green face to look at him and then let out a shrill cackle through jagged, pointy teeth. Goff's eyes widened as his skin tingled with fear. Lydia whimpered and hid behind him.

"Forget about that," Pam called out as the ground rumbled again, much harder than the last time. "Something much bigger is coming. We need to get inside."

Goff didn't move. Everything was spiraling out of control, and he knew it was precisely what Mathers wanted—to knock him off balance, distract him, make him run scared.

"I'm staying right here," Goff announced, surprising himself with the force of it. He suddenly felt a clear resolve. He would not run and hide, not from this witch, not from whatever monster was thumping their way, not from anything.

"Goff," Lydia pleaded, pulling his sleeve. "Don't be stupid. Get inside!"

Goff ignored her. He stepped forward, pointing at the witch, and shouted, "Show me what you got, you pathetic plastic decoration!"

The witch shrieked and spun her broom in Goff's direction. With a blast of green smoke from the end of her broom, she darted toward him, racing across the grounds of Town Hall like a crop duster dropping green fertilizer. Goff felt a sense of power rising up from the earth through his toes. He reached out to a white pine in her path, connecting with one of its long branches near the bottom. It became part of him, ready to respond to his will. Just as the witch reached it, Goff swung the branch like a baseball bat. It struck her with incredible force, and she disappeared in a cloud of black smoke.

"Home run!" Pam shouted.

"Dude!" Lydia gasped. "That was awesome!"

His heart racing with excitement, Goff watched the black cloud dissipate, leaving behind a bright red Nexi, oddly enough about the size of a baseball. It wobbled a little, as if unsure what to do, and then flew a few feet toward him. Goff could feel its angry, dark power.

"I think it wants you to be its wizard," Lydia said.

"Pick up the gun!" Pam shouted.

"Gun?" Lydia asked.

"Like in the movies," Pam explained. "Nobody ever picks up the enemy's guns. That's stupid. Goff should take this one for himself."

"Pam is right—we could use some magic on our side," said Halstrom.

Goff sensed that this Nexi would attach to him if he extended an invitation, but did he want that? This was dark, powerful magic, and having it attached to him would make him a full-fledged wizard. A tingle ran over his skin as he thought about that. His mind started racing with thoughts of how he could use its power to kill Mathers and all the reapers and maybe even stupid Ben. A delicious feeling rose from his stomach, and he stood there, staring at the Nexi, which began glowing brighter and brighter and moving closer.

"You okay?" Lydia asked, touching his arm.

"Get off!" Goff pulled away.

Lydia backed away. "What's gotten into you?"

"Shut up!" Goff shouted. "I'm thinking!"

"Excuse me?"

"You heard me."

"Goff?" Lydia turned him toward her. "What's going on?"

Goff clenched his fists, wishing she would leave him alone, but he suddenly felt like two people when he met her big green eyes. One was a new Goff boiling with rage and a desire to destroy anyone who got in his way. He could feel the Nexi calling to that Goff, filling him with a craving for power. But there was another Goff there, too, the one that had always been there, the one that was Lydia's friend, the one that felt like the real Goff.

"Dude," Lydia whispered, "you look all wrong."

"You're right," Goff exhaled, shaking his head to push away the new foreign part. He turned back to the Nexi. Picking up the gun wasn't the answer. That would just make him another bad guy with a gun.

"Go!" he shouted at the Nexi.

"Don't chase it away," Pam complained. "We need it!"

"No, we don't," Goff said. "I reject you! Leave!"

The Nexi spun in a circle before rising and being sucked back in the direction of Hallow Manor.

"You idiot!" Pam roared. "Now we have nothing again!"

"We don't need that something," Goff said.

Pam opened her mouth to say something but stopped when the ground shook again, this time so much that leaves showered down from the trees. Goff felt a sliver of fear cause his heart to speed up, but it soon galvanized into anger. "I'm going to go put an end to that before it hurts someone."

"I fear whatever is making that is too big to be swatted away with a branch," Halstrom pointed out.

"I'll find a way," Goff reassured them all, walking down the steps.

"Not alone," Lydia said, pulling Halstrom with her. "We're going with you."

"I can't let you guys come," Goff said. "It's too dangerous."

"You don't have a choice," Lydia said.

"I concur," Halstrom said, pointing at the garage where the Zippos were parked. "And might I suggest that ground speed would be helpful?"

"Good idea," Lydia nodded, running toward the Zippos.

"Lydia!" Goff shouted, chasing after her. "You guys get inside. This is my fight to finish, no one else's."

"Goff, we're all in this together. And we have magic, too, remember?"

"Chester only sparks," Goff said.

"Thanks for reminding me," she smirked.

"So then you know that's like taking a plastic knife into a sword fight?" He reached the garage where Lydia was already selecting her Zippo.

"Necessity can be a great motivator," Halstrom said, jogging up behind him. "Perhaps Chester and Occam will surprise us."

"Or perhaps you will both get killed," Goff frowned.

"Well," responded Lydia, "sorry, but I'm not getting *killllllled* without a fight!"

"Nor am I," Halstrom declared.

"Or me," Pam said, walking up to Goff, arms crossed. "So, what's the plan?"

"Do you ever do anything without a plan?" Goff asked.

"No. What's the plan?"

All eyes were on Goff, waiting for instructions. He thought for a second as the ground shook again, coming up with only one plan that made sense. "Lydia, Halstrom, you will come with me. We will deal with whatever is making the ground shake and get as many kids as we can back to Town Hall. Pam, you stay here and deal with them when they come. Use the flashlights, mace, and whatever else you can think of. If all that fails, barricade them inside. Got it? We'll be back as soon as we can." He turned to Halstrom. "Go get the walkie-talkies from the security desk so we can stay in touch."

"Pam," Goff added as Halstrom zipped off toward Town Hall. "I know it's a lot to take on alone. Are you okay with it?"

"I may not be G.I. Joe," Pam said hotly, "but I'm not a fragile little flower either. Bring it on."

The ground shook again, strong enough to throw them all off balance. Halstrom's Zippo faltered as he raced back with the four walkie-talkies and handed them out. Goff paused, looking at Pam, wondering if she'd be okay and if he'd ever see her again.

"Go," Pam said. "I'll be fine."

"Keep us informed," Goff said. "And let us know if things get out of hand as soon as possible. We'll come right back."

"Got it," Pam nodded.

Goff turned and urged his Zippo forward. Halstrom and Lydia followed, and the three of them crunched over the gravel out onto the driveway. The ground quaked again, and their Zippos wobbled back and forth.

A few blocks up the road, the red light of the beacon glimmered off a gigantic spider crawling down Main Street, its eight legs the size of tree trunks and its abdomen as big as a bus. Every step it took created a crater in the road, and its enormous abdomen bounced off the ground, shaking the buildings and rattling the glass. Behind it, the town's fire station was just a pile of rubble.

As they drew closer, the spider clacked its mandibles and let out a blood-curdling high-pitched screech.

Goff gulped. "Why is it always a spider? I freaking hate spiders."

"That's the spider that used to sit in the library window," Lydia realized. "It was just the size of a dog."

"Well, now it's big enough to destroy Town Hall," Halstrom said. "In about three minutes, by my projection."

"We can't let that happen," Lydia said, turning to Goff. "What's the plan, Mr. Mayor?"

Goff brought his Zippo to a halt. "I don't know. I figured I'd just wing it once we saw what we were dealing with, but I think Halstrom was right—a gust of wind or a tree branch won't take that thing down."

The ground shook as the spider brought its hairy leg down hard onto the roof of the donut shop, sending a pink ten-foot glazed donut with white sprinkles rolling across the street. The spider's abdomen struck the earth, and the tarmac cracked apart.

As Goff stared, lost for ideas, Lydia and Halstrom shared a private word and then darted off to the base of two telephone poles on opposite sides of the street. Snapping their fingers as fast as they could to make sparks, they managed to catch the tar on the poles on fire. Flames shot up quickly, spluttering and crackling along the tar-soaked wood.

Lydia and Halstrom raced back to Goff as he watched the flames climb, reflected as orange flickers in the black eyes of the spider. It reared back, sinking low like a crouching tiger.

"Guys, that was a cool trick, but this is like trying to stop a charging rhino with matches. Might work for a second or two, but—"

"Now," Lydia panted, "it's your turn."

"What?" Goff asked, confused.

Halstrom cleared his throat.

"There once was a young boy named Goff.

At the enemy, this boy did scoff.

He was the nicest of fellows.

But at times quite a bellows.

And that's how he sent the giant spider heading toward us and about to destroy Town Hall off."

"Terrible limerick," Goff shook his head.

"It's a parody of limerick form," Halstrom corrected. "Pam would have loved it."

"Whatever," Goff said. "I get it."

He closed his eyes and focused on feeling the strength of the earth beneath him, drawing power up through his core. The air around him began to move, and he connected with it, organizing it into a small tornado. When it was whipping fiercely enough, he unleashed it at the burning poles. It hit the flames and sent them horizontally as if shot out of a flame thrower. They struck the spider with great force. It rose on hind legs, standing taller than a four-story building, and raked the air angrily with its front legs. As flames swirled around it, a screech loud enough to wake the dead rattled the night.

"Get back!" Goff shouted.

The enormous flaming creature collapsed toward them like an avalanche of spider legs and gnashing mandibles. The trio backed up and covered their heads. Goff thought they were goners, but then the spider dissolved into a cloud of black smoke just as the heat became almost hot enough to singe their hair. Suddenly, other than the screaming of running kids and the crackling of the burning telephone poles, the street was empty and still.

A red Nexi became visible as the smoke cleared. It danced in a few circles, looking confused. Slowly, it grew brighter and moved toward Goff.

"Don't bother," Goff said to it.

Halting its approach, the Nexi shot back toward Hallow Manor.

Halstrom and Lydia pulled up next to him.

"A poem?" Lydia asked, turning to Halstrom and throwing her hands up with exasperation. "Really?"

"Inspiration struck."

"Regardless," Goff said, "one thing is becoming clear to me. If we're going to win, we have to play the weirdest game of chess ever. Finesse and form matter more than you might think when it comes to magic."

"Exactly," Halstrom said. "Hence the limerick."

Lydia shoved him, and while he didn't budge, the Zippo wobbled a little.

Goff turned to watch the telephone poles burning. Orange sparks escaped upwards in grand cascades. Main Street had become a battlefield, and he liked it. He hoped Mathers could see the glow from Hallow Manor. They had done some damage, and he wanted Mathers to know he wouldn't win this as easily as he might have thought.

Pam's voice burst from all three walkie-talkies at once. "What's going on out there? I see flames. Are you guys all right?"

Halstrom grabbed his walkie-talkie. "Yes, we are fine, and I incorporated a limerick as a form of communication—"

"What?"

"There once was a boy named—"

Lydia grabbed the walkie-talkie, "Ignore him."

"Ignored. What's your status?"

"Enemy neutralized."

"Casualties?"

"None. Your status?"

"No action here. Maxim and Bones are on the roof."

"Lookouts?"

"Supposedly."

"Ben?"

"Asleep."

"Good."

"Check back in ten."

"Will do."

"Over."

"Over and out." Lydia clicked off the walkie-talkie.

"Fascinating," Halstrom said. "Most succinct communication you've ever produced."

"Poetry has no place on the battlefield."

"Many poems have been composed about war," Halstrom said, taking back the walkie-talkie.

"Not during the actual battle!"

Halstrom was about to reply when a group of kids ran across the road two blocks down, chased by a herd of lumbering monsters.

"Two Frankensteins and three mummies, by my count," Halstrom said.

"Back to work," Goff said.

"Got a plan this time?" Lydia asked.

"Nope! Follow me anyway?"

"Of course," Lydia said, smiling broadly.

CHAPTER 33

March of the Reapers

ACROSS the street from the burning telephone poles, Bert's Best Sporting Goods store stood with its dirty front window reflecting the blaze in fuzzy detail. Bert had set up a sloppy display of teetering mannequins wearing big puffy black and red hockey gear, messy piles of brown footballs, and a rack of badminton rackets, hockey sticks, and baseball bats. Fake white spider webbing, corn stalks, and big orange and yellow plastic candy corns were haphazardly strewn about.

Goff sped over to the window and seized a rock from the ground, not wanting to walk into the next battle empty-handed and still loaded with adrenaline from roasting a giant spider. It was already halfway out of his hand before he remembered that throwing things didn't usually go well for him, but the glass shattered spectacularly, and pride warmed his cheeks.

"We need to arm ourselves," he explained, unable to keep a smile off his lips.

Taking care to avoid the glass shards, he climbed over to grab a bright-blue aluminum baseball bat and turned back to the others, tapping it against his palm. "Who wants one?"

"Better than nothing," Lydia shrugged.

Goff tossed it gently five feet to her. She yelped and let it bounce off the front of her Zippo.

"Dude!" she complained. "Why did you throw it at me?"

"*To* you," Goff said. "I threw it *to* you."

"The distinction is lost on her," Halstrom said. "She can't catch."

"It's like this disease I have," Lydia said.

Goff retrieved two more and threw one to Halstrom, who caught it deftly.

"Show-off," Lydia smirked, picking up her bat and climbing back aboard her Zippo.

"Don't let the wire touch you," Goff warned as he jumped on his Zippo and headed off, weaving around the sparking tentacle. Moving at full throttle, he led them down Main Street toward where they'd seen the last group of fleeing kids. He slowed a bit to take the turn onto Brandle Street, but only a little. With air pushing his hair back and making his jacket ripple, he felt like a knight racing to the rescue. A block further, they saw the group of kids on top of a van, each wearing military gas masks and night vision goggles. They were trapped by a ring of monsters jumping and grabbing at them from the ground.

"What do we do?" Lydia asked breathlessly.

"They move slowly," Halstrom pointed out. "We move fast. We have bats, and they don't. Those are the advantages we have to work with."

"So, we go fast and hit them," Goff said.

"That's it?" Lydia asked.

Halstrom shrugged. "It is a plan."

"I'll take the first swing," Goff said. "Lydia, you get the second, and then Halstrom, you follow her in case she falls or something."

"Hey!" Lydia protested.

"Sorry, but I'm just trying to keep everyone safe. We cycle around in that order until the monsters are all down, got it?"

Goff raced forward and readied the bat to strike, realizing he had no idea what would happen when his bat made contact. If these things were as flimsy as the witch, they would shatter, and he would just keep moving, but if they were solid, he might go flying. Before he had another second to think about it, he came up to the side of a Frankenstein. The ugly green stitched face turned to look just as he brought the bat around and made contact. Frankenstein exploded in a cloud of black smoke. Goff turned around to see another Frankenstein and then a mummy explode.

"Three for three!" Lydia shouted.

Goff circled back around. Three red Nexis floating in the remnants of the smoke flew off toward Hallow Manor. Goff headed back toward the van, where the remaining Frankenstein and mummy jumped up and tried to get to the kids on the roof. He stopped short, holding the others back with his hand. Something wasn't right. "That was too easy."

"Just because I got one, too?" Lydia asked.

"This could indicate," Halstrom said, "that these decorations are not a credible threat."

"We're playing into his hands again if we spend our precious time riding around like knights on white horses," Goff said. "These things are just a distraction."

"We should educate, not eradicate," Halstrom said.

"Exactly," Goff agreed. He turned toward the van and shouted. "Fight them!"

"Are you crazy?" one of them called back. He lifted a pair of night goggles hiding his face—it was Tom Sweeney. "They're monsters!"

"They're just decorations, Tom," Goff called. "They can't hurt you."

"Rip them to shreds, dude!" Lydia called out.

"Really?" Tom asked.

"Go for it," Goff called. "They won't even put up a fight."

Tom jumped off the top of the van, urging his two friends to join him. They all landed on the ground in front of the monsters, fists up. "Charge!" Tom roared.

Racing forward, they punched the decorations ferociously. A few seconds later, there was nothing left but black smoke and two red Nexis floating away.

"That's what I'm talkin' about!" Tom roared, high-fiving his friends.

"We've been running all night from nothing!" one of the others shouted.

"No more running," Goff shouted over their whoops and hollers. "Go tell other kids and spread the word. Tell them to get to Town Hall as soon as they can."

"Why?" Tom asked. "This is fun now."

"Actual monsters are coming soon, Tom," Goff explained. "There isn't much time."

"Actual monsters?"

"The adults," Goff said. "Black-eyed, soul-sucking reapers. They're strong and merciless. They won't stop until they kill all of us. Don't try to fight them. They're too strong."

Screams nearby preceded a group of teenage girls running out of the forest, hands in the air, their screams so high-pitched they sounded like a piccolo blown by a leaf blower. A second later, a herd of skeletons and zombies emerged from the forest behind them, jaws clacking and flopping as they moved.

"Go be heroes and then get them to Town Hall," Goff instructed the group of boys.

With big grins on their faces, they ran off in the direction of the screaming girls.

"What now?" Lydia asked. "We ride around educating and handing out bats?"

Goff closed his eyes and thought for a second. He had to think of some angle that played to an advantage he had. He needed to educate as many kids as possible quickly. His eyes popped open. "Wait—isn't there a big set of speakers on top of Town Hall for emergency announcements?"

"There is," Halstrom nodded. "Good thinking."

"We'll just yell fight, fight, fight!" Lydia hooted.

"Or something like that," Goff said.

Lydia grabbed her walkie-talkie and clicked the button to talk to Pam. "Status?"

"Under control."

"Good. Pam, do you know where the room is for emergency announcements?"

"Third floor, south wing, right side."

"Impressive. Go there now and tell everyone to fight!"

"No," Goff grabbed the walkie-talkie. "Tell them the decorations can't hurt them. Tell everyone to fight their way to Town Hall ASAP. Real monsters are on their way."

"Understood."

Lydia grabbed the walkie-talkie back. "Over and out."

Goff rolled his eyes. "I could have said that."

"But would you have?" Lydia clicked off the walkie-talkie. "I'm guessing you would have said bye-bye. Not cool."

They waited a minute before they heard a loud crackle and a pop, followed by Pam's booming voice. It was full of static but clear enough. "Attention, Spraksville, this is an important message from the command center. The decorations can't hurt you. Fight them and come to Town Hall ASAP. Real monsters are coming who want to eat your soul. I repeat…"

"C'mon," Goff said as they listened to Pam repeat the message over and over again.

Halfway back to Town Hall, Pam's announcement abruptly ended, and a moment later her voice roared out of the walkie-talkie, peppered with background noise and screaming, as if she was out in the street during a riot. "Warning! Warning!"

They stopped and Lydia hastily raised the walkie-talkie. "What's happening?"

"Avoid the pumpkins! I repeat, avoid the pumpkins! Someone said the jack-o-lanterns are dive-bombing. Victims end up frozen like wax statues."

"Broadcast that, Pam!" Goff shouted, leaning into the walkie-talkie.

"No can do," she answered as Lydia pulled the walkie-talkie away from Goff. "I'm on crowd control. I need backup."

"Roger," Lydia said. "On our way."

"Ten—four."

"Over and out."

"Bye bye!" Goff shouted to tease Lydia, but she'd already clicked off the button.

Shaking his head, Goff urged his Zippo toward Town Hall just as a group of flaming jack-o-lanterns crested the trees like a murder of crows traveling in a circle of orange light.

Panic surged through him. He pushed his Zippo to its maximum speed, Lydia and Halstrom at his side as they all kept just ahead of the flying pumpkins. They arrived at Town Hall to find absolute chaos. Hundreds of kids were running in from side streets, heading toward the big front doors of Town Hall as jack-o-lanterns flew at them. Goff watched as two of Amber's cheerleader friends—wearing cheerleader costumes, of course—raced across the tarmac but were struck by jack-o-lanterns fifty feet short of the door. A great orange flash and a cloud of smoke left both girls frozen like statues.

"We'll provide cover," Halstrom said, swinging his bat to ward off the attacking jack-o-lanterns, "while you drum up some natural magic to buy us time."

Lydia swung her bat awkwardly, like a toddler trying to scare away bees. "There're too many!"

"Ask Chester and Occam for help," Goff suggested, "and don't get hit!"

Halstrom and Lydia's bats started glowing purple and moved swiftly and accurately, like swords wielded by trained warriors. Blow after blow hitting dead on, sending sprays of orange pumpkin guts and seeds in every direction. Goff focused on the earth below him, feeling a connection with it that spread seamlessly to the air as if all part of one giant force. He urged the air to swirl, whipping it into a vortex. With one grand gesture of his arms, he pushed the army of air molecules at the flying pumpkins. The horizontal tornado rolled across the ground, sending the pumpkins sailing butts over stems. Flames extinguished, they flew far up into the sky and out over the trees across Main Street.

When the wind swirled to a stop, the night was suddenly still. Dozens of kid-popsicles stood on the front lawn ready to have their souls reaped without being able to put up a fight. Amber's friends were there too, their mouths open as always, but frozen in screams. Around them, dozens of kids stumbled toward the door, crying and whimpering.

Halstrom and Lydia walked over and leaned on their glowing bats.

"This is worse than I ever could have imagined," Goff said, eyes wide and breathing heavily.

Halstrom and Lydia looked at him, then at each other. "We agree," said Halstrom.

Without warning, the beacon on the hill extinguished. Goff felt the sudden darkness like a hand pushing him underwater, trying to drown him. All the kids stopped running and went silent. A steady beat pulsed through the air, distant but growing louder quickly.

"Marching," Halstrom said.

"The reapers?" Lydia asked with horror.

"Opening is done," Halstrom said. "Middlegame begins."

"Huh?" Lydia asked.

"He means," Goff said with unbridled fear pulsing through him, "that what comes next is life or death."

CHAPTER 34

Nice Try, Kid

AS the steady beat of marching reapers grew louder, Goff urged everyone to get inside. Halstrom swung the doors shut, and the mass of kids filling the entranceway, standing on the stairs, leaning against the railing, whimpering, shaking, crying, and some bleeding, all stared at Goff. He looked back at them silently. He'd never been the center of so much attention, and he didn't like it.

Tom Sweeney stepped forward from the crowd. "What do we do, Goff?"

When Goff failed to produce more than a croak, Lydia leaned in close and whispered in his ear. "Time to lead, dude."

Goff realized she was right and forced himself to speak. "The real monsters will be here soon. Their mission is to kill every one of us."

The crowd began screaming and shouting out questions.

"Quiet!" Lydia hollered at only a decibel she could produce. "Listen up!"

The kids settled and turned their frightened gazes back to Goff.

"There isn't much time," he said. "We are going to barricade ourselves inside to stay safe. Everyone needs to help. Those of you in front of me grab flashlights and bring in the kids frozen on the lawn and put them somewhere safe. Those to my left, go with Halstrom and Pam. Follow their instructions. Those on my right, follow Lydia and me."

No one moved. He started to wonder if maybe he hadn't been clear enough, but before he could add anything, Pam filled the room with the voice of a drill sergeant shouting at new recruits. "Move it, people! Now!"

The room exploded with action. A throng of kids grabbed flashlights and headed out the front door. Halstrom and Pam led their group to the west wing while Goff and Lydia headed east.

"Make sure every window is locked," Goff instructed his group.

"Move as much furniture as you can to secure every door," Lydia added.

As groups of kids strained to move heavy tables and file cabinets across the wooden floors, Goff went out on the front landing and surveyed the situation. There was only one kid left to be brought in, and he was large. Goff ran out to help. As soon as they were inside, he shouted, "Close the front doors and barricade them!"

Kids moved quickly in response, banging the large doors shut, bolting the locks, and then sliding tables and chairs and cabinets in front of them.

Halstrom came up beside Goff. "Everything is secured."

"Good," Goff said as Pam and Lydia joined them. "Now we wait."

Everyone fell silent and the sound of footfalls blended with the sickly bell ringing the last notes of the six o'clock chimes to create a nightmarish cacophony. Maxim and Bones came running down the stairs.

"Reapers in sight," Bones announced.

"Marching up Main Street," Maxim added. "Not far away."

Goff turned to Pam and Halstrom. "Get in position and wait for my command, okay?"

"Right," Halstrom nodded once, leading Pam up the stairs.

"Upstairs!" Goff shouted to the other kids. "Everyone upstairs!"

Kids rushed up the broad set of stairs. Goff and Lydia urged them to move quickly before following and running to the landing on the second floor, where a group of kids staring out the main second-floor window parted to let them past. It was pitch black, but the steady resonant beat of footsteps was louder than ever.

"Maxim," Goff said. "You have good night vision. What's going on out there?"

Maxim hopped up on the windowsill. "It's not good."

"Tell me!" Goff said.

"Hundreds of them are crossing the road, and hundreds more are right behind them. You might want to turn those lights on now, for what it's worth."

"I don't want to blow our only surprise," Goff said.

"Trust me," Maxim said. "I'd unleash whatever you have right now. There isn't going to be a better time."

Goff turned to Lydia. "What do you think?"

"Listen to the annoying cat," Lydia shrugged. "What do I know?"

"Right," Goff said, and then shouted as loud as he could, "Lights!"

A second later, bright white light flooded the front lawn, revealing a scene more nightmarish than Goff could ever have imagined. An army of reapers dressed in black robes with blank faces and dead black eyes covered the front lawn. They were writhing and shielding their eyes from the light.

"It's working!" Lydia yelped.

A joyful cheer filled the room and echoed off the walls, where rectangles of light held the shadows of jumping and yelping kids like a dozen old-fashioned movie screens. Goff looked around at all the lives he had saved and felt a huge sense of relief. He'd actually gotten a one-up on Mathers this time.

"Wait," Lydia grabbed Goff's arm worriedly. "Look!"

Goff turned back to the window. From the pockets in their robes, the reapers were pulling out dark sunglasses and putting them on. They straightened, and as if connected by one mind, began moving forward. All the joy and sense of pride Goff had felt immediately drained out of him, and his lungs felt like they'd filled with cement.

"He knew," Goff turned back from the window, his legs wobbly.

"Nice try, kid," Maxim said, hopping down from the ledge.

"Yes," Bones said. "It truly was a nice attempt."

Goff looked back out the window where the army of reapers had reached the front steps. It seemed that even their approach had been a ruse. These were no longer slow-moving rigid robots. They were agile, fast-moving army ants, determined to get inside and suck every soul he had not so cleverly trapped inside.

Working together, a group of them knocked over a bronze statue of the first mayor of Spraksville leaning on a musket and used it as a battering ram against the front doors. The impacts sounded like cannon shots. Kids started screaming and running in all directions. Goff stood frozen. The horror of the situation seeped deep into his bones. No amount of natural magic, no gust of wind, rush of water, or blow from a tree limb could even make a dent in the force bearing down on them now.

A heavy hand landed on Goff's shoulder. He turned to find Ben glaring at him.

"What a freakin' surprise," Ben said. "Your plan to shine lights on the enemy failed. This is the biggest joke I've ever seen, but I'm not surprised, since you're the one in charge."

"You think you could have done better?" Goff asked.

"Yes!" Ben said, his eyes flaring. "You should have gathered guns, not lightbulbs. We'd have a chance now if we had rifles and cannons and had made bombs and booby traps to kill those freaks!"

A group of kids had formed around them, standing behind Ben, glaring at Goff.

"We can't kill them," Goff said. "They're not monsters. They're our mothers and fathers and brothers and sisters."

Ben snapped his fingers. "Wake up, dork. They're tryin' to kill us."

"Maybe I should have killed you when you were possessed, and I had the chance?" Goff asked.

"A good leader knows when to kill."

"I disagree. You weren't you, just like they are not the enemy."

"That's war," Ben said, looking around at the nearby kids for support, most of whom were nodding in agreement. "It's kill or be killed."

Before Goff could reply, the window in the other room shattered, and a reaper rolled in like a football tight-end diving for a wide throw. Another followed, and the two of them headed for a couple of kids cowering in the corner.

"Run!" Goff shouted. "Hide! Don't let them catch you!"

Ben came up close to Goff. "You've killed us all. You know that? You're the worst leader anyone has ever seen."

"Go hide!" Goff said.

"I guess that's the only option you've left all of us," Ben said before running off.

Goff stood shaking as two more reapers climbed in through a broken window down the hall. He knew there was no escape for anyone in Spraksville. The reapers had the entire building surrounded. That meant there was only one hope left—him facing Mathers one-on-one.

"Goff, what do we do?" Lydia asked desperately, coming up beside him. Her headband was down on her eyebrows, and her glasses were crooked. Her eyes revealed an ocean of fear within.

"Go get Pam," Goff said. "Meet me up in the bell tower."

"What about you?"

"I'll get Halstrom."

"But—"

"Just do it," Goff said, running off. "Get to the bell tower! I'll join you there soon!"

As Goff ran down the corridor, he turned back to catch a glimpse of Lydia before she disappeared around a corner. His heart tightened at the thought that he might never see her again; the last thing he ever said to her might turn out to be a lie. It didn't matter, though. He couldn't save them here, and they couldn't come with him.

If he had learned anything about magic, it was that small things mattered. Going alone, with no protection or the comfort of companions, was foolishly heroic and would probably result in a quick death, but him making a foolish, desperate move was perhaps the only hope any of them had left.

CHAPTER 35

Moonlighting

ITH Lydia on her way to the bell tower, Goff turned and ran alone down a dark corridor toward a row of closed doors at the far end. The one he was looking for had "whatever" written in black sharpie in the empty space where the Men's room sign had once hung. Using the key he'd hidden above the frame after locking it earlier, he opened it and slipped inside, careful to lock it behind him. The screams and shouts of the kids were locked out with it, but not entirely. They slipped through the thick metal door like the sounds of a horror movie being watched in another room.

His heart pounding so much that his hands shook to its rhythm, he pulled his packed bag out from under the sink and checked the contents—a taser gun, a mace tank, a flashlight, and his notebook with a pencil slid into the rings. All useless for the challenge he was about to take on, especially the notebook, but he liked that it was there anyway; only a few weeks ago, he had never gone anywhere without one.

Hoisting the bag over his shoulder, he went to the window and slid it open. A short slate roof was just a few feet below. With screams, shouts, and breaking glass filling the night, he climbed out and made his way onto the top of a wall running over to the garage. Three reapers were jumping up, trying to get over. He recognized one of them as Pongo. The huge man was so large that he couldn't jump more than a few inches off the ground.

Goff walked across, minding his balance. As he passed by them, the reapers went into a frenzy trying to grab his feet. One of them hooked the wall with a set of dirty fingers with long painted nails. Goff jammed his foot down on it as if squashing a spider. The reaper, a heavy woman with big auburn hair, fell backward and landed hard.

"Sorry!" Goff called out instinctively, then felt stupid for apologizing, and continued across the wall and onto the garage roof.

From there, he had a good view of Town Hall. Half the facade was covered with climbing reapers, the windows were broken, the big red front doors smashed, and shadows of kids running from reapers raced across the walls. The side door burst open, and three kids ran out screaming "Help!" as a group of reapers came out after them. The reapers caught them easily and held them tight, opening their mouths to release serpents of black smoke that coiled them like boa constrictors.

Goff had an urge to jump down to run and save them, but he stopped himself. Three kids might be spared if he joined that battle, but the war would be lost. As the kids' souls began oozing out like ghosts, he turned away, not wanting to see any more. You're not abandoning these few for no reason, he reminded himself—you're trying to save them all.

His hopes of getting a Zippo were dashed when he saw dozens of reapers near the garage doors. He sighed with frustration. That meant he'd have to make the two-mile trip on foot and avoid any reapers. Drawing in a deep breath for courage, he climbed to the other side and jumped down to the road. The shadow of the garage left him in darkness, so he rummaged in his bag and took out his flashlight. When he switched it on, the light revealed a tall, black-eyed reaper running toward him, and not just any reaper—it was Frank. Goff's heart nearly jumped out of his chest.

"Frank!" Goff shouted. "It's me, Goff!"

Frank showed no sign of hearing him. Goff backed up against the wall, rows of hedges blocking his escape in either direction. He knew he would not be able to outrun Frank, and the panic running through his body made it impossible to organize himself enough to perform any natural magic.

"Don't do this!" Goff pleaded.

Frank wrapped his thick arms around Goff and opened his mouth to emit a snake of black smoke. Goff had seen this too many times. He knew the end was mere seconds away.

"No, Frank," Goff choked and struggled. "Please, it can't end like this."

Just before the tip of the black snake reached Goff's face, a deep voice called out from nearby. "Oh no you don't!"

A large man wearing a military uniform and a ski mask covering his face appeared from nowhere and threw a punch so hard it knocked Frank to the ground.

"Come on, kid!" the man said, grabbing Goff's shirt. "Darn things bounce back fast."

Pulled along by this giant man, Goff ran down the road away from Frank, who was already getting back on his feet.

The man pulled him down a road to the right. "This way."

"Who are you?"

"All in good time, kid."

"I don't have time."

"Ya do now."

"I don't understand."

"Just keep running."

They ran around the back of a building where a large military SUV with tiny horizontal windows was parked. The doors slid open with a soft hum as they approached, and the engine started.

"Get in," the man ordered.

Goff jumped up into the black leather seat as the man raced around to the driver's side. The doors slid shut, and a hundred dials and switches lit up along with a dozen monitors showing the outside from all directions. Racks along the sides held dozens of assault rifles, pistols, and even a grenade launcher. Crates in the back were marked with skull and crossbones, and Goff assumed they were full of ammunition and probably explosives as well. There was enough firepower here to take over a small village.

The man jammed the car in gear and sped off.

"Narrow escape back there."

"Who are you?"

The man lifted his mask and turned to Goff.

"Mr. Dempsey?" Goff couldn't contain his shock.

"In the flesh!"

"You've been moonlighting."

"Ha! Being a janitor was just my cover, kid."

"Cover?"

"You're a brave kid, Goff, but yer part in this is done now. The cavalry is here."

"You?"

"Me and about a hundred other soldiers who'll drop down in a few minutes. I finally convinced the BSI that this situation was real."

"BSI?"

"Bureau of Supernatural Investigation."

"So you know about Mathers' plan?"

"Ever since I stumbled on some old documents about a place called Monstraxen. Ever hear of it?"

"I've been there," Goff said quietly.

"Been there? That's not possible."

"I traveled back in time."

"You got that kinda power?"

"Want me to make a tree lift this van into the air?"

"I'll take a rain check on that."

They turned another corner, and Mr. Dempsey backed the van into a driveway ending in a big bay window of a ranch and set the parking brake. "This is a safe house we've arranged for you," he said. "It's off the digital and magical grid. No harm will come to you here."

"But what about everybody back at Town Hall?"

"We've got that covered."

"How?"

Mr. Dempsey pressed a button, and the doors slid open. "My objective is to get you safe. I'll explain everything else after we've neutralized the threat. You got nothin' to fear now. By morning, this place'll be back to normal. We know how to undo everything Mathers has done here."

They got out of the vehicle and approached the house. It was an ordinary brick house with black shutters, but magical symbols Goff didn't recognize had been painted on every window. These were not the symbols of protection he had seen at Mrs. Wicket's house. They looked darker, scary, and they were blood red. Goff's stomach tightened as he examined them. Mr. Dempsey unlocked the front door and held it open.

"Step in."

Goff hesitated, not sure why. Then he heard Brak barking.

"You have Brak?" Goff asked with amazement.

"Sure do! I rescued him. Poor creature was distraught. He's anxious to see you. Go ahead inside."

Brak barked again, but it wasn't the bark Goff expected to hear; it seemed more of a warning than excitement. Despite desperately wanting to see Brak, Goff didn't move. Something wasn't right. He turned to Mr. Dempsey. "How did you manage to avoid being turned into a reaper?"

"Step on in, kid, and I'll explain everything."

"How about you tell me here?" he said, the suspicion inside mounting.

"I don't have time for games, son."

Goff started backing up. "Brak! Come on, boy! It's me!"

"He's in a crate," Mr. Dempsey said. "To keep him safe until you got here. If you don't get in there soon, our plan to save everyone might be ruined."

Confusion raced across Goff's mind. Everything about this situation felt wrong, but what if Mr. Dempsey was telling the truth? What if his paranoia ruined their rescue efforts, and everyone died? He took a step toward the door. Brak started growling.

Goff froze. "Tell me how you avoided becoming a reaper first."

"You're gonna blow the mission, kid."

"Tell me," he said more forcefully.

"I have a device that protects me."

"What kind of device?"

"If you'll just step inside, I'll show you."

Goff sensed that whatever this evil trick was, he had to enter the house voluntarily for it to work. Once inside, he'd be unable to leave, and his natural magic wouldn't work either.

"I know you've been through a lot, Goff," Mr. Dempsey said. "I understand you being paranoid, but I'm here to help you, really."

"I guess it would be best to trust you," Goff said, trying to sound sincere.

"That's right."

"You are one of the good guys, right?"

"Yes, I'm one of the good guys."

"Okay," Goff said, faking a smile. "I want to see Brak."

"Great." Mr. Dempsey smiled, stepping inside and holding the door open wide with his arm.

Taking what was probably going to be his only opportunity to escape, Goff turned and ran, with no idea how he would outrun a trained soldier but not about to voluntarily step into that house.

"Get back here!" Mr. Dempsey shouted after him.

Goff ran off into the deep darkness of the night, barely able to see, and ran smack into a stone wall. He rolled over the top of it and dropped to the ground just before a beam of light pushed back the darkness and swept the area. He saw his glasses in the grass a few feet away and grabbed them before pressing up against the wall.

"Don't do this, Goff!" Mr. Dempsey called. "You are dooming everyone if you run! Mathers will find you, and then we'll be powerless to save your friends or anyone else. Come on, kid—trust me! I'm here to help!"

Goff crouched behind the wall, his mind racing. One thing he felt sure of was that Mr. Dempsey wasn't here to help. Crawling to the end of the wall, he found that it abutted the foundation of a house, leaving him nowhere to go if he wanted to remain concealed. Panic rose inside Goff as the light grew brighter, but he tamped it down. His only hope was to connect with the power of the earth below him. He took a deep breath and focused on his desire to save his friends and all of Spraksville. Power rose through his toes and up into his heart, and he became aware of the roots of a large tree nearby, a vast network of twiggy fingers running beneath him. Just as Mr. Dempsey rounded the corner and shined the light on him, Goff directed the roots to attack. They shot up out of the ground like a hundred zombie hands, knocking the flashlight to the ground and wrapping around Mr. Dempsey.

"No, Goff!" he screamed. "You're gonna get everyone killed!"

Goff walked toward Mr. Dempsey as he struggled to get free. The roots coiled around him tightly, and soon he could not move. Goff thanked the tree and picked up the flashlight.

"You've doomed everyone, kid!" Mr. Dempsey shouted.

"We'll see about that," was all Goff said.

Mr. Dempsey growled and struggled violently, so powerfully that the roots could barely contain him. Then all at once, he went still. Goff shined the flashlight on his face. His eyes were solid black.

Shaking, Goff backed away just as a screech split the air—Zig and Zag were heading this way, and by the sound of it were not far off. Goff turned off the flashlight and ran back toward the house to get Brak. *But how?*

Entering the house was out of the question, so he went to a window and shone the light in. Brak was pacing in a cage in the far corner, barking wildly.

Goff slid the window open. "Brak, it's me! I've come to save you. I just don't know how yet."

Brak stopped barking and growled.

"Don't worry," Goff responded. "I'm not coming in. But how do I get you out of there?"

Another screech arose, this one closer but still a little distant. Time was running out fast. How did this trap work anyway? Goff stared at the house, wishing it would reveal its secret, and with that thought on his mind, it did. The floor began glowing red.

"Aha!" Goff exclaimed, eliciting a bark from Brak. "That's why he kept asking me to step in. The floor is enchanted!"

He raced around to the front of the house and climbed into Mr. Dempsey's SUV. The engine was still running, and the doors slid open as he approached. He jumped in, jammed it into reverse, and hit the gas. The powerful engine shot the vehicle backward, smashing the big bay window and continuing right through the wall into the living room. He jammed on the brakes and stopped about six feet from Brak's cage. His heart pounding, he took his foot off the brake and gently pressed the gas, urging the vehicle back two more feet. Scrambling over the leather seats to the back hatch, he was able to reach the latch on Brak's cage and swing the door open.

"Get in!" he called. "Hurry, boy!"

Brak jumped in and started frantically licking his face.

"Okay, Okay, but not now, boy."

Goff quickly closed the hatch and climbed into the driver's seat just as Zig and Zag landed in the driveway.

"Control tower," Goff said, putting the SUV into drive. "We've got birds!"

He pressed down the gas pedal and the vehicle shot forward, giving Zig and Zag barely enough time to lift into the air. They tumbled and twirled as the car sped past and then rounded the corner onto the road.

Brak came up to sit beside Goff. He reached over and hugged him and ruffled the hair between his ears, feeling like he'd actually turned a table on Mathers for the first time since this whole crazy thing had started. He wasn't trapped in some awful little shack, and he had his dog back. The war was far from over, but he'd won a battle!

Suddenly, movement in the rearview mirror caught his attention. Glancing to see what was there, it became clear that he wouldn't get to enjoy his first victory for long. The next battle was already upon him. Zig and Zag were speeding toward him, flapping furiously, eyes hot with fire.

CHAPTER 36

Dead Man's Pond

ZIG and Zag's glowing red eyes remained dangerously close in the rearview mirror no matter how fast Goff pushed Mr. Dempsey's enormous SUV. The green speedometer needle read a hundred miles per hour. The steering wheel rattled in Goff's tightly clenched fists. A small plastic orange and black football helmet with the Spraksville High Warriors logo dangled from the visor and banged against the window. In the glow of the dashboard lights, guns were visible in racks all around him in this crazy military tank of a car, but trying to shoot out the window felt like a stupid idea. He'd probably fall out or break his wrist. Not what he needed right now. Plus, he didn't feel capable of shooting anything living, not even Zig and Zag.

But how to lose them?

A sharp turn in the road made him swing the wheel to the right. He took his foot off the gas as the car went up on two screeching wheels at a forty-five-degree angle. Brak fell off the seat onto the floor under the glove compartment, barking and growling. Goff held on for his life until the road straightened out and the car dropped back down, bouncing a few times before smoothing out again.

No sooner had he recovered and resumed full speed than the headlights revealed something sitting in the middle of the road: a blue plastic trash barrel. He didn't dare swerve this time out of fear of rolling the SUV. He white-knuckled the steering wheel, pressed the pedal to the floor, and drove straight at it. The impact was tremendous, sending it flying, along with bits of metal from the grille. He glanced at the rearview mirror. Zig and Zag hadn't lost any ground.

Goff's mind spun as fast as the tires under him. Where should he go? He was on the other side of the forest from Mathers, and even if he could find a way around it, it wasn't like he could drive right up to Hallow Manor. He certainly wouldn't get far if Zig and Zag were waiting as soon as he stepped out.

He turned to Brak. "What should I do, boy?"

Brak barked.

"Not helpful. I need to get them off my trail. Halstrom would state the facts of the case, so let me start with that. I'm a person driving a military SUV. They are two gigantic birds with talons. I have legs, and they have legs and wings. I have hands, and they have talons. I have eyes and ears—"

Brak barked again.

"Ears! Of course! Birds have very sensitive ears. I can use an explosion or something to disorient them and escape while they're recovering. I just need to throw a bomb or shoot a missile or something."

A panel on the dash lit up, and a soft female voice spoke in surround-sound. "Enemy targeting system ready. Identify target."

Goff's jaw dropped. *He was in an awesome talking SUV!*

He dropped his speed down a little and cleared his throat. "Flying enemy approaching from the rear."

A bullseye of light spun on the targeting screen, along with a graphic of the vehicle with two dots for Zig and Zag following behind it at the center of flashing red circles.

"Enemy identified. Terminate?"

"No!" Goff shouted. "Don't hit them."

"Disengage targeting?"

"No, just scare them off."

"I can't process that instruction."

"Explode something twenty feet in front of them."

A clicking sound arose from the back of the vehicle and then stopped.

"Missile ready to fire. Trajectory and detonation set for twenty feet in advance of the target. Fire when ready."

Goff didn't hesitate. "Fire!"

The SUV rocked a little as a flash signaled the firing of a missile from the back. A second later, an explosion lit up the sky. Goff could see the dots representing Zig and Zag in the targeting screen veering off to the side at a steep angle.

He turned his eyes back to the road just in time to see a vertical row of angled yellow and black lines catching the headlights a few hundred feet away where the road ended at the edge of the forest. He was rushing toward the barricade too fast to stop in time. Panic setting in, he slammed on the brakes. The wheels let out a horrible screech and sent up clouds of smoke. With a lurch, the vehicle stopped three feet from the metal divider. Heart pounding, Goff sat back and let out the breath he had been holding. When he inhaled again, the burning rubber in the air smelled like a dozen skunks had fired at once.

Goff unbuckled and was about to grab Brak and jump out when he realized that Zig and Zag would be back on his tail in a few minutes, and he'd be on foot and unprotected. He needed Zig and Zag to think he had crashed and died.

"Can you self-destruct?" Goff asked the car.

"Self-destruct system engaged. State delay."

He opened the door, pushed Brak out, and said, "Ten seconds."

"Self-destruct sequence initiated. Ten…"

Goff grabbed his bag and jumped out of the car.

"Nine."

"Come on!" Goff shouted to Brak, pulling him into the woods at a run.

"Eight."

Goff was about a hundred feet into the woods when he heard the car say "one." He crouched down, holding Brak tight and covering his ears. An explosion rocked the air, and a ball of fire shot upwards. A hot blast of air rushed over him. Through the trees, he saw Zig and Zag approaching, far enough away that there was no way they could have seen them escape. The timing had been perfect. Zig and Zag turned and headed off, apparently fooled.

With his ears ringing, Goff stood to watch the two giant birds fly away as the plume of smoke and fire billowed into the air, illuminated from below by the burning SUV.

"Okay, boy," Goff smiled at Brak. "We won another battle, but it's time for the end game, where I probably actually die this time."

Brak whimpered.

Goff rubbed Brak's head and ears and led him further into the woods toward Hallow Manor. The brush and brambles broke a little further on when they intersected a hiking trail heading in the right direction. With the light of the burning car illuminating their way, they turned and hurried along.

After a while, they came to the stone pillars that led to the entrance to Dead Man's Pond. The light of the fire had all but disappeared, leaving just enough to cast an orange glow on the tree trunks and make the water look like shimmering blood. Hesitantly, Goff walked down the path, nearing the pond. The trees began to rustle in an invisible breeze. The water drew his eyes. Something moved there.

He stopped. Was it just his shadow? No, it was still moving, slowly, like a ghost traveling deep at the bottom. Brak began a low, slow growl. Goff's own reflection appeared, broken into a thousand shards on the surface of the rippling water. He felt held there by some invisible force, staring into the water. At first, the reflections on it were all of him, but slowly, they transformed. Now, instead of his face repeated hundreds of times, they were reflecting faces he knew, the many faces of the kids of Spraksville, each with dead white eyes, staring back at him, expressionless.

Goff gasped.

A moment later, faint at first, but then as loud as a siren, a scream ripped through the air. The sound of it jabbed Goff's heart like a sharp blade.

Lydia.

Goff jumped up, wishing he could help Lydia, Halstrom and Pam, but knowing that wasn't part of his plan, and even if it was, he could never get there in time.

"Show me?" he begged of the water and trees and rocks surrounding him.

A wind whipped up, agitating the dry oak leaves still clinging to their branches. It grew so intense that Goff was forced to close his eyes. Instantly he was no longer standing at the edge of the pond. A room in Town Hall appeared before him as if he were standing in a corner. Shards of glass lay strewn on the floor as reapers climbed through the windows.

In the opposite corner, Halstrom, Lydia, and Pam huddled to-gether. Several reapers approached them, and Halstrom stood with his arms out in front of the other two, holding a taser in each hand. Fear was a strange enemy on his usually calm face. Two enormous reapers approached with their arms reaching toward him. Halstrom thrust the tasers into their chests. A popping and crackling sound echoed off the walls, but the reapers continued their advance. They overtook Halstrom and wrestled him away into a corner where one pulled his head back, and another sent out black pythons to steal his soul.

Pam growled and spread her arms, guarding Lydia as two more reap-ers approached. "Where is Goff?"

When the closest reaper reached out, Pam threw a punch and hit it square on the jaw. She might as well have swatted it with a fly swatter. The reapers, each twice her size, took down Pam, and a moment later, only Lydia remained, backed into the corner, trembling too much to put up a fight.

Pongo, black-eyed and huge, marched toward her and grabbed her shoulder. Her green eyes bulged wide with fear, her mouth dropped open, and she screamed louder than Goff had ever heard anyone scream. Remaining glass in the broken windows shattered. Rats ran for their nests. The siren billowing out of her gaping mouth consumed the space with misery and fear—the last scream of the last free soul in all of Spraksville. She kept screaming, eyes closed and shaking, until a black-eyed Pongo released his pythons to silence her forever.

Suddenly, the room fell sickeningly silent.

Goff opened eyes awash with tears. Sadness as deep as the shadow of the moon filled his soul. He stared at the faces in the pond as they moved around each other in a spiral. His shoulders heaved up and down, and he sobbed, not knowing if he could bear this any longer.

Slowly, the faces in the pond began parting, drifting away toward the far edges, leaving a space where three white circles deep below the water rose toward the surface. The pond rippled and bubbled. Goff took a step back, unsure what might emerge from the depths.

In a massive cascade, the water exploded upward. Three figures rose from the center of the plume, each translucent and dim. They paused just above the surface, arms spread. Slowly, they crystallized into shadowy forms of Lydia, Halstrom, and Pam. Their dead white eyes fixed on Goff's.

Goff went rigid and let out a silent scream, leaving him empty of breath and overcome with dread. In the rustling of the trees, he heard a faint voice, the voice of the Lady of the Tree. "Your friends have fallen."

"No," Goff cried mournfully.

The voice grew louder. "Your friends have fallen."

The phrase began repeating as the ghostly figures hovered above the water, staring at him. He dropped to his knees. He'd never felt such sorrow in his life. It was as if a clawed hand was pulling his heart from his chest. It all seemed so wrong, so pointless, so maddening.

"No!" he shouted again, standing up, feeling his body tense as anger colored his sadness red.

The voice kept chanting. "Your friends have fallen."

"No!" he screamed, stomping his foot.

A powerful gust of wind ripped through the forest, dissipating the figures and rattling the pond's surface so much that waves splashed the tree trunks. Goff's entire body swelled with rage.

"No!"

"Your friends have fallen," taunted him again.

As anger coursed through his body like molten lava, he suddenly understood. The Lady of the Tree wanted him furious, not defeated. He jammed his foot into the muddy earth again. The ground shook. Rocks tumbled into the water. Branches fell from trees.

"I will not let this stand!" he shouted up to the sky.

A steel rod of resolution formed in Goff's heart. Fists clenched, he turned from the pond and headed off into the woods, crashing through shrubs and branches in the direction of the enemy that had taken everything from him.

Growling and barking in support, Brak followed. Carried on by blustering winds and swaying trees through a long stretch of forest, the pair eventually arrived where trees ended and grassy field took over. Without slowing, Goff marched along a narrow path until they crested a hill, and Hallow Manor came into view in the valley below. It rose from the earth like a patch of fungus; a large black stone mansion with castle turrets and a wall as high as apple trees encircling it. The roof over the central portion was missing, and a red glow shown from it, not the beacon that had boiled the sky before, but an illumination that throbbed, almost as if alive. In a pulsing wash of crimson, an army of reapers was visible on the driveway and road leading from Spraksville.

A tear came to Goff's eye. Somewhere among them were the reapers who had harvested the souls of Lydia, Halstrom, and Pam. He missed them so much it hurt. He could almost hear their voices.

"Dude, that looks like a subdivision of hell."

"Hell is a singular construct," Halstrom would have said. "It doesn't have divisions."

"Guys, come on!" Pam would have shouted. "Time to kick Mather's butt!"

Goff wiped the tear away and resumed walking, scanning the giant, impenetrable castle-like mansion. With no plan in mind other than being in the right place with the right intentions, he felt like an angry toddler charging at a tiger. Right was on his side, but not might. The tiger would eat him; end of story.

When he reached the stone wall stretching many feet above his head, he stopped and searched it in both directions. There were no gaps, broken sections, or passages through. He looked up at the red sky, smelling candle wax and something acrid, like burning hair. There was no breeze now, nothing rustling the leaves. Everything was still… deadly still. A chill had settled, and Goff felt it as deep as his dismay. Shivering, he turned to Brak.

"Looks like I'm walking around to the front door. I'd understand if you don't want to follow me back in there."

Brak began sniffing the air as if a cat were nearby, and then he ran off. At first, Goff thought he had taken him up on his offer to wait out here, but then Brak stopped and started pawing at the wall.

"Brak!" Goff called. "Thanks, but don't bother. It's too thick."

Goff ran over and pulled him back. This section of wall was adjacent to a compact groundskeeping hut. Where Brak had scratched, a stone had come loose. Goff tugged at it, and it came right out in his hands. A hole into the little building opened up from which a familiar smell wafted out—dog food! This must have been where they had kept Brak. Goff pulled on the other stones, and they came out easily. Soon, there was a hole big enough for him to fit through. Brak went first, and Goff followed. The room was empty other than food and water bowls, but Brak ran over to a panel set into the floor and began to bark.

"Is this where they came up to feed you?" Goff asked.

Using the small iron handle, he lifted it, revealing a set of stairs leading downward.

"A root cellar! I'll bet it leads to a tunnel into the house. Nice work, Brak!"

Goff took the flashlight out of his backpack and descended, avoiding hairy spiders hanging in thick webs on the way down. The stairs ended in a windowless room ringed with shelves, empty but for a few cans of dog food. The room was tall enough to stand in, and another door was set into the opposite wall. Goff was relieved to find that they hadn't bothered to lock it. They entered a corridor with a dirt floor leading in the direction of the house. At the end was another door. Goff paused before opening this one and pressed his ears against it. Steady resonant drumming vibrated the door and rattled his skull. The muffled sound of Mathers' voice calling out names flowing through the wood struck his heart like a poison dart.

It was time to fight the tiger.

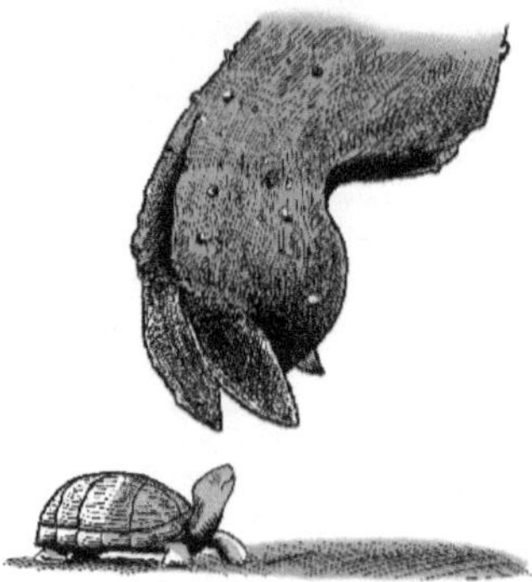

The Turtle and the T-Rex

WITH Brak shivering beside him, Goff pulled back and stared at the door, his heart racing in rhythm with the drums. This was it—his one chance. When he opened that door and stepped inside, he would face Mathers one-on-one, those dark eyes drilling into his soul. He wished he had time to think of some sort of plan before charging in there, but the ritual had already begun, and it could be over any second. It was time to act, plan or no plan.

Steeling his nerves, he placed his hand on the metal handle and pulled the door open a crack. The roar of drums poured through like the pulse of death itself. Pretending he didn't notice the fear that gripped his heart, Goff peeked through the opening. An enormous kitchen sat immediately behind the door, and the main hall was on the other side through an arched doorway. A hoard of reapers stood there, bathed in red light, staring blankly forward with glassy, dead black eyes. There was no way of entering unnoticed.

Mathers called out a name, and one of the reapers walked up to a large black cauldron. He gaped open his mouth unnaturally wide and leaned forward. A white wisp of smoke shaped like a distended human poured out and was quickly sucked down into the massive iron vessel. Goff watched, sickened by the realization that what he'd just seen was the soul of one of the kids in town he hadn't saved. How many names were left? Was this ritual all over once the last soul had been deposited in the cauldron? He looked at Brak, and Brak just stared back as if to say, "Don't look at me—I got you this far."

Another name was called. He couldn't wait any longer. No idea what he would do, he pushed the door open and stepped through. He couldn't feel his legs as he walked across the kitchen and then through the opening that led him into the main hall. As he crossed the threshold, a hundred pairs of black eyes turned toward him. The drummers stopped beating their kettle drums. The room grew completely silent. On a platform, Mathers turned to face him with the red glow of the cauldron washing him blood red and the light of the many candles flickering in his eyes.

The malice in Mathers' stare made Goff's skull rattle, and his knees went weak. It took every ounce of strength he had, but he held Mathers' glare. After a moment, with no idea what else to do, Goff cleared his throat and spoke words that felt wizardly: "I command you to release these souls and end this unholy ritual."

Mathers pressed his eyes deeper into Goff's and held his stare for a second before exploding with laughter. "That's what you came up with?"

Goff swallowed hard and kept his eyes set on Mathers. "I command you—"

"Spare me your ridiculous proclamations," Mathers interrupted, still chuckling darkly under his breath. "You have no power to wield here, Goff."

"I have more power than you know," Goff said.

"What power?" Mathers smiled confidently. "Wind? Water? Tree roots? Leaves? Or is it flowers and butterflies now? Those will do nothing here. I have won. You just haven't accepted it yet."

"You have not won. I am still alive and your enemy."

"True." Mathers walked forward, and the reapers parted to let him pass. "But you are a pitiful enemy, just as planned."

Goff walked toward him. With a ring of reapers around them, he now stood face to face with Mathers. He found it hard to look into those dark, evil eyes from this distance. The intensity made his head spin. "And yet, here I am."

"Yes, here you are."

"I've come to stop you."

Mathers raised an eyebrow. "If you have a move to make, then make it."

Goff stared back, unable to think of anything to do that would appear like a move. He felt no connection to the earth here, no ability to draw in a natural ally. This was a dead place, an evil place. He felt like a turtle standing up to a T-Rex. Bluffing was his only option. "Only a fool shows his hand prematurely."

Mathers shook his head. "Only a fool enters a fight without a weapon."

"Don't underestimate me."

"I'm not estimating."

"I won't let you kill my friends."

"It's too late for that. All but one soul is in the cauldron, and that's yours. Did you think faking your death would work? I've known your every move, your every strategy, your every plan. And as I anticipated, you arrived here at the perfect moment. Time to bring this to a close." Mathers stomped his foot on the ground. "Zig! Zag!"

The reapers again parted, and Zig and Zag emerged in human form, their ugly bald heads covered in deep hoods. They closed in on him, and despite his attempts to resist, they seized his arms firmly with hands as big as a gorilla's, rendering him unable to move.

"Time to collect the final soul," Mathers smiled, raising his arms.

Zig grabbed the hair on the back of Goff's head and pulled, arching him backward. Goff writhed, trying to wriggle free, but Zig was too strong. Zag opened his mouth wide, and his eyes went black. Unable to move, Goff watched as bolts of energy crackled from Mathers' fingertips, spreading across the room and out into the chests of the reapers. It brought them to life, and they moaned as they lurched forward toward Goff, mouths open wide, revealing empty black caverns within. Goff gasped. These were no longer the possessed people of Spraksville. Their souls had been reaped and were in the cauldron. They were empty, soulless bodies—mere vessels animated by the magic that Mathers had under his control.

As snakes of black smoke spiraled out of the reapers' mouths, encircling Goff, a horrible truth struck him—he and Mathers were the only two humans left in all of Spraksville, and soon his soul would be reaped and the ritual complete. The magical contour would collapse into Mathers. All his friends would be lost forever. The world would fall into darkness. Struggling to move but unable, he began to feel faint, weak, distant.

"We've waited centuries for this moment," Mathers said calmly.

Goff's mind began to fade, feeling like he was being pulled out of his body, taken from everything he'd ever known. Not wanting it to end like this, he desperately fought to hold onto consciousness, hoping against hope that something would occur to him or some miracle would happen.

"Don't worry," Mathers said, turning back toward the altar. "You'll soon be joining your pathetic Lydia, Halstrom, and Pam."

Upon hearing their names, Goff remembered their smiles, their laughter, and how good it had felt to have them at his side. How he missed them! How sorry he felt that he had failed them. Rapidly, sadness overwhelmed him, and he began slipping away until everything went dark. Then, their faces rushed up out of the darkness, pale and white-eyed. A shock ran through him. "No!" he screamed, forcing himself back to consciousness.

"Give in," Mathers said, spinning around with angry eyes. "You are only making this harder on yourself."

Goff fought against the force draining him, drawing on every ounce of energy left within him, finding strength in his core that he didn't know he had. The black serpents were pulling at him, trying to separate the last scraps of soul from his body. Knowing there were only seconds before he'd be gone forever, he reached out with his heart, pleading. "Someone help me save them, please. Majesty? Anyone? I'll do anything. Take my life instead of theirs. I'll suffer anything to save them. Please." He kept pleading until he felt himself about to fall off the ledge of life into eternal darkness. Then, just before he slipped away, a sound like a hundred crystal chandeliers shattering filled his ears. The thump of something enormous landing shook the ground. A blast of frigid air struck his face.

The hands holding him loosened. He felt the black serpents pulling away, letting his soul return to him. He regained consciousness and opened his eyes in time to see Zig and Zag transform into birds, screech, and beat their giant wings to rise into the air. A cold wind rushed in through the smashed window at the front of the hall, and in front of him, Majesty sat coiled in a ten-foot circle, hissing and snapping foot-long fangs at the reapers, chasing them back. Her presence was ominous, filling the space with power and ferocity. Mathers had been knocked down hard when she'd come through the window and now he struggled to get up.

"I felt you calling," Majesty said, turning her head to Goff. "Instead of pleading for your own life, you only sought to save others."

"They were counting on me."

"You aren't like other wizards."

"I'm pathetic."

"No, you are good."

"I would have tried to save you if I had known you were alive."

"I know that now."

A growl like a roll of thunder erupted from the front of the hall. "Enough!"

Mathers had gotten back to his feet. His eyes simmered with rage. He circled his hands, and crackling crimson energy shot between them. "Time to bring an end to your meddling, once and for all!"

The Queen

MATHERS raised his pale arms, draped in dark robes, and the sizzling ball of death grew to fill the space between his bony outstretched hands. Goff's heart clenched with fear—that thing would obliterate Majesty. He tried to move in front of her to protect her, but she swung her neck around to put herself in the line of fire. "Run," she hissed, leaning down.

Goff wrapped his arms around her and hugged her scaly body. "I won't leave you again."

"Trusssst me," Majesty hissed, pushing him away. "Go to the tower."

Before Goff could reply, Mathers flung the ball of energy forward. In a lightning-quick move, Majesty tucked her nose under

Goff and threw him into the air. "No!" Goff cried as he flew over the heads of the reapers, never taking his eyes off Majesty. When the ball of energy struck her, the explosion was incredible. The force of it knocked the reapers down and propelled Goff with even greater energy toward the back of the room. Holding his glasses on with his hand, he struck the large window, crashing through it and sending glass flying in all directions.

He fell rapidly toward the stone walk below, twisting in the air, but a rush of wind reached out like a friendly hand and lowered him softly into a bank of shrubs on the other side. Surprised he hadn't cracked his skull on the stone, he wrestled his way out of the bush and stood up to peer through the shattered window. The great hall lay in total disarray. Reapers covered the ground, moaning and trying to get up. Majesty was gone. At the front stood Mathers, his hair a mass of black snakes, his beard a twisted horn, and his eyes pure hatred. He looked up, and their eyes met, sending a jolt through Goff as if he had stuck his finger into a socket.

"Get him!" Mathers bellowed.

The fallen reapers rose like broken toys, lifted as if by magical springs. Mouths gaping and filling the air with piercing screams, they ran for the window. Majesty's last words reverberated in Goff's mind: Get to the tower!

Goff turned and broke free across the expansive yard and ran as fast as he could. The grass was wet with dew and strewn with cavorting shadows cast by a flickering blood-red glow shooting out of the windows. Howling reapers poured out of every door, chasing him, growling and snarling. Goff ran, and with the wind brushing his cheeks, he felt the presence of friends—trees, rocks, air, earth.

A hundred feet away, a gray stone tower with a circular room at the top rimmed with a cast-iron rail rose high into the night sky. Goff knew he wouldn't reach it in time with the reapers closing in so fast. Trusting that Majesty had good reason for sending him there, he pressed on, pushing his legs to move faster.

A snarling reaper, smelling of rot and burning flesh, pulled up behind him and tried to grab his shoulder. Goff gasped and dodged to the right. Another came close on the left and reached out, almost snagging him with its skeletal hand. Determined to get to the tower, Goff asked the air to create a tailwind to give him the speed he needed. Instantly, a gust formed, whirling up to him as loud as a train, lifting him into the air. Goff's heart jumped. Not sure he wouldn't crash right into the stone tower, he flapped his arms like a canary in a hurricane. The wind was too strong.

He rose higher and higher, soaring directly toward the circular wall of windows at the top of the tower, nearly seventy feet off the ground. Looking down made him want to throw up. He braced for impact, but a split second before crashing, another gust of wind intersected the first one, bringing him nearly to a stop. As if suddenly on an invisible conveyor belt, he moved forward slowly, his clothing flapping, over the railing to the little platform on the other side. The wind dropped away, and he lowered softly onto the walkway.

Standing on firm ground again, he stayed put for a second, clearing remnants of shock from his mind and gathering his breath before looking over the railing. The wind blew his hair into a tangle as he watched the mayhem below.

A sea of reapers flowed over the ground. Dozens were climbing the tower walls like spiders, and some rushed through the doorway at the bottom. Goff blanched. It would only be a minute before they would reach the top, and then he'd be stuck on top of the tower with no escape route and dozens of angry reapers surrounding him. What was he doing here anyway? Why had Majesty sent him here?

A tall window to the left flew open, hitting the wall with a loud bang. Goff jumped but relaxed when a familiar face peered out.

"Get inside!" Bones said. "Hurry!"

Goff ran to the window and hastily climbed through, landing hard on the floor with a *whump*. He looked up to see Maxim staring at him.

"Have a nice flight?" Maxim teased.

"What are you two doing here?" Goff asked, getting up.

"Delivering this," Maxim said, leaping down off a square block in the middle of the room.

Goff walked over to it. Etched lettering on top with 1775 sparkling next to it confirmed it was the Monstraxen stone, held together by a few turns of rope.

"Who told you to bring this here?"

"A mutual friend," Bones said.

"Remember when we told you that the names Von Grettel and Monstraxen didn't ring a bell?" Bones asked. "We lied."

"It was a big lie," Maxim said casually, licking his paw.

"And not the only one," Bones added, "but the biggest. Very big."

"Reapers are coming, guys. Get to the point?"

Maxim dropped his head. "None of us will ever forget that night. It was the night the greatest con man ever cost us our queen."

"You have a queen?"

"Had one," Bones said, flinching when the growls and shouts of reapers arose from the stairs a few floors below.

"I still don't understand," Goff said, shaking his head.

"This is your Traversal Gate," Bones explained, tapping the stone with his bony toe. "Created just for you."

"Me? Why?"

"So you can return to Monstraxen."

"Again, why?"

"We are just playing a small part in this," Maxim said. "All we know is that Cailin Wegot's grandmother made it for you, Goff, so you could return to Monstraxen on this very night."

"But I've already been there," Goff said as booming footsteps arose from just outside the door. "Everyone died. Why should I go back?"

"There are things even we don't understand," Maxim said. "Now, get over here quickly unless you want to end the night by having your soul sucked out."

The banging on the door caused it to rattle on its hinges, which seemed barely strong enough to last a few seconds.

"Quickly," Bones urged, "before it's too late!"

A hinge broke loose and fell to the stone floor. A pale hand covered in dirt reached around in an attempt to push the door open. Goff ran to the stone and placed his hand above it but hesitated. "I can't just leave. This is my fight!"

"You are not leaving," Maxim said. "You're taking the battle elsewhere."

"But what do I do there?"

"Follow your heart," Bones said as the door burst open and reapers poured in. "As you always do."

Several reapers raced through the open door toward him. Bones pushed Goff's hand down onto the stone, and the reapers disappeared, as did Bones and Maxim and the entire window-lined room. All that remained was movement, time, and space, rushing by as if he were being sucked down a tube. Then, as if awakening from a dream, Goff emerged, dazed, feeling slightly sick, lying on his back at the base of the statue in the center of Monstraxen.

Cold air struck his face, and tiny snowflakes landed gently on his body. Above him, the fanged gargoyle atop the statue leered down, its eyes glowing red. "You should not be here!"

"I agree," Goff said, standing up but not taking his eye off the gargoyle. "I don't know why I'm here."

"By all accounts, you should be dead by now."

"Happily, not dead, sorry to disappoint you."

"It's inconceivable that you are alive."

"Because I'm pathetic?"

"Exactly."

"I'm growing tired of people saying that," Goff backed a little away from the statue, fearful that the gargoyle might attack. Behind him, a handful of reapers marched by with blank black eyes, heading up the hill toward the mansion. "Not being dead seems pretty good evidence that I'm not as pathetic as everyone thinks."

The gargoyle spread its wings wide and flared its nostrils, "Regardless, your luck ends now with me."

With a flap of its magnificent wings, the gargoyle caused the sand and gravel at the statue's base to lift into the air in angry swirls. Baring its long, sharp fangs, the enormous creature hissed and swooped down. Goff dropped to the ground and curled up in a ball, expecting death to come swiftly, but instead, a crashing noise arose. The gargoyle screeched and howled. Goff scuttled forward, away from the statue. Furious hissing and screeching, like a tiger caught in a snare, filled the night.

The bronze figures of the four men at the statue's base had each extended one arm straight into the air. Their enormous metal hands clutched the legs of the gargoyle, which flapped its wings furiously as it tried to break free. The other arm of each of the men extended outward, pointing thick metal index fingers at Goff.

"Do what you came to do, Goff," a deep voice trumpeted above the gargoyle's howls.

Goff's heart did a flip. Was this what these men had been placed there to do? Save him from the gargoyle here on this very night? "Save them all," and "All for you," Calin Wegot's grandmother had said. *But how?*

The two stone men lifted and dropped their boots heavily, causing the ground to shake. "Go!"

As the ground continued to tremble, Goff turned and ran in the direction of the mansion. If nothing else, he would charge the tiger and hope for a miracle. He had nothing more to offer everyone who needed him to be a hero tonight.

"Don't listen to these foolish men," the gargoyle hissed and cursed as Goff ran. "Better for everyone that you should run the other way! Save yourself. You'll only make things worse! They will all suffer more because of you!"

As Goff raced up the hill leading away from the square, the gargoyle's voice faded, but not the fear churning in his stomach. At the top of the hill, the iron gates to the mansion came into view.

Unlike the last time he had seen it in the vision created by the Lady of the Tree, the mansion was still intact. The main building was one gigantic room large enough for an army. Tall arched windows repeated evenly along the length of the main wall, their panes like ribs through which a red interior glow spilled out. Deep resonant drumming pulsed the frigid air. A tower just like the one at Hallow Manor rose to the right. A surreal feeling tickled his mind as he approached the house with the drumming that was rattling his heart. This was all so familiar, yet different. He knew this place, and yet he didn't.

Fearing he might be spotted, he headed off to the side and made his way around the house under cover of bushes. A wide veranda opened up on the back of the structure, and he walked up six short granite steps to stand upon it. Through a window, he could see the dark interior and the red glow of the main hall splashing on the walls through an arched doorway. He tried the sash, and the old, weighted window slid up with a jerk. Just like at the mansion in his own time, he crossed the threshold with no plan and walked toward the throbbing light.

A booming voice called out a name as Goff settled into a nook outside the main hall. Such a familiar sight—a sea of reapers standing with dark hoods covering most of their faces, blank black eyes forward.

On either side of the door, two reapers banged steadily on giant kettle drums. Goff inched a little closer, and Mathers came into view. The resemblance to the present-day Harkland Mathers thirteen generations later was striking—same silhouette and dark black hair, but a trim-cut beard outlining his angular jaw.

Goff closed his eyes and felt the space. It was dead here. There was no natural magic available. Whatever he was going to do, he would have to do it without help. The reaper whose name had been called deposited a soul and then returned. Goff flattened against the wall as a voice arose from around the corner, a man's voice, speaking in a raspy whisper.

"You've come."

"Yes," a female voice replied, soft and round, not whispered but gentle. "You are Geoff Von Grettel?"

Goff flinched when he heard that name but stayed pressed silently against the wall.

"I am," came the reply in a voice that had the deepness of a man of battle, of hardship—scratchy from barking too many angry orders at weaker men.

"What I'm here to do is unprecedented," the girl said, "and were it not for the fate of all things magical and human resting in the balance, I would never have agreed."

"We are aligned in purpose, Your Highness."

Goff felt transfixed by the exchange he was hearing. Highness? Was this the queen that Bones had spoken of?

"But are we aligned on terms?" the girl asked.

"Did not the Lady of the Tree confirm our agreement?"

"She did, but I need to hear you speak the words myself."

Out in the hall, Mathers called another name, and another reaper shuffled forward.

"There is little time."

"Look me in the eyes and speak," the girl said sternly. "Or I will leave."

"If you leave, then we are finished. Mathers is too powerful for me to stop. Willingly or not, he will obtain my soul and complete the ritual. Is that what you want?"

"Leaving or staying is a decision I make based on my own judgment. Indulge me immediately, or I will judge it unwise to stay. What do you choose?"

"Very well," the man cleared his throat. "You will attach to me, which will allow me to direct your power, but only so long as it takes to bring this ritual to an end and save the people trapped here."

"And then?"

"Then I will release you."

"You do realize the trust I'm placing in you, I hope? I will be unable to release myself, and the feeling of my power within you will be overwhelming. Can you assure me that you are a man of strong enough character to resist the temptation of such power?"

"Has not the Lady of the Tree vouched for me?"

"Again, I need to hear you speak the words."

"I assure you that I will honor our agreement."

There was a pause, during which Goff's mind reeled. Confusion had been forming as he listened to this exchange. After all, he knew how this night had ended. Not with Von Grettel saving everyone, but with treachery and total devastation, the death of Monstraxen.

"Then we shall proceed as planned," the girl said.

"Yes, exactly as planned."

Adrenalin fueling him, Goff's body seemed to move before his mind caught up, and he stepped out from behind the wall.

Standing before him, stretching as wide as the door behind him, stood a giant, silver-haired Von Grettel. His angular, weathered face was half-hidden within a deep hood. A girl with large eyes and a slender face framed by shimmering hair rolling down her shoulders hovered inches off the ground before him. She wore a long flowing robe that billowed in an invisible wind, and her entire form glowed soft violet. She seemed made of light, transparent, sparkling as if super-charged, and Goff knew this was not really a girl at all but pure magic in the form of a young queen.

Moving as fast as a serpent, Von Grettel grabbed Goff and pulled him back, wrapping his thick, muscular arm around Goff's throat. "Who are you? How did you get here?"

"A boy?" the queen asked. "But that can't be. All souls must be in the cauldron. We are saved. The ritual will fail!"

"No," Goff said, struggling to find air to speak. "I don't count. I mean, I'm not really here, not as part of this crucible."

"The boy makes no sense," Von Grettel hissed, pulling a dagger from his robes and pressing it against Goff's neck. "I will slit his throat and end this trickery."

CHAPTER 39

Genie in a Bottle

GOFF knew death was just one quick movement of Von Grettel's wrist away, and, coiled within his massive arm like a rat caught by a python, he could do nothing to change that. The drumbeats rose to a cacophony, filling his ears.

"Stop!" the queen shouted, her eyes narrowing. "Drop the blade. This boy is an anomaly. I need to understand what his appearance here means."

Von Grettel held the blade in place for a second but then seemed to think better of disregarding her and dropped his hand away. He did not move otherwise, keeping Goff's throat compressed so hard that he could barely breathe. "We don't have the time."

The queen rose and floated back to him. Goff could see a candle sconce holding a black candle through her stomach. "Anomalies of this kind can carry great meaning, Von Grettel. I insist you allow his story to be revealed or our agreement is ended."

Von Grettel relaxed his grip, but just a little. "There is scant time remaining, your highness! Our mission is paramount."

"I agree, but indulge me," the queen said, turning her eyes to Goff. "Boy, explain your presence here."

"I've...come," Goff croaked, barely able to speak, his windpipe aching. To...warn."

"About what?" Von Grettel asked impatiently.

"This night," Goff said, coughing. "Ends in tragedy."

"That's certainly true if we spend more time listening to you," Von Grettel grumbled.

Goff pointed up at Von Grettel. "Because of him."

Von Grettel contracted his muscles and nearly crushed Goff's throat. "This is some sort of trick. I don't know by whom or what means it has happened, but someone sent this boy here to disrupt our mission. Let us not fall into this trap and fail in what we have worked so hard for!"

Goff felt the lack of oxygen begin to steal his consciousness. The room and the floating queen started to dissolve like a watercolor painting washing away, becoming nothing more than a cluster of fading outlines.

"Loosen your grip!" the queen commanded. "Or I swear I will go and let be what will be here tonight. I will peer into his mind. If this is a trap, it will be revealed."

"But—"

"Do it!"

Von Grettel's arm relaxed enough that Goff could draw a breath. The queen approached him, hand extended, and placed it on his forehead. A jolt ran through him, the feeling of which he found very familiar. *Maj-*

esty? But how was that possible? His mind raced, and like puzzle pieces finding their places, several things began to become clearer. The queen Bones thought they had lost had not been lost. Because of whatever had happened here tonight, she had been reduced to near extinction. The small, weak misfit Nexa he had bonded with and named Majesty had been none other than what remained of this queen after this terrible night's events. He felt her gaining access to his thoughts and then her confusion and surprise at finding his memories of her as a tiny, misfit spec of magic when they first met. She pulled her hand away abruptly.

"What sorcery is this?" she asked, a scowl on her translucent face. She turned to Von Grettel. "Someone has crafted a clever trick."

"Then let me kill him so we can proceed."

"No," she said. "You will approach the cauldron when called. I will emerge and bond with you at the critical moment."

"But what of the boy?"

"I fear he is of my world more than yours, so it would be unwise of you to harm him. It could backfire. Leave him to me."

"I do not like this change of plans."

"Nor do I, but any other path is unwise. The magical realm is churning in unexpected ways, and you do not possess the skill to navigate such gyrations."

As if on cue, Mathers' voice rang out. "Geoff Von Grettel."

Von Grettel's face turned grim. "You realize that the ritual is complete if I release my soul into that cauldron—either willfully or by force. There will be nothing you can do to stop it."

"We will bring it to an end before that transpires."

Again, Mathers' voice rang out. "Geoff Von Grettel!"

"Go," the queen ordered. "Be ready for me."

Von Grettel released Goff, hesitated for a second, and then pulled his hood over his face and walked out into the hall. "I approach, Your Greatness, with great honor."

"The honor is mine," Mathers said. "Tonight, you will pass through death to assist me in being the most powerful force this world has ever known."

Majesty turned to Goff. "I cannot explain you, but you are full of lies and trickery, and you will die. Soon, I will bond with Von Grettel, and after we have ended this ritual, I will ask him to direct my power to kill you before he releases me."

Goff raced through a thousand thoughts, trying to understand what she was saying. He had seen how powerful she was, yet she spoke as if she was without power. She had to ask Von Grettel to direct her magic? She had also said that what she was about to do was unprecedented. So, she had never bonded with a wizard before? Her power would overwhelm Von Grettel? A few more loose pieces of the puzzle suddenly fell into place within Goff's mind, and he clearly saw the con Von Grettel had spun. Von Grettel wasn't a failed hero. He was a monster, just like every other wizard, yet even more clever, clever enough to trick the Lady of the Tree. Von Grettel wasn't trying to stop the ritual at all. He only wanted Majesty to bond with him and become his personal magic. As Bones had said, he was "playing the situation" to obtain immense power. He had no intention of releasing her.

But one thing still didn't make sense—the night hadn't ended that way. It ended with Majesty destroying Von Grettel and all the people in the mansion. It had nearly killed her, too. Why? The truth hit Goff like a ton of bricks. He looked up at her, hoping against hope he could get her to listen.

"If you bond with Von Grettel, he will refuse to release you, and you will have to pay a terrible price to stop him from becoming the most powerful wizard imaginable."

"A terrible price?"

"The ultimate price."

"I still don't understand."

"If Von Grettel bonds with you, he has access to your full power, and he must release you, or you remain bonded, right?"

"Yes, but on the honor of the Lady of the Tree, he has agreed to do so after stopping Mathers."

"Yes, but he's lying. He's fooled the Lady of the Tree, too. He's the most brilliant con artist ever. All he really wants is your power for himself. He will refuse to release you. You will realize you've created a monster and do something extreme. You will sacrifice yourself to be free of him, taking everyone, including Von Grettel, Mathers, and all the people of Monstraxen with you to save the rest of the world. In the end, you don't actually die—I think because the Lady of the Tree heals you a little—but you end up as you saw in my mind: a broken, weak scrap of magic that has no recollection of ever being a powerful queen."

A look of horror flashed across her face. Her eyes locked on Goff's. "That's not possible."

"I've seen it. I was your wizard in the future."

"Prove it."

"Look inside me again. I'll show you."

She blinked and stepped forward, extending her hand to touch his forehead. This time, as she entered his mind, Goff drew up every image he had of Majesty. He didn't attempt to filter or organize, wanting her to know the whole truth, and thoughts and memories of her raced past in a rush—coaxing her out of the plastic spider; learning to light candles; making Tom Sweeney's pants drop; leading them to Mrs. Wicket's house as a pencil; stealing chips for Ben; losing her in a battle with Mathers, and how sad he was about that; her appearance as a snake; her saving him from reapers in Hallow Manor; and finally, the time in his back yard with Lydia and Halstrom, when she created Occam and Chester. A sadness welled up inside him at this thought, remembering what a magical, wonderful day it had been, a day that seemed a lifetime ago.

Her hand snapped back. "Oh, my."

"See?"

"That was genuine! I felt it in your heart, and the heart never lies. You are not a trickster at all."

"No," Goff said. "I'm your friend."

"I see The Lady of the Tree's hand in this, in you being here," Majesty said. "This moment had to happen, and you had to earn my trust by letting me see what we've experienced together. She knew there was no way to save this day, here in this time, and she cannot travel through time, so she worked to create someone I could trust who would travel back and change my decision. You."

Out in the hall, a commotion arose. Von Grettel's voice boomed loud and angry. "If there is help for me, for this night, let it come now!"

"Traitor!" Mathers bellowed.

Goff turned to see that Mathers had formed a ball of deadly energy.

"I feared trickery from you!" Mathers said, approaching Von Grettel. "I will reap your soul myself from your corpse!"

"You must stop this," Goff spun back to Majesty.

"No," Majesty said, approaching him. "You must stop this, Goff. I can do nothing unbound."

Before Goff could say anything else, she flew forward and entered his chest. The world disappeared behind a wall of color and light so bright it rivaled the sun. He'd felt magical bonding before, and it had felt incredible, but this time he felt as if the very cosmos were at his command. He felt as if he could easily make mountains dance, rivers rise into the air, oceans boil. He felt enormous, spatial, celestial. The feeling was so overwhelming that the situation before him seemed to disappear and grow distant. He was king of the universe!

"Remember your friends," Majesty said softly from deep inside.

Instantly, images of Lydia, Halstrom, and Pam filled Goff's mind, and his love for them filled his heart. It grounded him and brought him back to where he stood, into the present moment. It all seemed so clear now: All the power in the universe was worthless without friends. That was the secret that the Lady of the Tree had known.

He pushed away tears for the loss of his friends and turned toward the hall. Von Grettel lay on the ground with Mathers above him, about to strike him down.

"Stop!" Goff boomed, stepping into the room.

The drumming ceased, and a thousand black eyes turned toward him, reflecting the pulsing glow of the cauldron at the front.

Mathers turned to look at him. "Who dares to enter this space?"

"I've come to put an end to this ritual."

"I think not, little boy," Mathers laughed. "Somehow you slipped through the cracks. No matter, you'll join your friends soon."

Goff lifted his hand, and as if connected by magical strings, Mathers floated up into the air, away from Von Grettel.

"I call the shots from now on," Goff said.

Mathers twisted and spun, howling and cursing. "You cannot stop me!" He swung his arms in a circle, drawing all the magic within the reapers up into the air. Like empty shells, their hollow bodies thudded against the floor. Mathers swung his arms violently, orchestrating the released magic into a wave of attack at Goff.

Goff didn't feel even a sliver of fear. As if being approached by nothing more than butterflies, he smiled and drew his arms in an arch to create a domed netting of pure white light. Several Nexis struck it and came to an end like the mosquitoes that flew into Frank's bug zapper. The rest of the Nexis stopped short, quivered for a moment, and then floated up to the ceiling, where they gathered together in a jittery glowing cloud.

"This can't be!" Von Grettel jumped up and glared at Goff. "By what trickery did you steal her magic?"

"I stole nothing."

"Yet she bonded with you?"

"She did."

"But how?" Von Grettel hissed. "I've spent my whole life creating this opportunity. Then you show up, and in minutes she agrees to bond with you and makes you the most powerful wizard ever to live?"

"Amazing, right? Don't feel bad, though. It required the complex magic of being honest and brave and kind, and those are skills you certainly don't possess."

Von Grettel regarded Goff like a hungry lion does a gazelle. "Regardless," he snarled. "I possess all the skills you lack to use that power. If we formed a team—"

"I don't care about this power."

"What?"

"Do you not understand?" Mathers interjected, still floating up in the air like a rag doll. "No other wizard has ever even approached the kind of power you now have! The queen has bound herself to you! Join forces with me, and—"

"Stop it!" Goff shouted. "Look at the two of you begging me for a scrap of this power when I don't even want it myself. What you don't understand is that someone who wanted this power could never have gotten it."

"Fool!" screamed Mathers.

"I will have my revenge," Von Grettel fumed.

"I doubt it," Goff said.

He felt warmth rising in his heart, and a hazy form of Majesty crystalized in front of him. Realizing she wanted to speak to him, he froze time for a moment, which was as easy as blinking his eyes.

She stood before him, glowing bright violet, her eyes displaying wisdom that seemed timeless.

"I understand how this moment of victory is delicious for you," she said, "and you've earned it."

"I really didn't do much."

She smiled warmly. "You did plenty, Goff, and you should forever be proud. The universe owes you a great debt. I myself owe you an incredible debt. But now, I must implore you to consider how you'd like to bring this to a close."

"I'd welcome advice."

"Well, for the magical and human universe to return to normal, I must not remain bonded to you. I must return to my sovereign state, for I am the mother of all Nexis. The dynamics of the magical realm are complex, and my position within it is critical. My absence appears to have allowed even the gargoyles, who usually remain neutral, to influence that which they should not. Bonded to you, things cannot be right again."

"I never intended to try to keep you."

"I know that, but there is still the question of how to end this. Once you release me, I won't be able to work magic any longer. So, while you have my power at your disposal, what is your wish?"

Goff laughed. "You sound like a genie in a lamp."

"Genies don't live in lamps."

"Genies are real?"

"Yes."

"Wait, what about Vampires? Werewolves? Ghosts? All real?"

"I'm afraid you've only scratched the surface of the magic that moves amongst humans."

"Wonderful," Goff said drily.

"To organize your thinking, perhaps we should continue with the notion of me as your genie. Consider what you would request of me if you had three wishes before releasing me. The challenge for you is deciding in your heart what you want. Is it revenge in the form of suffering for your enemies? Riches, power, and prestige? What? Make them good because I will never again consider bonding with a human, not you or any other."

Goff spoke from his heart without even thinking about it. "Save all the people of Monstraxen. Save everyone back in Spraksville. Help me write a report about all of this good enough to get me into Amworth."

"And what of your enemies? The Mathers clan? Zig and Zag? Von Grettel? This boy Ben?"

"I'd be a fool to waste a wish on revenge."

"Just what I expected," Majesty beamed. "And that is why you are and will always be the greatest wizard who ever lived."

"Can you really make all my wishes come true?"

"Can you really give up all this power and release me?"

"Of course!"

"Then they are granted."

"And I release you."

No sooner had his words stopped hanging in the air than everything began melting away. The hall, Mathers, even Majesty washed away like a chalk drawing washed off with a hose. Soon, there was nothing but whiteness. As Goff slipped away, images flowed across the whiteness as if he'd been drugged with a sleeping potion. Children skipping down a cobblestone street, laughing. The boy in the red coat walking out of the Hoffstraden Family Bakery with his sister, carrying loaves of bread. Tom Sweeney flicking the ear of another new kid on the bus. Ben hitting a home run and pumping his fists in the air as he crossed home plate while Amber and her friends cheered on the sidelines. Downtown Spraksville full of leaf-peepers carrying coffee cups from Java Time and overstuffed shopping bags as orange, red, and yellow leaves fluttered down from the tall trees and blustered past.

The last thing he saw before he slipped away into oblivion was Halstrom, Lydia, and Pam, sitting together with him in a circle, laughing, and eating good chips, not the cheap SaverSpecial ones Ben hated.

Then, feeling as if his life and the entire world, everything about the existence he had known, was coming to an end, he, too, melted away and was gone.

CHAPTER 40

Three Wishes

THE sunlight streaming through the window struck Goff's face, filtering through his closed eyelids and rousing him to wakefulness. He sat there for a moment, feeling warm and comfortable as he pulled the soft flannel sheet up to his cheek.

Wait…

He shot up to a sitting position like a spring-wound toy, his heart racing. "Where the heck am I?"

"I've been pondering that as well," a familiar voice said from across the room.

Goff blinked three times before it registered that the speaker was Halstrom. His hair, unfettered by the usual beanie cap, stuck out like toasted cheese curls in all directions. He was wearing red flannel pajamas, and a look of confusion twisted his usually calm features.

"Was that all a dream?" Goff asked.

"This room is unfamiliar," Halstrom said.

"I agree."

"I'm wearing red flannel."

"I can see that."

Halstrom ran his fingers through his hair, smoothing it down, but not really. "And no beanie."

"You sleep in a beanie?"

"Always."

"What's the last thing you remember?"

"Telling you that I always sleep in a beanie."

Goff groaned. "I mean, you know, about all that happened?"

Halstrom stared at him, cocked his head and replied calmly. "A reaper sucking out my soul."

Goff's heart did a flip and his eyes widened. "Then it wasn't a dream?"

"You know what a reaper is?"

"I do."

"Then probably not a dream."

"Nope."

"You must have saved us."

"I did."

"Thank you."

"All in a day's work."

"Yet you can't explain our present circumstances?"

Goff looked around the room, taking it all in for the first time. It was a small room with only one window, through which blue sky and treetops were visible. Two desks sat on either side, each with tall stacks of books. The walls were bare, other than a corkboard above each desk. A small photo and a piece of paper had been pinned on the one nearest

Goff. He got out of bed and went over to it.

The photo, oddly enough, was of Brak chasing waves on a tropical beach with Maxim sitting nearby watching like an anxious mother. A skeletal hand was just barely visible resting on the sand next to him at the edge of the frame. The paper was curious too. It looked ornate and had a gold emblem on the bottom. He read it, and his eyes popped wide. He stammered with excitement as he described to Halstrom what was written there. "It's...an award...for me. First place for a paper entitled 'My Magical Adventure.' It's a fiction award...from Amworth Academy!"

"Isn't that the place—"

"Yes!" Goff shouted.

"Looks like you're in."

"You, too."

Goff noticed a postcard on the desk. The image on it showed a pretty little town nestled in snow-capped mountains. The streets bustled with shoppers, merchants, and kids. He picked it up, and his eyes filled with tears as he turned it toward Halstrom to show him that at the top it said Monstraxen. "She granted my wishes!"

"Who?"

"Majesty?"

"Was one of your wishes that I would no longer wear beanies?"

"No," Goff smirked. "Get dressed. Let's go see if we can find Lydia. I'll tell you all everything."

Goff went to the closet and found it full of clothes perfect for him. Jeans and T-shirts. Halstrom stood across the room in his signature blue sweater and beanie. Behind him, a closet door was open. Instead of hangers, it was full of shelves, each holding a blue sweater. A row of a dozen beanies hung on hooks on the door.

"I guess she didn't know what you sleep in."

Halstrom shrugged. "I'll forgive a few anomalies in exchange for being alive."

"Good attitude."

They left the room and entered a corridor that stretched in both directions for several hundred feet. Dozens of boys were scurrying up and down, carrying baskets of toiletries, hanging out in little groups chatting, running in and out of doorways. Goff and Halstrom walked to the doors at the end.

"When are we?" Goff asked, opening the door and heading down the stairs.

"That's not a question."

"It actually is for us."

"True. I'd guess fall, perhaps the year after our adventure?"

"So we're older, you think?"

"I don't feel any age-related changes."

Goff pushed the heavy glass door open and stepped outside. "Not sure that's how it works."

An expanse of manicured rolling green lawn with statues and fountains greeted them. Brick walkways sided by stone benches and shrubs cut worn trails in every direction. A ring of majestic trees encircled the campus, swaying beneath a deep blue sky dappled with cotton ball clouds and dropping a flurry of red, orange, and gold leaves. A little way off, the regal brick and stone buildings of Amworth's main campus spread along the horizon. It looked like a medieval village, complete with gargoyles leering down menacingly at students passing through arched doorways.

"I don't think I can afford this place," Halstrom said.

"I'm guessing Majesty didn't stick us with the bill."

"Dudes!" a voice called from behind them.

Goff whirled around and barely managed to avoid being knocked to the ground by a full-on hug from Lydia. She reached out and pulled

Halstrom in, and they hugged in a huddle for a few seconds before she released them.

"I've been looking everywhere for you two!"

"You must have been freaked out when you woke up here."

"I screamed so loud my roommate threw up."

"Fun for her."

"Last thing I remember is a reaper sucking out my soul!"

"Identical to my last recollection," Halstrom shared.

Lydia punched Goff in the arm. "You saved us, hero! How did you do it?"

"Wait," Goff said. "Pam isn't your roommate?"

"No," Lydia shook her head sadly. "I haven't seen her. Maybe she didn't make it in?"

"Maybe that was too much for Majesty to pull off?" Goff asked.

"Unlikely," Halstrom said. "The power required to do this must be nearly limitless. Time, history, location—it boggles the mind. I'll bet the truth is that in the depths of her heart, Pam is still bound to Ben. They need to be together and getting him here would require a character change."

"A nice, smart, hard-working Ben?"

"Impossible."

"Do you think she's okay?"

"Majesty has the biggest heart in the universe," Goff said. "So yes, I think Pam is just fine. She's where she needs to be."

"So," Lydia said. "Are you gonna tell us what happened?"

"I've already told the whole world."

"What the heck?"

"He's prevaricating," Halstrom suggested.

Lydia shoved Halstrom, though as usual, he remained immovable. "English, please?"

"I'm not being evasive, I'm being honest," Goff said. "I told the whole world."

"And they don't think you're crazy?"

"Nope."

"Really?"

"Apparently," Halstrom said. "They think he's an award-winning fiction writer. I'll have to read it to see if I agree."

"Frankly," Goff said, "I know it's amazing, even though I haven't read it, because it ends with me walking off with my two best friends."

"Dude, really?"

"Yup. Don't worry, I'll tell you everything. Now start walking."

Lydia took the middle and linked arms with Goff and Halstrom on either side as they headed off down the path toward Amworth campus. Goff began replaying for them everything that had happened, though for the entire walk he kept a wary eye on the gargoyles leering down at them from the tops of the buildings.

The End

Epilog (sort of)

UNDER a night sky full of stars like glowing sugar spilled onto black tile, a gentle, warm breeze blew through a bank of palm trees. The rustling of their broad fronds blended with the rush of waves crashing against the white sand beach. Just out of reach of the waves sat a small hut made of logs with a terra cotta roof. The windows were dark, as if no one lived there, and technically no one did. But it was not uninhabited. Two creatures, although neither actually alive, called it home.

As they had a habit of doing on beautiful nights like this, they had spread a blanket across the orange roof tiles to sit side by side, watching for shooting stars. A white line sliced across the sky, just a fleeting needle of light, but they both pointed and leaned in closer.

"I think we made it," Maxim said.

"Is it actually finally over?" Bones asked rhetorically.

"We've been here before."

"Not like this."

A big fluffy brown dog raced up to the side of the hut, just below where the happy pair sat gazing at the sky. He bounced up and down excitedly, barking loudly enough to drown out the sounds of the wind and waves.

"Brak needs to be fed," Maxim said. "Your turn."

Bones looked at Maxim and shook his head. "That's not his hungry bark."

"You speak dog?"

Brak barked again, louder this time, and then he growled.

"Somehow, dogs always know."

Maxim sighed and turned his face back up to the sky. "You mean—"

"Yes," Bones sighed. "Goff is in danger."

"Well, I guess we should enjoy this while we can then, eh?"

"Yup."

A quiet moment passed, filled only with waves and wind and Brak sending up his warning. Maxim broke the silence. "Still your turn to feed the dog, though."

Bones shook his head. "We're out of dog food."

"Not to worry," Maxim said, poking his friend in the ribs. "We've got plenty of bones."

"Funny."

Continue the Adventure in Shades of Winter

The snow has come early to Amworth Academy and so has something far more dangerous.

As winter descends on the campus, ancient evil awakens beneath the ice, threatening to trap it in an endless nightmare. Friends slip away into darkness. Old enemies return, unexpected allies emerge, and Goff's own powers begin to change in ways he doesn't understand. To stop a catastrophe centuries in the making, he must face secrets that challenge everything he thought he knew about magic, the nature of time, and himself.

Booklife Editor's Pick, Readers' Favorite Bronze Medal, Indie Reader Approve, Kirkus "Get It"

MISFIT'S MAGIC
SHADES OF WINTER

CHAPTER 1

Trouble

GOFF woke up with a start, sweat dripping down his temples. A chilly pre-winter moon sent its silver glow through the many panes of the tall dorm room windows. A dozen feet away, rectangles of light landed on Halstrom Fint, Goff's friend from Spraksville Junior High, lying in his wooden sleigh bed with arms crossed over his chest like a vampire.

Goff couldn't shake the dark feeling of the nightmare he'd just had. He felt as if he could still smell the rotting fish stench of the gargoyle and the scent of wax and oregano from the black candles. It all seemed as clear as if he had really been there.

The nightmare had started with the gargoyle coming through a window into a dark study lined with bookshelves. Goff felt certain it was the same nasty gargoyle that had tried to kill him a year ago, the night he saved the world. It had the same narrow, angled eyes and chunky snout, but it was hard to tell gargoyles apart. They were all a blend of gross and terrifying.

"Is it done?" the gargoyle had asked, his voice slick and oily. "If so, the book must be returned immediately."

"It is done," a man said in a deep, hoarse voice while sitting at an enormous mahogany desk inlaid with carved skeletons. He pulled deeply on a long reading pipe, turning the tobacco into a fiery volcano. The smoke scented the air with cherry and burnt nutmeg.

On top of the desk, illuminated by the light of a black candle, sat a large book opened to a page written in swirling letters and decorated with intricate drawings filled with dull colors. It looked like the kind of boring book they make you look at for far too long on museum field trips while a teacher prattles on about its history. The man exhaled a cloud of smoke and reached over to close it carefully as if moving any part of it too hastily might break it.

"Human hands have not touched that book in thousands of years," the gargoyle said. "I hope you have shown it due respect."

"I have," the man said, his bones cracking as he stood. "And, it has served its purpose."

He lifted the book, revealing what was set into the scaly green mackerel pattern cover: an eye with a hexagon pupil. It blinked and twisted around as if trying to figure out where it was and who was holding it.

"She's there," the man said, pointing to the far corner of the room, "no idea that she is no longer in the real world and no longer a threat to our plans. I've put ample protections in place to keep her there."

Where he pointed, a glowing sphere the size of a bowling ball rested on a tripod on a small table. Bits of light swirled inside it like a freshly shaken snow globe. In the center of the tiny storm floated a girl with long, flowing silver hair and blue eyes, wide open but blank and lost in a different world. Soft violet robes shimmered and swayed around her.

Majesty!—the queen of all magic frozen in glass like some prized sea shell. She had been Goff's magic and friend when he first became a wizard.

Carrying the book with the curious eye over to the gargoyle perched on the window sill, the man held it out for the creature to take.

"I hope you understand that what we have done here is

strictly forbidden," the gargoyle said, gently taking the book from the man's hands. "If they discovered you were in possession of this book, they would chop your head off. You must tell no one."

"No one will find out."

"And the boy?"

Sniggering, the man exhaled smoke through his nose, and it spread out in a cloud around him. "He got lucky last time, that's all. What could a clueless little misfit possibly do to topple such a masterful plan? He will cause us no trouble, and the days are numbered for him and his pesky friends."

"Let's hope that is the case."

"We have nothing to fear." The man shifted his gaze to a painting on the far wall and gestured toward it with his pipe. The painting's thick, broad strokes were streaked with cracks like a tile mosaic and depicted a tall, broad-shouldered man with dark, intense eyes and greasy black hair that hung from a lofty brow. "Everything is coming together, just as *he* planned."

"Excellent." The gargoyle turned and dropped like an owl targeting a fleeing field mouse. Several feet from the ground, it beat its massive wings to rise above a row of tall, pointy white pines at the property's edge. The man watched its silhouette pass in front of the full moon, then walked to the door, where he grabbed a cane with a gold gargoyle on top, then donned a long black wool overcoat and top hat, and left.

His cane clicked down the thirteen granite steps of an immense stone mansion as he descended. Walking along the mist-covered brick walkway, he passed an odd tree with fog swirling around it. Its branches were a tangle of gray pythons, but it was barely a tree anymore. A large crack ran down the middle. Both halves, devoid of leaves and brittle, fell to the side, almost touching the ground. He stopped to stand before it, inhaled deeply from his pipe, and exhaled a perfect little cloud. As the smoke floated toward the unfortunate tree, the man broke the silence with a raspy, wicked laugh and then clicked down the brick path toward the front gate, his breath freezing into a silver wake trailing behind him.

That's when Goff had awoken. His heart ached at having seen Majesty trapped in a glass ball in some wicked man's study, and the Lady of the Tree barren and split down the middle. She had been the magical creature who'd guided him to find a way to stop the ritual in Monstraxen last Halloween. At no point had the man's face been visible, but his voice was burned into Goff's memory, as was the cherry and burnt nutmeg smell of his pipe: sweet, bitter, and nasty at the same time. He almost felt like he could smell it now in the dorm room.

But it had only been a dream.

Yes, just a bad dream…

Goff stared up at the moon's shadow that was deepening the grooves of the basilica-patterned tin tiles twelve feet above.

Ever since he had arrived at Amworth after nearly losing his life saving Spraksville and the whole world last Halloween, nightmares were a frequent occurrence. They came in all shapes and sizes, but they all shared one common theme—the world of magic roaring back into his life and taking away everything he loved. There was nothing he feared more. He was truly happy now. He had good friends. He was a student at the greatest boarding school in existence and felt like he finally had a home. Losing that, being cast back into bouncing from home to home, having nothing to hold on to, and being lonely, rejected, and bullied, terrified him.

But they were just nightmares—his subconscious playing out his worst fears.

Nothing more.

There was no magic here at Amworth. That was all in the past.

An old-fashioned analog clock on the wall clicked steadily as the second hand swept around the dial. It was only five a.m. A bit early to get up, but he was too shaken to sleep; he put on his glasses, slid out of bed, and sat at his desk by the window to study. The moon's soft glow didn't provide enough light, so he turned on his green banker's lamp with a click of the beaded chain.

Instantly, Halstrom sat up as if his hips were a motorized hinge connecting his top half to his bottom half. As usual, he was fully dressed for the day—jeans, turtleneck, and beanie, all navy blue. Not a single curl of his black hair stuck out from his beanie despite being pressed against a pillow all night.

"I'm going buy you pajamas someday," Goff teased.

Halstrom came and sat next to him, opening a textbook. "I don't sleep fully dressed because I lack pajamas," he said in his typical mechanical voice, a slight accent around the edges adding a hint of cartoon scientist. "The efficiency of it benefits my schedule. You still have to change out of your pajamas before going to class, but I am already dressed."

"So, basically, you live in your pajamas."

"I do not. I sleep in my clothes."

"Which makes them pajamas."

Halstrom leaned back and crossed his arms over his chest. "Pajamas are attire designed specifically to be slept in. They are typically constructed of thin material and decorated with images evocative of slumber, like the juvenile flannel pair you are wearing decorated with tiny moons and sheep."

"Juvenile?"

"The brand is on the pocket—Kid-Jammies."

"Really?" Goff checked his pocket and sighed. "Got me there, but I don't care. I like them. They're very comfy!"

Halstrom shook his head and turned back to his textbook. For the next hour, he and Halstrom sat side by side studying. Goff took copious notes, but Halstrom just kind of looked at things. Somehow, that worked for him. He was a top student at Amworth. At 7:30, they started getting ready for school.

Halstrom brushed his teeth and then waited impatiently while Goff brushed his teeth, changed out of his Kid-Jammies into real clothes, and combed his hair.

"Very inefficient," Halstrom noted.

On the way out, Goff checked himself in the mirror. His glasses were smudged and slightly askew on his thin, pale face. As usual, despite being combed, his brown hair still looked like a bird's nest flipped upside down on his head. Distracted by Halstrom watching him, he'd chosen brown pants and a matching brown sweater.

He looked like a French fry.

Normally, he would have changed, but Halstrom was impatiently waiting at the door. Goff sighed and put on his wool pea coat, adding a crimson scarf for color and hoping it didn't look like ketchup.

The hallway rocked with the sounds of dozens of boys and girls getting ready for school, some wearing cheap polyester pajamas and others silk designer bathrobes. Amworth had two classes of students: those admitted based on academic merit and those admitted because their parents had donated buckets of money to the school. Designer clothes and well-coiffed hair were the hallmarks of the rich kids on campus.

After fighting through the crowd in the cavernous stone hallways lined with tall windows, they stepped outside and were greeted by a blast of chilly late-November air. The sky was a blanket of bumpy gray clouds; the first snow was not that far off. Goff shivered and buttoned his jacket. Halstrom doubled up the scarf around his neck. The Amworth campus spread wide around them like the grounds of a medieval castle, with a few modern additions sprinkled throughout. Even their dormitory looked like a mini-castle, with spire-topped turrets on each corner.

Lydia Garcia, the third member of the Spraksville world-saving team, was sitting on a nearby granite bench under a drooping willow tree. A large paper coffee cup in her hand released eggnog-scented steam, frosting up her gigantic red plastic-rimmed glasses; her headband hung at an odd angle, barely containing greasy brown hair that stuck out around the edges of her hood. A large textbook lay open on her lap, and sheets of paper covered in her swirly writing cluttered the ground at her feet. She regarded Goff with her eyebrows raised. "Dude!" she exclaimed, nearly spilling her coffee—Lydia never just said things. Her words were like little explosions. "Are you wearing all brown under there? You look like Tater Tot."

Goff pulled his coat closed. "Halstrom distracted me."

"He does that to people."

Halstrom stepped up beside Goff. "At least he is not wearing his Kid-Jammies to classes."

"You sleep in Kid-Jammies?" Lydia teased.

"They have tiny moons and sheep on them," Halstrom added.

Lydia laughed. "So cuuuuuute!"

"Well, at least I don't sleep in my clothes like Halstrom!" Goff said, leaning into Lydia. "What do you sleep in?"

"Uh…" Lydia cocked her head. "Big girl pajamas?"

"Perhaps Goff should buy some big girl pajamas," Halstrom suggested.

"I could loan him a pair."

"I'm not wearing Lydia's pajamas! My pajamas are fine!"

Lydia leaned back. "By the way—your scarf looks a little like ketchup."

Goff sighed. "Can we stop talking about my clothes?" He turned to Halstrom, and hoping to end this conversation, asked, "Isn't it time for you to call Pam?"

"It is." Halstrom began walking away. "I will tell her all about your Kid-Jammies."

"Please don't."

"Wait!" Lydia threw up her hands, sloshing some beige latte foam on her boots. "Before you go, do either of you understand the distributive property?"

"Of course," Halstrom said. "It's a means of simplifying expressions."

Lydia rolled her eyes. "I wasn't asking for a definition, Mr. not-helpful-at-all. I need help."

"Then why didn't you ask for help?"

"That's literally what I did!"

Halstrom tapped his chin. "You misuse the word 'literally'

often. I do not think you know what it means."

"I do!" Lydia exclaimed. "As in, this stuff literally makes my head spin, and I'm literally headed for Flunk City on my exam today unless I literally get some help!"

"Nearly every word of that was nonsense."

Lydia ignored him and turned to Goff. "Can you help me?"

"Yup." Goff sat on the bench next to her. "I found a few tricks that really help me with it."

Unlike Halstrom, who was at risk of becoming Valedictorian someday while barely doing anything, Goff and Lydia worked hard to earn grades that were good enough at Amworth. To remain here, you had to maintain a B average or better, and the teachers were strict. It was a great place that gave the students all sorts of independence and freedom, but the price was solid academic performance. That is, unless your parents donated tons of money, in which case you could putter around looking cool without lifting a finger and stay as long as you wanted.

Goff began going over various approaches to applying the distributive property while Halstrom walked away to call Pam for their morning chat—they talked every day before classes. Fifteen minutes later, Lydia was getting the questions on the practice test correct, and Halstrom returned.

"What's new in Pam's world?" Goff asked.

Halstrom thought for a second before answering. "She

wore a pink dress to school, but it was too much for her, so she had to wear all camouflage the next day to recover."

Lydia laughed. "Ben must have hated her wearing a pink dress."

"He did. He cut it up so she couldn't wear it again."

"Dude! I'll bet she was furious!"

"She was. She melted all of Ben's trophies in the microwave."

"Wow." Lydia shook her head. "Don't mess with Pam!"

"One should not."

Goff laughed and stood up to help Lydia pack up her things. "You'd think twins would get along better."

"She loves him." Halstrom carried Lydia's empty coffee cup to a nearby trash can. "But she often hates him too."

"A real love-hate relationship," Lydia said.

Halstrom nodded approvingly. "Literally."

When Lydia was all packed up, they trudged across campus through the early morning light, passing clusters of other students bustling along, talking and laughing, straps of heavy backpacks tugging on their shoulders. A few minutes later, they arrived at the city of fountains, brick buildings, keystone arches, white trim, lofty spiked turrets, and glowing paned windows that was the academic center of Amworth.

Halfway across the courtyard, they ran into Rolland Nolo and Becky Phipps, two seniors who were the king and queen of the rich kids at Amworth.

"Oh, thank goodness," Rolland said, his voice crisp and formal like a rich baron in an old movie. He was wearing his usual beige slacks, navy blue Amworth blazer, and yellow silk scarf that puffed out below his chin. Goff always thought he looked like he should be on a yacht; even his golden hair, glued with a gallon of expensive salon hair gel, looked like a wave cresting across his forehead. He pulled away from the brick pillar he had been leaning against and swaggered toward Goff, clutching a decorative triplet of leather-bound books he'd never read. "We're safe now, Becks—the Ghoul Patrol is on premises."

Becky sashayed over to stand next to Rolland. She came from money so old that nobody even remembered where it had come from. As usual, she manifested retro preppy to a cartoonish level—plaid skirt, white blouse, suspenders, knee-high socks, shiny black shoes, and black hair pulled back tightly with a tiny red ribbon. Plus, her friends called her *Becks*. "I thought I spied a ghoul this morning, but it was just *Garcia* pre-makeup."

"I don't wear make-up, *Becks*," Lydia shot back.

"Well," Becks batted her eyelashes, thick with mascara, disapprovingly at Lydia, "you should definitely buy some."

"Or maybe," Lydia jammed her hands into her hips, "I should just scrape some of the extra off your face."

Becks stuffed her nose in the air. "I use the best there is, but it still wouldn't make a difference on you."

Halstrom tapped his chin. "Then why did you recommend Lydia buy some?"

"Because—" Becks turned a hot shade of pink. "Oh, never mind."

When Goff first learned about Amworth a few years ago, he imagined that it was a place free of bullies and full of intelligent, respectful kids where he would finally meet perfect people who would make perfect friends. But that was before he met Lydia and Halstrom and learned that the most perfect friends are often perfectly imperfect people, proud outcasts and misfits, just like him.

He usually didn't engage with Rolland and Becks during their daily bully sessions, but he was still slightly edgy from his nightmare. He turned to Becks. "I don't know if you've heard, but a gorilla at the zoo is having trouble getting into Amworth. Perhaps your parents can help him by donating a few million like they did for you?"

Beck's nostrils flared. Goff knew that her hottest button was that neither she nor Rolland would ever have been accepted into Amworth if their parents weren't huge donors.

"Don't let these street urchins ruffle your feathers, Becks," Rolland said, draping his arm over her shoulder. "Someday, they'll be cleaning your lavatory and living in a paper carton in an alley."

"Street urchins?" Lydia challenged. "And who says 'paper carton' instead of cardboard box?"

"Snotty, entitled, rich kids," Goff said, "That's who."

"We are not snotty and entitled!" Becks fumed.

"Snotty, entitled kids say what?" Lydia asked.

Rolland furrowed his brow. "What?"

Becks stomped her foot and elbowed him. "Rolland!"

"Oh, goodness," Rolland whined. "I see the blunder I just made. Can I have another go at that?"

"Wow!" Lydia laughed. "You just tripled down on being a snotty, entitled rich kid."

Becks spun and strutted off, dragging Rolland by the hand. "Forget you losers."

"We're street urchins, remember?" Goff called out.

About ten feet down the path, Val, a broad-shouldered girl with short dirty blonde hair and a broad, dour face, stepped out from an arched opening right into their path. She bumped into Rolland, and he dropped his decorative pile of books.

"Oops," she said.

"Why don't you—" Rolland started to say before he looked up. Val dwarfed him like a wolf next to a poodle, and he went quiet as he bent down to pick up his books.

Val didn't offer to help and looked over at Goff, Lydia, and Halstrom for a second longer than was comfortable before wrapping her oversized brown wool coat tight around her and strutting off.

"That girl seems to never be more than a dozen feet from us," Lydia observed.

"She's more than that now," Halstrom said, pointing as Val reached the edge of the academic center.

"You know what I mean!"

"I rarely do."

"It seems like she wants to talk to us," Goff said as they hustled down the brick path leading to their first classes.

"How does someone seem to want to talk?" Halstrom asked.

"That's Goff's department," Lydia said. "I see a bad-tempered girl with a chip on her shoulder who gives us funny looks. Goff sees a lost soul in need of rescue."

"I just think she looks like she wants to be friends," Goff said.

"I saw only Val," Halstrom said. "The two of you often add things that are not there."

"I guess we all see things through different eyes," Goff said.

"We can't exactly swap eyes," Lydia said.

"Imagine if we could," Goff mused. "The world would be a much better place."

"No, it wouldn't!" Lydia yelped. "Thieves would steal those slimy little balls to sell."

"You do know they're attached, right?" Goff asked.

"No, they aren't!" Lydia rolled her eyes dramatically. "Look—they're just balls floating around in eye holes."

Halstrom regarded her with a raised eyebrow. "Have you

ever considered becoming a doctor?"

"No, why—Do you think I should?"

"Absolutely not."

Goff laughed and headed in the opposite direction, slipping among the other students. His first class was history, and he was anxious about it because they had a new teacher since their regular one was ill. Would this teacher be much more demanding than Mr. Hansplutt had been? That could mean trouble for his GPA; he was already struggling in this class—too many odd names and dates to remember.

When he stepped into the classroom, a woman wearing a long black dress was sitting behind the teacher's desk. Her kinky, salt-and-pepper hair spilled from the wide brim of a pointy witch's hat.

Goff's blood drained into his toes.

A witch?

Here at Amworth?

About the Author

FRED GRACELY grew up in Pennsylvania and now resides just outside Boston, Massachusetts. After attending six different colleges and studying many subjects (art, electronics, computer science, psychology), he earned a B.S. in Psychology from Framingham State University and, later in life, an M.A. in Human Relations, Specializing in Holistic Counseling Psychology from Lesley University (psychology is one of his passions).

He discovered his love for writing and storytelling as he read books to his children. On a whim, he started making up stories to tell them. They enjoyed them so much that he began to write them down. Now, there is little he loves as much as sitting down to craft language and bring characters and stories to life.

Website: fredgracely.com

Books by Fred Gracely

Misfit's Magic: The Last Halloween (book 1)
Misfit's Magic: Shades of Winter (book 2)
Misfit's Magic: Twisting in Time (book 3)
Moon Spirit
The Road Beside (coming summer 2026)

Acknowledgments

I owe a great debt of gratitude to the people who supported me while I went through the process of writing and publishing this novel, which was much more work than I expected.

First of all, none of this would have been possible without
the support of my wonderful wife, Nop, who showed great
patience with me as I snuck out of bed at 4 AM every morning to write and then wasn't able to keep my eyes open after
dinner. She also generously contributed her artistic sensibility
and common sense as I made decisions about the book, art-
work, and publishing (she has a well-developed compositional
sense and helped me see that I almost always overcomplicate
my designs).

I also want to thank my daughter, Caroline, whose honest
opinions helped me hone the story and related materials. She
did an early edit of the book and convinced me to remove
parts that didn't work (like a two-page cooking scene that
went into way too much detail and the idea that Goff liked to
drink vinegar water and called it pickle juice).

Thanks are also owed to my son, Adam, for his support,
encouragement, and interest in the process of getting this

book out into the world and for reminding me to live a little at the same time (he often got me outside throwing a football to take a break and pretty much forced me to plan at least a few vacations).

I owe a huge shout-out and thank-you to my friend Ethan Gettman, who created chapter illustrations and was also a valued (and patient) supporter and source of ideas throughout the process. His talent as an artist and keen sense for style and form helped me make the end-product and related materials much more professional (for instance, I now realize that Comic Sans is a tragic mistake, you really can't have five different fonts on the same page, and it's not ok just to stretch an image on a website to make it fit because it gets pixelated).

I was thrilled to find Candice Broersma as an illustrator for the updated cover. Her talent for creating narrative-based illustrations that are engaging and beautiful is simply remarkable. I was very impressed that part of her process was reading the book! I hadn't expected that, but she is very professional and dedicated. Working with her was a pure delight, and I think the new cover brings qualities of the story right out to the surface of the book.

I also want to thank my talented editors, Lisa Messinger and Gill Donovan, for their detailed reviews, support, and excellent suggestions, and my marketing consultants, Tina Koenig and Melanie Ann Galioto, for helping me understand how to launch a book in good form (I was just going to pop it up on Amazon in the spring and hope for the best until I met them).

A special thanks also goes out to my early readers, Margaret, Ethan, and Tina, who found inconsistencies and grammatical errors my eyes would not see, no matter how many times I re-read it, and to Priya Paulraj for her patience and talent in formatting the book to look beautiful. Finally, I want to acknowledge some wonderful folks who contributed to the KickStarter campaign for this book (in alphabetical order): Alexandra Hope, Betheny Thompson, Brian Lucky Skillen, Ed Dexter, Jacob H Joseph, James Gracely, John Miyasato, John Van Mulligen, L. Ana Ellis, Leslie Twitchell, Pam Wallace, Robert Brown, Sarah Langreder, Scott Markovitz, Sherry Mock, Stacey Kaczmarek, and Tom Stone.

MISFIT'S MAGIC: THE LAST HALLOWEEN